The Thistle Seed

By
D. J. Lane

PublishAmerica
Baltimore

© 2010 by D.J. Lane.
All rights reserved. No part of this book may be reproduced, stored in a retrieval system or transmitted in any form or by any means without the prior written permission of the publishers, except by a reviewer who may quote brief passages in a review to be printed in a newspaper, magazine or journal.

First printing

All characters in this book are fictitious, and any resemblance to real persons, living or dead, is coincidental.

PublishAmerica has allowed this work to remain exactly as the author intended, verbatim, without editorial input.

Hardcover 978-1-4512-5484-6
Softcover 978-1-4512-5485-3
PUBLISHED BY PUBLISHAMERICA, LLLP
www.publishamerica.com
Baltimore

Printed in the United States of America

Dedicated to my husband Frank, who patiently put up with late dinners, distracted replies to questions, and still gave me all his support wholeheartedly.

—D. J. Lane

Sylvia, abandoned at birth by her unwed mother, was raised by her maternal grandmother. When she was old enough to realize the different home life her schoolmates lived she began to question her grandmother about her mother. Eleanor told her she would tell her all about it when she was older. When at last the day came when Eleanor could no longer postpone the inevitable revelation, she told Sylvia how her mother had fallen in love with a married man who, according to Eleanor's daughter Rose, wanted nothing to do with her or her unborn child. As soon as the baby girl was born Rose had escaped her responsibility by leaving for parts unknown. A thread of hope still existed in Sylvia that one day she would see her mother and get an explanation. Granny had told her that life was strewn with seeds of wisdom, anticipation, despair, fortitude but the seed to be careful about was the Thistle seed, the one that carried only trouble if left to sprout untended. Don't let problems multiply unresolved for they can change one's life forever.

CHAPTER 1

The old woman sat before the mirror observing the wrinkled face in the reflection. Where had all the years gone? She hated the fact that her time was now limited. It didn't seem that long ago she could place herself half-way through a normal lifetime, smugly counting the years ahead. When she reached the age of forty, it was stretching things a bit to think she would live until the age of eighty. Well! Enough of this old woman's musings, she was expecting her granddaughter who had insisted on making a recording of her life memories. God! What had she gotten herself into? The sound of the door chimes echoed through the house interrupting her reverie.

Sylvia tapped her foot impatiently, waiting for her grandmother to answer the doorbell. She breathed a sigh of relief when the door finally opened and Eleanor stood before her, calmly stepping aside to allow her entrance into the hallway and then leading the way into the kitchen where the enticing aroma of fresh coffee infused the air.

"It took you long enough to open the door, what were you doing?" Sylvia snapped, trailing behind her granny's retreating figure. "I'm not any happier than you about doing this project, you know. The more nervous you become, the more the recordings will sound stilted. I want it to sound like you're speaking to a very dear friend recalling memories of the past. I know this will take time but I think it's important to have a firsthand recording of your life that your future grandkids will enjoy reading about. Don't you agree?"

Eleanor glanced at Sylvia, a slight smile tugging at the corners of her lips while pouring two fresh cups of coffee and setting out an assortment of cheese and crackers. She watched as her granddaughter placed a recording device on the table, plugged it into a wall receptacle, inserted a tape, and then sat comfortably sipping at the hot coffee.

"All you need do when ready to record is to push this button. When you want to stop, push this other button, it's easy as pie. When the tape is finished just pop it out and replace it with a new one." Sylvia felt the first beginnings of stress as she felt the muscles tighten in her jaw. She didn't want to argue, all she wanted was a little bit of cooperation on this project.

Ellie glanced at the recorder, a pained expression flashing for a moment and then disappearing from her face. Like it or not, it seemed this was a chore she could not avoid. She had always liked her privacy, had for years never delved into her past, nor discussed past difficulties with her grandchild, although she did give the wisdom of her experiences. With a final grimace of discontent she gave her nod of assent. She wondered what her granddaughter would think of her after she heard the accounting, whether good or bad, of her life.

*   *   *   *   *   *   *   *   *   *

The funeral was brief, exactly the way her grandmother wanted. Nothing fancy, just a respectful service at the small community church. She had asked that her ashes be taken up north to the old homestead abutting the state park and scattered where the wildflowers grew. Sylvia would keep her promise the very next day.

It was a four hour drive to the small upper Michigan town where her grandmother had been raised along with four brothers and a sister. Eleanor was the last of the original family, the others buried as far away as California. Turning onto the old dirt road it was only a short distance to the place she had been told about. Sylvia brought the car to a stop, turned off the ignition and sat quietly with closed eyes, head tilted back against the headrest, the arboreal silence calming her feelings of stress.

The chattering of a squirrel awoke her, it was almost twilight. She had dozed for several hours. Picking up the container with her grandmothers' ashes she exited the car and began walking along the road looking for a suitable spot, something with that special "feeling"…and there it was, a cluster of wildflowers at the edge of the forest, wildflowers she remembered being shown in her youth.

Standing upwind from the site she removed the lid and tossed the ashes into the breeze. For a moment they seemed to pause in flight, as though to say goodbye, then they were swirled away, scattering, gently falling into and around the scented petals of nature. It was finished. For the first time since her grandmother's death, tears welled up, streaming down her cheeks, even wetting the collar of her blouse. The reality that she would never again see that beloved face took her breath away for a moment. It was then she realized darkness was descending, and rather quickly at that. Clutching the emptied container to her breast she hurried to her car, climbed in, and turned the ignition key.

The silence that followed was shattered with a few choice swear words. "What in blazes were you thinking, you stupid moron?" She muttered to herself as she tried the ignition a few more times. "Damn, it's black as pitch out and you're stuck here for the duration." Resting her head against the steering wheel she felt like screaming but then, conscious of the darkness lurking outside her car windows, she smothered the inclination. After making sure the doors were safely locked, she made herself as comfortable as possible and settled in for the night. Hopefully the time would pass quickly. She would think about what to do in the morning.

A few curious creatures stopped on their nightly excursions for food to sniff at the metal monster sitting in their territory but finding nothing of interest, they hurried on their way. And as for Sylvia, she slept deeply, soundly, with only a few restless tossing's of her head and occasionally uttering a breathless murmur of discontent.

The feeling of warmth on her face and eyelids awakened her from a deep sleep, she must have been more tired than she realized. A glance at her watch showed 6:15a.m., she'd be home well before noon. Turning the ignition key there was still no response so with a groan of frustration she grabbed her purse and car keys, slid out the door, locked it, and began her walk. With luck she'd find a farm house and some assistance. Setting her purse strap comfortably over her shoulder she lengthened her stride, grateful she had worn jeans and tennis shoes.

Within a short time she reached the macadam-paved county road she had originally turned off from. Why hadn't she noticed how rural it was? There were acres of corn, an apple orchard, and even a large grove of pine trees in the far distance but not a house in sight. Taking a chance and turning the opposite way she had driven, she set her sights on the distant evergreens.

Gritting her teeth and trying to ignore the feeling that a blister was forming on her right heel she began to jog. The sound of a loud bicycle bell behind her almost gave her heart failure.

"Sorry about that, didn't mean to startle you, I didn't want you to make the wrong move and end up flat on the ground. Where are you coming from? I don't recall ever seeing you around here, are you visiting friends or relatives in the area?" He stood, balancing the bike against his hip, blue eyes doing a quick once-over of the tired-looking young woman standing before him.

Sylvia was conscious of two feelings, gratitude and also the sense that she did not look her best. Running her fingers quickly through her hair, giving her head a shake, she gave a grimace of frustration. Of all times to run into a guy who, in other circumstances, she'd have been thrilled to meet suddenly made her feel anger at the situation. "Do I look like I'm visiting someone? I'm tired, my car won't start and it's sitting back in the woods. I came up here to bring my grandmother's ashes and." Suddenly she choked up, tears spilling over her cheeks, deep sobs bursting forth that she could not subdue. Such a deep feeling of helplessness and embarrassment shot through her that she turned and sprinted off at a run.

She didn't get far. A strong pair of arms caught her up, tossed her over his shoulder and carried her back to his bike. "Look missy, I don't have time to listen to you right now. Just set your behind on the handlebars and I'll ride you home with me where you can sit down with my mother, have something to eat, and we'll figure out how to solve your problems. Does that sound logical to you?" Not waiting for a reply, he pushed off, beginning to peddle, Sylvia balanced precariously on the handlebars. Puffing slightly until he gathered enough momentum, they were soon speeding along the road, the forest of evergreens getting ever closer as the distance between diminished.

"Hey! By the way, what's your name? Mine's David, David Kendall, but you can call me Dave. I work with my father at our hardware store in town. Actually, it's more than a hardware store it's the town information spot too. We sell everything from fishing and camping equipment to household items. It's the best place to find out what's going on in the area, plus passing around the latest local news. I was just on my way back home for breakfast. I enjoy a good bike ride in the morning weather permitting. It keeps me in good shape, otherwise I'd likely start getting a bit too thick around my middle since my mom loves to cook and tries her new recipes out on us all the time."

"My name's Sylvia, everyone calls me Sy which suits me just fine. I never liked my name but mom had a best friend she grew up with, I'm her namesake." She tried not to groan as the metal handlebar seemed to dig deeper into her posterior when the front tire hit a depression in the road, it felt like a permanent ridge had indented itself in her tender skin. She clenched her teeth until her jaws began to ache.

David turned onto the dirt road, a rambling, white-aluminum- clad farmhouse not very distant ahead. She could see a red barn setting well back from it with a green tractor parked in front of opened double doors. She spotted a large vegetable garden on one side of the structure and on the opposite side, an orchard of trees. She had no idea what kind.

Reaching the front porch he curled his arm around Sylvia's waist and lifted her from her perch, letting the bike fall against the iron railing. He set her firmly on her feet and stepped away, a half smile tugging at the corners of his lips as he viewed the obvious discomfort of his passenger. Those handlebars were not built for sitting.

Sylvia experienced pain in places she hadn't known existed although she tried to not let it show. She was aware of his scrutiny but too stubborn to even exhibit a grimace of discomfort. "Thanks for the ride, David. I really appreciate your help but if I can use your phone to call road assistance I'll be on my way, hopefully sooner rather than later." She brushed the dust from her jeans, flipped her hair from her face and tried to act like she wasn't in complete agony. She'd love to be able to massage those sore, tender areas of her rear and get some blood flowing again but never in a million years would she succumb to the temptation. As he turned to resettle the bike more securely, she managed a few hurried rubs.

"What's going on here Davey? Why are you keeping your guest standing out in the hot sun? Hello! Young lady, I'm Davey's mom, come on in and make yourself comfortable. I just fixed breakfast, plenty for everyone. I was beginning to wonder where Davey had gotten himself off to." Holding the screen door open, she watched as her son escorted the young lady into the house, giving her a devilishly charming wink as he passed, knowing his mother would be hoping that maybe, this time, it was the young lady she'd been hoping for. There had been only one other, and that was a number of years ago. With a sigh she closed the screen behind them and followed the couple into the kitchen.

"Hi! Dad, I'd like you to meet Sylvia. Her car wouldn't start so I gave her a ride on my bike, I think she's hungry. Sylvia, this is my father David Kendall and I'm starved too."

They all sat, Sylvia next to David. The platter of golden flapjacks and another of scrambled eggs were handed about, then a plate heaped with browned sausages. Coffee was poured with its counterparts of rich cream and sugar available. It was the most delicious breakfast Sylvia had ever enjoyed. The chair cushion eased the discomfort of her derriere, and she actually smiled when she dug into two more of the light, fluffy pancakes, the very best she'd ever eaten.

As soon as breakfast was over the two men left for the Hardware store. Sylvia helped clear the table. Before she could phone for road service, David was back saying that a loose battery cable had caused her car problem and he'd be happy to drive her back to her vehicle.

His mother asked if she'd please phone to let them know she'd made it home safely. Sylvia wrote their phone number and address on a slip of paper and tucked it into her wallet where she'd be sure not to lose it.

She thanked Mrs. Kendall for the bountiful breakfast and hurried to the pickup truck where David was holding the door open for her. Thank God! She would be on her way home. At least it would still be early enough to check her grandmother's house, pick up any mail, and begin seeing to the many miscellaneous things that happened when a household was dismantled.

A feeling of relief overcame her when her car came into view followed quickly with the realization that part of her grandmother would remain here forever. She knew why Eleanor wanted her ashes brought so far away. No place close to home where someone would be mourning or shedding tears. She had not been the sort of woman to want someone to cry over what couldn't be changed. When David stopped the truck they sat in silence for a moment, both not knowing what to say.

"It was fortunate meeting you David, thank you so much for your help. I would have been in serious trouble otherwise, and thank your mother again for me. I really liked her a lot because she's much like my grandmother was, tough and independent."

David sat for a moment not replying, a slight feeling of anxiety lodging someplace in his chest. "Do you ever come up this way for vacations, or to visit friends or family?" He turned toward her, noticing the color of her hair and the green glints somewhere deep in her hazel eyes, she was actually rather nice looking. He hadn't paid much attention before, but there were little things that now attracted him. "Where actually do you live, I mean, how far away?" He watched the corners of her lips turn up. Her smile, as she turned full face toward him, seemed to make his heart lurch before settling back to beating normally. Suddenly he felt awkward, not as "in-control" as a man his age should feel.

Sylvia thought about how far she had driven, the distance roughly about 300miles. "It's quite a ways David, I don't know if I'll be getting up here again. If I ever do I'll drop in to visit your mom and dad, you also of course, you saved my hide. I don't know what I'd have done without your help."

For a while they sat in silence, only bird song echoing through the tree tops along with the chattering of squirrels. She realized what a nice place her grandmother had chosen. The peace and quiet serenity, yet it was teeming with hidden wildlife. Just sitting, listening to the music of nature gave her a feeling of contentment.

"Goodbye David, thank you again for your help, it was a blessing in disguise. Hopefully we'll meet again some time. I told your mom I'd call when I reached home. It likely won't be until late evening since I'll be at my grandmother's house immediately on my return. I've already disconnected her phone service." On impulse Sylvia turned quickly and planted a firm kiss on David's lips. Exiting the truck she pushed the door closed and turned away.

Sylvia felt her lips trembling as she walked toward the place she had scattered her grandmother's ashes. There, she reached out and touched one of the delicate blossoms Eleanor had loved so in her youthful wanderings. "Goodbye granny, I'll miss you. Rest peacefully, I'll always love you."

When she turned back toward her car she realized David had already left, she hadn't even noticed. She could see his truck at the end of the road just making a turn onto the pavement, his arm extended out the window waving a goodbye. He was gone from sight before she could respond.

With a sigh she walked back to her car and tossed her purse onto the seat. Settling herself comfortably she turned the ignition key and the motor purred to life. Shortly, she was turning onto the paved roadway and heading toward home.

Why was it so much quicker following the path homeward than when starting out, she wondered? As the miles flashed passed she was mentally ticking off the many things to accomplish. A stop at the Post Office to have granny's mail forwarded to her own place would be convenient. In fact, she'd better make a list once she reached home or else she'd be wasting time diddling around. She turned the radio on, pushing the "Favorite" button. Soft jazz drifted from the speakers. This was nice....the hum of the tires on the pavement, her favorite song playing, the tension she had been aware of seemed to slowly dissolve. The next thing she heard was a thunderous crash. Her car spinning out of control, she was thrown forward onto the steering wheel, her head smacking sharply against its edge, car upside down, she held in place by her seatbelt.

She regained consciousness slowly, the restriction of her limbs and the inability to move her head causing a temporary feeling of panic, then the awareness of hands that were gently soothing her, easing the pain that seemed to encompass her entire body.

"Lay still Miss, you've been in an accident, you'll be okay. You have a concussion from hitting your head on the steering wheel of your car and we're taking you to the hospital." They lifted her into the ambulance, secured the stretcher and closed the doors. One attendant kept watch over her while the other man turned on the wailing siren. Relieved that their patient was not considered critical, they sped toward the nearest medical facility.

For an interminable time in the emergency ward Sylvia was probed, x-rayed, and finally, when the day seemed to never end, she had been told she could go home. They told her it was a good thing she'd had her seatbelt on or things could have been much worse and, if there were any charges not covered by her insurance, they'd mail her the bill. The prescription for pain pills could be filled at the hospital Pharmacy. If she suffered any problems within the next several days pertaining to her accident, please contact them immediately.

With a sigh of relief Sylvia removed the hospital shift, put her bra and blouse back on, picked up her purse and headed for the exit door. What was she going to do now that her car was wrecked? She decided to phone her insurance company and see if she could rent something so she could at least get back home. What a mess, now she'd have to look for another car. She'd taken two weeks off work, figuring that would give her time to get all

Eleanor's affairs settled, not likely without transportation. Exiting the emergency section she headed toward the waiting area, looking for the telephones and the white pages phone book.

David saw her as soon as she pushed through the double doors. She had a big bandage on her forehead, looked pale as a ghost and there were speckles of blood on the front of her blouse, she hesitated a moment searching the room and then headed toward the bank of phones against the far wall. That's when David intercepted her. For a moment recognition didn't register, and then with a glad cry of relief she threw her arms around him.

Oh! My God! David, you're a lifesaver, whatever are you doing here? I was in an accident. I was just driving along, not speeding or doing anything reckless and out of a clear, blue sky someone smashed into me. You can't imagine how terrible it was. When I came to I was being lifted into an ambulance." Sylvia felt almost giddy reliving the experience.

David patted her shoulder, held her a little closer murmuring words of comfort. The aftershock of the accident had set in and Sylvia was shaking, recalling the trauma she had felt. "Come along young lady, I'm taking you back home with me, we'll get this all straightened out in no time. There is no need for you to fret over something you can't do anything about at the moment, right?" All the while David was talking he was leading her through the lobby doors and out to his truck. Opening the door he lifted her up and sat her on the seat, at the same time fastening the seatbelt snuggly across her shoulders. "There you go, isn't that better now? Just relax and I'll have you home in a jiffy."

By the time they reached the farmhouse Sylvia was feeling much better, although she did have a headache. Thankfully a police report had been made about the accident and the person responsible would be liable for any expenses she incurred. In the meantime her car was totaled, no possibility of repair. She gave a mental groan wondering what else could go wrong before she got back home.

David opened the truck door. She unfastened the seatbelt and he lifted her out, setting her firmly on her feet but keeping a firm grip on her elbow as he steered her toward the steps. Before she could protest, he lifted her into his arms, carried her into the house and deposited her in a comfortable chair.

Mrs. Kendall placed a foot stool close by where Sylvia could rest her feet. "There you go honey, you sit here and relax. We'll figure out what to do about your problems, don't you fret one bit, everything will be just fine, you wait and see." She gave her a motherly smile although there were a few worried lines etched across her forehead.

David placed her purse on the end table nearby. "I have a few things to take care of at the hardware store. I'll be back in an hour. We'll have some lunch and discuss a few ideas that I think you'll agree with."

Mrs. Kendall went to the kitchen to prepare Sylvia a cup of soothing herbal tea, very good for calming the nerves. David departed for the store.

Sylvia finally began to relax. She tilted her head back against the soft cushion, closed her eyes, just for a moment, and drifted into a deep sleep.

When Carol returned with the tea she placed it on the end table and reached for the folded lap throw on the nearby couch. Gently she tucked it around the sleeping girl. You poor little thing, she thought. All this trouble because you came here to bring your Grandma's ashes to a special place for burial. I can't fault you for that. I would have done the same thing no matter how much trouble I'd have had. You have a good heart sweetie, you're just the kind of gal I'd love to have my son hook up with. Who knows…maybe your Granny felt the same way, maybe she had something to do with keeping you here, anything is possible. I've always had closeness with the afterlife and I believe they sometimes give us a helping hand in ways we never realize. I'm positive your Granny had something to do with you being back here, and I think she and I would have been very good friends. You sleep well little gal, when you awaken we'll all sit down and figure out a sensible solution that everyone will be comfortable with.

When David returned home Sylvia was awake sipping a fresh cup of tea. Her color looked much better and there was even a bit of sparkle in her hazel eyes.

"Dad and I discussed the problem and the best idea we could come up with was for me to drive you home. I can stay overnight at my Aunt Rose's. She'll be happy to see me, plus catch up on all the news from home." David sat on the chair arm gazing down at Sylvia's swollen forehead, imagining the pain she must be feeling. "If we leave now you'll be home by dusk. I'll give my Aunt a call now and then we can be off." Rising, he brushed a strand of hair from her face and then headed for the kitchen.

Within ten minutes they were in his truck and on their way. Mrs. Kendall had packed some food, what she called "Lunch". Several cans of orange juice, half a dozen oatmeal cookies, baked chicken breasts, biscuits, a few apples, and of course links of her homemade smoked sausage. She made sure they wouldn't be hungry.

There was little traffic and the miles seemed to add up quickly on the speedometer. They finally pulled into a rest stop and after enjoying the lunch Mrs. Kendall had packed, they were back in the truck and on their way again.

"Davey, I think I'd rather have you drop me at my grandmothers' house. There's so much I have to do to get everything in order. If you take me to my apartment I won't have any transportation. Thank goodness Gram has a fairly new Chevy that I can use, I'm so glad I didn't rush into selling it. By tomorrow I'll be feeling myself again after getting a good night's sleep and can drive myself home anytime I like."

Dave glanced at her quickly, he'd been hoping to see where she lived, had wanted that little extra "tie" to her, even if it was only an address, maybe she didn't want him to know. He was surprised at the pang of disappointment that lanced through him. He mentally berated himself for acting like a schoolboy.

"Sure Sylvia, no problem, sounds like a sensible idea. But I thought you'd mentioned that the phone had been disconnected, I don't think you should be without one. At least until you're sure you won't have any after-effects caused by your accident. Of course, it's entirely up to you."

She had to admit his advice made sense but she wanted access to her Grams' car. "Okay, Davey, how about you dropping me off now so I can drive Grams car home? I can check that everything is okay at her place at the same time."

David gave a mental groan, this was not working out to his advantage. "Look here, Sylvia, you shouldn't be driving so soon after your accident. I'll take you to your apartment, pick you up in the morning and then take you back to your Granny's. You'll sleep better in your own place anyway. This is the wisest solution don't you agree?"

She was used to making her own decisions but in actuality, he was right. "Okay, I bow to your greater wisdom, but I really dislike all of my dependence on you, it makes me uncomfortable. I'm used to making my own way and not asking favors from others. Although I truly appreciate all you and your family have done for me I'm now in an awkward position. How can I reciprocate?"

David could think of any number of ways she could reciprocate. He'd like nothing better than to take her in his arms and kiss her until she begged for mercy. The longer he was around her, the more her presence affected him. It had been a very long time since he felt like this. The pain of losing his first love in a boating accident seven years ago still haunted him, but since meeting Sylvia a welcome change had occurred. The ability to feel emotions again felt like a rebirth, he actually felt like laughing. A bubble of merriment burst from his lips surprising himself and Sylvia too. She could see laugh wrinkles in the corners of his eyes which were alight with warmth. She felt a smile tickle the corners of her lips and suddenly she too was laughing aloud, not really knowing why but it felt good.

"David, you are full of surprises. Just when I think you're too serious and rather staid for someone about my age, you turn my assumptions upside down. I find I like you." Sylvia was still assimilating the change in attitude she felt. She'd felt he was a nice person from the very first they'd met but now there was a stirring of interest. She turned toward him, taking advantage of his concentration on driving, for the first time really taking a good look at him. She liked his coal-black hair. His dark blue eyes were mesmerizing, she could lose herself looking into their depth. He had a nice strong face and she couldn't fault his build. Someone looking that good was usually married, had baggage, or was engaged. An unexpected feeling of disappointment dampened her good mood.

"We're almost there, David. Make a left turn at the next main street, we're not far from my place now. Okay! Now turn right at the flashing yellow signal light...see that two story grey brick apartment building at the end of the block? That's where I live. There are only four apartments in it, two upper and two lower. I live in the lower right, Apt#2."

David pulled next to the curb, turned the motor off and inspected his surroundings. It was a nice neighborhood. Two story brick residences with wide side-drives and brick two-car garages in the rear. There were old-growth trees creating an arched canopy over the street. He checked the address on her apartment building, #45 Candler, and the town was Highland.

"Come in for a moment Dave and have a cup of coffee. You can phone your Aunt, let her know you're in town and want to stay over. That will give

THE THISTLE SEED

her a chance to get things ready. Does she live very far from here? Is she your moms' sister or your dads'?" Sylvia felt suddenly awkward, he had done so much for her but the onus of obligation she felt was uncomfortable. She should have taken a bus home…but still, there was the kindness of his mother and dad. How could she ever repay them or Dave?

"Aunt Rose is my moms' sister, they could be twins they're so much alike. She's only about five miles from here, has lived here all her life, decided to stay on even after Uncle Bob died. Luckily she got his pension, so along with social security she does just fine and not to change the subject, I'd love a cup of coffee if it's not too much trouble.

Dave followed her into the apartment where they entered a neatly tiled vestibule. A stairway in the center led to the two upper apartments. Sylvia unlocked the door on the right hand side, the #2 in brass fastened to the door just above a peephole. He followed her onto a small 5ft. square tiled area with a clothes closet on the right. A nice sized living room carpeted in light grey and to the left a dinette, kitchen and to the right of that a short hallway to a bedroom and bath. It was unexpectedly elegant.

"This is really nice Sy, how long have you lived here?" Dave liked her taste in colors and the style of furniture was pleasing, inviting an instantaneous feeling of relaxation. Uninvited, he settled himself into an easy chair and placed his feet upon its' matching footstool. "Ah!....this is fantastic. I haven't had a moment of rest since I got the phone call from the police telling me about your accident. Good thing you had our number in your purse, no telling what could have happened to you otherwise. At least you're now home safe and sound."

Sylvia was already in the kitchen getting the coffee maker set up and turned on. The gurgle of the heating water made her realized how much she needed that cup of coffee, the anticipation was almost unbearable. Setting out coffee mugs, slicing the remains of a coffeecake from the refrigerator, she placed everything on the polished maple table in the area she liked to call a dinette, although it was actually an extended arm of the kitchen. She retrieved sugar, cream and the coffee decanter, which she placed on a pretty, wooden, apple-shaped heat shield. "Coffee's ready, come and get it." She called, turning toward the living room. Extending her hand to Dave, he reached out, they clasped hands, and she gave a strong tug to help him from his seat. She then led him to the table where they settled themselves in the comfortably upholstered seats.

"That's a very pretty picture you have hanging over there, Sy, I recognize it's a Thistle plant. I've come across them many a time when I was a young lad playing with friends out in the fields. We loved seeing all the little wild things. Like Banana spiders, our name for them because they were yellow and black, field mice, garter snakes. I brought one home once, wanted it for a pet but mom vetoed the idea. Said I wouldn't like catching mice to feed to it, which was true. I liked the Praying Mantis insects a lot. They lay their eggs on milkweed plants. Another thing we used to do is catch bees. We'd grab both wings at the same time so as not to get stung. We never hurt them, let them go immediately, but I did get stung a few times. Unfortunately that was bad for the bee because it would die after that, made us feel sad. We finally stopped doing that trick. Would you believe we even had picnics? We'd gather scrap wood and then beg for some matches and a salt shaker. Of course everyone brought the biggest potato their mom could find. We'd dig a pit, build a fire and tuck all the potatoes in it. After about an hour or so we'd dig them out, let them cool enough so we could handle them and then make pigs of ourselves. They tasted so good but we'd get our hands and faces all black from peeling the burnt skin. Of course our shirts were our napkins." David gave a chuckle recalling the look on his mothers' face each time he returned from his potato roasts, it was a priceless memory. He would have been surprised to know how much she treasured those same moments remembering that dirty face so beloved, those blue eyes so alight with pleasure, she wouldn't have wanted to miss a single moment of those times. "Gee! I sure got sidetracked asking about your Thistle picture. Is there something special associated with it?"

Sy gazed at the picture for several moments, a smile spreading across her face at the memory of her grandfather. "Actually, I bought it, came across it at a yard sale and couldn't resist the impulse. Granddad was part Scottish, even took a trip there when he was middle aged, retired, and pining for something to do. When he returned home with all his tales of Scotland, one of the things he recalled was the Thistle plant and the folk tales about the honesty and nobility of character it depicted. Granddad had fallen in love with the Thistle plant. It portrayed how he had tried to lead his life. I gave him the painting a few years before his health began to fail. Now my mornings at this table enjoying my first cup of coffee, admiring that Thistle painting with its simple message of living, is always an excellent beginning to my day. I love it as much as he did."

David sat silently, musing about the folklore and her grandfather who sounded so much like his dad. Suddenly the lateness of the hour reminded him he had to phone his aunt. "Mind if I use your phone, Sy? I'd better place that call, Aunt Rose is usually in bed fairly early and I'll let her know I'll be staying overnight."

Dialing the number, it rang several times before he heard her soft voice. Thank goodness she was still up. "Hi! Aunt Rose, this is David. I'm sorry to call you at the last minute but I had to make an emergency trip down here for a friend, would you mind a little company? I can sleep on the couch and will be up and off again early in the morning." He smiled listening to her protest about the couch but he succeeded in convincing her he would be quite comfortable. "I'll be there in fifteen minutes."

Dave had a grin on his face as he hung up the phone and turned to Sylvia. "She's such a sweetheart. I'd better get going, don't want to keep her waiting. I'll be here bright and early in the morning. Would seven o'clock be okay with you?"

Closing the door after David's retreating figure Sylvia felt thoroughly exhausted, it had been a harrowing two days. After a nice hot shower with freshly shampooed hair and the silky feeling of body lotion soothing her dry skin, she settled snuggly into bed. Within moments she fell deeply asleep and into dreamland.

She was standing alone in a house, brightly lit from an unknown source, only one large room with not a single piece of furniture. The windows were empty of frames or glass and beyond them was pitch darkness.

Suddenly, from the far wall, through the empty frame of where a door would have been, Granny emerged. She was laughing softly as she walked toward Sylvia.

"You poor child, I didn't really die, it was my body that could no longer support my spirit. I could see and feel the pain you were going through. I waited, hoping you would stop grieving. The days passed and still you were steeped too deeply in sorrow. Finally I couldn't bear to see you suffer so, I knew if we could meet and I could talk to you it would help ease your pain."

Sylvia didn't understand what was happening. She was angry at herself that all this time she had thought Granny dead. A huge feeling of relief swept over her, the sorrow and pain slipping away.

Sylvia slept on but the memory of the house sitting in darkness, light blazing forth from the vacant window openings would always remain, the meeting with Granny a permanent balm that soothed her soul.

The remainder of the night passed uneventfully. The sound of the ringing telephone woke her from a deep sleep. Bounding from the bed she raced into the kitchen and picked up the receiver.

"Good Morning sleepy head, I was almost ready to hang up, thought I'd dialed the wrong number. I'll be there in fifteen minutes then we can stop for breakfast before I drop you at your grandmothers. Does that sound agreeable to you?"

Still half asleep Sy glanced down at her nightgown taking a moment to analyze the time she needed to get ready. She gasped a "Yes" and replaced the receiver, not even considering she had not said goodbye. When the doorbell sounded seventeen minutes later she was dressed, composed, and smiling when she admitted David inside. "I just have one more thing to take care of and then we can be off." She said as she hurried toward the bedroom. Quickly she made the bed, fastened on her favorite pair of opal earrings, grabbed her purse from the bedside chair and then joined Dave at the front door.

When they reached the restaurant and had settled themselves comfortably at a table, David ordered for them both, scrambled eggs, hash browns, country sausage, toast and coffee. Sy was famished, normally would have protested that amount of food but she could almost hear her stomach growling. When their order arrived she consumed every morsel, almost giving a groan of pleasure. This would carry her the entire day. She gave Dave a huge smile of contentment, he returned it with a grin.

"Um! Sy, you have a piece of something stuck in your teeth." His grin widened as he saw a rosy glow brighten her face. He choked back a laugh, trying to contain his mirth as Sylvia bolted for the ladies room. Why, he wondered are women so sensitive?

When Sy returned, composed as much as she considered possible under the circumstances, she saw David had already paid the check and was waiting by the door. Thank God for that, she thought, I'm embarrassed enough without being the focus point of the other diners. Hurrying through the door that he held open for her, she didn't even glance at him. Complete silence, only the directions to her Granny's house, a short "Thank you, have a safe trip home," and then she was out of his pick-up truck and fumbling with the keys at the front door.

David could not believe he had acted so foolishly, he really liked her. He'd been feeling much too comfortable around her, acting natural like a family would. Somehow he had to get back in her good graces. As he pulled away from the house his mind was formulating ideas. Maybe it would be wise to spend another night at his aunts' house. He'd call mom, tell her what had happened, maybe she'd have a few answers about what he should do. "David, you're a jerk," he muttered to himself. You better hope you haven't ruined things permanently. How many more years might it be before you find another woman you are so deeply attracted to?

He drove directly to his aunt's home and phoned his mother. After explaining everything to her, she told him. "You're old enough to figure out what to do without my help. Call me after you've given Sylvia your apology, I'd like to know if it is accepted. You have a second chance, son. It's taken you a long time to recover from that first loss of a loved one. Since you already have feelings for this young lady you'd better put your best foot forward. Aunt Rose will likely enjoy your company for a few more days so make the most of them. I'll tell your father what has happened. I'm sure he'll feel the same as I."

Giving Aunt Rose a hug he asked if there was anything she needed from the store, he had errands to do and would likely be gone most of the day but would shop for her on his way back.

"No Sonny, I don't need a thing, and don't worry about what time you get back, here's an extra house key so it won't matter if I'm up or abed." She pressed the house key into his hand.

"Thanks Aunty. I don't know what time I'll get in. I promise to be quiet and not waken you." With a quick hug he was out the door, into his pickup, and on his way to the nearest florist.

"Not Roses, she isn't the type, she's different." David stood at the counter glancing into the windowed glass panels behind which an array of arrangements and varied groups of flowers were on display. Bright yellow Jonquils caught his eye. "There, that's what I'm looking for, something dainty but colorful."

The sales lady retrieved the container from the cooler, placing it on the counter. "This is not an arrangement, sir. It's for planting outside after it finishes blooming. They'll come up every spring and you'll be able to enjoy them for years. They're very similar to Daffodils, just smaller and more delicate. Would you like me to wrap the base?" Receiving a nod, she chose pale green foil and then added a pretty white bow. By the time she finished, David had a pleased grin on his face, sure that this token would show his regret for his rudeness and make amends with Sy.

On the way to granny's he was careful not to make any sudden stops, didn't want to topple the flowers. When he arrived he pulled onto the driveway, turned off the motor and sat in contemplation. He couldn't help noticing what an attractive place it was, a red brick, two-story colonial, not overly large. Attractive black shutters adorned the sides of the windows. The front door was white, beveled glass side-panels etched with polished brass curlicues framed each side. At the side of the house the driveway led to a red brick two car garage. Exiting his vehicle he strode to the porch, mounted the steps and rang the doorbell. He couldn't see through the side panels, shirred curtains blocked his view.

Sy swung open the door, a smile spreading across her face. She'd been sorry for her over-reaction at breakfast. Of course, he shouldn't have laughed at her but it wasn't that big a deal. Thinking back at what she must have looked like with that "something" stuck to her teeth and smiling a mile wide, she must have looked pretty funny. She had always been able to laugh at herself when in embarrassing situations and normally she would have then. It was just that she really liked David, had wanted to make a good impression. "Well! Look who showed up on my doorstep, just when I had been thinking about you. I'm glad you came, I was hoping I'd have a chance to apologize to you for the idiotic way I behaved this morning." She actually felt a blush spreading across her face.

Dave brought his arm from behind his back presenting his gift to her, giving a lopsided grin of embarrassment and hope. He needn't have worried. She reached out, a wide smile of pleasure lighting her face and then, just as quickly, tears of happiness bringing a glow to her eyes.

"Oh! Davey, these are beautiful, I love them. Whatever made you think of Jonquils? They're one of my favorite flowers. Come in, I'll set them on the kitchen table where I can admire them while we have a cup of coffee. There are so many things I wanted to talk to you about. I also have some serious decisions to make, wanted someone else's opinion on what would be the wisest thing to do."

She stepped back allowing him entrance. Closing the door, she led the way into the kitchen. Placing the Jonquils on the table, she proceeded to make a fresh pot of coffee.

David relaxed, leaning back in his chair watching Sy set out the coffee cups, sugar and cream. She placed a prettily painted cork-clad trivet in the center of the table setting the pot of Jonquils atop. They looked very cheerful, presenting an atmosphere of pleasure. He decided they could very well be his favorite flower also. He liked where the table sat, right in front of a large window giving a nice view of the flower beds, a birdbath and several feeders hanging from shepherds' hooks. The kitchen, though not too large, was laid out in a utilitarian way that was conveniently handy for whatever the cook wanted to do. A low wooden cabinet ran the length of the wall opposite the table holding several plants, a pair of bookends holding what looked like cookbooks, and several wooden carvings, one of a male mallard, the other of an owl. On the wall above the cabinet an oil painting of a winter snow scene drew the eye. It had an old fashioned feeling to it, warm and inviting.

"Hmmm, this coffee is delicious Sy, is this some special blend? I don't think I've ever tasted this flavor before." David took a generous sip, savoring a slight hint of spice, all the while watching the play of emotions flickering across Sy's face.

"No, nothing special David, I picked up the habit from granny. She loved cinnamon, often added a sprinkle to the coffee grounds just before brewing." Sylvia sat down opposite Dave, pushing the flower aside so she'd have a clear view of his face.

"David, I've decided to give up my apartment and move here. Originally I only thought of selling this house, putting the money in the bank and enjoying the feeling of security it would give me. Then I thought of how expensive my apartment rent was and how ridiculous to keep it when this place is free and clear of debt. My furniture will fit nicely into this living room. Of course I'll also keep a few pieces of Granny's. Her rocker I'll put upstairs into the front bedroom, that's the one I plan on using. The extra furniture can be stored in the garage. Would you be able to help me begin moving in today?"

"Sy, this is weird how things are turning out. I already made plans to stay over, at least for another day, already talked to my Mom too. If you're ready, let's finish up our coffee and get on the road. I bet I can have you all moved in by this evening."

They made four trips to the apartment, not in the same day however. The second morning, on their final trip, they picked up the kitchen set, the easy chair and foot rest. She had her apartment phone disconnected and her grandmothers turned on. She also phoned the apartment management and made arrangements to send a check for the next month rent in lieu of a months' notice. It was accomplished.

"Would you like to stay for lunch Dave? I can make some scrambled egg sandwiches in a jiffy." She felt exhausted. It had been a whirlwind of lifting, lugging, shoving, but finally, everything was here and set in place, even the items in the garage.

"Sorry Sy, I'd like to but I had better get going. I already told Aunt Rose I wouldn't be returning this evening, she likely phoned my mom with the information. Before I forget, give me your phone number, I'll give you a call as soon as I get home. I'm really glad I was able to help get you moved. I think it was smart of you keeping the house. There's something so warm and inviting about it, I felt it the minute I walked in the door. There must be something of your grandmother's love of the place that still lingers. It surely seems to welcome you. You already seem to feel very much at home, as though you've lived here for years." He reached out, pulled her gently into his arms and held her closely nestled against his chest. "I find I like you a lot Sy. I hope to see you again soon. Who knows, maybe there's something the future has in store for us." Grasping her chin he tilted her head up and then cradled the back of her head with his hand as he pressed his lips warmly, tenderly against hers. He felt an electric shock tingle all the way to his toes as Sy lifted her arms, encircled his waist and pressed herself tightly against him. It was almost more than his poor heart could bear. With a sigh he removed her arms from his waist and stepped away. "This is dangerous territory little girl. It's not that I wouldn't like to carry you upstairs this minute and make love to you, it's the fact that we're not at that special place in time yet. We have a lot to learn about each other, I hope we get that chance because I have no intention of taking advantage of you.

Sylvia felt herself trembling, at first thinking there was something wrong because he had backed off so quickly. But then, the gleam in his eyes, the yearning look on his face and the roughness in his voice made her realized it was because he wanted her.

With a deep sigh, acknowledging the wisdom of his actions she flashed a devilish smile at him. "You are so right David. The last thing I'd want to do is completely lose all my self control and act like a wild woman. Goodness sake, what would you be thinking?" She almost giggled out loud at the expression on his face when imagining the scene. She managed to keep herself from bursting into unrestrained laughter, her nervous reaction to the feelings she was experiencing.

"Ah! David, I'm sorry. Sometimes I do act a bit silly, it's just that I have an odd sense of humor. I'm glad you respect me and I admire you more than you will ever know. I know you should be on your way, here's my phone number. I still have yours somewhere in my purse. As soon as you get home please call me."

She walked him to the door, brushed a light kiss on his cheek and watched as he got into his truck, fastened his seatbelt, started the engine and gave her a wave as he backed out of the driveway. His disappearance from view made her suddenly feel very much alone. Was it really less than a week since she took Granny's ashes up north? It felt like a long, long, time ago, but then so much had happened. She reminded herself that she'd have to look for the car keys to the Olds, it wasn't too old. Grandmother hadn't driven it very much, only for shopping or occasional visits to a few old friends. Tomorrow she'd check in the ignition, the most likely place the keys had been left. Locking the front door she returned to the kitchen.

That evening, finally snuggled into bed in the front bedroom, she had trouble falling asleep even though she'd slept like a baby the previous night. Thoughts of David kept wheeling through her mind, she cared for him more than she wanted to admit. He hadn't phoned even though he had left early enough to reach home at a reasonable hour, he should have been home by seven p.m. at the latest, and it was now after ten. Soon her eyelids fluttered closed and she was deeply asleep, the exhaustion of the past several days taking its toll. She didn't hear the creaking and popping of the homes construction settling in for the night. In the silence the repeated ringing of the phone echoed through the downstairs unheard by the sleeping young woman. Someone else would spend the night worrying also. The night passed uneventfully, house locked up tightly both front and back. As snug as any house could be.

Morning dawned with grey clouds and intermittent rain drops hitting the windows making rivulets of tiny streams trailing down to the ledges and then dripping into the flower beds below.

Sy sat at the table sipping coffee, contemplating what to do first. She had to dispose of Granny's clothing she had retrieved from various closets and drawers. Quite a few kitchen items would also be included. This would be a good time to phone her best friend Sally Rose. If she wasn't busy maybe she'd like to stop over, visit for a while and check to see if there were any items she'd like to have.

Within an hour the doorbell rang. When the door opened Sally quickly closed her umbrella giving it a vigorous shake. Sprays of raindrops spattered them both but it didn't dampen their joy at seeing each other. They had been friends since 9th grade in intermediate school, had gone through the trials of puberty, double dating, shared stories of first crushes and even, at one time, shared an apartment. At least until Sally had lost her job and moved back with her parents. Sally had rushed into marriage at age 22. Within a year she became pregnant, had a baby boy, and then filed for divorce because of her husband's irresponsibility and abandonment. She had, since then, met the man of her dreams and remarried. They were a perfect couple and deliriously happy. Al had even adopted her son. From the first Sally had joked that she had won the race for marriage and children, which Sy didn't mind one bit.

Placing the closed umbrella in the tall ceramic cylinder that sat near the door, Sy led the way into the kitchen, Sally trailing close behind. The teakettle was already steaming as Sy retrieved two delicate china cups, matching saucers and a teapot from one of the cupboards. She scooped a heaping spoonful of chamomile tea from a small ceramic canister sitting nearby, placed it in the pot and immediately poured in the boiling water. She covered it with a tea cozy to keep it hot while it steeped. She set out a plate of crackers, butter, a jar of Strawberry jam, two small serving plates with utensils, two linen napkins and finally a small pitcher of cream.

"My Goodness, Sy, what's the special occasion? When have we ever been this fancy just sharing a tea or coffee get-together?" Sally inspected her friends face closely, not seeing any sign of stress, but yet, something had happened. A peculiar glint in those hazel eyes, a look she couldn't exactly figure out. "What's going on? Has it something to do with Granny's passing, I know how close you two were, or has something else happened to upset you? Come on, spit it out, we two do not keep secrets from each other." Sally continued examining Sy's countenance.

Sy gave a quick glance at her friend as she poured the fragrant tea into their cups. "Let's enjoy our tea first since I'm not sure where to begin telling you about my adventure, I'll have to sort it all out first."

"Are you crazy, Sy? There's no way in heaven that I can sit here trying to eat when I wouldn't be able to keep my mouth shut from asking a million questions. I don't care where you begin your tale. Just start from the time you got up on the morning your story begins."

Thoughtfully, Sy spread a little butter on a cracker, took a bite and began to chew, her mind reliving her experiences from the time she had arrived at the forest road. Not thinking about manners she began to speak. Between bites of cracker and sips of tea, she related the entire story, right up until yesterday when David left to return home.

Sally had watched every play of emotion that flickered across Sy's face. There were some serious feelings involved between those two. Her intuition told her that her friend had finally met someone who was of serious interest. She couldn't remember anytime previously, other than crushes when they were in their teens, that Sy had been so intense about a guy. Good…it was about time, she thought.

"You're in love with him, aren't you?" Sally couldn't help grinning at the look of surprise that flashed across Sy's face. "Don't tell me you didn't realize that he had you wrapped around his little finger, I know you Sy, and you know yourself pretty darn well. All kidding aside, tell me you haven't felt that heavy-hearted yearning whenever you were close to him. Even now you have a disgustingly silly look on your face just listening to me talk about him. Ah! Ha! Right there it is, I dare you to go look into a mirror.

"I do NOT want to talk about this Sally, and I'm not in love with David either. He was very nice to me, bailed me out when I was in serious trouble, and even helped me move. That's the extent of it. He did kiss me, I admit, but he caught me at a weak moment. He lives 300 miles away and is a partner with his dad in a hardware store. I have my own life that I enjoy very much and have no intention of changing, or moving again. I like my job and people like my "Common Sense" advice column." Sy felt irritated and wondered how they ever got into this sort of conversation anyway. She was not in love. He was just a very good-hearted fellow who had been of great help in a couple of tough situations. She almost groaned aloud recalling the bike ride.

"Let's change the subject. What have you and Al been up to for the past month? I can't believe it's been that long since we've spoken." She examined her friends' face, for the first time noticing how pretty she looked with her blonde hair, fair skin and blue eyes. She actually seemed to glow.

"I have news of my own Sy, I'm pregnant again. I didn't want to mention it before I was sure it would "Take" and not be another miscarriage. Al is as ecstatic as am I, and at last Donny will have a sister or brother, just like he's been asking for. I'm due sometime in the middle of December." With a wide grin Sally tried to keep her enthusiasm in check but instead, was off on a happy tangent talking about baby clothes, furniture, repainting the extra bedroom and of course, reciting the list of names she and Al had come up with. She wanted everything in place before her girth became too uncomfortable and curtailed her activities. "I wanted to ask, would you be Godmother at the baptism?"

Sy couldn't help smiling, "Nothing would make me happier, and I'd love to. This reminds me of some of our youthful daydreams we used to share, this was one of them." She retrieved the pot, poured fresh tea into their cups, and then spent the remainder of the morning in serious discussions about all the little things that best friends talk about.

Later, after Sally had left for home and she had neatened up the kitchen, she decided to check Granny's car to see if the keys were there. She pushed the remote button on the wall near the back door that opened the garage. Once inside, out of the rain she peered through the cars window. The keys were in the ignition, just as she suspected. Retrieving them she checked the glove box and then the rear seats. There was a small parcel resting in the corner. Leaning far over, she was able to retrieve it. Whatever it was, Granny had been much more particular about not leaving things lying around. Closing both the car and then the garage door, she returned to the house.

Placing the package on the counter she unfastened the string and opened the wrapping. The recorder, extension cord neatly wrapped about it and several tapes secured with a rubber band, was exposed to view. "I wonder why she didn't leave it here on the counter where it wouldn't have been in the way." Sy mumbled to herself. It made no sense putting it in the car and in the back seat no less.

Not in the mood to listen to the tapes at the moment, she carried the recorder into the laundry room and placed it in the tall wooden cabinet used to store miscellaneous items. There were five shelves, each carrying a variety of odds and ends. Envelopes of both sizes, postal stamps, cookbooks, boxes of greeting cards for Christmas and other holidays, writing paper, tax records, extra pens and pencils, Bank records and checks. She had to make room near the envelopes where the recorder fit perfectly. She gave a sigh of pleasure that grandmother had actually used the thing. It would be interesting listening to the stories of her grandparents' lives.

There were a few things she had yet to do before she could truly say she was completely moved in. Picking up the cloth wrapped parcel from the laundry table she carried it upstairs into her bedroom, laid it on the bed and unwrapped the toweling that had protected it. The beautifully oil-painted picture that her grandfather loved so dearly was exposed to view, "The Thistle Plant." Sy couldn't help smiling to herself as she hung it on the best wall, one that would keep it from direct sunlight yet give her a first view when awaking each morning. Stepping back, she straightened it just a tiny bit more. "There, that's perfect, I can't think of another thing to do to make the room feel cozier." With a contented smile on her face she headed downstairs, carrying the terrycloth wrapping with her, hurrying a little faster when she heard the phone ringing. By the time she reached the kitchen the ringing had stopped….whoever it had been would likely call back. She was correct.

"Hello, yes, this is Sylvia Fields. I beg your pardon? What? What are you talking about, do I know you? I have no idea what you're referring to. Yes! I write a column for our local newspaper. It's the "Common Sense" advice column. I'm sorry sir, I don't" ….The caller hung up abruptly leaving Sy wondering who and what the man had been referring to. He had spoken with such a soft, gentle voice at the onset of the conversation but with each of his questions unresolved, his voice had gradually raised, eventually becoming loud, aggressive, and downright threatening. Sylvia felt a chill travel through her body making her tremble with nervousness. "I wonder what in the world that was all about?" She asked herself, knowing she would not be able to answer her own question, knowing there was no one alive who could give her a sensible reason for the phone call. She glanced about the kitchen, walked to the back door and secured the lock, checked all the windows and even the front door, however the sense of threat did not go away.

The rest of the afternoon was spent doing laundry, house work, cleaning both the upstairs and downstairs bathrooms. Not that they really needed it but only to keep her time and thoughts occupied. It was evening when she finished, not even noting the lateness of the hour.

Exhausted, she treated herself to a hot, leisurely shower using her favorite scented body shampoo. She then donned one of Granny's flannel nightgowns, one of several that she had saved for those times when she needed the feeling of coziness, warmth, and the long ago childhood memories of Gram's arms holding her closely when she had been hurt or frightened. Surprisingly, Sy fell asleep immediately, sleeping through the entire night, every extra ounce of energy having been entirely used up.

The warmth of bright sunlight warming her face awakened her. When her eyes focused on the painting it seemed to glow with its own inner light. What a wonderful beginning to the day it seemed to offer. Teeth brushed, hair groomed, dressed in her favorite jeans and tee, wearing comfortable tennis shoes, she made up the bed and stuffed yesterdays garments down the old fashioned, but very handy, laundry chute located on one of the bathroom walls. Too bad modern houses don't have these any more she mused, she'll enjoy the convenience as much as granny did.

Sy was already downstairs preparing scrambled egg on toast, pouring a glass of juice, when she suddenly recalled the upsetting telephone conversation of yesterday. It didn't seem so threatening this morning, just some fellow getting upset because the people he'd wanted to contact had passed away. That'd make anybody angry she thought, knowing if you'd been a few months earlier you could have had your questions answered. She dismissed the entire episode from her mind. She had too many other things to occupy her time today, for one thing, picking up the mail packet from her boss that contained letters from people who wrote asking for "Common Sense" advice on all sorts of problems. Her Sunday column was very popular, provided her with a comfortable salary, plus she adored reading about all the trials and tribulations folks experienced, some quite hilarious. Her boss, Mr. Simpson, had taken a huge chance on her when she had applied for a job promoting her idea of the column and giving him a reasonable time-limit for its success. Thankfully, it was greeted with enthusiasm and her employment was secure.

Breakfast over, she neatened the kitchen and retrieved her purse and car keys. She was out the door, into Granny's car, now hers she realized, and on the road. It was a four-door cream-colored Oldsmobile with leather seats and all the amenities a person could ask for. The computer monitor told her the tire pressure was low. She stopped at the next gas station and bought gasoline, filling the tank. She had the fluids checked, and then asked the young man to fill and gauge the correct tire air pressure. His wide smile told her he hoped that would gain him an advantage, maybe even a phone number. She did give him a tip which he considered a second best award.

When she reached the office she headed directly to Mr. Simpsons office. A quick tap on his door and then, observing his nod through the glass panel, she entered, a wide smile greeting his welcoming grin.

"Glad to see you Sy, I'm really sorry about your grandmother, I know how close you two were. Where the heck did you get that bruise on your forehead, did something happen on your trip up north with her ashes?" He gave her a piercing look, realizing there was something vaguely different about her. He couldn't exactly put his finger on what that difference was. He waited expectantly for her reply, giving her a smile of friendly encouragement as he passed over the packet of mail that asked for Sy's "Common Sense" advice.

"I was involved in an accident and unfortunately I totaled my car too." Sy replied. "Thank goodness one of the locals was kind enough to give me a lift home. It was also convenient that he could overstay at his aunts because he ended up helping me get moved. I gave up my apartment and I'm now living at my grandmother's house. I still can't believe she's gone, I swear I can still feel her presence everywhere about the place." Sy felt if she didn't change the subject quickly she'd make a fool of herself. The sudden realization that her Granny was truly gone forever had her on the verge of a serious crying spell. She had to get out of there, and soon.

"Thanks, Ken, I just wanted to collect my mail and give you a rundown on what has been happening. I really should get going. I can feel by the bulk of this package that there will be a slew of letters to answer." Sy arose from her seat. Turning toward the door she gulped, "I'll phone you in a few days," and then she was hurrying through the office compound, out the doors, and practically running to the parking lot. She was able to hold back her sobs until she was safely secluded inside her car where the tearful storm broke releasing all the tears she had been holding back for so long. It was quite a while before she was able to get herself under control but surprisingly, she felt much better.

Tilting down the visor she inspected her face in the mirror attached to its backside. A little powder and lipstick applied with a touch of toner to hide the hint of blue under her eyes and she looked presentable. At least she could get the shopping done without looking like a forlorn waif.

The remainder of the day was spent selecting fruits, vegetables, canned goods, fresh containers of herbs and spices, all the comestibles necessary for a nicely setup kitchen. When she returned home she tossed the mail packet on the counter and then busied herself clearing the cupboards of old supplies and restocking with the new. The refrigerator and freezer were cleaned and new purchases neatly arranged in both sections. At last, with a satisfied sigh, she relaxed at the table a fresh cup of coffee steaming before her, an onion bagel, sliced, with cream cheese slathered on and sprinkled lightly with freshly ground peppercorns. No wonder she'd felt starved, it was already mid afternoon. Appetite satisfied, she felt contented. For the first time since the trip north with Grannies ashes she was able to sit quietly and relive all the things that had happened. Mentally she revisited the Kendall's and David, both before and after her accident, they'd been so kind, truly concerned about her recovery. She remembered the kiss she and David had shared, the excited thrill that had seemed to touch every part of her body. True, she was very attracted to him, but to no avail. The many miles between them put up a wall too high for commitment to overcome. She would never move up north, he would never move down here.

With a sigh of frustration she carried the luncheon utensils to the sink where she washed, dried them, and put them away. Retrieving the mail packet she sat back down and tore open the bundle. A myriad of multicolored envelopes tumbled onto the table. A smile lit her face at the profusion of questions she would be examining, some quite serious, others so outlandish they would cause outright laughter. Once in a while there was that oddly tragic note that would almost bring her to tears.

Stacking the letters into a pile, she opened and began to read the first of many. Only a sentence or two told her if this was a "Keeper" or one for disposal. Slowly she depleted the correspondence into those she would respond to. She did place one aside that she wanted to show her boss. Normally this type was nothing to worry about. However, in this instance, the person described her Granny's Oldsmobile, the car she was now using.

The afternoon passed quickly. In the morning the Cable Company would be out to hook her up to the internet. She'd be able to write the responses to her selected letters, email them to her boss Mr. Simpson, who would then give them to the printing department. The thought crossed her mind that it was sad she couldn't have persuaded Gram to purchase a computer. It would have been fun exchanging emails with her.

Sy liked sitting at the kitchen table, being able to enjoy the view outside while still doing work related activities. "What wouldn't anybody give to have this pleasant office?" She really liked her lap top computer too. It was lightweight and would set on the long, low cabinet built against the wall when not in use. The printer/scanner would be concealed inside the shelf below, hidden behind its closed door. "I wish tomorrow morning would get here quickly." She murmured to herself. "Everything that needed to be done has been accomplished. I'll be able to relax, work on my column and enjoy my new home but, Oh! How I miss seeing you Granny. You were my rock through good times and bad, a solid support knowing that the love you felt for me was my warm comforter protecting me from the cold world. It helps that I'm living in your house, I still feel your presence." At that moment it felt like a gentle puff of air, a soft word whispered into her ear....she had forgotten Granny's recordings.

Reaching into the storage cupboard, moving a few items out of the way, she retrieved the recorder along with the tapes and carried them into the kitchen. "Oh! My! God! This is going to be harder than I realized," she thought, "I never imagined I would be listening to her dear voice after she had passed away." She placed the recorder on the table, the same spot it had been placed when she had coaxed Gram into doing the recording and plugged it into the same receptacle. Sy could not bring herself push the "On" button. She had no idea what those first words would be, but she knew, as surely as she lived and breathed, they would remain in her mind forever. "Fraidycat," Sy remembered. That's what Gram would say when you were afraid for no logical reason. Gram would show, explain, touch, examine go through every motion and emotion with you to build your confidence until you yourself could honestly say, "I'm not a Fraidycat, there IS a logical reason for everything." Sy felt a smile tickle the corners of her lips recalling many of those long ago lessons about bravery. Gram had been correct. There was always a plausible explanation.

With a deep sigh and a little hiccup of nervousness she pushed the rewind button and waited for the tape to stop. Hesitating only a moment, she pressed "Play." For a few seconds only silence and then Granny's voice filled the room.

(Tape)…"Well! I'm doing it Sy, just like you said I could, I can't believe this little skinny thing is going to record everything I say. Where should I start? You said at the beginning, so I guess that would be at my very first memory. I have a lot of years to travel back through. My mother Fern, (your grandmother), told me one day when we had been reminiscing about my childhood, that I began to walk at the age of about one year. Until then I hadn't known how old I was but I could always remember those steps very vividly, it was the first outstanding moment of my young life. I recall the parlor very well, I realize now that the couch and chair were a matching color of deep burgundy but at that time it only attracted my attention. Someone was sitting on the couch, I knew it wasn't mommy, maybe it was daddy. I was sitting on the floor next to the chair and I had pulled myself up until I was standing, hanging on to the edge of it. Everything across the room looked blurry but I could see the person's image and hear that the person was coaxing me, holding their arms out to me. I didn't think of crawling as I looked down at my feet. I didn't know what they were called but I knew what I wanted them to do. They each tried to obey, but they were confused, sort of making little circles in the air before setting down. Finally they both stayed on the ground and I managed to place one in front of the other, stumbling-staggering almost to the couch where the person grabbed hold of me before I could fall. I remember they called out, and of course they were telling somebody that I'd taken my very first steps. That's what I remember about that first important, life-changing event. I don't believe I ever crawled again." (End)

Sy turned the tape off, this was enough for today. She was amazed that Gram could remember something that happened so many years ago and at so young an age, she did believe her however, it wasn't in her character to lie. She placed the recorder in a corner on the counter. "In sight, in mind" as the family saying went. She would listen to the recordings whenever she had time to relax, it was something to look forward to. Instead of feeling sad she had felt as though the two of them had been sitting together once again, the feeling of love and companionship a strong, unbreakable bond. The sense of comfort she experienced was tangible and not to be denied.

She would be busy tomorrow catching up on her letters, but right now she felt starved and it was too late to cook. Tomorrow she would have to begin making sensible meals, but what to fix for today? She checked the small pantry and found the makings for tuna salad. She removed two slices of bread from the whole wheat loaf in the freezer, the slices would be defrosted by the time the tuna was prepared.

At last she sat before the large kitchen window enjoying her hot chocolate and tuna salad sandwich as she watched evening descend and the first stars began to make their appearance. She hadn't realized until now how closed-in her apartment had been. There was a certain harmony of spirit just watching nature slowly change late afternoon into evening and then into night. She hadn't turned the kitchen lights on so the spreading colors of twilight looked extraordinarily brilliant fading into lavender, deep purple and then darkness. It had happened so gradually she had not even been aware of the time. Just as she reached to retrieve her cup and plate, a sudden flash of movement in the backyard near the side of the garage caught her attention, when she tried to focus, nothing was there.

"Likely a late nesting bird or even a stray cat," she mused as she reached for the light switch and the kitchen was illuminated, seemingly somewhat brightly after sitting in the darkness for so long. Just to be sure, she checked the backdoor lock before turning the light off and heading upstairs. She could hardly wait to hit the bed.

Edging his way across the yard, staying within the shadows to avoid any chance of exposure, he watched the young woman through the large uncurtained window as she sat eating. He'd been positive she had spotted him when the dove he'd startled had drawn her attention for a moment. Fortunately he was safe from exposure now, tucked within the overhanging branches of a rather large lilac bush. This was the first chance to get a really close look at her, the bitch, she had ruined his marriage. He was still pissed at what had happened up north after he'd followed her there. He'd seen her alone in the woods too, if he'd been the blood and guts type guy that would have been the end of her. Then that good-looking' dude came along. He almost choked, laughing at the memory of seeing her on those handlebars. He'd thought his chance at revenge was over for the time being but something told him to stick around for awhile. Good thing he had because the perfect opportunity presented itself after the young stud dropped her off at her car. As soon as she was on the highway, no cars in sight, he'd fastened his seatbelt, stepped on the gas and done a "cop-spin" on the back-end of her car hoping it would spin out of control, do a flip and send her to never-never land. Bad vibes because her car only spun three or four times and then came to rest at the side of the road. Good thing he'd managed to maneuver his car down that overgrown side road before any traffic appeared. He'd waited, hiding in the brush, watching for any movement from her vehicle when a cop car came along. It hadn't been too long before an ambulance was on the scene. That's when he'd decided to head back home and hang around her apartment. Sooner or later she'd show up, he wasn't the sort to give up easily when something this important had to be taken care of. He gave a silent laugh to himself feeling smug. He was exactly where he could pick and choose the time and place for his "pay-back", she wouldn't have a clue what hit her.

When the lights when on for only a moment, he got a great view of Sy as she checked the back door. She wasn't a bad looking broad, great body too. For a few moments he imagined getting his hands on her, maybe having s little fun before he turned her lights out. The thought made him realize it had been a while since he'd had a piece of ass. His last had been his wife Rita after he'd beat the shit out of her for refusing him. She had managed to grab his whiskey bottle and brain him with it. Then she'd skipped out taking his paycheck and the dog too. He had no idea where she disappeared to, didn't really give a damn. The last thing she'd done was leave a note on the kitchen table, it was the reply to a letter she had written to "Common Sense." He remembered picking it up and reading it, with every word his rage kept building until, with a choked yell, he'd tossed the whiskey bottle through the kitchen window. He still recalled each word….

Dear Sy, my husband is a bully who likes to drink too much too often. When he's drunk he gets mean and I'm afraid all the time. What should I do?
Rita

Dear Rita, I can't advise you on marital problems. If the marriage road is too rough, only you can decide the best way to rid yourself of those bumps, they will not disappear by themselves. Good Luck, Sy

THE THISTLE SEED

Sy awoke suddenly, possibly because of the suns' brightness or maybe just the lateness of the hour. One moment she had been deeply asleep, the next wide awake. She glanced at the bedside clock, 9:15a.m., "Good Grief" she thought, all set to bounce out of bed until she suddenly realized she had nothing to be in a hurry about. No appointments, not a solitary thing that needed her attention. Giving a leisurely stretch she relaxed, laying there for a moment and letting her thoughts wander through the various items on her agenda. Maybe this morning she'd listen to Granny's tapes again. The thought spurred her into action. A quick shower, her hair washed and towel dried, with a light touch of makeup and dab of her favorite perfume she was on her way downstairs. Maybe just coffee and toast this morning since it was so late, she glanced at the clock, almost 10a.m. already. She detested these late starts but the extra sleep she'd enjoyed gave her a feeling of enthusiasm and energy just waiting to be tapped.

After refilling her coffee cup she retrieved the recorder, pushed the "Play" button and then leaned back in her chair. Granny's voice filled the silent void.

(Tape)...."Hmm! Now let me see, I think I must have been about three years old. As I recall now, this was after the Great Depression when things were very tough for everyone. My grandmother Ella, (your Great-granny) owned the house and a few pieces of property which, little by little, she'd had to sell. It came to the point that she had to rent the entire upstairs of the house to make ends meet, we moved into the basement. My grandpa and my dad were gone, looking for work. There was just Granny Ella, my mom Fern and myself. Granny had made me a pretty rag doll from scraps of cloth. She was sewing it together but was having trouble rethreading her needle. I remember watching her try over and over again. Finally I said, "I can do it Grammy." She carefully handed me the needle, showing me how to hold the thread. I remember it as being very easy for me to do and didn't take very long. Both mom and granny were excited about it and praised me no end. Of course, now that I think back, who knows how long I tried? But I did learn that it's a good thing to be patient and not to give up easily. At the bitter end, because of the depression, Granny lost her home. She couldn't find the funds to pay the property taxes. Grandpa moved to his sister's house in Holly, Grandma rode with her second eldest son Ted, his wife and two sons out to California. She got a job working for a wealthy gentleman who owned a lot of property including a lodge named "Paradise" high up in the mountains. She cared for the cabins that vacationers and hunters rented. It ended up that the wealthy man became her son-in-law after her youngest daughter became widowed and traveled out to California to visit her mom and became that rich man's wife. The great depression changed so many peoples' lives, mine and your granny Ferns' also, some few for the better, at least those who had employment and no debts, but so many more were drawn into poverty. Once-proud people could be seen trying to sell apples out on street corners, their sense of security gone, disappeared. There were food lines at places that fed the hungry and flop houses where men without jobs, without hope, went to spend their nights, no longer having a home or family because they could no longer feed or support them. Some people sent their children to orphanages out west, hoping to one day find them again but unfortunately, many never did. I hope we never have another time like that. The heartbreak of broken homes and lives were never fully repaired. It was many years before things began to get back to normal. (End)

Sy turned the recorder off, sitting in silence yet still mentally listening to Granny Eleanor's' voice. She could almost place herself in the episodes Gran had been talking about. How she wished she had taken more time to talk to her, listen to her stories. Sy placed the recorder back into its resting place on the counter. A feeling of frustration and disquiet settled upon her putting her in a rare bad mood which lasted only moments, until the doorbell rang.

"Good morning! Cable Company Miss Fields, so sorry I'm late. I had a few problems at the last appointment which delayed me. If you'll show me where you want your Cable hookup, I'll get right to work on it."

Sy led him into the kitchen, pointed to the place she wanted her computer connection and watched as he wrote up the request. Then he was out the back door and the next thing she saw was him carrying a ladder to the telephone pole that sat behind the garage. Within an hour the line was strung and attached to the house, wiring led from that to the site where he drilled through the outer wall, pushed the cable line through, screwed on the metal connector, hooked up the modem, and then attached that cable to her laptop. He asked that she turn it on and within moments she was online. "Terrific, I can't believe we're already finished, I thought it would take much longer than it did." Sy had a huge smile on her face, her moody feeling completely gone. He handed her the receipt to sign and then removed her yellow copy of the work order, waited until she filled out a check handed it to him, and then wrote "Paid in full." She saw him to the door and closed it behind his retreating figure.

"At last" She murmured softly to herself. "Now I can reply to my Common Sense letters and email them to Ken. That will be my first project for tomorrow morning. I adore my job, the convenience of no fighting traffic. I'm well paid and I'm sure glad I applied for a copyright to my column name, no one else can steal it from me." She gave a huge sigh of contentment, what more could a person ask for?"

She didn't feel like working on her Common Sense letters, it was now late afternoon. Peering out the window, really taking note of the condition of the flowerbeds, she saw that some needed pinching back to encourage growth, a few weeds were gaining a foothold too. "What the heck," she thought, it won't take that long and at least I won't feel lazy when I look out and admire my handiwork. She found a pair of work gloves in the laundry cupboard and headed out the back door, pushing the garage door- opener button on the wall as she exited. She'd need a trash container, a rake and a shovel.

Working her way from the side of the house and then along the side fence to its corner, she weeded, dug, pulled and groomed the flower beds until they looked fantastic. In a short time she also toiled along the back fence, removing every unwanted growth, pruning every stray tendril until she finally ended up at the lilac bush.

Someone watching her would have thought she had taken ill. She turned pale, her hands began to tremble as she nervously picked up her tools and the trash container returning them quickly to the garage. She pressed the "Close" button situated on the inside edge and then hurried into the house, securely locking the door behind her.

Before pulling off the gloves she reached into the cabinet, extracted a small plastic bag, and watched as numerous cigarette butts dropped in. They were dry, dropped there after the rain the day Sally had visited. She clenched her teeth as a shiver of fear travelled up her spine. She sealed the bag and pulled off the gloves, stuffing them into a corner of one of the shelves, all the while hating the feeling of fear and distrust she was beginning to feel about the safety of her environment. She wondered if she should contact the police but then, what could she tell them other than the fact that she'd found some cigarette butts out in her yard? As anger began to fulminate, her fear began to diminish. "Take precautions", common sense told her, "get some outdoor floodlights installed, maybe an alarm system, and most important, take your time."

Glancing at the clock, the time showed 6:15pm. She realized she was famished, having eaten only a slice of toast with her morning coffee before listening to Grams' tape. Searching through the pantry she decided on something quick and easy. She opened a can of vegetable soup, poured it into a micro-safe container and placed it into the microwave oven that hung below a section of the cabinets. She also retrieved crackers, soup bowl, spoon and napkin, placing them all on the table. Just when she was reaching out to remove the hot soup from the microwave, the door chimes sounded their musical melody, startling her for a moment.

"Who in the world could it be this late in the day?" she wondered, not for a moment sensing that any sort of danger could be possible. Hurrying to the front door, peeking through the shirred curtains of the sidelights, she could see the tall outline of a man who looked vaguely familiar. "Oh! Good! Grief!....It's David." She glanced down at her soiled clothing, realizing her hair was a mess and her face likely not very clean. Gritting her teeth with exasperation at what a sight she must look, she opened the door. She couldn't help that a wide smile lit up her face because she truly was happy to see him.

When Sy swung the door open and David saw that wide grin he thought she was the cutest little thing he had ever seen in his entire life. He picked her up, swung her around and planted an enthusiastic welcome kiss on her lips that made her blush to the very roots of her hair. She couldn't help but wrap her arms tightly around him, losing herself completely in the absolute joy of seeing him again.

"Come in Davey, I was just about to have something to eat, there's enough for two." She latched the door and then led him into the kitchen where she got another place setting and then ladled hot soup into their bowls, all the while talking a blue streak, telling him everything that had happened since she had last seen him, everything, that is, except for the stranger and the cigarette butts.

David told her all the news of his family, also that Aunt Rose was in the hospital. He had driven down this morning after she had phoned his mom and said she was coughing quite a bit and was having trouble breathing. "Doc put her in the hospital and she'll be there until she recovers. I tried to phone you earlier but got no answer." Dave's eyes twinkled and a mischievous grin tickled the edges of his lips as he gave Sy's soiled clothing a once over. "Did you plant any veggies?"

Sy almost choked on the cracker, she had completely forgotten about her grubby appearance. She glanced at the clock, almost 9p.m. where in the world had the time flown. Clearing the table she rinsed and then placed everything in the dishwasher.

"You're welcome to stay over Davey. The back bedroom is already made up, even has towels and soap in its bathroom, I have an extra toothbrush for you too. I'm exhausted, I need a shower and a good night's sleep. I don't mean to rush you but I truly am ready to drop I'm so tired." Sy checked that the side door was locked, David followed her up the stairway. She indicated the bedroom where he was to sleep and with a quick "Goodnight," she entered her room and closed the door.

David inspected the pleasant surroundings which gave the warm feeling of an old-fashioned atmosphere. The maple bed had a patch-work quilted spread. A maple dresser and chest were positioned against two walls, while a rocking chair with a padded seat matching the bed quilt sat in a corner of the room. The floor was thickly carpeted in neutral beige. The full bathroom had warm rose-colored tile half-way up the one wall that the door opened against, and ended at the tub/shower. The end wall tile extended from the tub/shower, under the edge of a frosted, curtained window, over to the corner and behind where the commode sat. Next to the commode, the double sink/vanity, covered with square "oatmeal" colored tiles, extended along the wall and back to the edge of the door frame. A very large mirror covered the entire wall over the double sink vanity. The floor was tiled in small ½" x 1" multicolored beige, pink and rose tiles that was visible at the outer edges of the rose hued carpet which ran the center length of the 12 ft. room. Sy's grandmother had great taste, he thought. Who else would have considered covering the cold tile so nighttime trips would not shock a barefoot person completely awake?

He looked into the wall cabinet that hung over the commode. There were towels, wash cloths, toothpaste, shampoo, hair spray, cologne, perfume, extra rolls of tissue, body lotion, and even a canister of room spray. He reached for two of the thick bath towels and a bottle of shampoo. There was already a new bar of soap in the shower.

Stripping off his clothes he leaned in, adjusted the water temp, stepped into the tub and slid closed the heavy frosted glass shower door. "Ah! This is pure heaven," he muttered to himself, suddenly feeling the weariness of the long hours of driving from home, the time spent at the hospital getting Rose admitted and then waiting with her for an available room.

Stepping from the shower he quickly towel dried his hair and his body and then tossed the towel over the shower door. He wrapped the extra towel about his waist and headed for the bedroom. Removing the bedspread he folded it and draped it neatly across the rocking chair. He turned back the covers, clicked off the bedside light, dropped the towel from his waist and crawled into bed. Within moments he was sound asleep.

Sy had been in bed listening to the sound of the shower, enjoying the feeling of security it gave her knowing there was someone she knew and trusted spending the night in her home. Maybe in the morning she'd tell David about the cigarette butts, the evidence that someone had been watching her. It gave her the creeps just thinking about it. Soon her eyelids became too heavy to keep open and she fell deeply asleep, the beginnings of a familiar nightmare looming on her dreamland horizon. It was always the same....

The sky and land met at the horizon, both a golden yellow, blending together so well she could not separate the two. Not a living creature to see or hear existed, only the deadly silence. Far away, at the edge of the horizon, a tiny black speck hovered, sending out a powerful but still distant HUM of evil. She was frozen in place, nowhere to run or hide. The speck grew larger and larger the sound louder and more powerful until she was filled with total panic, the monstrosity hovering directly overhead. That was when she awoke covered in perspiration, her body so paralyzed with fear and muscles so rigidly tensed that they were as stiff and unresponsive as a board. There was nothing to analyze, the total encompassing power of sight and sound completely overwhelmed her, making her feel as though she would be obliterated into nothingness. It took a while for her breathing to return to normal, her heartbeat to slow and her muscles to relax.

Turning onto her stomach she pulled the other pillow close and willed herself to sleep. In a minimal amount of time she was breathing lightly. She would sleep through the remainder of the night. The patter of rain drops against the window awoke her at 8:05a.m.

She made up the bed before getting dressed in jeans and a cotton blouse. Even though it was raining she felt in a very good mood, didn't mind the grey skies one bit. She caught herself humming a tune she didn't recognize at first until she realized it was a popular love song, the title name lost to her. She noticed David's door open, his bed remade, everything neatly in place. "Please don't tell me he already left," she muttered to herself as she hurried down the stairs and headed toward the kitchen. It was then that the aroma of fried bacon tickled her nose.

David turned toward her with an embarrassed grin spread across his face. He held out a platter containing fried bacon, four sunny-side-up eggs, and buttered toast, the other hand held the carafe of freshly made coffee. The table was already set with plates, utensils, cups and two small glasses of orange juice, cream and sugar. He placed the platter in the center of the table and the coffee carafe on the heatproof pad. Pulling a chair out and seating Sy, he then took his place opposite her.

"This is a surprise David, the last thing I expected was a big breakfast, let alone having it prepared by someone else, a fellow no less. Do you make a habit of doing this when staying overnight at someone's house?" Although she was not in the habit of indulging in such a cholesterol laden meal, she felt hungry enough to consume every bite.

David couldn't help grinning at the astonished look on Sy's face as she helped herself from the selections on the platter, he enjoyed seeing a woman dig into a meal and from the sized portions she took, she must be starved. He felt famished also.

Neither felt like indulging in conversation, at least not until both plates were wiped free of egg with the last piece of toast, and their last bite had been washed down with a sip of coffee. When they give a sigh of contentment, almost simultaneously, it brought a smile from both.

"That was the most delicious breakfast I've ever enjoyed Dave, you're a very good cook, and do you bake too?" Sy watched as a bashful grin spread across his face. Most guys didn't know how to scrambled eggs, let alone do a complete meal.

"My mom taught me. She said that someday I'd have to know how to feed myself, take care of a house, do laundry and even sew. At first I was ashamed because none of my friends had to learn any of that stuff, but the more I learned, the better I became. I like being able to take care of myself. Now when I need some clean clothes, or lose a button or decide my bedroom needs cleaning, I don't have to ask, I can just do for myself. I like the independence it gives me, takes away the feeling of being helpless. I'm a self-sufficient young man. Eventually a wife will appreciate my talents."

Sy couldn't contradict him about being appreciated, he was honest, hard working, and definitely would be quite a catch for someone. If she felt she was ready for marriage, she'd nab him before someone else did, but marriage was not yet on her agenda. She liked her life just the way it was with no permanent attachments. Being able to come and go as she pleased was definitely her style. She couldn't imagine having to explain to someone where she was going, or what time she would be home. Just thinking about a situation like that made her edgy and uncomfortable. Nope!. Being tied down like that would strangle her. She realized David was looking at her expectantly, waiting for a possible reply.

"Oops! Sorry David, I was lost for moment thinking about something and got a little sidetracked. I'm really amazed at you and your accomplishments. You're right, not many guys would bother learning how to do "Woman's work." You deserve a lot of credit and so does your mom, she's the one that taught you."

Sy began to clear the table, rinsing the dishes and then stacking them in the dishwasher. She wouldn't turn it on until it was filled, which usually took about a week or two, depending on visitors. This practice saved water and liquid dish soap since she detested any kitchenware sitting in the sink. It took a while to use up a twelve piece place setting. She smiled recalling Granny's logic about things. "You can never have too many dishes or silverware settings, she'd admonish. Don't be stingy with cookware either, you should always have a variety of sizes."

David broke into her reverie with a laugh, he had been watching her, so serious about rinsing the dishes and silverware well, wiping the counter, cleaning the glass top stove, making everything neat as a pin, as his mom always said. She also did things like his mom keeping everything neat and in its place. Maybe that was why he thought her so interesting. He walked over to her taking her hand, "I'll be leaving in a short time for the hospital to check on my Aunt Rose, Sy. I'd like it a lot if you could come with me. I know she'd love to meet you." For a moment Sy was very tempted but her intuition brought a common sense response. "Normally I'd jump at the chance Davey, but your Aunt wouldn't appreciate a visit from me at this time, she won't be feeling her best. How about giving me a call when she's back home again?"

"That was a little dim-witted of me Sy, and you're right. But if you don't mind, I'll give you a call when I reach the hospital and let you know what's happening. If you have nothing planned for this evening, would you like to take in a movie, maybe grab a bite to eat?"

Maybe it was the slight discomfort she felt because of the big breakfast, or maybe it was the feeling of just a little too much pressure about meeting his Aunt, Sy felt resentment flare. She almost had to bite her tongue to keep herself from snapping an angry reply but she stopped herself in time. "I have some work to catch up on, and letters to reply to David, I'm really sorry. I've enjoyed your company and I hope we can get together again soon." She was steering Dave toward the front door as she was speaking, not noticing the puzzled, hurt expression on his face. I hope your Aunt is better and able to return home.

He turned to thank her for letting him stay over but the door was already closing in his face. He couldn't believe what had just happened. There had been no harsh words spoken and he knew for a fact he hadn't said anything rude to cause her to act in such a manner, but something weird had occurred and now he was in a rotten mood which would stick with him all day…on second thought, maybe more than a day. He hurried down the steps not even bothering to look back to see if she was watching, jumped in his truck and sped off, first to the hospital to check on his aunt and then back to her house. He had things to do.

Sy leaned against the door completely baffled by her actions. What had caused her to be so short tempered? Dave hadn't done a thing to deserve to be literally tossed out on his ear, yet a feeling of relief seemed to settle over her. She was not ready to make a commitment and David seemed too comfortable making plans for her involvement with his family. Not that she didn't like them, she in fact did. But enough of this self analyzing she thought as she pushed away from the door, she had laundry to do bedding to change. She headed upstairs to strip the bed Dave had slept in, at the same time grabbing towels and her soiled clothing. She felt a need to fill her time with something that would keep her mind occupied and too busy to dwell on things she really didn't want to delve into. "You're nutty as a fruit cake," she told herself, "get to work, make yourself useful." And she did.

By the end of the day the house was spotless. Wood floors shone, furniture polished, carpets vacuumed, the light scent of lemon oil a testament of her hard work. From the kitchen the aroma of homemade chicken vegetable soup was the finale. Just like in the old days when she came home from school and Gram waited with milk and oatmeal cookies to tide her over until the soup was ready. With a reminiscing smile she ladled a scoop into one of the set of stoneware bowls they had used since she was a child and then she sat at the table enjoying the rich flavor. It had been one of Grannies favorite recipes.

She now felt drained of every ounce of energy she had expended, but it was a good feeling. She had accomplished every single thing she had set her mind to do and now the house shown with love and care. Checking that both doors were securely locked she ambled up the stairs and into the shower. Afterward she used the hairdryer and then slipped into one of Granny's old soft flannel nightgowns. Within moments of her head hitting the pillow she was sound asleep.

The gentle sighing of the wind moving through tree branches began to strengthen, low clouds were beginning to appear on the horizon, signals that a storm was on its way. In the distance, flashes of lightening lit up the underside of black clouds that billowed and swirled. A loud crack of lightening and powerful growl of thunder rolled across the sky, seeming to go on for miles, passing over the house where Sy lay deeply asleep.

Far away the spinning tip of a cloud began to drop earthward, stretching, reaching, elongating until it became a whirlwind sucking everything within reach into its powerful maw. Debris began to attach itself as the funnel grew larger with every mile it progressed.

Sy was in the yellow house waiting for Granny. Wake up child, granny seemed to be shaking her, you must go into the basement, Wake up Sylvia, you must hurry. Granny would not stop shaking her. Sy pulled the pillow over her head and held on...

The bed was shaking so vigorously that Sy was toppled onto the floor, mattress and bedding landing on top of her. Wind was screaming past the windows which no longer contained glass panes. It seemed an interminable amount of time passed as she huddled under the bedding and then, just as quickly as the shattering sounds had begun, all became silent. After a few moments Sy pulled herself from under the bedding and then wrapped the blanket about her shivering body, she stood in the midst of the rubble surveying the damage. It was a mess, glass and pictures scattered about the room, the front windows completely wrecked. Placing her feet carefully so she wouldn't be cut, she made her way through the debris to the bathroom where only a few things were out of place. Slipping on her shoes which she'd left on the floor before taking her shower, she inspected the other three upstairs rooms. It seemed the only repairs needed would be the front windows of her bedroom. She retrieved slacks and a blouse from the closet, underclothing from a dresser drawer. Returning to the bathroom she brushed her teeth, combed her hair, applied a light touch of lipstick and then donned her clothing. She hurried downstairs to see what the storm had wrought. Again, the front windows were shattered, the living room in disarray but the front door and sidelight panels were undamaged, maybe because of the added support of the brass insets. The kitchen and dining room were also untouched.

Sy reached for Grams little black phone book, the insurance company would be listed there. Unfortunately, it was not under the "I's." She searched page by page and finally found it listed under its name, Universal Insurance. "Sure." She mumbled to herself, "It had to be the very end of the alphabet." She picked up the phone, ready to punch in the numbers…No dial tone. "Oh! Good! Grief! What am I supposed to do now? No electricity, no coffee….no phone, and I can't just leave the house open and unattended while I look for assistance. She sat at the table disgruntled, nervous, and wishing for either coffee or tea to sooth her nerves and warm her insides. It was then she heard a horn honking from outside in the driveway. Before she got to the front door a hand reached through the open living room window holding a Styrofoam cup and a voice said, "Peace offering, can I come in?" David's head popped around the corner, a shy grin on his face. "I'd heard the storm had hit in your area, thought you'd like some company, maybe even some help in case there was any damage."

Sy opened the door, stepping back to allow him entrance. "I'm so sorry David. I don't know what got into me yesterday. After you left I felt embarrassed, couldn't understand why I had acted so badly. The only thing

I could think of was that I'd suddenly felt pressured, but about what I have no idea."

David checked out the broken windows, also the upper story didn't look too bad. He could probably have them repaired in two days time at the most. He followed Sy into the kitchen and sat with her at the table while they drank the coffee and ate the donuts he'd brought. He glanced at her occasionally, thinking she looked darn good, even relaxed for someone who'd just been hit with a storm. As for Sy, she was grateful that David wasn't the type to hold a grudge, she'd actually changed her attitude about him and she needn't be concerned about marriage. If the subject came up she always had the option of saying "No." Suddenly a friendly smile lit up her face. "Davey, you're quite a guy, and I'm awfully glad you came by. Do you have any ideas about the windows that need fixing? Sy watched him expectantly, waiting for his reply.

Don't worry about a thing Sy, I haven't worked at the hardware store these many years and not learned how to do maintenance on a home. Dad taught me from an early age. You clean up the glass while I remove the damaged frames and take measurements. I'll also pick up some heavy duty plastic and cover the upstairs windows to keep the weather out, but the ones downstairs should be done today to secure the property. Measuring the frames, David found they were standard size, vinyl-clad, double-hung and readily available at the do-it-yourself complex, as were the double windows in the front bedroom upstairs. He left immediately. Once he started on a project he seldom stopped until it was finished.

Sy couldn't believe her eyes. By the end of the day the downstairs windows had been replaced, the drapery re-hung, and the room completely restored to its previous neatness. Not a sign remained that a storm had caused damage. Tomorrow David would do the upstairs. The replacement windows were already resting against the upstairs wall waiting to be installed.

They'd had a lunch of scrambled eggs and ham, thanks to the power being restored by mid-morning. For supper Sy had fixed baked-breaded chicken breasts, with garlic potatoes and a tossed salad. They finished the meal with cups of fresh brewed coffee.

"I'm not staying overnight Sy, I want to stop at the hospital and visit with Aunt Rose for a bit, and then I'll head over to her place. The Doc said she may be able to go home in a few days and I want to surprise her and have the house clean as a whistle. She wasn't able to do much when she became ill and knowing her, she won't be able to relax if she sees anything needing dusting or vacuuming."

Sy was surprised at the disappointment she felt. Glad, of course, that he'd be back in the morning to install the bedroom windows so everything would be back to normal, and yet, a feeling of depression loomed, as though some intangible thing was going to be missing from her life. Maybe the storm bothered her more than she realized. Whatever the reason, she wasn't going to dwell on the mystery this evening.

"I'll see you tomorrow then Dave. You did a beautiful job and I'll sleep comfortably tonight knowing the house is safe again. Give me a call when you're on your way tomorrow morning, I'll have breakfast ready. How does that sound?" Sy watched as a wide grin spread across his face.

"Sounds wonderful Sy, I guess I neglected to mention that I think you're a terrific cook, you're every bit as good as my mom. I'll call as soon as I leave, likely around 8a.m. I'd better get going now. I want to spend a little time with my aunt before heading back to her place. Supper was delicious Sy, thanks for feeding me, I enjoyed every bite."

She followed him to the front door and watched as he got into his pickup and backed out of the driveway, she waved goodbye but wasn't sure he had seen. After closing and locking up she returned to the kitchen to finish some minor cleanup. She checked that the back door was secured and then turned out the lights. Heading up the stairs she realized she felt exhausted, it seemed a long time ago that the storm hit but it was only yesterday. Dropping her clothing to the floor she stepped into the shower and as quickly as possible did her ablutions. Within ten minutes she was snuggled under the covers. Her eyes fluttered closed and she was asleep, unaware of how lucky she had been to have David arrive, her home now secured against intruders.

Ed Grogan ordered another beer for himself and a round for his buddies Luke Agee and Al Freman. They'd been sitting in the bar most of the afternoon, sometimes playing pool but most of the time just griping about the hard times and wondering when they'd be called back to work. All three were employed at the local steel mill. Al and Luke had a good 10 years more than Ed who had only worked there for the past three, about the longest he'd ever stayed at any job. He was the sort who hated being bossed around and sooner or later an employer would notice he was slacking off, taking too many days off, or sometimes even showing up for work half loaded with a hangover. He always managed though, to stay long enough at a job to qualify for unemployment. Trouble was, it was never enough to pay all the bills so he'd borrow money to tide himself over until the next job came along. He'd been on easy street when Rita was still around, she was a hard worker and her paycheck came in handy. Now that she'd split, life wasn't so great. The apartment was always a mess, no meals ready, bills piling up, and he was the one who had to take his clothes to the Laundromat.

"Hey! Ed, I gotta get going, promised the old lady I'd be home before three to take her to see her mother. It's the old bags birthday and if I don't show up on time there'll be hell to pay. I'd rather stay on the good side of her since she's got us in her will." Luke gave a coarse laugh, blowing out a stream of cigarette smoke as he picked up his winnings from the table, swigged down the last drop of beer from the bottle and then banged it down on the table where it tipped over and rolled onto the floor shattering into brown shards of shiny glass. "Oops! Sorry 'bout that Ed." He turned and headed for the door, his best pal Al right behind him.

"What the Hell," Ed muttered, "You bums just suck up the drinks and then run." Now he was ticked, he'd bought two rounds of beers, it was again Luke's turn to get the next and then Al's. They'd stiffed him again. He picked up his change and headed out the door where he saw that they had already left the parking lot.

He climbed into his old Ford truck which had seen better days but still ran like a top, and then sat for a moment, undecided about what he wanted to do. Not in the mood to go back to the empty apartment he decided to swing by his favorite place of interest and in less than twenty minutes he was cruising past the large brick house. Irritated, he saw that the downstairs windows had already been replaced. That sure messed up his plans for the evening, he'd thought it an easy access to the trouble maker who he owed big-time for the mess he was now in. It was her fault Rita had left him, had to be. He hadn't heard a peep out of Rita in all the five years they'd been together, not a single complaint. He gritted his teeth, his anger building and making him grasp the steering wheel tightly, just as tightly as he wanted those same fingers wrapped around that trouble-making broads neck.

Trying to relax, he loosened his grip, circled the block once more to see if there was a chance she was outside. No movement, everything quiet. It was still too early to park and check the backyard, maybe do a little more spying but people would notice a stranger lurking about and the last thing he needed was running into a cop. They'd check his record for sure and he might find himself spending a few years back in prison. They'd never had caught up with him on his last caper when he'd tracked and followed that blonde. He'd enjoyed every minute. She was in the hospital for quite a while recovering from his assault. He doubted she would ever forget and neither would he. His thoughts drifted back to the years of his childhood recalling his father's periods of drunken stupor, the beatings inflicted on his intimidated mother who never said nor did anything to protect her two kids from the bullying, angry tirades. The older Ed became, the more he resented her. When he was old enough to leave home he struck out on his own and never looked back, never contacted them again either. Somewhere he had a younger sister. She had suffered just as much as he but what had become of her was a mystery and he didn't really care. He resorted to petty theft to feed and clothe himself, slept in flop houses, and did menial jobs when they were available. He began to drink and smoke weed which had seemed to ease the misery of his everyday existence. Finally, one "hang-over" day he'd met up with a wise old bum who gave him a word of advice. "Clean yourself up, shave, get a haircut and look for a good paying job. Once you get enough time in, you got it made. You'll never be out on the streets again." For the most part, it'd worked and he'd ended up with a Golden Goose egg, the steel mill job that was getting him unemployment at this very time. He grinned at the thought of getting paid every week and not working....

Finally realizing he'd circled the block a second time, he turned at the next corner and drove away. "You stupid jerk," he growled at himself, "you don't need some busybody remembering the old red Ford truck circling the neighborhood." He headed for home.

Claire, Sylvia's next door neighbor, had definitely noticed the old red, rusted truck making another trip down the street. She had seen it slow down on its first pass but only became concerned when she saw it again. The driver looked a bit scruffy too, not a very trustworthy-looking fellow. She made a note of the time, date, and description of the truck on a piece of paper, took it into the kitchen, and anchored it to the refrigerator door with a magnet where it rested among a multitude of other notes. Claire worried she was beginning to forget things, her little memos gave her a feeling of confidence every time she looked at them, they were her memory bank. She smiled as she returned to the living room and sat down in the window chair. This was as good as watching television, not as many things going on that were sometimes confusing, but just enough to keep her life interesting. Edna, her friend across the street, exited her front door and made her way over to Claire's. She let herself in and closed the door firmly. "Did you see that ratty looking fella, Claire? That was the third time I spotted him. I bet you didn't know that he'd parked three houses down from us and was looking between all the houses, sneaky like, maybe trying to see if someone had left their garage door open. That must'a been maybe a week ago. It'd already gotten dark, one minute he was there, the next gone like the wind. Didn't know where he'd disappeared to but toward midnight I heard a motor start up and I looked out the window. Saw that old truck sneakin' away, trying to ride quiet-like. Figured he'd been up to no good but didn't hear a peep out of anyone so didn't mention it. I think we better keep our eyes open. That new girl that moved in across the way is living alone, I think we better mention to her what's been going on. Forewarned is forearmed and I'd dislike seeing anything bad happen because we were remiss about warning her."

Edna patted Claire's hand, "I'll fix us up a nice cup of tea, honey, be right back."

Sy awoke early, maybe because of a light morning breeze rustling the plastic which covered the bedroom windows. A quick peek at the dresser clock told her it was 7:15a.m., she'd better hurry and dress, David would likely arrive by 8 o'clock. Although it had been only a few days since the storm damage, it felt so much longer. She wanted things back to normal as quickly as possible so she could concentrate on writing her column, it was impossible when her mind wanted to wander elsewhere.

Bed made, room neatened, she hurried downstairs to start the coffee maker and begin preparing breakfast. Hash brown potatoes prepared in her electric fry pan, with sunny side up eggs nesting nicely on their top. In the microwave oven she cooked a rasher of bacon on a paper plate lined well with paper towels and covered with another to prevent spatters. Bacon always turned out perfectly browned. Buttered whole wheat toast and orange juice completed the meal. She was just setting the plates and silverware on the table when the door chimes pealed. He was just in time…

THE THISTLE SEED

David thought the breakfast fit for a king and showed his enthusiasm by digging in with gusto. Sy couldn't help smiling since she had seldom been subjected to seeing a man eat so heartily. It had been years since Grandpa passed away but he had never been one to take much interest in food, anything placed in front of him was satisfactory.

David headed upstairs to begin the work of replacing the bedroom windows. Sy cleared the table, rinsed the dishes and placed them in the dishwasher. She thought about watching David work but second thoughts told her he liked working without interruptions and would finish much quicker without distractions. At a loss for something to do she pulled out the packet of "Common Sense" letters and opened the top one.

Dear Sylvia,

I am 15, my mother said I am too young to go on a date but all my friends do. This is so unfair, how can I change her mind?

Sandy

Dear Sandy,

Arguing will not solve the problem. Sit down with her and have a question/answer session. You may be surprised at the outcome.

Sylvia

Sorting through the pile, any crank mail she tossed, others too serious to take on were also relegated to the trash. Finally there were only about a half dozen letters remaining. These she began to read through, formulating her responses as she went along, making pencil notations. The time seemed to pass so quickly that when David came down to tell her he had finished installing the windows, she was startled. It had seemed just a short time ago that they'd had breakfast. Glancing at the wall clock she saw it was already past 2 p.m.

I'm so sorry David, I would have had lunch ready but got sidetracked on these letters. Sit down, I'll fix some sandwiches, be ready in a flash.

"Nope, don't worry your head about food. I'm taking Rose home as soon as I leave here. If it's okay with you, I'd like to leave you her phone number and give her yours. She's stubborn about calling when she's not feeling well. I know it's presumptuous of me to take you for granted but it would be a huge relief to me, and of course my mom, if we didn't have to worry so much."

David looked uncomfortable about his request but Sy thought it a great idea. It was the least she could do in return for all the work he'd done for her, especially since he refused to accept payment.

"It's a sensible plan David and I'll be more than happy to check on her and let you know how she's doing. Actually, since it's not that far from my office, I could even drop in occasionally and visit with her on my way to or from picking up my mail."

Dave jotted Roses' phone number on a slip of paper and handed to Sy, he'd already memorized Sy's, knew her number by heart. Suddenly he realized he likely wouldn't see her again for quite some time. That realization caused actual pain, a feeling of loss that struck him numb. He felt tongue-tied, didn't know what to say or how to express his consternation that they would be separated by several hundreds of miles. Silently, he cursed himself for being a fool, falling for someone who wasn't interested in him other than for having him as a friend. He turned away and headed for the front door.

Sy followed him, wondering at the sober, unhappy look she had glimpsed as he had turned to leave the kitchen. "Don't worry Davey, I'll let you know immediately if anything happens regarding your aunts health, you can trust me, I always keep my word."

He turned toward her, his eyes searching her face hoping to find any indication, no matter how small, that she felt more than just friendship towards him. Her smile was friendly, face upturned to his, beautiful hazel eyes with their glint of green looking at him expectantly. He was lost. Reaching out he pulled her tightly against him and covered her mouth with his own.

At first Sy tried to step away, but as the kiss deepened she was swept up in the heat of its passion. She wrapped her arms about his neck and opened her mouth to his kiss. When David realized what was happening, he grasped her arms pulled them from his neck and stepped away.

"I'm so sorry Sy, I don't know what got into me, I swear it won't happen again." Hurriedly he turned, swung open the door, stepped through it, and closed it quickly behind him. Practically running to his truck he was in it, and then out the driveway and gone so quickly, that when Sy had regained her breath and reopened the door, he was out of sight.

Sylvia was stunned. The kiss was a huge surprise, not so much the kiss but the feelings it had evoked in her, she felt embarrassed about her reactions. She couldn't believe she had flung her arms around his neck, likely almost choking him. Then she acted exactly like a hussy hanging on for dear life. What would he think of her? She cringed imagining his thoughts as he left, and he did leave in a big hurry, couldn't wait to get away from her. How could she ever face him again, let alone keep in touch with them about the health of Aunt Rose. Well! She wouldn't go back on her word, she'd keep her promise and make the phone calls, even stop in to visit Rose. At least he wouldn't have to run into her very often, good thing he lived so far away. She wondered why she didn't feel very happy about that.

The moment David sped away he regretted it. He should have stayed for at least a few moments instead of racing off like a frightened scatterbrain. "Too late now," he muttered to himself, "you made your bed, now sleep in it."

He sped toward the hospital, parked in the pick-up zone and hurried to the service desk. "Hello, I'm here to pick up my aunt, Rose Ryan. Is everything in order for her to be released?"

The nurse checked her registrations, "I'm sorry sir, she was released this morning. We were told you were staying at her house but when we phoned there was no answer. She was quite comfortable taking a taxi home and she said to tell you that she was well and feeling fit as a fiddle." The nurse smiled, "She's quite a strong lady, and she had us jumping through hoops making sure she got on her way as quickly as possible."

A bit un-nerved by the information David hurried back to his truck and sped away. Reaching his aunt's house, he turned off the motor and sat for a few moments trying to settle his mind and stomach which felt like it had been wrapped with barbed wire. He couldn't recall the last time he had felt so miserable. "I've got to pull myself together. I can't be moping around like some lovesick puppy dog. I've got to get my mind off her and think about something else." His heart hurt just picturing her standing at the door just before he'd kissed her, the kiss that had opened a new door to his emotions. Now he was in trouble.

Exiting his truck, he sorted out his aunt Roses house key from the others and unlocked the front door, closing it behind him. He liked her place. Solidly built, it was an old fashioned two-story, yellow brick bungalow with three bedrooms and a bath under the gabled roof. The downstairs had a living room with a fireplace, dining room, and a kitchen large enough to accommodate a kitchen table and four chairs. It also had a full basement. David headed for the kitchen, Aunt Roses favorite place to keep herself busy, and there she was. She turned with a smile, holding out a spoonful of something she was cooking.

"Taste this, David. I really think it needs a touch of something but I can't quite figure out what."

David took the spoon and took a small taste, then consumed the remainder. "Hmm! This is very good Aunty, what is it?" He actually licked the spoon and then placed it in the sink.

"Chicken with tomato sauce, onion, garlic and mixed California veggies. I was tired of the regular chicken soup I usually make, so I added a small can of tomato sauce. It's quite tasty Davey, better than the usual, don't you think?"

David had to agree it was the best he'd ever tasted. Aunt Rose always amazed him with her innovative creations. He couldn't recall a recipe that hadn't been outstanding.

"Sit down Honey, I'll get the bowls and the hot pad. Would you like crackers or biscuits, which I just made fresh this morning?"

"I'm perfectly satisfied with just the soup Aunty. Come and sit down, you shouldn't be standing for so long, you just got out of the hospital."

"Silly boy, do I look ill to you? I'm back to feeling like my old self again. You know I recover from these asthma episodes very nicely, it was just a little more serious this time." I'll be around for a long time to come" Now eat honey, before it gets cold.

Lunch over, table cleared and soup ladled into a freezer container setting out to cool, Rose packed a sandwich and a few goodies for David to take on his trip back home. "You be careful driving, sonny and as soon as you get home phone me so I won't be worrying about you, okay?" Rose handed the paper sack to him and then gave him a hug and kiss on the cheek.

"This feels heavy, what in the world did you stuff into it? The lunch you just fed me will last me until suppertime." He gave her a quick squeeze and brushed a kiss on her wrinkled cheek. "I'll call the minute I get home, I love you aunty." He was out the door and into his truck, with a quick wave out his window he drove away.

"What a sweet young man he turned out to be, just like his daddy. He'll make some woman a good husband one day," she said aloud as she closed the door. Rose had a habit of talking to herself, sometimes even laughing at herself if she'd misplaced an item and then found it in an odd location. Anyway, it was pleasant to hear something besides silence. She realized suddenly how very tired she felt. Maybe she had overdone things a bit just getting out of the hospital. Although it was only early afternoon, she needed to lie down and maybe take a little nap. Pulling herself up the stairway, hanging on tightly to the railing, she made her way into her bedroom where she slipped off her shoes and stretched out on the bed, at the last minute flipping part of the bedspread over her body to avoid feeling chilled. Within moments she was soundly asleep.

Afternoon passed into evening which seemed unusually dark because of the moonless sky. Everyone in the neighborhood eventually retired for the night and Rose slept on, not hearing the latch click on the front door which she forgotten to lock, nor the muffled footsteps traversing the downstairs rooms and then making their way up the stairway. Into each of the upstairs rooms the steps went until they stood at the doorway to Roses room.

A short burst of muffled laughter escaped, but not before a pillow was taken from the bedside and pressed firmly over Roses sleeping face. A weak, short struggle ensued but after only a few moments all was quiet. Lifting the pillow, Ed Grogan made sure not a breath was forthcoming from the supine body. It was done. Now he had all the time in the world to search, relax and do exactly as he pleased. He had checked this place out for several weeks and the old lady never had company except for that fella who lived up north, the same guy who had rescued that broad Sylvia from her so called "accident."

Ed's coarse laughter filled the room, who knew what treasure he'd find? Old people always had good stuff hidden throughout their homes, money, gold jewelry or coins, silverware, and that wasn't counting household things. He had a good fence to take the stuff to, the guy always took it across the state line to another pawn shop he ran. In all the years they'd done business, there was never any trouble about the stolen loot or any cops nosing around and he was known as an honest guy, what a joke. He'd even nicked a few things from his own family.

Suddenly Ed felt the letdown, his nerves shot from too much beer, the buzz he'd gotten from icing the old broad had faded. He needed some food and a good sleep. This was a safe place to crash for as long as he wanted, no danger of any visitors. He made his way into one of the other bedrooms and flopped on the bed, not bothering to remove his shoes, he stretched out and was soon sound asleep. He didn't hear the ringing of the telephone, he slept until morning. Awaking and feeling famished, he remembered the carton he had seen sitting on the counter, it had smelled like something tasty. He made his way downstairs and, not bothering to heat it up, consumed the entire contents giving a huge burp of satisfaction after downing the last mouthful. He spotted a mound of something covered with a towel. Flipping the towel away, his mouth watered at the sight of homemade biscuits. His hungers sharp edge not yet satisfied, he looked in the refrigerator for something to spread on them and found instead something much better, a jar of homemade apple butter. "That old bag sure knew how to cook," he muttered to himself as he polished off a half dozen of the biscuits slathered in the cinnamon scented mixture. "Now," he mumbled as he licked the last of the crumbs from his lips, "It's time to check out the house and look for any valuables the old broad has stashed. This'll be a very satisfying game of search and find." He gave a grin of greedy delight.

Through the basement he wandered, peeking in every crevice, every cupboard and even into the pantry where jars of home canned products lined the shelves. He retrieved a jar of spiced peaches while searching. Finding nothing else of value except for the tempting jars of fruits and vegetables, he returned to the main floor. Into the kitchen cupboards he went, delving into vases and cups, ceramic pots and jugs. There in a Chinese tea pot he found a nice wad of folded twenty dollar bills which he stuffed into his pocket. He knew he needn't search here any longer, he'd never seen a "Double-stash" in one area. It was on to the dining room. The glass front cabinet didn't interest him, he headed for the bureau and sure enough, the sterling silver set along with two trays and serving pieces were nestled in the tarnish resistant cloths. These were prime pieces, solid sterling no less. He burst out in gleeful laughter, he'd be set on easy street for quite some time and he hadn't even found her jewelry yet. By the time he finished going through the upstairs bedrooms, her gold and diamond rings had him actually drooling with the thought of all the money he'd make. He found a spacious leather suitcase that would hold all his treasures and packed everything into it. As soon as nighttime came he would be out of here, no sense sticking around, he'd found more than expected. It was just a matter of killing time.

Almost evening, in another hour it would be dark enough and he could leave unnoticed. He leaned back in the kitchen chair thinking that maybe he'd move out of this burg, head for a different town and start a new life. Except this time he'd keep a clean record and act respectable so the cops wouldn't be pulling him over every time somebody stole something or a place was broken into. He was sick and tired of their suspicions even though they were often right. He was getting up in age, getting tired of spending so many years stuck in prison. He leaned his head back letting his thoughts drift. Soon he was sound asleep, head nodding, snores beginning to make his lips tremble with the passage of air, his lips sputtering with each outward breath.

In front of the house a car pulled to the curb, the motor was turned off and the person sat quietly as though trying to reach a decision. The car door opened and the young woman exited the vehicle. Striding confidently she climbed the stairs and strode across to the front door. Her hand trembled nervously as Sy reached out and rang the doorbell. She hoped that she and David's Aunt Rose would like each other.

The sound of the doorbell woke Ed with a start, almost causing him to fall off his seat. Again the bell rang but he remained sitting quietly. There were no lights turned on so whoever it was would likely think that either the person was sleeping or not at home. Soon after the third ring he heard a car motor start up and then it drove away. "Phew! That was too close a call, it's time I got out of here. He stuffed the remainder of the biscuits into his pockets, grabbed the suitcase and slipped out the back door. Pitch black, no moon, and perfect conditions for not being spotted. Just a quick hop over the back fence and then he'd make his way to his truck parked on the next street. He'd be out of there in seconds, he almost strutted his confidence was so high. Unfortunately when he arrived at the place where he'd parked his truck, it was not there, not anywhere in sight either. "What the hell's going on, where's my truck?" He felt the first stirrings of panic grip his gut, his stomach muscles tightened, his sphincter muscles loosened and a thin stream of fluid soiled his underwear. "Damn it to hell, must'a been that soup. Jeez! He tried walking bowlegged to ease the discomfort but the smell assaulted his nose and made him feel like puking which further tightened his muscles. Finally he slipped behind a garage, removed his pants and the soiled underwear and cleaned himself the best he could with a handful of leaves. At least he felt a lot better. He'd find the nearest gas station and call a cab, he could afford it. Just thinking about that wad of dough he'd lifted from that old hag made him smile, his discomfort forgotten.

It seemed he walked for miles before finally spotting an all night station. He used the bathroom first and then used the wall phone to call a cab. Within an hour he was back in his apartment, filthy clothes shoved into a plastic bag, the stink washed off his body in a hot shower, and he was sound asleep in his own bed dreaming of high living, fancy cars, and available broads hanging onto his arms. An old lady hovered close by who kept scratching at his body with sharp nails. It was driving him crazy. He kept swatting at her trying to make her stop but she wouldn't go away. He pulled back his arm and tried to hit her as hard as he could with his fist, but the blow just seemed to float through the air as lightly as a butterfly. He tried to grab her by her neck but she remained just out of reach yet somehow her nails kept scratching his skin. He let out a scream of rage and immediately awoke.

He couldn't lay still another moment, he was in misery. It felt like his entire body was on fire. He turned on the light and looked at his skin, at least the part he could see. He was covered in a rash, even his butt itched. A painful grimace crossed his face when he realized what had happened, the distant memory from the days when he was a kid returned with all the misery attached to it. He had poison ivy.

When he realized he didn't have transportation to get to a drugstore he went crazy. He searched through the cupboards for something to relieve his agony but all he found was a fifth of Jack Daniels, a bottle he had lifted from the local liquor store. He grabbed a glass from the sink, pulled a chair up to the kitchen table and poured himself his first drink. He liked beer better but the old saying, "Liquor is quicker," he knew to be the truth, at least he hoped to hell it was. Slowly he drank himself into a stupor. An occasional twitch would indicate a bit of discomfort, but that could have been from the awkward angle his head was tilted, surely not from any sense of irritation caused by the poison ivy. That he would have to deal with in the morning.

The Holly Village police department had received the call about the abandoned truck and had checked the registration before towing it to the impound yard. "Hey! Walt, this guy is bad news," Officer Jack Adams commented to his best friend on the force. "He has a record a yard long, I'd bet he's somewhere in that area, maybe hiding out in a house where folks are away on vacation. D'you think we should do a check to see if there's any vandalism or evidence of a break-in in the area?" Jack walked over to Walt's desk, waiting until he'd finished writing the last of the report he'd been working on before showing Edward Grogan's rap sheet.

"Hmmm! That might be a good idea Jack, especially since the truck had been there overnight, that's not a good sign. If the guy was lurking about for that long of a time, there's a possibility he broke in someplace. Let's hope nobody got hurt if any pilfering when on. We haven't received any calls but it wouldn't hurt to check. I'll send a couple of squad cars and have them do a routine search of the area. Maybe even a walk-through might turn up something." When Walt had one of his hunches, which bugged him occasionally, he'd found it wise to check them out because more than a few times they had been right on the money.

The officers were sent, the area checked out. One officer, Philip Owens, phoned in his findings about a pair of dirtied briefs discarded in a back yard among a growth of poison ivy. He'd bagged them just in case they were needed as evidence. Meanwhile a police car had been sent to check out Ed Grogan.

When Officer Daniels arrived at the apartment and Ed answered the door he looked miserable. The rash had spread to his face, arms and, with the itching he was doing, over a large area of his body. Immediately the officer scanned the room, the expensive leather suitcase caught his attention immediately. "Turn around, put your hands behind your back, you are under arrest for possession of stolen property." Ed was handcuffed. The Officer retrieved the suitcase and escorted Ed to the police car securing Ed in the back seat. He placed the leather case in the trunk.

When they arrived at the station house and Ed had been placed in a cell, they checked the contents of the suitcase and knew immediately that they had a serious problem. A major crime had been committed, the volume of wealth displayed would send Ed away for quite some time but so far they had not been able to find out from the suspect where the theft had occurred. This made them suspicious that something more serious had happened. They would have to search house to house in the area.

On the morning of the second day they knew the location of the house where an elderly woman had been murdered. The only reason they became aware of that information was because the victim's nephew had repeatedly phoned her and not getting an answer, became worried. It was luck that they already had the suspect incarcerated.

David was heartbroken and so were his parents. If only he had stayed with her for a few days maybe this wouldn't have happened. He felt so guilt-ridden he doubted he would ever be free of the feeling.

Aunt Rose had already made plans for her cremation and funeral services years ago. There was nothing for him to do. He would take her ashes up north where she wanted to be interred in the family plot at the town's older cemetery. All he could do for now was wait for the results of the coroners' examination.

David felt restless and at loose ends. Rather than sit around his Aunt Roses' house waiting for the Medical Examiner to release his aunts body, what he really wanted to do was go see Sylvia. Remembering the kiss that he had smothered her with the last time he had seen her, he was hesitant to phone. "What the heck!" he muttered to himself, "I'll go see her. All she can do is tell me not to bother her again. You can't be that much of a chicken to face her, can you?" he asked himself. Unfortunately, he knew what the answer would be but maybe seeing him face to face would put a damper on her telling him "No" like she might over the phone. Not giving himself a chance to "chicken out," he almost laughed at the thought, he hopped into his truck and took off.

On the way there he realized he had a legitimate reason for seeing her, she didn't know about Aunt Rose and the break-in. Feeling more confident about the meeting he kicked up the speed a notch and arrived at her place in record time. Jeez! He could have gotten a ticket, he thought as he pulled into the driveway, practically leaping out of his pickup and then taking the steps two at a time. He was out of breath as he rang the doorbell. It seemed to take forever before the door opened, but by then at least he was breathing normally.

"David, what in the world are you doing here? Why didn't you phone first?" Sy wore an old faded shirt and torn denim shorts. She was barefoot, her hair was pulled back into a ponytail, and there was a dab of beige paint on her cheek. She held a paint brush in her hand. Although not a touch of makeup was evident on her face, it held a glow that actually made his heart do a flip, at least that's what it felt like to David.

You look great Sylvia, it seems forever since I last saw you. I hope I'm not interrupting your hard work. What are you painting? I don't recall seeing anything that needed redecorating. David let his eyes travel the length of her from head to toe. It made Sy think he was talking about her and she could feel the blush begin at the top of her head and travel down her entire body. She dropped her eyes, too embarrassed to look eye to eye.

"Come in David, I just finished the last of the painting in the laundry room, I want to clean this brush before it dries. Pour yourself a coffee, it's fresh. There's also some cookies in the cookie jar sitting on the counter next to the refrigerator, help yourself. Sy strode away, David at her heels heading for the kitchen. He admired the shape of her legs. The shorts sure looked good on her, showed off the curves of her body. Under the odor of the paint he caught the faint scent of her. He was well aware that every person had their own natural human scent. This had nothing to do with perfume or grooming products, this was pure nature and hers was drawing him like a magnet. There was a scientific name but for the life of him he couldn't remember.

As soon as Sy cleaned and dried the brush, not a big deal since she'd used satin finish paint, looked like flat paint when on the walls but it could be washed easily. She placed both paint can and brush in the laundry room cabinet.

While they drank their coffee David told Sy about Aunt Rose and what had happened to her. When Sy told him she had stopped in to check in on his aunt, they were both uneasy about it being close to the day that his aunt had been killed. David reached out caressing the slender grace of her delicate hand. He brought it to his lips, planted a kiss in its palm and then closed her fingers over it.

Sylvia pulled her hand away quickly, "David, what are you doing? I'm certainly not in a romantic mood, you just told me about your Aunt Roses murder. It makes me nervous knowing the killer was likely there when I rang the doorbell, in fact it gives me the creeps just thinking about it." Sy arose from her chair and headed for the coffee pot, intending to refill their cups. When she realized the carafe was down to its last dregs she proceeded to make a fresh pot, anything to keep herself busy. For some reason she felt unusually nervous and on edge and she suspected it was because of David's presence, she was much too attracted to him. In fact she felt if she dropped her guard she'd be lost in a romance that she was not ready for. "Okay, be honest," she told herself. "He'd be quite a catch and you can picture yourself living the rest of your life as his wife but you're not ready to marry yet are you, not ready to have kids? That would be the first thing on the agenda, wouldn't it?" Realizing she had been standing there far too long, she returned to her seat. "Coffee will be ready in a moment Davey, what were you saying?"

"I asked if you would like to go out for dinner this evening. I can't leave town for a while because when the coroner releases Aunt Rose's body it will then go to the crematorium so I'll be here for several more days at least. I just don't want to sit in her house waiting and imagining what went on there. I don't think I'd get a minute of sleep." He looked at her hopefully, a sad look on his face and a slight tremble in his voice.

"Oh Good Grief," she thought, "I'm going to be a fool and ask him to stay," and before she could stop herself, the words fell from her lips faster than a speeding bullet. "You can sleep here David." She almost groaned aloud but the smile that lit up his face almost compensated her for the invitation, she may as well go whole hog. "I'll fix dinner too and even make dessert. How does that sound?"

She loves me, David thought, she just doesn't know it yet. "I'd love to stay over Sy, you've sure eased my depression because my aunt's house is so gloomy without her. My suitcase is still in my truck, I never thought of taking it out and I guess I should phone the coroner's office and give them your phone number so they can reach me.

"Get your suitcase David and you can get settled in the same room you had when you last stayed over. If you like, take a shower and freshen up also. I have to shower and change before starting dinner so I'll meet you down here in about half an hour. How does that sound?"

The grin he gave her almost did her in. God! She was such a fool, she thought. Promising herself that this visit would be strictly as friends only, no romance, she hurried upstairs to her room closing the door and latching it behind her.

Within a short time she was showered, her hair washed and blow-dried, clean jeans and a lime green tee shirt chosen for comfort, she hurried downstairs. She wondered what to fix for supper, then decided steak and baked potatoes would be quick with a tossed salad. She pulled two rib eyes from the freezer, filled the sink with cold water and dropped in the plastic-bagged steaks. They'd be defrosted in an hour. She scrubbed two baked potatoes sliced them in half, placed thinly sliced onion and a pat of butter on each and sealed the halves together with foil, they would bake for an hour and be ready when the steaks went under the broiler. For dessert she'd make strawberry short cake using homemade biscuits with a scoop of ice cream on top.

David felt like a million dollars now that he was freshly showered and shaved. Wearing blue denim and a soft, sky-blue cotton shirt, he headed downstairs, not aware of how the colors brought out the brilliant blue of his eyes. For a moment sadness overcame him remembering his aunt Rose, her loving warmth now gone forever. It felt strange knowing she was no longer living. Although she had lived a distance away they'd had the comfort of knowing she was "There." Now an empty space had taken up residence in the comfort zone of his family. His parents would be arriving from up north tomorrow. His dads' best friend, Bob Nelson, would take care of the hardware store while they were here getting Aunt Roses estate settled. Once his parents arrived he would stay with them at his aunt's house.

David watched as Sy began preparations for their supper. The potatoes looked like they'd be tasty, he'd never eaten them fixed like that before. By the time they sat down to eat he dug in with gusto although Sy didn't seem to have much of an appetite.

"What's wrong Sy? This is a terrific meal you've prepared, you're a very good cook." David laid his fork down on his plate and gazed at her, wondering why she looked so disconsolate. She made no attempt to even taste what was on her plate. He reached over and took her hand which felt as cold as ice. "Look here, Sy, I know you don't want to get serious, I'm not as dense as you think I am. You like me, I can see that, and that's just fine with me. I'm not the sort of guy who wants to rush a young lady who I'm very fond, of into a romantic relationship, that's not my style. I'm quite contented just being friends with you with no pressure on my part to take steps any further. This is completely up to you, and don't even think that I'll be angry or upset if things aren't going exactly how I'd like them to go. I want you to want me, to think about me when I'm not around and miss me. When, and if, you ever reach that stage in our relationship, that's the time that will belong to both of us. I know I stepped out of line when I came on to you too strong. I put too much of my feelings into that last kiss and I promise I won't do it again although I won't promise not to kiss you."

Sy pulled her hand away, a slight smile twitching the corners of her lips. "Actually, David that was not what I was thinking about. You're the first man that has me wondering what I want my future to be. I've tried to picture myself married to you and even imagined our children, but somehow I'm not yet comfortable with that scene. I'm just not ready to settle down with those responsibilities. I have true feelings for you, but I can't call it love, at least not yet. I suppose that's a step in the direction you're aiming for but it's much too soon for me to get that serious about you. I'd really like it if we remained in touch, getting together occasionally and letting fate take its course. If we're meant to be, then so be it, but I do not want to rush into a relationship and end up feeling uncomfortable about it. Knowing you, I bet you wouldn't want me to make a commitment only to have me change my mind months down the road. You're a good guy Davey, the last thing I'd want to do is hurt your feelings so give me my space, ease off." Sy could see the disappointment that David tried to hide without success. She wanted so much to ease his hurt but knew that would be the wrong action to take, it would only make him feel he still had a chance. She wanted only to be his friend, but he wanted her to be his wife. It was an impasse that may be insurmountable for them to remain friends.

David looked down at his dinner, no longer interested in finishing his meal. He left his fork where it lay on his plate and making a split second decision, also placed his napkin on the table and arose from his chair. "I can't play games with you Sy, and I won't tag along behind your skirts hoping you'll change your mind about your feelings for me, I just can't stand waiting anymore. I'm going back home today as soon as I pick up Aunt Roses ashes. Dad won't have to worry about the hardware store with me back home, that's a little less pressure off them. The meal was very nice Sy, thank you. I'll grab my suitcase from upstairs and be on my way." Without waiting for a response he turned and walked out of the kitchen. Shortly afterward she heard the closing of the front door and then the sound of his pickup truck pulling out of the driveway.

Sy was shocked. Not really sure what had caused his departure to happen so suddenly. She prided herself on honesty, knew she'd done the right thing telling him about her feelings but had she done it gently? At least she thought she had but maybe he was more sensitive than she realized. Aloud she reprimanded herself "Sy, you're stupid. You never look before leaping into a situation and this isn't the first time you've greased your slide into regret by flapping your mouth too quickly. When will you ever learn to be more considerate?" Unfortunately the reprimand she gave herself wasn't sincere because she actually felt a huge wave of relief that the pressure was gone. She felt not a hint of regret.

After clearing the table and then starting the dishwasher, she couldn't make up her mind what to do. It had been quite a while since she had listened to Granny's tapes. This would be a perfect time to just sit and listen to that sweet old voice tell stories, just like when she'd been little. Hurrying, she retrieved the recorder from the laundry cabinet and plugged it in. She fixed herself a cup of tea and then sat at the table and pushed the "play" button.

Tape….Hmmm! Let me see, the last tape was about my Grandmother Ella losing her house. That's when everything turned really bad for my mom Fern, my dad Al and me. There were very few jobs and for a short while dad, who was a lithographer, found odd jobs to earn a little money but it wasn't enough though to keep us fed and a roof over our heads. Now that I'm older I realize why we moved during the night so often, no money for the next months' rent. This went on for about two years. The last place we stayed is very vivid in my memory. It was a very old two story unpainted house sitting right behind where the trolleys' (Streetcars) did their turn-around. I liked playing in the attic. It was old and dusty but I liked looking out the back window. I still had my ragdoll that granny Ella had made and I had a few of the trinkets gas stations gave when people stopped to fill up. My Uncle Ray saved these for me. Tiny flying red horses from Standard station and a few other little trinkets from other stations. Maybe a total handful, I loved them. That Christmas we had a real tree with lights. When I went to bed I tried hard to stay awake and meet Santa but fell fast asleep. In the morning there was a tricycle with my name on it. It was painted green with red, green and yellow reflectors on the front and a real bell that I could ring. I couldn't believe how lucky I was. I rode it up and down the sidewalk in front of the house. But one day something terrible happened. A big truck pulled up in front of the house and a man took all our furniture away, he took my tricycle too. He said he was very sorry, he was just doing his job. He let me keep the rag doll that granny Ella made but I cried when he took my bike, it was the prettiest thing I ever had. I think the reason I remember that last house so well was the Christmas, the green bike and I also remember that was where I caught Measles and mom had to keep me in a dark room until the measles went away. She said that was to save my eyesight because the measles could make them weak.

Years later I learned that the bike was from my Uncle Ray the one who save all those gas station trinkets for me. Years later I was able to repay him for his wonderful kindness. I had a dog I'd named Timber, called him Timmy for short. Uncle phoned me, said there was a contest in the News paper to name a dog. I told him to use Timmy's name Timber. Uncle won a consul color TV set. He called and told me about it, said he'd pay me half of what it was worth. Of course I told him "No." My little green bike meant so much more to me than he could have realized. It was a bright star shining from my childhood, something so precious I would remember it all the years of my life. His winning that TV set was a way for me to tell him "Thank you" for that special Christmas memory..... (end)

For a while Sylvia sat in silence, reliving the words she had listened to. She recalled Granny laughing about Grandpa giving her a nickname saying that he always called her his little "Thistle Seed" because she seemed to manage things in her own quiet, stubborn way. She'd actually bristle at anyone who felt she couldn't handle a problem. Sy decided the name fit granny perfectly. Thoughtfully, Sy took out the tape and returned the recorder to the cabinet. She located a perfect sized box to hold the tapes she had listened to, large enough that eventually they would all rest in it. Someday she'd have a family and want her children to listen to them. When she had talked Granny Eleanor into recording her memories she'd had no idea they would be a wonderful treasure worth passing on. Thinking about her own childhood, she couldn't imagine what kind of person she would have become if she had lived Granny's life. She also wondered about her own mother. She had always assumed that Gram would tell her about it when she was old enough to understand, so she hadn't pressed for the information. She should have asked years ago but it seemed time had slipped away too quickly and here she was now almost 27 and not knowing a thing about either of her parents a rather weird situation and Gram was gone, her chance to find out lost forever. Why hadn't she ever asked Gram about them? Maybe she'd been afraid of finding out, losing her home with Gram and then having to go live with strangers. She would have hated that. Maybe there was something Granny knew that would have been hurtful to me.

Finally, disgusted with herself for all the questions plaguing her mind, Sy went into the living room and turned on the television set. It was already into the early evening hours. Maybe the local news would have something interesting, although she seldom bothered with watching.

THE THISTLE SEED

Red Alert! A prisoner has escaped from the local hospital where he had been confined and under treatment for a seriously infected rash which will help identify him. He is a murder suspect, and considered dangerous. Please be on the lookout for a heavy set Caucasian, brown hair, brown eyes possibly wearing an interns blue shirt and pants. If you see anyone matching this description call your local police immediately. Please do not attempt to apprehend him yourself. Red Alert! A prisoner .

Sy turned off the television. She needed some distraction but didn't know what. It was still early evening, maybe Sally wouldn't mind a last minute visit, it had been a while since they had gotten together. Dialing the number, waiting for someone to answer, she finally hung up after the tenth ring. Maybe they were out somewhere, she thought. Restlessly, pacing the kitchen floor for several minutes trying to think of something to do or someone to visit with, she finally admitted defeat about finding a distraction and plopped herself down into one of the kitchen chairs and just as she was considering the idea of soaking for an hour in a bubble bath 'til puckered skin made her look like a prune, the front doorbell rang.

Edna and Claire waited at the door hoping they hadn't chosen a bad time to drop in on their new neighbor and when the door opened, they practically pushed Sy out of their way as they entered and closed the door firmly behind themselves. If they hadn't been so old and infirm looking Sy would have felt nervous but having seen them occasionally when leaving or returning home, she was simply curious. Truthfully, she was relieved at their intrusion, her ennui finally at an end.

"Hello ladies, is there something I can help you with?" Sy could see they were seriously upset about something. Whatever it was, she'd be happy to assist with any problems they could be having. The two glanced at each other and then Claire gave a nod to Edna who took Sylvia by the arm and led her into the kitchen, Claire followed close at their heels.

"You better sit down honey, we have a few things you should know about, but would you mind first making a pot of tea? It sounds rather forward to ask, but when you get to our age, the less time spent wasted, the better."

Sy was so happy about this curious distraction she was almost giddy with relief. "Ladies, I'd love a cup of tea myself." She filled the teakettle, placed it on the electric burner and turned the knob on "High." She got out cups and saucers, cream and sugar, also setting out a plate of butter cookies. She lifted down the china teapot from the cupboard and filled it with hot water. After it was well heated she poured that water out and then prepared their tea using fresh hot water. Finally she sat down with them.

"I'm Claire, your next door neighbor and that's my friend Edna, she lives across the street from you. We've been meaning to talk to you but after seeing the police report on the telly, we felt it necessary we do it immediately. That fella they showed was the same one we saw driving past your house several times. He'd even parked and was lookin' between the houses, did a quick disappearin' act too. We were worried because he seemed so interested in your place. Being as he escaped from the hospital he might start lurking around here again. We didn't want you to accidently forget to lock your doors or maybe not pay close enough attention to what's going on around you. We wanted you to be a bit wary, extra careful. He's driving an old, rusty, red Ford pickup truck."

This was the last thing Sy had expected to hear. She'd thought they were just curious old gals who felt like getting acquainted. Instead they were two guardian angels who kept their eyes out for anything out of the ordinary, anything that might prove to be something dangerous for one of their neighbors. She was grateful for their concern, especially recalling those cigarette butts she'd found in her backyard.

If she had been a mind reader she'd have known that Ed Grogan was edging his way through the city, making his way toward her residence at that very moment. He had already found a change of clothes from some laundry that someone had left out to line dry and forgotten to take in. Fortunate for Ed that the man of the house was just about his size, although the pants were a little short. Now that he was wearing a presentable outfit including a cap and jacket, he was confident that he could navigate his way to the other side of the city without any hassle from the cops. Twice he hitchhiked, his excuse being that when he'd left work his car wouldn't start. The last guy had been too good hearted, saying he'd be willing to take him all the way home, so he directed the way to a street not too close to where he wanted to go. With a wave goodbye to the jerk, he had walked to the front door feeling safe because the house was in darkness, the people either asleep or not at home. He pretended to use a house key as his free ride took off. Geez! Some people were stupid. If he'd been making a fast getaway, that would'a been a perfect sucker to take advantage of. He'd of had the guys car, money, home address and ATM access, but with the cops on the lookout for any unusual heists, he would've been a sitting duck. He'd get his chance once he reached that dame's place. That dumb-assed broad didn't know what she was in for since messing up his life. The more he thought about it the more pissed he got. "I can hardly wait to get my hands around her throat," he muttered aloud.

He arrived at his destination at last. Her place was all lit up inside as though she had company, so he eased back between two houses and prepared to wait it out. Within a half hour two old biddies came out the front door talking a blue streak although he couldn't catch the drift of the conversation. He watched as one ambled over to the house next door, and the other made her way across the street to the home he was hiding near. He pressed himself farther back into the shadows and was unseen as the old lady climbed the stairs and entered the front door. He heard the lock click immediately.

Across the street her downstairs lights went off and almost as soon, the upstairs front windows lit up. Now he was ready, he made his way around to her back door.

Sy turned on the spigots and ran bathwater, adding a generous scoop of skin softener to the tumbling spume of water that created an inviting, colorful mound of bubbles. Dropping her clothing to the floor, she stepped into the steamy warmth sliding down until only her head was visible. "This feels like heaven," she murmured with a sigh, reaching for the wash cloth and scrubbing her skin until it tingled. When she finished bathing she opened the drain, closed the glass doors and turned on the shower. She shampooed her hair, rinsed herself off and then applied a skin moisturizer. It was after she turned the water off that she felt a cool draft bring goose bumps to her skin.

"I couldn't have picked a better time to visit." The coarse voice whispered. "Let's get a gander at you bitch, I've been waiting a long time for a chance to get my hands on you." The shower door slid open and Sy stood naked, the sight causing instant arousal as Ed's eyes checked out the places of her body he was interested in, it had been a long time since he'd had a woman, this one would do nicely. His groin actually ached in readiness. "A nice tight piece of ass, girlie is what I'm wanting right now. He grabbed her by her neck, pulled her from the shower and headed for the bedroom.

Sy fought as hard as she could but the tight circle of his hand about her neck was almost choking her, she could sense the darkness closing in around her. "Oh! No! The thought came unbidden to her mind, this was not what I saved myself for." Although she tried to speak, the words were only an echo in her mind. She made a last horrific effort to strike him, scratch his eyes out but instead felt a sharp blow to the side of her head and then the blackness closed about her.

Ed stripped the better to enjoy the coupling. Looking at her lying there, sprawled open invitingly, he stretched out beside her and let his hand explore her body. This is great he thought, nice tits, good body and perfect silence with no "No" words. He rolled on top of her ready and eager. When he entered her, the resistance he felt almost made him lose it, he'd never had a virgin before. With a groan he worked hard until he climaxed then he rested for a while and then worked at it again. Completely sated and exhausted, he fell asleep. A few minutes later he woke with a start. The broad was still out like a light, he wasn't finished with her yet but he knew he couldn't stay here. Gathering her clothes from the bathroom floor, he wrapped a blanket around her, lifted her to his shoulder and then headed downstairs. Enough moonlight was coming in to be able to see well enough to do a little searching. He set her on a kitchen chair and leaned her head upon the table. Then he inspected every cupboard, finally going into the laundry room where he found her purse in the cabinet along with car keys and some money. "Got it made," he told himself. Within a short span of time they were on the road. She, wrapped tightly in the blanket and unable to move should she awaken, and he, feeling more satisfied than he had in ages.

There was an old cabin up near the Mackinaw Bridge that a pal he'd done some hard time with had told him about. The guy was dead, didn't have any family either, so it was a good bet this would be a perfect place for him to lay low for a while with his new playmate. He remembered the directions the old guy had drawn out in the yard dirt. He grinned to himself, one good thing he had was a memory. On the way he stopped at an all night grocers and bought food. Mostly canned stew, soup, cheese, tinned milk, instant coffee, sugar and a few things for minor injuries including aspirin. Before morning he arrived at the destination.

It was a shack with a saggy tin roof about the size of a one car garage but it had a fireplace. There was also a large shed big enough for the car to fit in. Carrying the supplies inside and then the still unconscious broad, he put the car in the shed and pulled the doors closed.

Inside the shack a rickety table and three chairs took up the center of the room. A small wood burning pot bellied stove sat in one corner and a bed slightly wider than a cot sat in the other corner. It had wooden slats but no mattress. At night they could sleep in the car which would be more comfortable. The only other item was a worn straw broom standing in the corner. No window coverings, but at least the door closed to keep out critters. He'd stay here for a while until things cooled off and then sneak over the border with her into Canada. Right now he was dead tired and needed sleep. He checked to see if she had regained consciousness. Her breathing was light and he was sure she was sleeping soundly. Pulling one of the chairs to the table he rested his head on his arm and was soon fast asleep, a few muttered words interspersed with occasional snorts of heavy breathing. He didn't awaken until morning.

Sy awoke with a start, unable to move she couldn't understand what was wrong. When she turned her head she saw a man sitting in a chair sound asleep and at the same time she realized she was lying on a dusty floor wrapped tightly in a blanket unable to move either arms or legs. The sun shone brightly through dirty windows lighting up the small barren room and for a moment she thought she could be dreaming. The thought didn't last very long as pain hit her with a vengeance. Her head was splitting, the agony traveling down through her entire body and yet, at the same time, she could feel the blanket against her skin telling her she was nude. She tried to piece together what had happened, her last memory was of standing in the shower. Slowly the sequence of events returned full blown, the shower door opening and the fight that ensued trying to protect herself. Now the unfamiliar pain between her legs was the horrendous results of what had occurred while she had been unconscious. With a groan of abject misery, uncontrolled tears welled up trailing down her cheeks, wetting the edges of the blanket wrapped too closely about her neck.

Ed awoke, the muffled sobs pulling him abruptly from a vivid dream of handcuffs being locked about his wrists, ready to fight tooth and nail trying to escape. The babe was awake. He looked down at her wrapped in her wooly cocoon, she'd put up a pretty good fight before he'd whacked her. At least she wasn't one of those screamers, he'd give her that.

"If you shut up that noise I'll unwrap you, even give you your clothes to put on but if you try one slick trick you'll find yourself back on the floor. Got that?" He watched her expression, sly to the tricks that she might try, knowing by the look in her eyes if she was going to attempt pulling a fast one. He'd learned well how to read people. Prison was the best teacher of all. She gave a slight nod of agreement watching him warily as he reached down and encircled her shoulders pulling her onto her feet where she swayed unsteadily while he began to unwind the blanket. It dropped to the floor. She stood before him nude, not bothering to try and hide with an arm across her breasts or her other hand covering her thatch. He had expected her to cringe, and in that startling moment of her self-pride, a modicum of respect for her made him turn away, reach for her clothes and place them on a chair. He walked to the door, exiting without looking back.

Sy dressed, the lime green tee shirt seemed like she'd worn it ages ago. She pulled on her jeans, her mind sorting how long it had been. It seemed forever, but was it only the day before yesterday when David had walked out angry, leaving his dinner? Only two days? Her mind couldn't grasp the fact.

Outside, Ed decided to check around the area hoping to see a stream or any source of water. He spotted an old fashioned water pump. Problem was, it needed priming and there wasn't any water to prime it with. We have to have water, guess I'll just have to wrap her up again and take a look around the area, might even find a better place to stay. Just the thought made him smile, a place with a real bed and bathroom. Even a regular stove to cook on so he wouldn't have to worry about the smoke from that old wood stove. His mind made up he turned back to the shack.

Sy was sitting at the table. She had pulled her hair back and it now hung in a ponytail secured with a rubber band she had found in her purse, the car keys were missing. She had to escape. He couldn't watch her every minute. Sooner or later he'd slip up and she'd have her chance. She noticed the indecision on his face and couldn't help that a spark of glee flashed through her mind. Maybe her chance to escape would be easier than she thought. He wasn't a very sharp minded guy. She concentrated on her hands, not wanting him to see any expression that might make him feel wary. Her nails had a ridge of dirt under their edges so she tried to clean out as much as she could, keeping her head down, eyes focused, giving him a sense of domination, as though she was too afraid to look him in the face.

He had to wrap her up again, Ed thought. No way he could trust that she was subdued enough to obey his orders. Women were too tricky, they had all those sneaky ways of doing what they wanted while making it seem they were following their husbands' rules. His wife Rita had been like that, the bitch was always going behind his back making his life miserable. Not only that, he'd suspected she was stashing money away out of her paycheck but he could never find her hiding place. Looking back he could see that she had been too submissive just before she had taken off. Why hadn't he suspected? She'd never been that way when they first married. He recalled the laughter and light that seemed to shine from her face every time he'd come home from work. She used to sing while doing dishes or when listening to the radio. He'd looked forward to going home, being greeted with a big hug and kiss. When did it all change? Was it because of his stopping too often at the bar or racetrack? Losing his money too many times? Slowly a distance grew between them, no more kisses at the door when returning home, the fumes of liquor unpleasant to her. They'd grown apart and that had made him mean and miserable. He recalled the note Rita had left on the kitchen table. It wasn't even addressed to him but to the bitch sitting next to him right now. He almost choked on the anger that flared so quickly and not thinking, he backhanded her tilting her chair and sending her sprawling onto the floor.

"If it wasn't for you my wife would still be with me you piece of shit, I could kill you for that." Ed stood looking down at her as she cringed, curling into as tight a ball as possible to protect her body from blows. He levered a kick against her ass and then reached down, grabbed her by her hair and pulled her upright welding a stinging slap across her face. "For a while I forgot why I wanted to catch you, maybe it was that tight piece of ass that fogged my mind but I'm back to normal again. You screwed up my life, now I'm going to screw up yours. Strip babe, it's playtime for Eddy boy.

The next hour was a haze to Sy. She had been turned, her body bent or folded into positions that were agony to her. No matter, the monster wouldn't quit until finally, near the end, she lost consciousness.

Ed had done everything he could think of, even made up a few new poses just for the fun of it, but the thrill was gone, she was just another used up babe and he was tired of her, sick of this cruddy shack too. It was time for him to hit the road and head for Canada. He dressed, grabbed the car keys and hurried out to the shed. Within a few minutes he was headed north on the highway.

Sy awoke finding she was lying on the floor half covered with the blanket and with a splitting headache making her feel physically ill. If her stomach hadn't been empty she would have heaved all over herself. Ed was nowhere in sight. Grabbing a chair for support she pulled herself upright standing shakily for a few moments until the dizziness passed. She pulled on her clothing and then sat, waiting for him to return. As she waited she tried to think of a way to escape and then suddenly realized that he hadn't rolled her in the blanket. Wherever he was, she had her chance right this minute. Pulling the blanket about her shoulders she pushed through the door, ready to sprint for the nearby woods as quickly as possible but then, through the open doors of the shed she could see that her car was gone and fresh tire tracks led down the dusty road. She began following the unfamiliar trail that she didn't recall seeing before, and had no idea how far she'd have to walk before finding a busy thoroughfare. After what she'd been through this was a piece of cake. She lengthened her stride, the fresh air invigorating, her headache easing and the queasiness of her stomach forgotten. It seemed to take forever but she finally reached a macadam paved road. She stayed near the tree line just in case she spotted her white car returning, this was not a busy roadway and he'd stick out like a sore thumb. In the distance a vehicle slowly grew in proportion as it neared, a green minivan pulled up in front of her and a young woman, looking puzzled at Sy's blanket wear, asked if she needed assistance. As they drove off Sy told her about being kidnapped. The woman, named Patricia, immediately took her to the local police station where she escorted her inside and after explaining her part in finding Sylvia, she left to complete her errands.

Officer Stan Jorgenson took Sylvia's statement and then issued an APB (All Points Bulletin) for the cream colored 4-door Oldsmobile and the kidnap suspect Edward Grogan, possibly headed for Canada. Officer Jorgenson then drove her to the local hospital where rape evidence would be collected and she would be examined for any other injuries. A news photographer took her picture as they entered the hospital. Sy was upset but unable to do anything about it. All she could feel was abject shame and embarrassment about what had happened to her. She knew it was none of her fault but she wanted to hang her head and hide from all who would find out through the newspaper. She was ruined, damaged goods so to speak and her life destroyed. This was not what she'd planned for her future.

She spent the night at the hospital. After the examination for evidence she was then X-rayed for head damage and given a physical, the results

THE THISTLE SEED

available in the morning. Later, the hot shower was heavenly, at least she felt partly clean again, and after a good supper, the bed felt like sleeping on a cloud. She felt better in the morning except for the fact she had no money, no car and no way to get back home. Her outlook on life had changed one hundred percent, there would not be that rosy future she had so often thought about, that "Once upon a time" daydream that young women sometimes took out to look at and reexamine occasionally, making minor changes as the years grew closer to their fruition. A lump formed in her throat as she now realized how much she had looked forward to that "Someday."

She dressed in her soiled clothing from yesterday, picked up her purse and went to the main nurses' station where she signed the release papers, once again showing her health insurance card to affirm coverage. Getting instructions on what elevators to take down to the main floor she exited and headed for the revolving doors. A firm hand took her arm and the rush of fear caused her to raise her fist, ready to strike. She was turned around, pulled into a pair of strong arms and held closely. In panic she tried to break away, ending up face to face with David Kendall.

"I got here as soon as I saw the morning papers Sy, your picture and story was on the front page….No! Don't turn away from me, you don't have anything to be ashamed about, you didn't do anything wrong. For God's sake, LOOK at me Sylvia," David turned her face toward his, forcing her to look into his eyes. "You DID NOT DO ANYTHING WRONG."

For a moment she stood gazing back at him with a confused, lost expression. Tears trembling on the brink of spilling down her cheeks, she felt miserable. There was nothing in the world he could say that would fix what had happened to her. All she felt like doing was to crawl into a hole and hide. She turned her head away. She didn't want to look at him, or at anyone. For the first time she realized she had no family to find a haven with. Granny was gone, the one person she could have leaned on and gained strength from. If she had felt terrible before, desolation now added its burden. She was alone. "David, I need to borrow some money for bus fare to get back home. I don't want you to drive me. I couldn't bear the thought of someone sitting so near me in that close of an environment. I need to get home, be by myself for a while."

Sy wouldn't even look at him while making her request. She was so "closed off" that he could almost imagine a feeling of cold emanating from her and infusing the atmosphere, he stepped back a pace. "If that's how you feel I'll drop you off at the bus terminal, it's a ten minute ride from here if you think you can bear my presence that long. Here's an extra twenty for cab fare when you get back to town. He steered her through the revolving doors and out to his truck where he helped her in. His next stop was the bank and then it was on to the bus terminal where he purchased her ticket. Turning he handed her the ticket and walked her to the bus where he gave her a quick kiss on the cheek before walking away. It was the hardest thing he had ever done.

Sy selected an aisle seat hoping that no one would bother about the window seat Thankfully the bus wasn't crowded so she rode relatively peacefully all the way back home to Highland Township. At three p.m. the taxi dropped her off at her door.

The shock of seeing where her assault took place almost undid her. The bathroom messy, towel and washcloth tossed on the floor. Realizing that the clothes she now wore were the ones she had taken off that day, made her skin feel creepy. She shed them on the spot. They'd go out in the garbage. Nude, she walked into the bedroom intending to select clean clothes to don after showering, but seeing the sight of her bedding all mussed and the faint trace of bloodstains where she had lost her maidenhead, Sy broke down and sobbed her heart out. She had no memory of the assault, but the evidence of her attack was heart wrenching. Slipping on a robe, she tore off the bedding, retrieved her clothing from the bathroom floor and wound it all into a bundle. Carrying it downstairs, she located a large trash bag and stuffed it all inside, this would go out on garbage pick-up day, she never wanted to lay eyes on the items again.

She remade the bed turning the covers down, and then she stepped into the shower. She shaved her legs and under arms, scrubbed her hair and smoothed on a moisturizer to her skin. Finally, after her hair was dried, she donned one of Granny's flannel nightgowns, the soft warmth was what she needed to sooth her nerves, she was desperate for good night's rest. Curled under the coverlet she was soon deeply asleep. From afar she could hear Granny's voice calling to her and then, in the blinking of an eye, she was in the Sunshine house and Granny was talking to her.

"Poor darling girl, you've been through so much these past days. If there had been a way to help you I would have, but you're going to be just fine

THE THISTLE SEED

Sylvia. I'm sure you realize by now you're a very strong woman, it's lodged in your genes, something passed down to you from your ancestors. Your bruises will heal and you will get on with your life. In the morning it's time for you to listen to the next tape, there is something you can do to take your mind off the hurt you are experiencing. Sleep well my dear granddaughter. I love you dearly."

Sy slept deeply through the night waking up feeling refreshed and surprisingly, no lingering bad thoughts on her first awakening. Of course later the memories landed with a crash, almost making her spill her coffee. She needed some distraction so she retrieved the recorder, plugged it in and inserted the tape. She pushed "Play."

Tape....After the truck left with all our furniture and my green tricycle, we had to leave that house. In fact I don't recall ever seeing my father again, I don't know where he disappeared to. Mom and I started walking. I remember it was cold and the next thing I remember is we are inside the empty upstairs of a house. There is no furniture or food and it is now night. Mom has a candle that she lit with a wooden match. We sat and watched the candle burn, it is getting colder. There's a back porch and an old wooden chair which mom takes and breaks up into pieces to put in the fireplace. I fell asleep near the heat. In the morning we left and walked again for a long time. It was almost night, we went into an old building that was filled with cots with people sleeping in them, all the lights were off except at the far wall there was a man sitting at a desk and Mom talked to him. He put us in a storage room where stuff was piled up but there was a cot and a chair. Mom laid me down on the cot but something started biting me. Mom looked and there were a lot of little bugs, so she went and asked the man for some matches. She would light the match then blow it out and run the burnt end around the seams. I don't know how long it took her, seemed forever but it killed the bugs and she put me down to sleep while she sat up in a chair. Poor mom, when I was older I then understood how terrible this must have been for her. I'll leave more of my story for the next tape.

This part of my story made me think of your mother Sy. There is one important thing you must do and it's about the unanswered question in your mind, the one you never asked me about it. You know what that question is don't you, about your mother? I had to promise her I would never search for her, she was adamant about that. She was my only daughter and I loved her too much, even doted on her, and gave her anything she desired. I was so wrong, it spoiled her. She fell in love but the affection was not returned so she decided to trick him and became pregnant. Instead, he gave her money for an abortion and left for parts unknown. I would not allow the abortion. After you were born she said she never wanted to see me again. I tried many times over the years, to find her, she is out there somewhere. She is 46 years old now.

Try your best to find her Sylvia. I have a feeling that she needs help and would be very glad to meet you and see what a wonderful person you became. In fact I wouldn't be surprised if she had been thinking about you all these years, it would be human nature. Rosemarie was 19 when you were born, I'm sure age may have mellowed her, maybe even gave her regrets about her sudden decision. I love you dear granddaughter. When you find your mother, tell her I never stopped loving her. End.

At last, Sy knew about her mother. The knowledge that she was out there, maybe waiting to be found, made Sy want to pack her bag. The problem was where to begin the search? She turned off the recorder and put it away, all the while wondering where she could find information. This was worse than not knowing. There was a chest in one of the bedrooms, a search through it couldn't hurt. Sy practically ran up the stairs and into the side room that was basically unused although it held a full bedroom set along with the beautiful cedar wood chest that had been handed down from her great-great grandmother Ella. Who knew what she might find there. The scent of cedar was strong and clean smelling, permeating the entire room. Sy began lifting out all the surface items. Old family photo albums, scrapbooks, two beautiful handmade rose patterned Afghans, a large, pink-dyed-eggshell-decorated box which when opened revealed an array of family jewelry tagged with the names of deceased relatives. Some items were almost one hundred years old. Diamond and ruby rings engraved watches, even an ivory letter opener. Two large manila envelopes held a multitude of loose photos, these she set aside. Sy closed the eggshell box and then sat on the floor dejected and disappointed, there was nothing here to help her search. Once everything was returned to the chest and the lid closed she carried the packages of photos downstairs to the kitchen and placed them on the table. Just then the doorbell chimed.

"We've been worried sick about you, honey," Clair took Sy's arm and guided her toward the kitchen feeling a little out of breath. Walking and talking at the same time was sometimes challenging. "You remember Edna? We're so relieved you're home, where in the world did you disappear to? Come along Edna, don't dawdle. D'you happen to have some tea handy? We'd sure love a cup while we catch up on all the news." Sy was on the verge of laughing out loud at their brazen attitude. Maybe that's what happens when people age, she thought, they just don't want to waste time.

"I surely do ladies, sit down and make yourselves comfortable while I get it ready." Sy was so busy heating the water, getting down cups and saucers and something to nibble on that she didn't notice pictures were now scattered across the table and the two women were busily looking through them.

Edna got excited, "Look Claire, here's Eleanor and Raymond when they first moved into their new house, she sure looks pretty. They were a good looking pair, weren't they? I can't believe it's been that many years ago, and now they're both gone. We used to play cards at least once a week. We three couples were the best of friends, even went out to dinner and dancing occasionally." Edna gave a sigh of regret for those happy days of long ago. "Oh! And look, here's a perfect picture of Rosemarie. I wonder how she is, it almost killed Ellie and Ray when she ran off."

Sy was so startled she almost dropped a cup. Hurriedly she brought the tea settings to the table and set out the remaining articles, finally pouring the fragrant tea into their cups and sitting down to join them. "You will never know how happy I am to see you two. If you're not in a hurry I'd love to hear all about the wonderful times you had being friends with my grandparents. I'm curious about Rosemarie too."

For the next hour or so the three women looked at pictures, they talked of the good old days, drank tea, munched on cream cheese and crackers, and became friends. Edna said she had an old letter tucked away someplace, if she hadn't tossed it away unthinkingly. Rosemarie had sent it to her after she had run away. "I'll look for it as soon as I get back home. I'm sure the last time I saw it, it was in my bureau drawer. I keep cards and letters, it's nice to sometimes reminisce over old times and friends that have either passed on or moved away." For a moment Edna's eyes seemed to shine with unshed tears. She gave a nervous "Harrumph" of embarrassment and turned her head away until she had control of her emotions again. "I'm very happy you moved in Sylvia, it's such a comfort to look across the street at night and once again see the warm glow of lighted windows. I loved your grandmother and miss her terribly. It has to be twice as desolate for you with her gone. Anytime you feel lonesome just get yourself over to my place, honey. The company will be good for all three of us, Claire loved Eleanor too."

Gathering the pictures into their manila envelopes, Sy placed them on the counter and then refilled their cups with the last of the still hot tea. "Thanks Edna, I may take you up on that offer." Sy had no intention of telling them what she had been through. "I've had a tough time up north. For a while I was sort of "tied up" with a project but I'm relieved to be home again safe and sound. I'd enjoy it if we could make a point of getting together at least once a week, have our tea-party and catch up on all the latest things we've been up to. How does that sound to you? We can take turns at each other's houses, that way there's a change of atmosphere. What do you think?" Secretly, Sy felt the need for the comfort of having the two women actively close in her life. Her Grandmothers' physical existence had been an anchor for her own well being. With her gone it felt like being in a room filled with people who then suddenly disappeared, a lonely, frightening feeling like floating in space without a tether.

"It will be like the old days." Claire said. "There wasn't a week went by that we didn't get together and make plans or just relish each other's company." She had a wide smile on her face as she picked up her emptied tea cup and placed it on the counter. "I'll look forward to it. Next tea party is at my place. I'll even bake a pie, haven't made one in ages, I hope I didn't forget how."

Edna followed suit with her teacup and then followed Claire to the front door. "It was a lovely visit Sy, and seeing those old pictures brought back wonderful memories that made me feel young again. If you need anything let me know honey, I'm glad to help."

Sylvia closed the door after the two elderly women left. Locking it, she leaned against it with a smile of contentment thinking it was the best she'd felt in a long time. There was something special in the companionship of women that was not only soothing, but actually therapeutic. Retracing her steps she then proceeded to hand wash the delicate china cups she had selected for the occasion. After they were put away, she sat back down at the table looking at the picture of her mother. Of course it had been taken long ago and wouldn't be much use in finding her, but just having her image, the way she must have looked when Sylvia was born, made Sy feel closer to her.

"Do you ever think of me mother, or wonder what sort of person I grew to become? Did you ever try to watch me as I walked to or from school? Were you curious, the way I've been curious all these long years? I don't want to bother you, I just have to find you, see the person that gave birth to me, ask you why you didn't want to stay and be my mother." Sy felt afraid of what might happen if she found her.

Rosemarie Henderson had just finished her day shift at the Old Country restaurant. It had been an unusually busy Friday because of the holiday weekend and she was exhausted. Her shoulders ached and so did her back. What she really wanted was a nice long soak in a soothing bubble bath but it would likely be another hour before she could indulge herself. Removing her frilly apron and hanging it on the hook in the back room, she pulled off her flat soled shoes and placed them in her locker. Slipping her feet into the spiked high heels that showed off her shapely legs and added a few inches height to her diminutive figure she pulled the pins from her hair letting it fall to her shoulders. A touch of lipstick and she was satisfied. Calling a goodbye to her boss Lenny, she exited through the back door and headed for her little blue two-door Chevy. She'd owned it outright for three years after making that final payment. What a relief that had been and it wasn't that she didn't earn a decent wage. Her customers liked her and by the end of each week their tips often added up to an extra hundred dollars which she always placed into her savings account. Settling herself into the front seat she started the car motor, once again hearing that odd noise from under the hood. Making a right turn out of the rear parking lot, she headed for the auto repair shop.

"Hi! Nick, thanks for taking me at the last minute. I don't know what the problem is but the noise just started this morning. I thought it wise to have it looked at as soon as possible, I'd be lost without my car."

"No problem Rosy. Pop the hood and leave the motor running, I'll take a look-see." Only a second or so elapsed and he told her to turn the motor off. She heard a sound of metal against metal.

"There, you're all set kiddo. I won't even charge you except for a free coffee tomorrow morning when I stop in for breakfast."

"What was the noise, it was nothing serious?" Rose felt a wave of relief. "I can't accept favors, Nick, wouldn't want you to get in trouble. Seriously, what was wrong?"

"It was only a loose fan belt, you could have done it yourself, so don't worry your little head. It didn't need any parts so, no charge. Now get on your way so you'll miss most of the heavy traffic, I'll see you bright and early tomorrow morning." Wiping his hands with a cloth he closed the hood and waved her on her way.

Rose felt a lift to her heart and gave him a big smile, she'd treat him for breakfast, and it would be worth every penny. She turned the car toward home and the bath she had been thinking about. Within twenty minutes she was walking up the stairs and through the door of her tiny apartment at the upper rear of a large red-brick, two story house. The living room had an oriental type rug, grey couch and matching chair, two end tables and a cocktail table in front of the couch. At the far left of the room was the hallway leading to a full bath on the right, a bedroom straight ahead, and the kitchen to the left. The back stairway door was on the left wall when entering. Rose loved the place. It had radiators, steam heat was clean, the walls real plaster with fancy swirls that were beautiful. The home owner, an elderly lady, lived in the upper front apartment. Rose owned the living room furniture but the maple bedroom set and kitchen table and chairs belonged to the old lady who'd put a new mattress on the bed

a few days before she had first moved in. It'd been a measure of comfort knowing she was the only one to use it. Tossing her purse on the bed she quickly stripped and then proceeded to the bathroom where she let the tub fill while she retrieved clean clothing and a towel. With a sigh of intense pleasure she stretched out and relaxed.

After dressing in slacks and tee, she popped a frozen dinner in the microwave and while waiting for it to heat, sat at the kitchen table scanning her hometown "Highland Township" newspaper she'd subscribed to, the smartest thing she'd ever done. She was so proud of her daughter, every day she read the paper from front to back keeping up with all the local news. The "Common Sense" replies Sy gave in her column were truly sensible and sometimes quite comical. The micro's bell rang and Rose, using a hot pad retrieved her dinner. It was baked chicken, mashed potatoes and green peas. Between reading and eating, time slipped away until she finally pushed her plate aside. It was an article on one of the inside pages that caught her eye and almost made her heart leap with shock…

* * * * * * * * * *

Local police are investigating the murder of an 86 year old local senior citizen.

They apprehended the suspect Edward Grogan at the Canadian border. He is also being charged with the kidnapping of Sylvia Fields, a young woman who writes for news "Common Sense" column. Police have solid evidence to support conviction. "He will go to trial as soon as possible." said the Prosecuting Attorney.

* * * * * * * * * *

She needed to know more. She recalled writing Edna a letter right after she'd run away, her last name was Shaw. On the spur of the moment she called information and asked for the Shaw phone number. It was unlisted. Damn!!…what was the other old woman's last name? Claire…what? Her husband's first name was Peter. When Claire was irritated with him she used his full name and that time he'd been BBQing. The table had been set. All the food displayed, potato salad which was my favorite, deviled eggs, baked beans, I was starved as were all us teenagers. We were ready to sit down when Pete tripped, the ribs went flying everywhere and Claire had yelled, "Mr. Peter Delaney, what did you do." How could I have forgotten?

Once again Rose called information but this time she was lucky and got the phone number. She dialed and waited, finally hanging up after the tenth ring. She'd keep calling if it took all night, sooner or later Claire would get home from wherever she was off to.

Eventually the days long hours caught up with her, she rested her arm on the table, her head on her arm and began to doze. She dreamed of her mother Eleanor and of the older man she herself had fallen in love with, became pregnant by and later learned he had been married and temporarily separated from his wife. It was not the first time because of his philandering. She had been such a fool but it was the first time she had experienced love. She'd told her mother it was a young wealthy man that had abandoned her. She still couldn't forget that first time he had made love to her, it had spoiled her for younger men. She was content to remain single but maybe one day she'd meet a man she would want to spend her life with. Rose awoke with a start, she'd been dreaming about her youth. A glance at the clock told her only an hour had passed. There was still time to make that phone call.

Once more she tried the number. This time the phone was picked up and Claire answered.

"Hello Claire, this is Rosemarie, remember me? It's been quite a few years since we last saw each other, how have you been?

"Who did you say this was? Rosemarie? Claire had no idea who the person could be. "Hold on just a moment, I have to check something, I'll be right back." Clair hurried to her refrigerator to check the notes she had attached as reminders but search as she may, there was no one there named Rosemarie. Hurrying back to the phone, she had forgotten why the person had called. "What can I help you with?" She sighed.

"Thank you Claire, I wanted to know about your neighbor Sylvia Fields. I'm an old friend and happened to see the story in the newspaper. Is she alright? I was a bit worried about her."

"Don't you worry, Miss Rosemarie, Sylvia is just fine and dandy. Edna and I were just having tea with her the other day, we've become great friends. We plan on having our little tea get-together parties quite often. In fact we're having one the end of this week. You're welcome to come, we'd be happy to have you." Before Clair had finished speaking the call was disconnected. Hmmm! She thought, I wonder what that was all about.

By the time Claire hung up the receiver she had already forgotten it, having become sidetracked by one of her notes that had fallen from the refrigerator door. Carefully she placed it under the magnet and straightened it. With a step back she was pleased that all the notes hung neatly. Thank goodness for her memory bank, she would be lost without it.

As for Rosemarie, she felt a little more relieved knowing Sylvia was home, but there was a lot of dissatisfaction with the information she had gotten, not much more than before she'd made the call. Somehow she'd figure a way to find out more without revealing her identity. On the spur of the moment she decided to take a trip back home. She doubted anyone would recognize her from the girl she once was when she ran away so many years ago. She was due a vacation, tomorrow she'd tell Lenny she wanted a weeks' time off. Her decision made she felt much better.

When she arrived at work she waited until the morning rush was over, knowing Lenny would be in a much better mood. Taking him aside, she told him she was taking her vacation starting Monday and she'd be back the beginning of the following week. He was slightly peeved but since he'd called her occasionally to fill in for other waitresses who had been taken ill or begged off work, he wasn't about to turn her down. She was the best worker he had.

"Sure Babe, anything to please you. Having problems with someone or something? You know all you have to do is ask, I'm here if you need me." Lenny was old, overweight and had a heart of gold. He was the one who had told her about the apartment and since he knew the old woman who owned it, she hadn't had to pay a security deposit.

"Thanks boss, you're a peach." She watched a blush spread across his face which always made her smile. He was such a shy guy for someone his age and compliments made him light up like a Christmas tree. She was actually quite fond of him. Turning away to save him more embarrassment, she hurried to wait on another customer. It would seem like a very long Saturday.

That night, after packing her suitcase, she had everything ready to leave early the next morning. The fridge was cleaned out, car gassed up, extra money in her purse and she had disposed of any trash. The apartment was neat and clean, ready for when she returned. Finally settling down into bed she realized how very tired she was. It had been a long day but much had been accomplished. Her mind drifted to her daughter which it had often done, wondering what sort of person she had grown to be. She, herself was likely despised for leaving right after the birth but recalling the frantic state she had been in, she doubted being a good mother would have been possible.

The alarm clock woke her. It was still dark but a good time to miss some of the holiday weekend traffic which shouldn't be too busy on a Sunday morning. Within minutes she was on the freeway heading home to Highland Township. She had packed sandwiches, a coffee container, a few mini chocolate bars and three bottles of water. She intended to drive all day and should be able to complete the 425 miles by evening, God willing. Her car was purring like a kitten, thanks to Nick.

At midmorning she pulled in at a rest stop, used the bathroom and sat at a picnic table sipping some of her coffee and munching one of the chocolate bars, then back on the road. At noon another rest stop for lunch and the same later in the day. She reached the outskirts of Highland just as dusk was falling. Wending her way through the city she finally reached Shady Oak Inn, which was only about five miles from her old home. The price was reasonable.

She felt light headed, her back hurt and she was exhausted. Who would have thought just sitting and steering could be so tiring. When she slipped under the covers sleep claimed her almost as soon as her head hit the pillow. She didn't awaken until morning when the sound of a barking dog intruded into her dream. When she opened her eyes it took a moment to realize where she was. Giving a stretch and a yawn she slipped out of bed and made her way to the shower. Within a short span of time she was dressed and back in her car, wending her way toward home while talking to herself about what she intended to do. Confident that no one would recognize her, she planned on checking out the neighborhood.

Pure heartache set in as she cruised down her old street, passing her mother's house, recognizing her old girlfriends' place which looked so different, maybe new owners. She wondered how her mother was getting along. She'd be up in age now, in her late seventies. Where had all the years gone? She herself was now middle aged, only a few years shy of the age her mother had been when Sylvia was born. How did mom ever stand it, me running away and leaving her with a baby to care for? I know I could never have done it. I wouldn't blame my daughter for hating me if I were in her shoes.

Suddenly, the possible results of her long ago actions landed like a ton of bricks on Rosemarie's conscience. "What a spoiled brat I was." She thought. "How could anyone have tolerated my self-serving behavior? Everything had been "me-me-me," with never a thought or concern for someone else's feelings." Putting herself into her mother's place she couldn't keep her eyes from welling with tears, almost causing her to pull over to the side of the road for safety. With a quick swipe she brushed them away and promised herself she'd make it all up to her, she would not run away again. Making a spur of the moment decision, Rose circled the block. When reaching her mother's house she then pulled into the driveway and turned off the motor. She could feel her heart palpitating so rapidly she felt faint but steeling herself against panic, she exited the car and made her way up the steps. Hand shaking, she almost missed the doorbell finally pressing it firmly while holding her breath, hearing the old familiar chimes echo through the house. It felt like forever but eventually the door opened and a young woman stood before her with a questioning look on her face.

For several moments neither spoke, the unexpected surprise of gazing back at a familiar reflection, one older and the other younger was a phenomenon that left both women speechless.

"Sylvia, I'm so glad I finally decided to come here, I've thought of you almost every day for all these years wondering how you were and what sort of person you had grown up to be. I'm Rosemarie. I gave birth to you twenty seven years ago when I was too immature and self centered to accept the role. I hope my mom doesn't hate me. So many times I was tempted to take a chance and come home to ask her forgiveness. The years slipped by too quickly until finally I realized I couldn't delay it anymore." Rose bowed her head, shame overcoming her like a leaden weight. She felt so guilty that she could hardly bear to look her daughter in the face. What's my mom doing, is she out visiting her friends? Before anything I need to see and talk to her, tell her how sorry I am about running away. I've missed her so much."

Sy stood in shocked silence, the idea that her mother finally stood before her, the real flesh and blood image that she had wondered about for most of her life, was almost more than she could assimilate. Realizing that she had stood too long not speaking, she reached for her mother's hand and drew her inside, closing and locking the door behind them. Without a word she put her arms around her. "Mother, I'm so sorry, what a terrible thing to have to tell you when we just meet. Granny passed away just this spring, it was a heart attack. I took her ashes up north to her favorite spot near where she grew up." Sy couldn't help the tears that blinded her as she relived the loss but the sound of sobbing made her realize the terrible pain her mother was feeling. No chance to tell Granny she was sorry or how much she had loved and missed her.

"Granny forgave you Rose. She said you were much too young to accept so much responsibility, she told me to try to find you. Come sit down, do you like tea? I'll put the pot on. Of course you'll be staying here. Oh! For heaven sake, listen to me talking a mile a minute. I'm so sorry you didn't get here while she was still alive. She left some recordings that you might like to hear." Sy gave a nervous laugh as she pulled out a chair for her mother and then set herself to filling the tea pot and getting something out for snacks. Finally settling down across from Rosemarie, Sylvia gave her a timorous smile as she waited for her mother to speak.

"Odd! But I had a sixth sense mom had passed away. It was around last spring when I awoke in the middle of the night thinking I'd heard her call my name. I lay awake for a while thinking about her. The feeling that she was close by was wonderful, just like being back home in bed knowing she was downstairs, busy doing last minute chores before retiring for the night. I loved her, she had been so patient with my wild ways. I didn't know what was wrong with me, I couldn't sit still for long, always had to be on the go running about like a scatterbrain. It wasn't until I ran away and tried to manage on my own that I realized what a wonderful life I'd had but I was too stubborn to return home and admit my mistakes. The money I took with me was enough to pay for a room for a month at a local residence and have enough left to last about a week. My first job was at a furniture store in their office answering the phone and entering customer payments on their accounts. I only had that job a short time. The boss told me that "Balance due" should be put on late payments. I mistakenly put it on each statement I sent. Of course the customers had to be appeased and I was fired. I decided I didn't want anything to do with office work but at least I'd earned a few dollars to keep me going. I happened to see a "Help Wanted" sign in a restaurant. I applied, got the job, and have been working there ever since. I really enjoy meeting people and I couldn't ask for a nicer boss." Rosemarie sat pensively recalling her first week of work. The customers had been overly generous with their tips after seeing how hard she was trying. So many of them were now die-hard friends after all the years she had been serving them. Twenty six years, she couldn't believe it until she looked at her daughter, now a full grown woman and a perfect stranger.

Sy returned the look, a feeling of friendship toward her mother, something quite surprising. "I always wondered about you. Granny never said a word, just told me about you running away. She said when I felt ready she'd tell me anything I was curious about, I was at that point when she passed away. I was not only devastated because of her death, but also about losing any little bit of information about you. I'm so glad you decided to come home, I hope you stay. There was an empty feeling inside that nothing could satisfy but now, with you here, we can get acquainted and fill in all those years we missed."

"There's nothing I'd like more, I'll go get my bag and then I'd like to take you out to breakfast Sylvia, I'm starving." Rosemarie was already heading for the front door.

It had happened so quickly that for a moment Sy sat in surprise. So, this is my spur-of-the-moment, quick-decision, mother, she thought. I recall granny mentioning that fact. A wide grin brightened Sy's face when she realized there would not be many quiet moments wondering what to do with her mother here.

Later, they settled themselves in a booth at the Boulevard Grill, a new establishment opened after Rose had left. She liked a hearty meal in the morning, it kept her going full steam all day. Ham and eggs, hash browned potatoes, wheat toast, coffee and orange juice. She ordered the same for Sylvia.

Sy felt foolishly happy, this would be their first meal together. She liked the idea of dining on the same food, enjoying the same flavors like people do at family dinners. A warm glow began at her toes and spread upward through her entire body, it felt like the times she'd cuddled into granny's flannel nightgowns feeling love surround her. Shyness overcame her and a blush spread across her face as she looked across the table at her mother who was finally there, within reach. This was real, not a dream.

"I hope you can stay mom, I'd like to learn all about you, I've wondered about you so many times."

Rosemarie sipped her coffee, not sure if she wanted to stay. She really liked her life back in Indiana and all the friends she had there. This was something she'd have to seriously consider. She hated to think of giving up all her friends, yet on the other hand, being close to her daughter would be lifelong satisfaction. Someday there could also be the pleasure of enjoying grandchildren. There was actually no doubt of the choice she should make, she owed her daughter big-time. At least there were plenty of years left to grow together in love and mutual respect. Her mind resolved, a feeling of relief settled over her, the anxiety now gone since the decision was made although thinking about the loss of her friends was hurtful. Setting her cup down, she reached out and took Sylvia's hand. "Honey! You're right about me moving here, we've been apart far too long. I'll stay for the remainder of the week and then head back home. I'll give my boss a months' notice and also my landlady." Rosemarie's mind was already running through some of the things she'd have to do, like leaving the furniture so the old lady could rent the apartment furnished. All she'd need to do would be to close her bank accounts, as easy as pie.

When they returned home the phone was ringing, Sy got to it in time before the call was disconnected. It was Officer Jorgenson from up state.

"Good morning Miss Fields, we apprehended Ed Grogan and have your vehicle. Lucky for you there was no damage to it. You can come pick it up anytime."

"This is great, thank you so much sir. I was hoping I'd get my car back but was worried it had been damaged. I think I can get there by dinner time, would that be okay?"

"That would be fine Miss Fields, see you later then. Drive safely."

"Mom, would you mind driving me up north to pick up my car? I'll tell you all about what happened on the way. We can stay there overnight and in the morning I'll follow you back here. This is such a relief, I thought I'd never see it again." Sylvia was so excited about getting her car back she wanted to leave immediately.

"Let's hit the road Sy, no need to pack anything either." She exited the booth, dropping a tip on the table just before heading for the cashier, Sylvia trailing close at her heels. Within minutes they were in the car. Rosemarie stopped for gas and then they were on the northbound freeway pushing the speed limit.

Twilight was fast approaching when they reached the small town and made their way to the police station. Sylvia showed her identification, the car keys were turned over to her when she signed the release form. Rosemarie followed her to the nearest auto care facility. After the car had been vacuumed and washed Sylvia felt more at ease now that all reminders of her abduction had been erased.

Her mother followed her to the nearest motel/restaurant where they paid for their room and then had a late light supper. After a good night's sleep, the ride back home seemed much quicker than the ride up, they were home by noontime. It had been a whirlwind trip but the close proximity had been the best thing that could have happened to them. Mother and daughter became friends.

"I'm going to do a little laundry, mom, so go change your clothes and get comfortable. There are some recordings I want you to hear that Granny made."

Sy retrieved the tapes she had already listened to. When Rosemarie returned, she sat at the table listening to her mother Eleanor's' voice. Although the painful loss was almost unbearable, the life history was so incomprehensible that the image she had maintained of Eleanor's life was shattered into fragments.

When Sy finished the laundry, all folded and put neatly away, she sat quietly with her mother listening to the ending of the last tape. Sy felt embarrassed sitting with her mother when granny spoke about Rosemarie wanting an abortion. It was such an awkward situation, the feeling that she might never have been born had Granny not put her foot down and forbade it. For a moment she felt a twinge of resentment but then, seeing how ashamed her mother looked, she reached over and took her hand. Pressing it against her heart she found the words to release them both from their uneasiness.

"Mom, feel the beating of my heart. It's there because you gave me life. Regardless what you may have thought when you carried me I am here, a living breathing person you created. Look at me mother, see me? My eyes that look at you with love, my lips that smile with humor because you are my mother and I know you love me. Do you realize how clever Granny was to relate the incident about abortion? If she had not, it would have been a guilty burden you would have hidden from me all your life. Now the air is clear between us with no secrets. I have no feelings of ill will about what you had been thinking so many years ago. This is today, a new beginning for the two of us. Can we go on from here?"

Rosemarie began to cry heartbroken sobs that seemed to emanate from her very soul. "You'll never know how sorry I am that I even thought about an abortion. The longer I carried you inside me, the more I became attached to you. When you were born it almost killed me to leave you, but I knew I couldn't stay and give you a good life, I had to get away. I couldn't bear the thought of running into the man I had loved to distraction, didn't want to be anywhere we might meet. I couldn't have survived the humiliation and shame of his abandonment. I thought of you every day, pictured how you might look. When you reached adulthood I began to think of you getting engaged and then married. I even thought I might be a grandmother but the hometown newspapers I subscribed to never carried any information. Then one day I happened to see an item by Sy Fields and I knew immediately it was you. Many times I was tempted to write but how would someone in Indiana know about your "Common Sense" column?" Rosemarie gave a sniffle and dried her eyes with a tissue Sy handed her. She felt so much better now that the air was cleared about her outrageous idea she'd had so many years ago. Eleanor had been so right to mention it in one of the tapes. She'd never feel guilty again about keeping it secret from her daughter. She sent a silent "Thank You" to her mother Eleanor, her heart aching that she'd not been able to see her once more before her death but hearing her final words of love on the tape had healed a tremendous rift that had been between them when she had fled the city.

"Your Grandmother taught you well, sweetheart. I'm relieved my secret is bared and you accept it as the meaningless idea it truly was. Hmm! I'm feeling a little hungry, how about you? I make a mean omelet, if you have the eggs, I have the time." While Rosemarie fixed the eggs, Sylvia heated frozen hash browns in the microwave, she also popped two sliced bagels in the toaster and then spread them with cream cheese and strawberry jam for their dessert. The table set, tea poured, the two women sat to enjoy the fruits of their labor, and it was delicious.

* * * * * * * * * *

CHAPTER 2

    Alexander Jason Williams sat quietly in his office contemplating the final plans for finishing the development of the Highland Township shopping Plaza. The construction itself was completed, merchants rental contracts signed with more than half already moved in, minor tile work to be finished on the far end of the site. Within the week every last detail would be taken care of. Thank heaven it was over. It had been a hassle from the very beginning. This was definitely the last building project he wanted to set eyes on and it wasn't that he was too old. At age 58 he was fit, active in sports, and really enjoyed going head to head on making business deals but lately he had become restless and bored. Maybe this was some type of man's "Change of Life" he thought, like what women go through. If so, it was plain bull and he wanted no part of it. At his yearly physical the doc had said he needed a hobby, something to occupy his spare time like golf, some activity that would use up his excess energy. That was a joke, he got enough action dating. It hadn't always been like this. Once he had been happily married, at least he was. His ex-wife Alicia had been a social climber, always looking to improve her station in life. She'd snagged him good, she was all he could think about so they'd married, stayed married until she set her mind on a big- wheel executive who was known for being foot-loose with women. He had what she wanted though, a big mansion, servants, and deep pockets.

    When Alicia divorced him he got to keep their two year old son Ryan, who was now twenty eight. He never wanted to be tied to a woman again. They were just gold-diggers looking for an easy ride through life. Dating suited him just fine. Just then the phone rang interrupting his reverie. His secretary had his son on the line and put the call through immediately.

    "Good morning son, what are you up to on this fine day? No! I have nothing important scheduled. Everything has been finalized and thank God, we'll be finished with it as of next week. Did you get those last rental contracts signed? That's great! Then we're done with it. Do you have anything planned this evening, will you be home tonight or out on a date? Great, then how about if we celebrate, it's my treat at anyplace your heart desires. Okay! I'll see you at home around seven." He had a smile a mile wide when he hung up the phone. It wasn't often they got together, in fact they sometimes crossed paths during their coming and going. He buzzed his secretary Wanda. "If anyone calls, I'm gone for the day. Ryan and I are going out for a good time tonight. You may have the rest of today off, go shopping enjoy yourself. I'll see you in the morning."

"Gee! Thanks boss. You two have fun, you deserve some relaxation the way you've worked your heads off. I'll see you in the morning." Wanda would wait until her boss left just in case something unexpected came up. When she heard his private exit door close she knew she could leave.

Alex entered the underground parking garage and headed for his classic 1957 white Corvette convertible, 4-speed trans, 350hp, racing cam, and about 9 miles per gallon. He loved it, specially the way the rag top stored nicely into the section behind the seats when its lid was closed. When he pulled out of the garage exit he was glad the top was up, a light shower had begun. It rained all the way home.

After his divorce he'd kept the residence, all Alicia wanted was the money. He and Ryan had been quite comfortable with their living conditions. Esther came in twice a week taking care of cleaning and the laundry. He had a gardener who trimmed the shrubs and mowed the lawn in summer, winters he removed the snow. Alex was extremely satisfied with the arrangements. Neither he nor his son wanted nor had time to bother with housework. They were neat about not having "stuff" laying about the place so Esther Rodgers was very pleased with her Tuesday and Thursday schedules. Tuesday cleaning the upstairs and changing the beds. Thursday was for cleaning the downstairs and doing laundry. She was widowed, her only son killed in an automobile accident years ago. She had come to work for Mr. Alex right after his divorce and her family tragedy, when Ryan was just a tyke not even in school yet. At first she'd come each morning and then, after work, he drove her home, taking Ryan with them. It was too much for all three of them. Finally he'd raised her pay promising a bonus at the end of each year if she'd move in with them until Ryan was older. She agreed and ended up staying until Ryan graduated from school, fifteen years of having a family to care for and love. She had spoiled them with good old fashioned cooking, homemade cookies and milk when Ryan came home from school. All the little things a mother would do for their family. It had saved her sanity and at the same time had given the boy a stable home life. During those years she had at first rented out her home, later selling it at a nice profit. Alex had invested the money for her and she was now sitting pretty with a comfortable old age she could look forward to, but that was a few years away. She liked to stay busy so on the two days she came to clean she usually cooked dinner for them before leaving for home. Alex had given her a new Ford sedan a few years ago and driving herself around was the best feeling in the world, a true feeling of independence. Just then the phone rang interrupting her reveries.

"Esther, don't cook dinner, Ryan and I are going out tonight to celebrate. We finally completed that contract. Yes! No thanks, that's sweet but honestly, we'll be just fine. You go home and relax but be careful driving, it's raining. I'll talk to you soon." When she replaced the receiver the phone rang again immediately.

"This is the Williams' residence. No! I'm sorry, he's not available at the moment, would you care to leave a message? What is your name? Mr....would you spell that? Yes! Mr. Farthwald, I'll relay the message to him. Thank you for calling." She left the message next to the phone so Alex would be sure to notice it.

With a last glance around to make sure all was tidy, she slipped on her jacket, retrieved her purse and exited the house, making sure the door was securely locked behind her. A few steps she was in her car and backing out the driveway heading for home. She didn't notice the black sedan parked a few doors down the street. Two men were sitting in it, their faces turned away as though looking at the home they were in front of, she didn't get a look at their faces.

When her vehicle was out of sight the two exited their car and made their way to the rear of the vacated residence. Within moments they gained admittance and placed themselves in areas where they wouldn't be readily seen when the occupants returned home. According to the report of their accomplice, Alex William was even now on his way home. They hadn't heard from the man who was shadowing the son Ryan. Timing was of the essence and they were being paid very well.

Looking at the two men it was a sure bet that they were not ordinary people, a little too well dressed to be skulking around. When Alex entered his residence they subdued him with little resistance. Blindfolded, wrists tied, he was taken to the waiting car. Although he tried to question the men, not a word was spoken. At first Alex had thought it a joke being played by his son but the silence seemed ominous. Within a short time the car came to a halt and he was led into a building where he was placed on a chair and told to stay. Shortly, he heard footsteps and then someone was placed in a chair next to him. He could feel his hands being released and then the blindfold was whipped off.

To say he was shocked would have been an understatement. The entire work force including office and labor personnel were present. Balloons, colorful swags decorated the ballroom, caterers began to place trays of food on the banquet tables, and next to him sat his astounded son, as amazed as was he. A huge banner was draped across the room from wall to wall reading, CONGRATULATIONS, JOB WELL DONE. A loud cheer burst forth and Mr. Leon Farthwald himself made his way over to shake Alex and Ryan's hands. A waitress, carrying a tray holding champagne and glasses, wended her way through the crowd toward them.

"You did it Alex, I knew I'd selected the right man for the job, right on time and with excellent workmen who knew their trade. As promised, you get the bonus. I have the $1,000,000 check right here and you earned every dollar of it."

A lopsided grin spread across Alex' face as he took the check. Ryan was slack-jawed for a moment until his dad nudged him in the side, then he was laughing outright at the subterfuge that had been played on them.

"I have to tell you Leon, you sure had me worried for a while. I thought I was being kidnapped." Alex felt embarrassed about not putting up a fight, but all in all, what did it matter. It was all in good fun.

The remainder of the evening was enjoyed by all. The food was fantastic and there was even a small band that did a good job coaxing dancers onto the floor. At the end of the evening, everyone replete with good food and companionship, the celebration began to break up. Mr. Farthwald had a limo waiting to take Alex and his son home. It had been a memorable evening.

It was a relief to step into the shower and then crawl into bed. Alex slept nude, he liked the feeling of not having things get twisted and uncomfortable. A restless sleeper, he used the entire bed with his tossing and turning from one side to the other. Regardless of the time he retired he was usually up and about by six, a confirmed early riser. Ryan had the same habits. They usually met in the kitchen, whoever got there first made breakfast. The aroma of fresh coffee and bacon had Alex grinning.

"Good morning Dad, how does bacon, cheese omelets and toasted bagels sound? The omelets are just about ready, bacon is draining on paper towels and you can pour the coffee."

The sun was brightening the eastern horizon when they finished breakfast. The rinsed dishes and silverware went into the dishwasher, random crumbs brushed neatly from the table and disposed of in the trash, the two men looked askance at each other wondering what they'd do with their time on this early Friday morning, their first day of leisure.

Alex's face lit up as an idea sprouted like a fast growing weed. "Look, I have to get to the bank and deposit that check. How about if we go shopping at our new Mall? We spent so much time working on it that it might be fun seeing it from the consumers' angle. I need a few new shirts and socks. That new men's store, "Graystons" might be an interesting place to visit, how about it?" Alex didn't like sitting around idle as Ryan was well aware.

"Sure dad, d'you think they carry jeans? I could use some new ones to bum around in. That last project took its toll on the few pair I had, I'm game, let's go."

It was warm enough not to need a jacket so they scooted out the door like kids chasing the ice cream truck. After they stopped at the bank, the drive to the mall took only about half an hour. They were pleasantly delighted seeing the crowd looking for opening sales in the newly stocked stores, a terrific sign that the mall was on its way to being a favorite site. Good thing they were shopping today, Saturday would have been too much of a hassle.

Typical guys, window shopping was not high on their "to do" list and so they headed directly to the men's store not paying attention to any of the side displays. They drew the eye of more than one woman. Both were tall, at least six feet, broad-shouldered and well proportioned. Both had brown curly hair, the younger had sun-lightened highlights, and the older with attractive touches of gray at his temples. It was obvious they were father and son, completely unaware of the attention they attracted.

They spent several hours browsing, buying and trying on jackets. Alex had coaxed Ryan into getting a new suit with the works. He was measured meticulously for a perfect fit, also selecting several shirts and ties to compliment the outfit. When they emerged from the store it was noon.

Ryan pulled Alex across the atria towards a Coney Island. "My treat dad, I've been dying for a Sloppy Joe ever since I found out they were moving in. Since we're here we may as well take advantage of our shopping spree." The booths were all filled. They found the only two available seats at the far end of the counter and ordered. The Coney's were piled high with chopped onion which overlaid the chili sauce that was ladled over the hotdog. Alex took a big satisfying bite, glad that he didn't have a date lined up for the evening, it tasted fabulous. Ryan managed to down three of them.

"Thanks son, haven't had one of those in years." He glanced about as they made their way toward the door, almost past the last booth until belated recognition flashed and he stopped in his tracks, Ryan bumping into him. He turned, stepped back and leaned toward the woman who stared at him in shock.

"Rose?...Rosemarie, is that you? Where have you been hiding all these years?" He saw she was sitting with a younger woman who bore a close resemblance, possibly a relative.

"My God! How long has it been? It's got to be almost thirty years or close to it." She was still as beautiful as ever. He began to recall their last moments together and how angry he'd felt when she had told him she was pregnant. He hadn't believed her. She wasn't going to play him the fool the way Alicia had. More enraged than he'd thought possible he'd thrown money at her and left. Afterward he'd had regrets.

"Rosemarie, this is my son Ryan Williams. Ryan, this is Rosemarie Fields, a young lady I knew years ago. May we join you?"

Rosemarie was stunned, this was the last person in the world she wanted to run into, especially with her daughter Sylvia sitting next to her. Well! She thought, nothing ventured, nothing gained, and I'll take the bull by its horns. She gave a wicked smile up at Alex, more interested than she could ever have imagined in wan

ting to see the expression on his face.

"I'm very pleased to meet you Ryan. This is my daughter Sylvia Fields. Sy, meet Alex Williams and his son Ryan."

When recognition suddenly registered on Alex's face, it was all she could do to hold in her gleeful exultation seeing his dilemma. It was a priceless payback for all those times she had relived their last moments together.

"You're more than welcome to join us Alex, and Ryan also. We were just about to order coffee."

"Good idea, I could use some caffeine, how about you son?" Alex was afraid to look Rosemarie in the face, afraid of what might be revealed. He was devastated at the possibility that he'd had a daughter all these years, never contributed to her support nor even bothered to find out about the abortion that Rose had mentioned. Since he hadn't heard a thing from her he had assumed it had been accomplished, the pregnancy had been terminated and he was free of all responsibility. He glanced at Sylvia, examining her features, trying to find any indication that she was his daughter and there it was as clear as day. He found himself gazing into his own eyes, the same ones he saw in Ryan every morning, hazel with that glint of green. He thought his heart would stop because of the shock.

"Do you ladies have anything planned for today? If not, I'd like to invite you to my home. We can have a nice relaxing afternoon and get acquainted, I'll even fix dinner."

Rosemarie felt a surge of triumph at his request, if he thought he could get back in her good graces that easily he was sadly mistaken. She didn't care about getting to know him again, and she sure as hell wasn't going to tell Sy anything about him being her father.

"That's very nice of you Alex but unfortunately we already have plans that would be impossible to change this late. Maybe another time, give me a call. Right now we really have to get going. It was a pleasure seeing you again, and very nice meeting you also Ryan."

Picking up her purse she tugged at Sylvia's elbow helping her daughter slide across the bench seat. Once Sy was standing, she steered her quickly toward the door, only pausing momentarily at the cash register to toss a twenty on the counter and tell the cashier to keep the change. The two women were out of sight by the time Alex and Ryan exited the restaurant.

"What's the hurry mom, we don't have any appointments today? It might have been fun going to Mr. Williams' house. He acted as though he liked you, and you couldn't seem to take your eyes off him. I thought his son was very nice looking, I wouldn't mind dating him and he sure seemed interested in me. Who knows maybe we could even double-date sometime."

The more Sylvia talked, the more nervous Rosemarie became. Somehow she had to get them away from here for awhile until things simmered down. It was almost time to head back to Indiana.

"Sylvia, can you get a little time off work? Seems the days flew by and I have to get back to work. I'd love to have you come along. At least meet my friends and help me close up everything for my move back here. What do you say?"

"When are you planning on leaving mom? I actually don't have anything pressing that can't be remedied."

Rosemarie thought a moment, "Okay, how about the day after tomorrow, Sunday. The traffic won't be that heavy, we'll have tomorrow to clean the house, do any laundry and pack. If we leave early in the morning we'll be there by evening."

"Mom, let's take my car it's full of gas and ready to go. Park yours in the garage, there's plenty of room and no sense having it just sitting out baking in the sun. They accomplished their miscellaneous chores, retired early Saturday night to be fresh and well rested for the next morning. Claire had volunteered to pick up their mail while Edna, across the street, said she would keep an eye on the property while they were gone.

The drive back to Owens, Indiana seemed to take half the time that the trip from there had taken. It must have been their "catching up" conversations that made the miles slip away so quickly. When Sylvia pulled up in front of her mother's large brick apartment and turned off the motor, all she could do was smile at the different image she'd had of where her mother had resided. With every bit of knowledge gained she became closer to Rosemarie. She wished Granny had lived long enough to have seen her daughter again. How wonderful it would have been, the three of them living together in love and companionship.

It was still early enough for a visit to the landlady. Rose knocked on her door and when it was opened, she gave the old woman a hug and kiss on her wrinkled cheek.

"Well! Rosy, have you been a good girl while you've been gone? I've missed you. Come in honey, would you like some soda pop or something cold to drink? Who is this cute little gal you have with you?"

"Hello! Mrs. Gilliam. I'd like you to meet my daughter Sylvia. She came with me to help pack, I'll be here a week before heading to Michigan but I'll give you a month's rent in lieu of notice and will also leave all my furniture so you can rent it furnished, maybe charge a little more rent. My mother passed away this spring and left the house to the both of us. It's time I moved back home."

"Aw! I'm sorry to hear about your mother, Rosy, sorry too that you're leaving. I surely loved having you here and thanks, the furniture will bring a little more income but you don't have to pay any extra because you're leaving. I've had several people on a waiting list hoping to rent here. They'll be moved in quick as a wink." After visiting for a few more minutes mother and daughter took their leave.

Sylvia liked the apartment. It was immaculate, cheerful and roomy. The lime green walls and white trim in the bedroom was eye catching, a very pretty combination. The bath was all white tiles with black edging and she loved the old fashioned tub with its lions feet. She could see why her mother had liked living here, she would have also.

Rose had put two frozen dinners in the oven. When the aroma of baking chicken made her stomach growl, she smiled at Sy, knowing she must be hungry also.

After eating, dishes washed, clothes put away, they each enjoyed a hot bath and then, bone tired, they went to bed. They both slept soundly until morning.

The next day Rosemarie took her daughter to meet her friends at the Old Country restaurant and also give Lenny her weeks' notice. This was going to be tough, she'd worked here for so many years that they were like a second family to her. Steeling herself for the eminent heartbreak in store for her, she settled Sylvia in a booth and made her way to the kitchen. As soon as Lenny saw the look on her face he knew what was coming. He'd had an idea this would happen.

"Lenny, do you have a minute? I'd like you to meet my daughter Sylvia. I guess you know that I'll be moving back home but I'll work the week, it'll give you a chance to hire another girl. I'm so sorry about putting you in a bind like this. You've been so darned good to me." Rose felt her eyes begin to well with tears. She quickly brushed them away, this was no time to get maudlin. Leading him to where Sylvia sat in the end booth she couldn't help feeling exceptionally proud of her daughter.

"Sylvia, I'd like you to meet my boss Leonard Greenfield. Lenny, this is my daughter Sylvia Fields."

"Hi! Sylvia, I'm pleased to make your acquaintance." Lenny reached to shake her hand, surprised that she didn't have the same dark blue eyes as her mother Rose although their facial features were very similar. "I'm going to miss your mother, she's been a fixture around here for quite a few years and the customers will be complaining at the top of their lungs at the slow service until I can find another waitress who's as good." Lenny couldn't help smiling at the blush that colored Roses' face but she knew she was top-notch and deserved the compliment.

"Rosey, I need a few words with you. I'll have your mom back in a flash Sylvia." Lenny led Rose into his office at the rear of the restaurant and sat her down in a chair opposite his desk. He pulled some papers from a drawer and then sat facing her, a serious look on his face. "I remember when you first came here. I thought you were too small to handle those big trays but then you settled in and within a month you were one of our best waitresses. Other help came and went, but you stuck it out for all these years. Sometimes you were so sad that it almost broke my heart. I decided that I'd try to help you in some way. At the end of each month I added one dollar a day as an extra tip for each day's hard work. I put it into a special savings account for you. With interest, it's my thank you for your loyalty and dedication." He handed her a large pink envelope.

Rose opened it and pulled out a large fancy "Bon Voyage" card. A check fell onto the desk. Hesitantly she reached out, turned it over and then sat, tears streaming down her face, mascara running, and sobs almost choking her. It was for ten thousand dollars. "I can't take this Lenny, it's too much." She pushed it toward him.

"Oh! Yes you can Rosy. You made more than a dollar a day in tips, this is minimum. You'll take this and say "Thank you Lenny." You were my best girl and I'm going to miss you more than you'll ever know. You were like a daughter to me. Now go fix your face, you don't want to keep Sylvia waiting." He had a hard time keeping control of himself, this was so much harder than he'd imagined. He got up and as he walked passed her he planted a kiss on the top of her head. "Goodbye Rosy girl, I'll miss you."

Sylvia could see that her mother had been crying. "What's happened, mom, did he give you trouble about quitting?"

"I'll tell you when we get to the car Sylvia, I don't want to start bawling here in the restaurant."

Sylvia steered her mother to the car while Rosemarie tried to stop the tears that began to flow down her cheeks. At last, with a final hiccup, she dried her eyes. She glanced at the check still clutched in her hand. "I can't believe that he did this. All those years, times when I was irritated with him, even flipping him off when I was in a bad mood. I feel so ashamed and embarrassed. He didn't even know my real name. I was afraid mother would find me so I used an alias. Come on, honey, let's get out of here, I don't want to make a spectacle of myself. There's nothing to keep me from leaving today."

When they returned to the apartment there wasn't much to sort through. Sylvia didn't want a thing since Granny had everything a homemaker could want. They stopped at the bank so Rosemarie could close her accounts and leave her forwarding address. She would deposit Lenny's gift when she opened her accounts at the local bank back home in Highland Township. The return trip was uneventful, they arrived at dusk. After parking the car in the garage they carried their suitcases indoors setting them on the counter in the laundry room, they'd sort out the washables in the morning.

Sylvia began preparations for tea while Rose got out cups, saucers, cream and sugar. She also checked in the cupboard for any munchables since neither one felt like cooking dinner. Finding nothing, she looked in the freezer section and sure enough, there was a loaf of raisin bread. She brought it out, separated four slices and popped them in the toaster. By the time the tea steeped the buttered toast slices were ready.

They had just finished eating when the phone rang.

"Hello, who's calling?....Just a second. Mom, it's for you, Alex wants to speak to you."

"Hello! Alex, how did you get this number? You're kidding, you didn't? It's too long ago. Honest?" Rosemarie had a huge smile on her face listening to the conversation. It was too outlandish not to be true, and truthfully, she was impressed. "I'll think about it Alex. We just got home from a long drive and we're exhausted. Give me a call in the morning. We'll talk then, okay?...Tomorrow. Goodbye."

Deep in thought she helped clear the table while Sy waited for an explanation about the call. When none was forthcoming she couldn't control her curiosity.

"Was it anything important mom? I knew Alex liked you. I could see by the way he looked at you. Did he phone to make a date? Hopefully Sy waited without success.

"Sy, I'm not sure I want to get involved with him, he's from a different class of people that I would never fit in with. I told him I'd think it over and for him to call me tomorrow. I was very flattered that he'd saved this phone number all these years. I wondered how he'd gotten it since it's unlisted. I'll talk to you tomorrow, Sylvia."

They turned off the lights and headed up stairs. Although it was still early, Rose wanted to relax, maybe read a little, and hopefully decide what she wanted to do about Alex. She hated to admit, just seeing him again had stirred feelings she had thought long buried only to have them flare up again as torrid as ever.

As for Sylvia, she wondered what the mystery was all about. She felt the attraction between the two when Alex couldn't take his eyes off Rosemarie. There was more here than meets the eye. She decided to wait and see what happened, no more questions.

The morning passed. Alex was, at that moment, reevaluating his options. After all the hassle he'd been through completing the shopping plaza project he needed a rest. Didn't want any deep involvement where he'd be poised on the brink of another disaster like the last time he and Rosemarie had been together. He was still youthful and fit, enough that young women were drawn to him but he wasn't the "hit and run" type guy. What he truly wanted was a loving, lasting relationship, maybe even a second try at marriage. But then, what he'd gone through with Alicia's cheating had made him mistrusting of what women really wanted. It was likely just money, the more the better. He decided to back off any contact with Rosemarie. His decision made, he felt relief.

Ryan strolled into the kitchen starved, the aroma of bacon sizzling in the pan causing his mouth to salivate. Dad had breakfast ready so Ryan poured the juice and filled the coffee cups. They spoke not a word as both men cleaned their plates of every morsel. Finally satisfied, just sitting while finishing their coffee, David cleared his throat and making a spur of the moment decision broke the silence.

"Ryan, I've decided to take off on my own for a while, maybe a couple of weeks. Would you let me borrow one of your cars? You know what lousy suspension my '57 Corvette has. Although I love the thing and wouldn't trade it for love nor money it's like riding on your fanny, you feel every bump in the road."

THE THISTLE SEED

"Sure dad, d'you want the Jimmy or the Jeep? Take your pick, and I promise I won't touch your vette, you'd hang me if anything happened to it. How come you decided to take off, I thought you were going to get together with that woman you once knew, that Rosemarie?

Alex wasn't in the mood for questions. Sometimes Ryan was too inquisitive, wanted to check on him every minute and it ticked Alex off to no end. "Look son, I need some free time. Maybe it was the combination of finishing up the big job, that chance meeting with Rosemarie and the feeling that suddenly I'm hanging out in the wind with nothing to grab on to, that has upset me. Whatever the reason, I'm getting away. Just the thought of complete peace and quiet with no phone calls, no bills to pay or dinners to fix sounds exactly what I need, and No! I'm not checking in with you every day, you'll be lucky if I phone you at all and if you don't mind, I'll take the jeep. It has four-wheel drive and I expect to do a little sight-seeing, some off-road exploring. It's been years since I enjoyed the experience, it was fun never knowing what was around the next bend in the road." His face lit up with the thought, enthusiasm coursing through him like an electric charge he wanted to leave immediately.

Ryan could see the sudden determination, typical for his father, of immediate action. "Go pack dad, I'll take care of cleaning up this breakfast mess later. I'll take the jeep to the station and get it serviced and gassed up. By the time I get back, you'll be ready to take off." The wide grin he got from his dad was worth the little extra kitchen work.

Ryan had the jeep washed, vacuumed inside, battery checked, all fluids checked, tire inflation checked. He picked up two packages of cheese crackers with peanut butter filling and tossed them in the glove box just in case his dad was in the boonies and got hungry. He also bought a roadmap and placed that in with the crackers and then two bottles of water were added to the collection which made Ryan feel better. For good luck he added a tin of roasted peanuts.

Alex was ready when Ryan returned with the jeep. After the midmorning breakfast he knew there would be no stopping for lunch, he was free as a bird to spread his wings. Ryan was a responsible young man so this wouldn't be the first time he'd be on his own while his dad was off gallivanting.

"Thanks son, it looks brand new all clean and shiny. He gave Ryan a huge hug and pat on the back, then tossed his duffle bag on the floor in front of the passenger seat. He climbed in, started the engine and with a last wave of his hand was away.

Ryan watched as the jeep grew smaller, finally turning a corner and disappearing from view. A dreadful feeling of loss loomed ever larger, the farther away the vehicle became, until Ryan wanted to run after his dad and try to stop him. Too late, he was gone.

After the kitchen was cleaned up and the dishwasher turned on he was at a loss of what to do. He thought of Rosemarie's daughter Sylvia and how he had felt a connection to her. Maybe he'd give her a call and take her out to an afternoon movie and then supper, a good chance to get acquainted. Reaching for the phone he pushed "redial" which would bring up the last call made, quickly he wrote it down as he waited for the phone to be answered.

"Hi! Is this Sylvia? I'm Ryan Williams, we met at the Coney Island a few days ago. I know this is short notice, but I was wondering if you would like to take in an afternoon movie and then have a bite to eat later. You would? Great, what is your address? Okay, I'll pick you up in 20 minutes. Nope, I'm wearing jeans and a shirt so don't get dressed up. You can invite your mom too if you'd be uncomfortable. Oh! Well, maybe leave her a note then. Okay, bye.

Half an hour later the young couple was at the mall doing a little window shopping to kill time before the movie. They talked about their likes and dislikes, favorite foods and wines. They found that they both loved the same kind of music so Ryan invited her to an outdoor music festival later, one of many going on most summer evenings and a favorite gathering place for both young and old. Sylvia wondered how she could have missed the enjoyment all these years.

After the movie, which had Sylvia crying toward the end, they stopped at a local grille for a late lunch. Then it was on to the outdoor arena to get a good seat. It was almost ten o'clock when Ryan pulled into the driveway to drop her off. It had been a wonderful afternoon and evening with open conversation, laughter and mutual likeability. She couldn't recall ever having such a great time on a date, it was apparent that Ryan felt the same way.

Sylvia gave Ryan a quick kiss on the cheek, told him not to bother walking her to the door as she exited the car and then watched as he backed his car out of the driveway and gave a wave of his hand as he drove away. She was still smiling as she entered the house. Apparently her mother had not yet returned home, so she tossed the note in the trash.

She was sound asleep when Rosemarie peeked into her bedroom, relieved to see her daughter was at home. She herself was exhausted, had spend too much time playing cards with Edna and Claire, talking about the old days when Eleanor, Rosemarie's mother, had been alive and the good times the three couples had enjoyed. The memories as fresh today as they had been so many years ago.

Rosemarie had bags under her eyes when she looked at herself in the mirror the next morning. What a night. She'd had a wonderful time but had indulged in too many gin and tonics, a slight hangover made her wince when she pulled the comb through her hair. Even her scalp hurt. She was positive that Claire, being so forgetful, had likely double dosed the drinks but she was such a sweet old soul that Rose didn't have the heart to reprimand her. Before the evening was over they had taught her some of the old songs that were once so popular and they had ended up singing their lungs out. It was the best time Rose had enjoyed in years. She was so glad she had returned home but for a moment the loss of her mother was overpowering.

She heard Sylvia stirring. Knowing she'd be taking a shower before coming downstairs, Rosemarie hurried down to the kitchen to get breakfast started. Just thinking of food made her feel ill, likely dry toast and coffee would be her fare but maybe French toast would sit well. She gathered the ingredients together and began preparation.

By the time Sylvia sat down at the table the French toast was ready. Sylvia preferred maple syrup while Rose chose to eat it plain. Fresh coffee topped off their meal.

"So mom, what did you do last night?" She couldn't help smiling at the puffiness under her mother's eyes, a sure sign of late hours and not enough sleep.

"I was at Claire's house along with Edna. We played cards, drank gin and tonic and sang old songs. Those two are outrageous, they had me laughing so hard at some of the antics they used to pull, that now I realize why mom and dad enjoyed their company so much. They did everything together, even vacations. I hope when I'm old and gray I have some wonderful memories like that to remember and laugh about." Rose had such a wistful expression on her face that Sy wished she could think of something to make her smile. Instead she went to fetch two pain relievers. She knew now was not the time to tell her of all the fun she'd had with Ryan.

Soon after breakfast Rose returned to her bedroom to lie down for a while until the headache went away.

Sylvia sorted through the mail she had picked up yesterday while out with Ryan. As usual there were a few crank letters, one from a pervert, three sexually explicit asking for dates, and three worth answering, one that sounded very heartbroken. The remainder went into the trash.

Dear Sy,
After many years I found the one I love and I'm sure the feeling was mutual. For some reason we've lost touch, maybe because of work schedules, I don't know. What would you suggest I do?
Sincerely
D. R. K.

Dear D. R. K.
By all means get in contact, don't take chances. Forever could last a very long time, with or without her/him.

Rosemarie awoke around noon feeling much better. After showering and washing her hair she felt almost human again, ready to face the remainder of the day with no after effects of last night's indulgence. Wandering into the kitchen she heated water to fix herself a cup of herbal tea, also asking Sy, who was busy answering "Common Sense" letters, if she'd like a cup.

She placed Sys' tea near to hand and then sat opposite her daughter watching her work until finally the last letter had been responded to.

"How did you manage to get this job, Sy? It's perfect, your working hours are set at your convenience, the pay is excellent, and you're very popular."

"It was a "try out" mom, I talked my boss into it and thankfully, it was an instant hit. The first few editions I actually wrote myself and answered until the mail started arriving. You'd be surprised how some folks actually lack common sense, so I give them a hint. I did have big trouble with that deranged husband, but that was the first time and it's something I'm happy to forget." To change the subject, Sy began to talk about yesterdays date with Ryan.

"We had a fantastic time mom, finally ended up at an outdoor concert. I really like him and I believe the feeling is mutual…Why are you looking at me like that, mom? You look pale as a ghost, is your head still hurting? You're scaring me badly, if you don't say something in the next minute I'm calling EMS, you look like you're on the verge of a stroke." Sy was frightened, ready to reach for the phone when her mother began to speak.

"No! Don't call, sit down honey it's time we had a mother-daughter talk, something I've put off for too long." Rose tried to compose herself, the last thing she wanted to do was break down and cry. It was too many years ago, years that she felt were over and gone forever, but seeing Alex had reawakened old memories and feelings. She felt like a fly caught in a web, not able to disentangle herself. There was no way out other than telling her daughter the painful truth.

"You remember tape #4 that Eleanor made mentioning me trying to trick my lover into marrying me? Actually, I happened to get pregnant and didn't tell him hoping he would propose simply because he loved me. When I began to gain a little weight I knew I had to tell. Unfortunately it happened to be at the same time he was considering leaving me. He didn't believe me but threw the money telling me to take care of it. I don't think he was referring to an abortion. It would have been easy to misunderstand what he meant. Sylvia, that man was Alex Williams, and his son Ryan is your brother."

Both women sat in silence. Rosemarie relieved that Sylvia now knew about Ryan. Sylvia, because she was trying to change her image of Ryan from being a date into being her brother. Surprisingly, it wasn't that difficult to do.

"You know mom, I really don't mind. I like Ryan a lot but not in the same way I'd felt about David who I haven't mentioned to you before. I won't say a word to Ryan though, this is something he should hear from his dad. I may still go out with him and keep it casual, at least if you think its okay."

Rose couldn't believe she had made such a big deal out of something that had turned out so simple. The relief she felt was overwhelming. This was turning out to be a very nice day after all.

There was a definite change between the two women. A strong new bond had been formed between mother and daughter, both well aware of and thankful for.

For the first time in quite a while Sylvia thought of David and how he had been there for her when she had been released from the hospital after the kidnapping, he had even driven her to the bus terminal. She had never written nor called to thank him for his kindnesses. A huge wave of embarrassment swept over her. What an ungrateful wretch she was, granny had taught her better manners than that. She decided to phone immediately and apologize. Digging through her purse she found the scrap of paper and dialed the number.

Carol Kendall picked up the phone on the third ring. "Hello? Well for goodness sakes, how are you Sylvia? We've wondered how you were doing, that was a pretty horrifying experience you went through. That's wonderful dear, we would have called but Davey said we shouldn't bring back such dreadful memories to you. Oh! We're doing just fine, we miss Davey a lot though. What? Oh! No! Nothing has happened to him. He just decided that at his age he should be living on his own so he moved into Aunt Rose's house. Yes! That's where he lives, it was shortly after the trouble you'd had. Sure, do you have a pencil handy? Got it? When you talk to him give him our love. Yes! It was wonderful talking to you also honey, bye-bye."

Rosemarie had finished her tea while Sy had made the call. She was aware of a hint of excitement in Sy's voice when she had asked about David.

"I don't recall hearing you speak of this young man named David. Is he someone important in your life?"

"I thought so at one time, mom, but that was before I was snatched by that maniac. When I took Granny's ashes up north David was a life saver when my car wouldn't start. He rode me to his home on the handlebars of his bike, I thought I'd never walk again. Odd, now that I think about it, he's been around a number of times when I needed help, even replaced some windows that had been shattered by a tornado."

Sy fished out her little black phone book from under the counter near the phone and entered Aunt Roses number and also the Kendall's. She immediately dialed David. The phone rang three times and then the answering machine picked up. Sylvia left her number. Then she sat and told her mother all about David, his family and the many things he had done for her. The more she talked, the more she appreciated what a special person David truly was.

When the phone rang later it was David returning her call. They talked for quite a while, Sylvia invited David over for dinner at 6pm.

Rosemarie called Claire and Edna, the neighbors, and made plans to play cards, Sylvia would be on her own.

THE THISTLE SEED

When David pulled into the driveway with ten minutes to spare his hands were shaking, his heart racing, and his mouth felt dry as a desert. Steeling himself for the encounter, he marched to the door and rang the bell. When it opened and Sy stood before him he froze.

"David, you'll never know how happy I am to"…before the sentence was finished David pulled her into his arms.

*   *   *   *   *   *   *   *   *   *

CHAPTER 3

Alex felt the exhilaration of being on the road to God knows where, encountering anything other than the usual, boring, everyday rituals. He was heading north, as far as possible. He loved the North Country with its scent of pine trees and the sightings of wildlife. He'd left his credit cards home even though Ryan thought it risky, but there were rural places that accepted only cash, and so he'd decided that pay-as-you-go was what he'd enjoy experiencing.

It was a beautiful day, traffic not too heavy on I-75 and since he wasn't in a hurry he kept the speedometer around 65, not caring how many cars passed. The feeling of contentment grew with each mile traveled. Flint city drifted away and soon Birch Run was left behind. When he passed the off ramp to Bay City, he watched for the Kawkawlin exit, intent on taking the side road to Pinconning near Saginaw Bay, and then traveling route 23 all the way along the edge of Lake Huron until he reached the Mackinaw Bridge crossing to the Upper Peninsula.

The scent of fresh air was invigorating as he cruised at the local speed limit along route 13. In Pinconning he stopped at a place to buy smoked fish and then further along he stopped at a store that specialized in cheeses. There were so many varieties he couldn't make up his mind so he purchased several. Before he left the area he bought a small cooler, found a store to buy dry ice, and had the cooler packed with the bottled water Ryan had provided, the smoked fish, the cheeses and two sandwiches from a local Deli. He wouldn't have to stop anyplace except for gas.

When he reached Mackinaw city he rented a room at a motel. He showered, and then with the towel wrapped about his midriff, he sat on the edge of the bed munching one of the sandwiches and sipping at a bottle of cold water. Hunger satisfied, feeling too restless to settle in for the night, he dressed in jeans and tee, and went for a walk.

It was a tourist town, folks bustling about, Mackinaw fudge stores selling their trademark sweets and souvenirs of the fantastic Bridge itself. He purchased a picture postcard, addressed it to his son and wrote a short, "Wish you were here," note. When he dropped it into a mailbox he thought that maybe it would have been nice if he had invited Ryan along. Pensively, he headed back to the motel.

The next morning he overslept. Before dressing he consumed the remaining Deli sandwich, still cold from the dry ice. What he really craved was a good cup of coffee. Back in the Jeep, he filled the gas tank at a nearby station and then parked at the next restaurant he spotted. The coffee was passable but better than none. By nine-thirty he was driving across the five-mile-long Mackinaw Bridge. The view was magnificent, the waters of Lake Michigan on one side, Lake Huron on the other.

At the end of the bridge he made a spur-of-the-moment decision exiting left. From that moment on he would follow his nose and hope that he would always find a gas station. In Manistique he topped the gas tank and then bought food. Foil packages of tuna, pop-top sardines, oysters, and clams, anything that would tide him over for a short spell when he was off the beaten track. He was on highway #2 and from now on he would only travel north or west. He checked the compass attached to the dash, the compass needle pointed west.

Alex loved taking drives, he hadn't felt this free and foot loose since he was young. He recalled one summer when he and two of his friends made plans to rent a cottage on Higgins Lake. At the last minute they'd had to work, said they would get there for the following weekend. He'd been royally ticked off. The second morning he was there he decided to take his camera and go sight-seeing. At that time he owned a sweet little 1941 Plymouth coupe, blue with whitewalls, double spotlights and skirts. The inside door upholstery was matching blue plaid. The final touch was the suicide knob attached to the steering wheel which could turn that honey on a dime. Riding along, looking for an interesting place to investigate he had noticed a dirt road meandering through a field and up a hill into woodlands. On the spur of the moment he'd turned onto it and drove to the top and into the trees. Exiting his car he walked to the very top of the incline. Down below, through the branches of trees he saw a beautiful lake, several cottages scattered around its circumference, he began to take photos. He became aware of a rustling sound through the dried leaves of the previous autumn. When he turned to discover the reason, he'd almost wet his jeans at the sight of a black bear. He would have won a marathon and that little coupe would have too they were out of there so speedily. He laughed at the memory. Unfortunately, the only picture he had was of some tree branches and a lake....

Alex almost missed seeing the side road leading north, he turned onto it and continued until he came to a clearing where he stopped for lunch. He ate one of the packages of cheese crackers with peanut butter that Ryan had stashed in the glove box, they were good. He rinsed them down with a few sips of water and then continued onward. The day was fading rapidly into twilight, the time had passed more quickly than he realized, likely because of all that day dreaming he had indulged in. The road was getting so steep that he gunned the motor, tires sliding a bit in the loose sandy soil. Suddenly finding traction, the jeep barreled up the incline over the top and out into space, Alex could only grip the steering wheel and pray.

When he regained consciousness, it was the next morning and he was stretched face down on a narrow barren beach. There was a high precipice behind him, only sand, water and driftwood in each direction that he looked. He didn't know where he was or how he had gotten there. Not far away a small container floated near the shore. He went to retrieve it. When he looked inside he found an assortment of food. Maybe someone had lost it. It would be nice to keep in case he got hungry. He picked it up by its handle and began to walk along the narrow edge of sand. Suddenly he realized he was soaked through and through but didn't remember being in any water, maybe it had rained while he was sleeping.

There was only a short distance to walk in each direction and then the beach disappeared, deep water lapping against rocky walls. He was sleepy again, he went back to where he'd awakened and curled up. Between dozing and just sitting, the day passed and night came. He curled against the rocks hoping to find a place where the wind couldn't reach him. Finally he piled stones as high as he could, it reminded him of something from long ago when he was young, but he forgot what it was called.

The days passed, he ate and slept, walked the short span of sand and wondered why he was there, why was he all alone? He wanted to go home but he couldn't remember where it was.

Once the last of the food was consumed Alex became desperate. It would have been impossible to scale the escarpment so he thought he'd try swimming, although he couldn't recall if he knew how. Grasping the handle of the cooler he waded into the water, after only a few steps the bottom dropped away. He found he could side-stroke while keeping a grip on the cooler with his left hand. It was awkward but at least it was something to hold onto when he tired. He made his way around the edge of the cliff. There was nothing in sight but an extension of the stone walls. He returned to the narrow beach, disappointment furrowing his brow and a hint of panic hovering in the back of his mind. When rested, he again entered the water and made his way in the opposite direction. This time the cliffs meandered downward until, in the far distance, he could see where a pier jutted out into the lake. His spirits rose even as his strength waned. He paddled and swam, the image growing larger as the distance closed.

At last, totally exhausted, he pulled himself up on the beach, lying on his back until he could breathe normally again.

It was a relief not seeing the stone wall hovering overhead. The wide expanse of woodland was a beauty to behold after viewing only water for the past elapsed amount of time. On closer inspection he realized the pier was decayed, half collapsed and unused for years. The building itself looked abandoned with missing window glass, but the log walls looked solid even though part of the roof was gone. At least it was better than the sliver of beach he'd lived on for God knew how long.

Staggering slightly, he made his way to the dilapidated structure. The door hung askew and when he squeezed through the opening several small, long-tailed critters skittered away. With a sigh of relief he settled into one of the spindle-backed wooden chairs that sat beside the square table where an assortment of glass jars and other odds and ends were scattered about its surface. Right now he didn't care about anything but sitting and relaxing, enjoying the improvement in his living conditions. Oddly enough he fell fast asleep sitting up, a nice change from cuddling up to cold rocks.

When he awakened half an hour later he felt better although thirsty. Picking up one of the jars, he made his way to the lake where he scoured the glass with sand and then filled it with fresh lake water. He drank until his thirst was slaked, refilled it and then carried it back to the cabin. His stomach growled, he had only the water to fill it. He explored the surrounding area finding no other buildings in the vicinity.

That night he slept once again sitting up at the table, not however, a deep sleep this time. His bodily aches and the discomfort of hunger pangs kept him restless. When morning dawned he decided to follow the rutted road that led into the dense forest. He carried the water-filled jar with him.

Swarms of mosquitoes engulfed him, welts covered his face and arms and it seemed hours before he finally reached a rural macadam-paved road, the torture of the blood-sucking insects finally over. He saw a small gas station in the distance and headed toward it, his step quickening with the thought of rescue.

Roscoe Jenkins had just opened up, ready for any early morning patrons who happened by. When the door opened, no sound of a motor alerting him to a customer, he became alarmed, even more so when he viewed the creature standing before him. Of course he knew it was a human, but the bloodied gash near the hairline, the red welt's covering every inch of exposed skin, and the haunted look on the man's face startled Roscoe, the guy was in bad shape.

"Please, help me. I'm lost, I don't know how I got here or where I came from. I don't even know where I was going, but I'm so hungry I'd give anything for something to eat. He reached deep into his side pocket and pulled out a wad of bills. Here, take what it would cost."

Roscoe's eyes widened at the sight of the money. Twenties, fifties and even some hundreds, all crunched together. If he hadn't been so honest he could have taken it all.

"Hey fella, sit down, relax. You can have my lunch and thermos of coffee, no charge. People in our town don't take advantage of those who need help." He seated the man at his desk and unwrapped the sandwich. He poured coffee into the thermos lid and then sat on the stool and watched as the food was consumed, wolfed down in the blink of an eye. He passed Alex a banana and finally the last of the cupcakes his wife had made.

"So, what's your name and where do you hail from? I don't recall ever seeing you in these parts before, course this being a rural road, out of town travelers seldom come by."

Alex had a blank look on his face soon followed by panic. He searched his pockets, only the money and nothing else. He tried to remember where he had been but the only memory was of the sliver of sandy beach and then the ramshackle cabin. He raised his hand to his brow, fingers spread to brush his hair back. He felt the gash that was scabbed and dry, something that had happened days ago that he had no memory of.

"I don't know, I can't remember anything." He looked down at his clothes, not recognizing them as his. He was wearing no watch, nor ring. He must have had shoes but he was barefoot, didn't recall if he'd ever had shoes on. He stood and walked over to a discolored mirror hanging on the wall and peered at his reflection. He didn't recognize the face, a perfect stranger. He turned toward the other stranger, "You've never seen me before? What's your name, sir?"

"Just call me Roscoe, fella. I'm calling the Sheriff, he'll know what to do. I bet you were in an accident somewhere nearby and there'll be a record of it. You'll be back home in no time."

Sheriff Hatch arrived in record time. There wasn't much ever happening in his jurisdiction. A few locals having too much to drink and spending the night in the hoosegow, a domestic disturbance, sometimes bored teens getting into mischief. This was out of the ordinary, a guy who didn't know who he was. Oscar was sure it might be someone who was too drunk to know his name but still, this wasn't an ordinary occurrence.

When he entered the gas station and saw the fellow, he knew for a fact he'd never laid eyes on that face before. Scraggly beard, face sun burnt to almost beet red, brown curly hair, and hazel eyes with a glint of green.

"So fella, you can't remember your name or where you're from? Then the first thing we do is get you to our local hospital and have you checked out. It's possible this is only temporary amnesia. Hey! Don't worry, we'll take good care of you, I know you're scared, but we'll get you back home. I promise." He helped him to the squad car, waved goodbye to Roscoe, and headed for the emergency ward. Twenty minutes later they arrived at the hospital. He escorted the man inside where a nurse took charge. Sheriff Oscar Hatch gave what information he had to the attending Physician, Dr. Ted Snyder.

"You seem healthy enough sir, nothing that a good meal and some decent rest couldn't cure. As for your amnesia, it's hard to tell. Sometimes memory returns quickly, although there are cases where it is permanent. Health wise there is nothing wrong with you, I'm sorry but we can't keep you here. Sheriff Hatch may have some suggestions, good luck to you." The Doctor hurried on to his next patient, no time to waste on someone healthy. However he did stop to inform the sheriff that the patient would be released to his care.

This wouldn't be the first time Oscar'd had charge of someone with no place to go. He'd put him up at one of the motels, at county expense of course, until they could track down his family. In the mean time there was always labor needed at local farms.

"So! What shall we call you, buddy? I guess "John Doe" would be best until we learn your true name, we'll also help you get some work so you can earn your upkeep." He helped "Joe" into the squad car passenger seat, closed the door and then walked around to the driver's side, settling comfortably behind the steering wheel.

Alex fumbled in his pocket pulling out all the paper bills, some dropping on the car floor.

"Hey, what have you got there? Where did you get all that money? Good God! Man, you shouldn't be carrying that around with you, are you nuts or something. That's a big wad of cash, you could end up dead someplace." Oscar was so upset he almost sputtered trying to get his cautioning point across to the idiot sitting next to him. "Nobody in their right mind"…Oscars voice trailed off, he had no idea what to do or say. The guy didn't have any ID, he could be a thief. Well! That took care of that, no way could he ask anyone to hire him, and he didn't want the fellow wandering the streets. He didn't want to jail him either, no evidence of wrongdoing. The only place he could keep an eye on him would be to settle him in the tack room of the barn.

"I Think I'll use your alias initials, call you J.D. Put your money away and pick up what fell on the floor too. I'm taking you home, my wife Angie will fix you up with a bath and some clean clothes. You're about the same size as my eldest son who's also a cop and works the nightshift. He leaves when I get home. My youngest son is home for the summer, he's 17 and begins college this fall. There are enough of us to keep an eye on you in case you get confused or need help. How does that sound to you?"

J.D sounded like a good sort of name, and he liked the idea of having his own place in the barn. He'd have felt uncomfortable in Oscar's house knowing that as a stranger he'd not be fully trustworthy. He was actually looking forward to meeting the family. He looked over at Oscar who was busy concentrating on the minimum of traffic they encountered driving through the small town. Oh! How he wished he could remember if he had a family, a wife, maybe even a kid or two. He wondered where all the money came from too. Was he an honest man? But what if he was a crook, had robbed someone and was wanted by police somewhere else? This not knowing was going to drive him crazy, but what if there was something wrong with his mind other than memory loss? It frightened him not knowing what he was capable of doing. He actually

couldn't trust himself. He sat quietly the entire ride pondering his predicament. When Oscar pulled onto the gravel driveway leading to his sprawling ranch style home, rather than stopping near the side door, he proceeded to the barn at the rear of the property. It was medium sized, painted the usual barn red, its double doors trimmed in white, and it was topped with a white shingled roof. There was a small separate side entrance with a wooden ramp. This was where J.D. followed Oscar who opened the door and led him to the tack room, a snug wooden-walled room with one swing-open window, a pot bellied stove in the corner with handy firewood stacked nearby. A bunk bed, mattress swathed in plastic, stood in the far corner and a 5 shelf cupboard was attached to the wall beside the door opening. The room was clean and had a pleasant woody aroma.

"This is where you'll bunk J.D. You can have your meals with us and Angie will do any laundry. She'll get the bed made up and ready for you while you enjoy a nice bath. I have extra shaving articles you can have. Will, my eldest son will provide you with some clothing. He'll take you into town tomorrow so you can shop for what you'll need.

"Thanks Oscar, I appreciate this. I hope I get my memory back, I can't stand not knowing anything about my life. I swear to you someday I'll repay you, and it's not about money. I seem to have enough for my living expenses of room and board."

"Well! Let's get back to the house, no sense standing out here wasting time. You can soak as long as you want, but when you're finished bathing, you clean the tub and be sure to put the towel and soiled clothing in the hamper. Angie won't stand for laziness and sure won't clean up after us. She always tells us we're not babies for a momma to be coddling." Oscar had a bashful grin on his face about being bossed around by his wife but a person could tell that he loved it.

Later, when J.D. settled into the hot water, he reveled in the luxury of soaking and scrubbing until his skin began to pucker. He washed his hair with the shampoo Angie had provided and after he was satisfied he was completely clean, he opened the tub drain and then stood under the shower rinsing away all the soapy residue. He felt like a million dollars. For a moment, something in his mind clicked, he seemed to recall something about that sizeable amount of money but nothing further came to mind.

Oscar could barely recognize J.D when he entered the kitchen. He was a nice looking fellow if a person disregarded the scarlet sunburn and the healing gash on his forehead.

"Come sit down and help yourself. Angie made meatloaf, corn on the cob, baked potatoes and a nice garden salad, and there's apple pie for dessert." Oscar pulled out a chair next to himself for his guest to be seated.

J.D. tried to contain his enthusiasm about his first real meal in a while. Although he felt ravenous, his stomach had shrunk and he could only consume a small amount of food. It was however, immensely satisfying.

After dinner everyone helped clear the table, Angie took care of the rest. Will left for work, his younger brother Chris had a date to take his girl to the movies, and Oscar and J.D. went to sit on the front porch, watch the sunset and discuss what sort of work J.D could do to occupy his time and earn a few dollars. As twilight began to drift over the landscape a few fireflies began to appear, flashing their amorous greetings to the females of their species. With yawns the two men departed, heading for bed.

J.D fell asleep immediately. The first goodnights rest he'd had in as long as he could remember when he awoke early the next morning. He stretched, gave a huge yawn and just laid there, perfectly contented to be in a real bed that was soft and comfortable. His mind wandered back to when he had awakened on the sliver of beach and he wondered once again how he had gotten there, where he had been and where he had been heading. Nothing in the area reminded him of family or home.

There was a knock on the tack room door, Oscar called out that breakfast was ready and since he'd be leaving immediately afterward, if he wanted to go into town he'd better get his body moving. He could spend the day there and then ride back home with him later.

"Okay, I'll be there in five minutes." He needed his own clothing, didn't like borrowing someone else's. When he walked into the kitchen he had already brushed his teeth, combed his hair and looked presentable. He'd made sure he left the bathroom neat.

"Good Morning everyone, I had a terrific sleep thanks to you all. And Will, I'll get myself some clothes today and save some wear and tear on yours, thanks for lending them."

Today Angie had fixed a pancake and sausage breakfast. When they were finished eating the two men said their goodbyes and headed out the door. Oscar dropped him off at the local department store that carried everything including kitchen sinks. "When you've finished shopping come over to the police station. You can leave your purchases there while you inquire about finding some sort of employment. This isn't a large town but folks do take vacations or sometimes are short of help due to illness or even increased business. At least it will keep you occupied until we find out where you belong." With a wave Oscar was off to do his routine inspection of the territory to insure all was well.

J.D. had fun finding things. After personal grooming essentials he drifted over to the men's section and purchased socks, briefs, tees, two pair of jeans, two shirts, two pair of slacks and a jacket. Then he went to the shoe section for loafers, dress shoes and finally a pair of Nike's. In the luggage department he bought a duffle bag. He couldn't think of another thing he'd need except a few books to read would be nice. He'd have a reasonable excuse to give the family more privacy. He was able to find two that sounded interesting, one a murder mystery, the other international intrigue. Even with the money he'd spent he still had plenty left. He couldn't help wondering where it had come from.

He was smiling when he entered the police station. He put his new possessions, all neatly packed in his new duffle bag, in Oscar's office and then left to make the rounds of the establishments searching for a job. He found one at the local Coney Island. He'd receive minimum wage, hours 8a.m. to 4:30p.m., with one-half hour for lunch. The hours would mesh with Oscars. He had a definite jaunt to his step as he made his way back to the police station.

On the way home Oscar expressed his pleasure. "You did great J.D. You got clothes and happened on a job too. This is going to work out just fine for us. Now our only problem is trying to find out who you are and where your home is. I have an idea that may bring results, I'll try an APB tomorrow. Sorry, J.D., that's an "All Points Bulletin.""

"I thought an APB was only used for criminals, Oscar. I don't think I'm a crook, at least I don't feel like I'm one. D'you think I'd have some kind of inkling if I'd done something dishonest?" J.D. felt his nerves tense up, just the thought of having a run-in with Oscar because of something crooked he'd done in his past made him feel ill.

"Take it easy J.D. Personally, from my experience with all sorts of folks, I think if you were a felon your true nature would have shown itself by now. You seem like an honest, hard working guy who likely went on a trip, got into an accident, and temporarily lost your memory. Although I have checked the accident reports from all the surrounding areas and there's no one missing, all persons have been accounted for. I even checked with private airports but found no missing planes. I haven't been sitting on this J.D. but actively seeking info from everywhere. I even checked for escaped prisoners, you do not fit any of their descriptions. I'm at a complete stop and don't know where to go from here. For sure, you're a missing person, we'll just have to wait and see. Somewhere, someone is going to realize that you're not where you're supposed to be. From the healing of the gash on your head, I'd say that happened about a week ago, not a long time. Let's say you were on vacation, eventually you'll be expected back on a certain day, Right? Well! There you are, we'll get a heads-up on a missing male Caucasian, brown curly hair, hazel eyes, and the complete description of you." Oscar pulled up near the barn so J.D. could grab the duffle bag from the back seat.

"Angie likely has supper ready, get up to the house pal and stop worrying, I'll get you back to your home, that's a promise." Oscar backed the squad car to the driveway and got out. He felt sorry for the guy and wouldn't ever want to be in his shoes, lost with no memory. He wouldn't wish that on his worst enemy. He was a meticulous cop, always searched for that needle in the haystack, but this time he was stymied. Where in God's name had the guy come from, and where was the car he'd driven? If he could find it he'd have the plates to trace, it would solve everything but he'd driven all the roads in the area with no results. Sooner or later something had to give.

That night Angie had outdone herself. Stuffed cabbage rolls, mashed potatoes, homemade coleslaw and strawberry shortcake for dessert. She almost blushed from the compliments but with a, "Pshaw, it was nothing," she brushed them off and filled the passed plates. Afterwards, when table had been cleared, J.D wished everyone a "Goodnight," excused himself and returned to his quarters.

It took a while to remove all the price tags, pins, and paper insets. Once everything was folded and neatly stacked on the shelves, he also folded the duffle bag placing it at the very top and out of the way. He changed his clothes, actually Wills, and wrapped them in the shirt to place in the laundry hamper in the morning. Wearing only briefs and a tee, he relaxed on the bed and opened one of the books.

Simply reading the first paragraph he could tell it would be interesting. Thank God for books. From the time he had been a kid and his mom had punished him by banning him to his room, he had lost himself in them. It wasn't punishment at all, it was pure pleasure and he loved it. Surroundings faded away and he was living in the written pages, not just the words but the ability to absorb them and turn them into a living experience walking the paths of the phantom lives someone had created. He lost himself in the story....

He awoke in the morning, book lying across his chest forgetting where he was, remembering a dream where he had been talking to someone named Rose. He wondered if it was someone he'd known in his "other" life. Putting the book aside he dressed for his new job in jeans, a tee and Nikes.

Angie's breakfast treat this morning was hash browns with sunny-side-up eggs nested on top, something he had never eaten before, at least he didn't think so. This was enough fuel to keep him going all day long.

Oscar dropped him at the Coney Island, wished him good luck at his new job, and proceeded on to his office. Yesterday there had been reports of two escapees from the maximum prison in Jackson. He wanted to find out if they were from this area so he'd keep an eye on any local relatives they might contact. He pulled into his parking spot.

Patty Shelds, his all around office manager was talking on the phone, likely to her son Brad who, Oscar opined, was spoiled rotten and got away with too many high-jinks. At sixteen he already owned a car Patty had bought him for his birthday, but he had no job for after school or even during summer to pay for its upkeep. She had a hard time controlling him. What he needed was his father but unfortunately the guy had skipped town, no one knew where he'd disappeared to. He'd been one of those restless sort of fellows who had to be on the move constantly or get bored. He signaled to her, she hurriedly said goodbye and hung up.

"Brad giving you trouble again Pat? I can always stick him in the local jail overnight to teach him a lesson. That might quiet that sassy mouth of his for a while, you know I'd be happy to do it." Oscar couldn't tolerate smart-mouthed kids and boy, was Brad a bad one. "Anything new on the docket? I sure wish we'd hear something about J.D. and where he hails from, maybe soon I hope." Oscar went into his office, deciding to stick around today just in case something turned up.

Mid morning the Coney Island got busy. J.D found the routine was fairly easy as long as he didn't drop anything. It was…plate…open buns….dog…chili…and then customer's choice….onions…mustard or hot sauce. As long as he remembered to open the buns, the rest went like clockwork. He enjoyed meeting the customers. When it wasn't busy he got to know a few regulars. At noon he savored his free lunch, he had to admit, it was darn good. The day passed quickly and before he knew it, Oscar was parked outside waiting to take him home. He felt great, the activity had invigorated him and the pleasure of doing something useful pleased him immensely. He had a broad grin on his face as he settled himself in the passenger seat, and Oscar couldn't help grinning back.

"You sure look chipper this evening J.D. Don't tell me you found your niche this easily and are a natural born Coney Island slinger. Pleased-as-punch is how I'd describe you, and not as serious looking a fellow as the one I dropped off here this morning."

"I was happy Oscar, it felt good doing something besides sitting around wondering. I liked meeting the locals and I even liked the free lunch. After a while the work became automatic, I didn't even have to think about it, just talk with the customers, joke a little, and before I knew it, the day was over and there you were, waiting to pick me up. Did you hear anything today, any inquiries about missing people?

"J.D, it's only been a week since I found you and maybe a week you were stranded.

and I've told you before, it takes time for people to realize someone is really missing. There are always excuses. Maybe they stopped to visit someone, or were in an accident, any number of things come to mind. I expect any day now I'll be contacted."

The next morning when Oscar arrived at his office there was a faxed picture and missing person report from Highland Township. It certainly looked like J.D. The person's name was listed as Alex Jason Williams, age 58. In the picture he carried a little more weight but it was definitely him.

Oscar arranged for a relay delivery, the only sensible thing to do because of J.Ds amnesia. He didn't want to take a chance on anything happening that would get him lost again. Each county would deliver him to the next until he reached home and the local police. The delivery system would begin in the morning when all the arrangements had been completed. Although Oscar was relieved and delighted that all questions would now be resolved, he was truly sorry to lose him as a friend.

Later that day, before they drove away from the Coney Island, J.D. gave them notice he would be leaving. He was relieved to know he belonged somewhere but anxiety made him feel jumpy and nervous.

At supper he was introduced to the family as Alex Jason Williams. It felt strange to be called Alex. He had no appetite and later in the tack room he couldn't relax. He packed all his belongings in the duffle bag, just leaving out the clothing he'd wear in the morning. He slept restlessly, tossing and turning all night.

At breakfast he could only get down some scrambled eggs and a piece of toast. The food did not set well on his nervous stomach. Angie had packed sandwiches, two apples, several hard boiled eggs and two large dill pickles to tide Alex over till he reached home.

The "Goodbyes" were painful. Angie hugged him, and then he shook hands with son's Will and Chris. They felt like family, the only family he knew and it hurt to leave them. When he settled into the squad car next to Oscar, he felt close to tears, his throat hurting from trying to control his emotions.

Oscar drove him to Manistique, turned off the motor to have a few words with Alex before handing him over to his next ride. He slipped a paper with his address, phone number into Alex's pocket.

"I won't forget you and I'd like for us to keep in touch. Maybe someday you'll want to come up this way for another vacation. When you get home call me, we'll all want to know you got there okay. You're a good man Alex, good luck."

Alex grabbed his duffle, and then shook Oscars hand hard. "I'd have been lost without your help Oscar. You welcomed me into your family, fed me, gave me a place to sleep, and kept my spirits from flagging. I won't forget you my friend."

Theo, the next relay officer was recently engaged, the wedding was in two months. He talked about his fiancé, the big wedding and where they had decided to go on their honeymoon. He was just getting started on the cooking lessons his soon–to-be-wife was taking when they arrived at his next relay site, Mackinaw City.

Roger was the silent type, maybe five words passed his lips during the entire ride from Mackinaw to Roscommon. Alex thanked him. "You're Welcome" was the retort.

Les liked to tell jokes. From Roscommon to Bay City, Alex was laughing almost the entire way, his sides actually aching by the time they reached Bay City. He thanked Les for the most enjoyable entertainment he'd had in a long time.

Floyd loved the water. From Bay City to Flint he told about all the best fishing places where to find Walleyes, Perch, and even favorite recipes for preparation. Alex got so hungry he shared the lunch Angie had made. They consumed every bite. Floyd dropped him off at the Bay City police station and waved goodbye.

Alex stood in the parking lot for several minutes knowing his son was to pick him up and drive them back home. He felt so many emotions overwhelming him that he was on the verge of panic. From the corner of his eye he noticed someone hurrying toward him. He turned in that direction seeing a good looking young man, tall with curly brown hair. He thought the face looked familiar until he realized it resembled his own. Unbidden, he recalled the name Ryan and a smile spread across his face as he reached to give his son a ferociously hard hug, while glimmers of memories seemed to swirl around in his mind… almost, but not quite ready to become recognized.

"What happened to you dad? When you didn't phone or try to contact me I was worried sick. Were you in an accident? What happened to the Jeep?" Ryan was talking a mile a minute and Alex had trouble keeping up with the questions.

"Slow down a little Ryan, I have no idea what happened. Even now my mind isn't working at full capacity. I had a head injury, didn't know who I was or where I came from. They couldn't trace any license plate because there was no sign of any vehicle. I may never know because of memory loss. Just out of curiosity, what sort of car was I driving?"

Ryan was totally shocked that his dad couldn't even remember driving the jeep. He turned to look at him as he opened the door of the Jimmy, tossed the duffle bag in the back seat, and then closed the door after his dad was seated. Walking around to the driver's side he swung into position and turned the key.

"It was my Jeep, dad. You didn't feel like driving this one, nor your Corvette either. Maybe we'll never know what happened, but I'm thankful you're alive. I keep thinking we may never have found you if you had been stranded someplace and couldn't get out. First thing we should do is get you checked out by our family doctor and make sure you're okay. Maybe Dr. Franklin can explain about your memory loss and if you'll get it back."

Alex recalled disliking doctors. The memory of invasive procedures where he was probed with instruments in his ears, mouth and nether regions made him want to cringe. Maybe though, if it was just examining his mind, it wouldn't be so bad. Alex gave a nod, not realizing that Ryan didn't see it, he was concentrating on driving.

When Ryan pulled into the driveway of the red brick colonial, Alex didn't recognize it and turned to his son with a questioning look on his face. "Is this where we live?"

Realization of the true ramifications regarding the loss of his dad's memory hit Ryan like a ton of bricks, hard facts that couldn't be ignored. First thing he'd have to do would be to get their housekeeper Esther back full time so she could keep an eye on him, and he couldn't take a chance of him driving anyplace either. Suddenly Ryan was aware of the reverse switch in their positions. He hoped to God he could do as good a job as his father. Patience, Fortitude and one day at a time.

* * * * * * * * * *

CHAPTER 4

David loved the convenience of living at his Aunt Roses' house. It had been signed over to him by his parents but he still couldn't get used to referring to it as his. From being a footloose bachelor living at his parents, to now owning a home and almost being engaged was a mammoth step. He hadn't asked Sy yet but he felt positive she'd accept his proposal. Well, almost positive.

Sitting at the kitchen table he poured over the receipts for deliveries to the new hardware store that would open in three weeks. When Aunt Rose died and his parents urged him to keep the house, that of course meant he'd need a job. He could have gotten work at a number of places since he was adept at everything pertaining to maintenance or even building a home. The years working for his dad, assisting customers and doing installations had primed him for opening his own hardware store right here in Highland. He'd be a good source of "How-To" information for anything his customers needed to fix. A quick glance at the clock told him he'd have to get moving, he was due to interview a few who had already submitted their applications.

When he arrived there were three people standing by the entrance. He led them indoors and had two sit on a bench placed outside his enclosed office, the older man he brought inside for the interview.

Scanning the application he could see that the man, Karl Ward, age 60, had been employed for thirty years as a handy man at a large school which had closed permanently. He'd been looking for another job since last summer. David could see that he was well muscled, his hands calloused from hard work, the writing and spelling on the application legible. An intelligent hard working man, just what he was looking for. "Could you start immediately? I can use you today, the foreman will tell you what to do. On your way out send in that next fellow, would you?"

THE THISTLE SEED

"Yes Sir. I'll also phone my wife and let her know I have a job." Karl was on his feet unable to contain his excitement. "Thank you, Mr. Kendall, you won't be sorry, I'm a hard worker, always on time and never miss a day of work." He shook David's hand then turned to leave, cell phone already in his hands making the call.

Ralph Noland was 48, single, and honest as the day was long. He'd been a whiz with a computer at keeping track of supplies at a well known supply company. Unfortunately he didn't realize someone was stealing, placing dummy orders to cover up the loss. When the shortage was discovered Ralph was arrested, later exonerated when the real thief was caught. He was offered his job back but did not want to work for someone who hadn't believed him. David hired him on the spot, he'd already checked out the story.

Jennifer Pryor was a looker with golden hair, golden eyes and a figure that would stop traffic but that wasn't why David wanted her. She was a terrific accounts receivable/payable clerk. In between office work she could also work as cashier. She thanked David nicely when he told her she had the job, but the look she gave him when he turned away had a predatory gleam. Like a feral cat contemplating its next victim.

In two days deliveries would start arriving, the shelves would be stocked. The huge grand opening in one week would be the finale.

When David arrived home that evening he phoned Sylvia immediately. They had a date, one he hoped to use as a springboard for making his proposal of marriage. Over the past months they had reached an unspoken agreement that they were a couple. It was time it was evident to everyone, he had already purchased a ring. He could hardly wait to slip it on her finger.

"Hello! Oh! Hi! David, you sound happy this evening. It must have been a very good day for you. Did you get those new employees you were hoping for? That's great, one less thing for you to worry about. Davey, if you don't mind I'd like to cancel our date for this evening. Do you remember when I told you about Alex Williams being a missing person? Well, Ryan has just phoned, his dad is back home but he'd suffered a head injury and has amnesia. Ryan thought that since Alex had seemed interested in Rose, it would be a good idea for Rose to come over for a visit. My mom is very upset and I don't want to leave her alone tonight. Thanks honey, I knew I could depend on you. I'll call you tomorrow then. Bye bye."

It was a restless night for both women. In the morning they could hardly wait to get ready and leave. Rose had been rather quiet for most of the drive and then half way to their destination, she broke her silence.

"Sylvia, honey, I have to tell you something that I've been fighting myself about for years. It's kept me from feeling close to any other man. I never recovered from my love for Alex. When he left he took my heart with him and I'm going to do everything I can to help him regain his memory, even if I have to stay with him twenty-four hours a day. I can't help myself, just being in the same town with him is emotionally draining. This is my chance to get close to him, he won't reject me because I'll be a stranger to him and his natural courtesy will prevent rudeness. Maybe by the time he regains his memory he'll want me to stay." A smothered sob escaped that Rose couldn't hold back.

If Sylvia hadn't been in traffic she would have pulled her car over to the curb. "Mom, please don't cry, I want to help but I don't know what to do. This is something that has to work itself out. I noticed when we met them in the restaurant, Alex was very interested in you. I'm sure, from the way he acted, it was more than just a passing fancy. Dry your eyes Mother, you don't want to meet him looking a mess. Use the visor mirror and fix your face, take that shine off your nose too, you look like Bozo the clown. There, isn't that better?" Sy glanced at her mother, realizing in that moment she was still a young vibrant woman, someone any man would be proud to be seen with. When Sylvia pulled into the driveway of the Williams home both women were ready for anything.

Ryan was waiting at the door, a relieved smile of welcome on his face as he ushered them into the house and closed the door.

"Good morning Rose, I'm so glad you decided to come, nice to see you again Sy. How about a cup of coffee? If you didn't have breakfast I'll fix some scrambled eggs."

The offer of eggs was declined but the coffee was accepted. They were just seated when Alex walked into the kitchen, a look of intense curiosity on his face as his eyes settled on Rosemarie.

"You look familiar, have we met before? He filled his cup and then settled down next to her, gazing into her face, a look of wonder and excitement lighting his eyes. "I know you from somewhere don't I? I couldn't forget someone as beautiful as you. Where have you been all my life" Those age old

THE THISTLE SEED

pick-up lines, stale as old bread, brought a smile to everyone's face, including Rosemarie's, the very same line he'd used on her all those years ago. She couldn't help the feeling of déjà vu that brought her back full circle to their first meeting...

"You're the cutest little redhead I've seen in a long time." The man said to her as he came walking across from the car lot where he had been looking to purchase a new car. She was eighteen at the time, had used Egyptian henna on her hair which gave it a glowing highlight and she was dressed in her four inch heels. She still lived at home and was on her way to her new job at the furniture store where she was learning to handle customers. This was the first time a fellow had been so brazen in their approach. He intrigued her but also caused a feeling of intimidation. She dropped her eyes and walked on.

The next morning and each weekday afterward he was there to greet her until she began to look forward to seeing him. There was a feeling of assurance and magnetism about him that she had, until now, never encountered in a man, at least in the young men her age she had dated. She didn't realize he was so sexually attracted to her that the main thought on his mind was making love to her and eventually he did, completely overwhelming her with his ardor. When the heat of their first lovemaking cooled, he grasped her tightly, "You're mine, and "This" belongs to me....Say it." He was overpoweringly sexually explicit in what he wanted her to promise, and she did.

He took her on weekend trips out of town, anyplace where there was something of interest to see but always with the urge to possess her, oftentimes waking her in the middle of the night with his caresses. When she became pregnant, her world collapsed....

Rosemarie's reverie came to a halt when she realized Alex was waiting for her response. She replied softly, "I've been waiting for you Alex, and where have YOU been all my life?" She quickly blinked the sudden shine of near-tears away and gave him a tremulous smile. No matter how hard she tried, she still felt she belonged to him.

There was something in her eyes that caused Alex to move closer to her. He felt tension building and a strong urge to put his arm around her couldn't be controlled. He drew her to him, scenting a long forgotten fragrance that brought familiar feelings he remembered from long ago. She was his, only his, he knew this even though he could not recall her name. He looked into her eyes feeling confusion and attraction mixed together. He took her chin in his hand and turned her face to his, slowly drawing closer until their lips touched and they were lost in the reverie of long ago.

Sylvia and Ryan sat quietly, neither speaking a word, both wrapped up in the intense display of affection their two parents had exhibited.

When their kiss ended Alex gave Rose a huge smile. "I know you from somewhere don't I? There's something so familiar about you, I hope you'll come and visit again soon. I'm sorry, but for some reason I feel a little ill, I'm going to my room and lie down for a while." Alex rose from his chair and left the room, a look of distraction on his face. He glanced toward Rosemarie, a puzzled expression flashing for a moment then disappearing just before he turned away.

Rose followed his exit with sad eyes. All those years lost but maybe it wasn't too late for them to have a second chance. She wanted to leave as soon as possible, she could feel the tears building, ready to blind her with their torrent.

"Thanks for the coffee Ryan. Sylvia, I really need to get home. Do you mind if we leave now?" She didn't wait for a response, but rose from her chair and was already half way to the door before Sylvia could reply.

When they arrived back home Rose went immediately to her room. The meeting with Alex had undone her, his kiss bringing back too many memories of the misery she had felt so many years ago when he had walked away without even a backward glance. She was almost sorry she had ever returned to her home. At least living in a different place with no chance of ever seeing him, she had been able to manage her life. Why would she even consider getting together with him again? She needed a chance to think. Maybe a vacation for a month or so, maybe even a job someplace else. Anything to leave this suspense behind, get back her confidence again by living the same predictable existence she'd had in her previous life far away. No ties, no commitment to anyone, her resistant walls built high to keep everyone out. It had worked very well all those years.

While she had been pondering the unhappiness dealt her so many years ago, and the tumultuous feelings she had experienced today with Alex, she had unwittingly packed her suitcase. When she realized what she had done, it seemed like a very good idea. She slipped her checkbook in her purse and then went downstairs to face Sylvia.

When Sy spotted the suitcase it felt as though her heart had lodged itself in her throat. "What's with the suitcase, Mother? You never mentioned anything about a trip.

Rose set the case down on the floor and then went to her daughter giving her a big hug. Honey! I have to get out of here. All these years I've managed to put my troubles aside and face each day knowing things would be better the next day, and as each day passed, it was true. Now I feel that I'm right back where it all started and I can't go through it again. I'll call you, but I can't say when, or even if I'll be back. Trust me, Hon! I know what I'm doing."

The torment Sy could see on her mother face was as upsetting to her, as was her obvious misery displayed for her mother to see. With their arms about each other, the tears couldn't be withheld. With a laugh-sob they finally separated and Sy walked her mother to the back door and then out to the garage where her dusty blue Chevy was parked. "Get a car wash mom, it'll make you feel better driving with a clean car. Please call me when you reach where ever you're heading. I'll never sleep tonight otherwise, Promise?

Rose nodded her assent as she slid her suitcase across the front seat and climbed in to settle herself comfortably behind the wheel. The engine purred to life and she backed out of the garage. With a final wave she sped away.

Sylvia felt lost immediately, she had become accustomed to having her mother's presence in her life. It was a joy every morning to see her and a comfort every night knowing she was in the next room fast asleep. There was now a strongly knitted bond between the two regardless of the years they had been apart. That empty space her mother had filled so lovingly now felt like a yawning precipice where, if not careful, Sy could lose her equilibrium. She did not want to feel that emptiness again, it had plagued her since the age of reason. Heartsick, Sy returned to the house locking the door securely behind herself and then, aimlessly, she wandered about the house not knowing what to do with herself. She walked into the laundry set on doing a load or whatever needed doing. That was when she spied the tape recorder up on the top shelf, it seemed ages since she had last listened to them. Gathering the tapes and recorder, she set it up on the kitchen table, plugged it in and selected the next numbered tape. Inserting it into the machine she pushed the "Play" button.

Tape....I remember more about that big room with all the sleeping people. The next morning that same man told mom he was very sorry for the trouble she'd had with the bedbugs, he handed her something, at first mom didn't want to take it, I didn't know what it was. We walked again for a long time, then we went into a tall building. She talked to someone and gave them whatever the man had given her. Then we went into a small room. It had a bed a chair and a metal cabinet against the wall near a window. The floor didn't have a rug. Mom went to bed and fell asleep, maybe I did too. The building had a cleaning lady, she let me go with her when she cleaned the rooms but I had to promise her I would not touch anything, I was good and I didn't. Mom kept sleeping and I got very hungry. I was down in the main room where people came and went. Somebody ask me if I could sing. That was something I liked to do. I sang and the man gave me a whole nickel. I ran out the door and not very far away on the same side of the street there was a building that was all white and looked like a castle but they had food. I gave the person my nickel and he gave me a big hamburger. I ran back to the room we were living in and woke mommy up to share it with her but she said she wasn't hungry so I ate the whole thing. Down the street there was an old house that nobody lived in, I didn't know it at the time, I went to see if there was someone I could play with. The house was empty but part of the lattice, (I learned when I was older what it was called), around the porch was gone. I looked underneath, it was all nice clean sand and nothing else. (Thinking back I still feel scared.) I don't know what drew me to that exact spot because there was nothing sticking out of the sand, but when I put my hand down and started to dig I pulled up a very pretty "vase." Gee! This is something nice to play with I thought. I took off the top and "Lo!" it was also filled with sand. Just as I was ready to pour it out, the sand trembling at the vases edge, an old man's voice screamed in my ear, "DON'T TOUCH THAT." There WAS no old man and I was terrified, so frightened I dropped the vase and scooted away as fast as I could. Even to this day I can still relive that feeling of frantic, unbridled terror, hear his voice and feel my fright. Of course now I know it was his cremated remains, poor soul. I wonder what happened to his ashes after modernization leveled those abandoned buildings.

 I don't know how long we stayed in that room but one morning Granny and Uncle Ray came to get us. I don't know how they knew we were there. In the metal cabinet I remember there was a small can of pork&beans sitting on the shelf, (what a strange thing to remember.) Granny and Uncle took us away. This is enough until next time….End.

Sylvia knew her granny didn't lie but it was difficult to believe what she had said about the ashes and the old man's voice but there was no reason for her to include it in the tape if it hadn't been the truth. She felt the hair on the back of her neck rise giving her goose bumps.

She replaced the recorder and tapes in the cupboard, picked up her purse and car keys and headed out the door. She had mail to pick up at the office, it'd be a good chance to see her boss, Ken Simpson, and possibly get a raise if he was in a good mood.

He was happy to see her. As editor he received mail regarding customer's opinions on articles and Sy's column was very popular. He handed her the correspondence bag, no longer just a small package, his smile spreading across his entire face thinking about all the new subscriptions Sy had engendered. She was a goldmine.

"Just want to mention Sy there'll be an increase in your salary. Just remember that when you balance your check book since it's an automatic deposit in your account. You've done one heck of a job with your column, keep up the good work."

"I was just going to ask for a raise, you must have read my mind. Thanks Boss that was a great boost to my morale."

Sy hefted the small mail bag, thinking gleefully that she'd be kept busy for quite a while, exactly what she enjoyed. With a wave of her free hand, she gave Ken a smile and hurried away. When she got to her car there was a folded slip of paper tucked under the windshield wipers. She slipped it into her pocket, tossed purse and mail onto the front seat and drove away.

Once home she could hardly wait to read through the correspondence. The thrill of suspense opening each letter was exciting, never knowing what to expect. As usual there were miscellaneous requests which were silly or inane. She finally whittled them down to about two dozen worthy of a reply. Since it was getting near suppertime, she put them aside for the day, she needed something to eat, and she had missed lunch and felt starved. Rising from the table she noticed the crackle of paper in her pocket. She unfolded it and read.

I know your type, you stupid bitch, you're ugly. I hope you drop dead and make the world a better place without you around.
Guess Who

Sylvia was sure she knew this person. She would bet it was some guy from the office who was jealous about her popularity. She decided to answer it.

Dear Guess Who.
As an intelligent person I reply to your letter thusly. I appreciate your interest in my column. You have helped promote it by writing me. Thank you.
Sy

Sy couldn't help grinning at her reply, she'd bet it would rile the heck out of the writer because her reply was polite. What she wanted right now was food. Opening the fridge there wasn't a leftover in sight. Thank goodness for eggs, half a green pepper and two leftover breakfast sausages. She pulled out the small Teflon coated omelet pan, drizzled a small amount of olive oil into it and turned the heat on high, adding the minced pepper and sausage. When the pepper was tender she poured in two scrambled eggs, covered the pan and turned the heat medium. After a few minutes she flipped over the egg mixture, waited a few short moments and then enjoyed the fluffiest stuffed egg omelet in town. It was exactly what she needed to stop her stomach from complaining so much, she was ready to tackle the world.

She picked up her purse and car keys and headed out the door on her way to see David and his new hardware store which was open for business.

When she parked in the ample lot she could see it was a perfect spot for the hardware store which sat in the center of assorted establishments. At the far left corner sat Acmes Grocery, next Ligget's drugstore, then a small Men's shop. David's Hardware was next and then a Beauty Shoppe. The very last one was an Ice Cream Parlor, all creating enough customer movement to assure drop-ins at the hardware. She had a grin on her face as she entered, her eyes immediately scanning for David's familiar image. What greeted her as she passed the checkout was a pair of golden eyes glaring at her, the heat of rage aimed in her direction. Sy was puzzled at the obvious animosity.

When David caught sight of her his pleasure at seeing her was quite evident to everyone. He drew her to the rear of the store and his office. Closing the door he pulled her into his arms and kissed her soundly, Sy happily returning the affectionate embrace.

"Sit down sweetheart, I'm so glad you stopped by, I was just going to phone you, wanted to know if you'd made any plans for this evening. I know how sometimes you and your mom like to take in a movie now and then but I was hoping, now that I have everything under control here and have more free time, that you and I could finally have a real date."

"David, mom decided to take off for parts unknown which makes me more than a little nervous. I couldn't tell her "No" because she would have lost her temper. She was upset about something that happened at Alex's, something that brought back hurtful memories from the past. I'm afraid not to be home just in case she phones and needs me. If you don't mind, you could come over, I'll make dinner and we can just talk or even watch TV. It's been a while since we've spent any time together and I miss you."

David was delighted at the idea. "Look here, don't cook, I'll bring carry-out, something romantic with a bottle of good wine and, if you don't mind, I'd like to stay overnight. Completely respectable of course, I'll sleep in the spare bedroom." One thing they'd agreed on was waiting until their wedding night for any intimacy.

The decision and time agreed upon, David walked her to her car and kissed her soundly before seeing her settled into the seat. He closed the door firmly and watched her drive away, his mind already thinking of what specialty to bring for their dinner. He already had the engagement ring in his desk drawer.

Jennifer watched their every movement with cold eyes. The heat of her antipathy toward Sylvia caused droplets of perspiration to form beneath her hairline dampening her forehead, creating a sheen of moisture. She drew the back of her wrist across to wipe it away. This couldn't be allowed, she had better make plans, and quickly. Before David had taken two steps Jennifer was already in his office, had the engagement ring in her pocket, and was in the restroom with the door locked. Standing on the commode seat she lifted one of the ceiling tiles and placed the ring box inside. No one would ever think of looking there. She exited, a satisfied, gloating smile on her face.

David felt the day dragging by much too slowly, he was anticipating the surprised expression on Sy's face when he slipped the ring on her finger. Once they were engaged then the wedding plans could begin. Daydreaming, thinking that possibly within a year he would have Sylvia as his wife, David didn't notice the cat-grin on Jennifer's face as she rang up purchases for a customer, glancing at him several times as he absentmindedly stacked merchandise near her register.

Only two more hours until closing time, Jennifer thought. David would be frantic about the missing engagement ring. She'd help him search, offer him her sympathy and a shoulder to cry on. All she need do is get him to really notice her. Once he really looked at her, instead of through her, she was confident she'd have a chance to entice him and once he took that step, she'd be in like Flynn. Just thinking about the size of that diamond made her drool.

As expected, at closing time the doors were locked, the registers cash counted and balanced to receipts, overhead lights dimmed. Jennifer was in the stock room retrieving her purse, stalling for time when she heard David's voice calling the employees into the office.

His face was pale, more from shock than anger. "Who of you has been in the office this afternoon?" Seeing all four heads shake in negativity, he asked if any stranger had been seen near the office within the past day or two. Again he received a negative reply. Near panic, not revealing the reason for his inquiry, he told them they could leave. Jennifer lingered until they were out of the building.

"What's wrong Davey, you're pale as a ghost. Did something upset you, something we did? Jen put on her sweetest, worried looking face. She forced a few tear ducts to leak a modicum of fluid. Trembling on the edges of her eyelids, it would make David want to sooth her fragile feelings. She would use that to full advantage.

When he noticed how distraught she was, he put his arm about her shoulder telling her about the engagement ring. She turned to him, making sure her lips brushed across his collar leaving a ruby trail.

"I'm sorry to hear about that Davey, what a wonderful surprise that would have been for Sy." She forced a few hiccups and a deep sigh. "I'll help you search if you think you misplaced the ring, it may even have fallen under the desk." She dropped to her knees pretending to reach knowing that her blouse had opened and bare skin was exposed.

"Come on Jen, this isn't necessary. Maybe I got distracted and stuck it in my pocket. If it's not here it might be back at home, anything's possible but I'm sure it's around somewhere." When helping her up her high heel got caught in her skirt hem and she fell heavily against him, her lips once again leaving a crimson trace, this time on the front of his shirt.

"Thanks Davey, I'm sorry to be so clumsy. I'm sure you'll find your ring. I'd better get going, I have a date tonight. I'll see you tomorrow bright and early." As she turned to leave, a satisfied grin flashed for a moment, her little ruse had worked perfectly.

David stopped at the Italian deli. He purchased two cannoli for dessert. Raviolis, antipasto, and instead of champagne, Chianti wine and a loaf of Italian bread. He was relieved he hadn't told Sy about the ring. Once he had it in hand again he would be more careful. He was positive it was only misplaced.

Arriving at Sylvia's near seven, David had his hands full but managed to press the doorbell, the chimes sounding from within. Sy opened the door, a wide smile on her face knowing that a nice dinner was in store without any effort on her part. Stepping aside to allow him entrance, she closed the door and followed David into the kitchen. The aroma, wafting from the packages, titillated them with the anticipated pleasure of a fantastic meal.

The table already set, Sy found appropriate serving dishes and when the food had been transferred to them and set about the table, Sy settled herself in the chair across from David. It was only then that she noticed the red smudge on his collar. Her breath caught in her throat for a moment leaving her unable to speak a word.

David saw that Sy was sitting motionless, staring at him. "What's the matter honey, you look terribly pale, are you feeling faint or sick to your stomach?" David rose from his chair and hurried to her side, her eyes following his every step. As he drew closer she saw the smear on the front of his shirt.

"Did anything unusual happen today Davey, anything out of the ordinary?" Sy watched his eyes, waiting to see what they would reveal to her.

The pause seemed to last too long before his reply. "Nope, all went well. The three handymen did a terrific job and my new cashier, Jennifer was all that she promised, fast and very friendly. Some of the customers even complimented me on hiring her. I think she'll be a goldmine." David has a wide grin on his face which soon turned to puzzlement at the expression on Sy's face.

"I'm happy to hear that." Sylvia responded frostily. "The food is getting cold, we'd better get to it before it's ruined." She ladled a small portion of ravioli onto her plate helped herself to some of the antipasto and tore off a small piece of the fresh bread. She watched as David poured the Chianti into their glasses. Without another word she proceeded to devour her meal until every morsel on her plate was gone, then she downed the ruby wine in only a few gulps. She waited until David had finished eating and then proclaimed that it was late and she was very tired. Would he please excuse the brevity of their evening together and leave?

David could see Sylvia looked upset, he had no inkling why. "Anything I can do for you, Honey? I'd really like to stay, I can even fix breakfast for you in the morning."

"I'd rather you not David, I'd like to be alone, get a good night's rest. Hopefully, I'll feel more capable of making a logical decision in the morning. I have some serious things I have to reconsider, I'm glad you understand."

She walked him to the door and before he could turn and give her a goodnight kiss, he was standing outside wondering what in the world had happened. Shaking his head wonderingly at the mysterious workings of the female mind, he gave a final look backward at the now darkened windows. He must have said or done something that riled her, he thought. Else why would she have almost pushed him out the door without even a word of thanks for the meal, or a good night kiss to show her affection?

Starting the truck engine he backed out of the driveway. An agitated feeling of irritation rising within him soon turned into downright anger. She'd have to call him. It would be a cold day in hell before he picked up the phone to call her. His mind resolved, the next move would have to be hers.

Jennifer Pryor watched as David pulled his truck into the garage and then entered the rear door of his "Rose" home, as she had heard him refer to it. She was thrilled at the short stay he'd had at Sylvia's. She knew it had to do with her lipstick tricks. She had used them more than once and they never failed to produce fireworks between couples.

She liked the way David looked, tall, well-built and rich. At least judging by the size of that diamond he was. She had checked the price out at the Jewelry store in the shopping mall after she had seen the ring in his desk, very expensive. She had plans to make it hers legitimately and it wouldn't take much effort. She has seen the way he had looked at her when she had pretended to search for the ring.

When the lights went out in his house she drove away, heading for her little walk-up apartment which was only good enough for a doghouse. It was small, two and a half rooms with bath. She had to laugh at the half-room which was her kitchen, the size of a closet. Just a 3ft long walk area between two walls. On the right side wall was a single sink, next to it an apartment sized stove. On the left wall a small fridge, next to it a metal cabinet which held her toaster and electric coffee pot. A small 2x3 table and chair sat in the living room right next to the kitchen access. A couch and chair with end table in the living room and a long hallway running down the left side wall where you pass a full bathroom and at the end of the hall a bedroom. That was it.

Once home, she tossed her purse on the bed and stripped. She admired herself in the full length mirror attached to the bedroom door. She had to admit, she looked good. Slender, high breasts, nice legs and a tight ass. That was from all the walking she did at work, it kept her muscles toned. She liked to keep her hair long, it attracted men's attention. It was long, below shoulder length, had a loose natural curl and such a shiny black that it looked silky. Men would have loved to run their hands through it and see the sparks friction produced. Her eyes were a golden honey-color with long black eyelashes that fanned her cheeks. Even her skin had a golden hue, inherited from her south sea island mother.

She stepped into the shower. The water stinging her skin made her nipples harden, as thoughts of David caused an ache that only he could alleviate. Maybe soon they would be together. Nothing would stop her from accomplishing her goal.

She slept soundly, dreamt of David making love to her and bringing her to a wild orgasm. When she awoke in the morning she felt free of sexual tension but did not recall the dream.

She dressed carefully for work, didn't want to seem brazen but wanted the allure of specially fitted clothing that drew the eye to her assets yet looked sweet and wholesome. She knew the sort of man David was, he wouldn't be attracted to a woman that looked like a tart.

Satisfied with her choice she then sprayed a mist of her favorite musky perfume into the air and walked quickly through it. The scent would envelope her without being, as she liked to say, "Overkill."

When she arrived at the store David was already there busily showing the new stock boy how he wanted the display set up. When she walked past him, his casual first- glance turned into a serious once over. He hadn't realized what a stunning looking woman she was, he must have had blinders on. His interest jumped into high gear.

This was working out easier than I imagined Jennifer thought, as she noted, from the corner of her eye, the interest David was showing in his appraisal of her. One of the reasons she was setting her sights on David was because she was ticked at the reply Sy had posted in her Common Sense column. When she'd read the response, the first thing she had thought of was revenge, and trapping David was perfect. Actually, he'd be a good catch, a handsome, hard working guy with all the right attributes. Once she hooked him with a marriage license she'd have it made. The thing was, she needed him to ask her out for dinner.

"Good morning David." She moistened her lips and lifted her arm to run her fingers through her hair so her blouse would tighten over her breasts, lifting them and exposing a glimpse of a voluptuous curve. She was woman personified. With a sensuous glance at David, she walked past him on her way to the office where she would leave her purse.

David's eyes followed her all the way until she was out of sight. He wouldn't mind taking her out, he thought. Especially after the way Sylvia had acted, making it obvious she wasn't as attracted to him as he'd thought. For sure he wouldn't sit at home and mope over a lost cause.

As the day progressed toward closing time David made his move just as Jennifer was getting her purse to leave for the night.

"Say Jen, do you have anything planned for tonight? I know its short notice but if you aren't busy would you like to take in a movie or maybe go out to dinner?" David couldn't help hoping she'd accept, why hadn't he ever notice how captivating she was?

Jennifer didn't want to seem too anxious so she hesitated a few moments, waiting until David was about to speak before nodding her head and giving him a smile of acceptance. She gave him her address and he said he'd pick her up at eight.

She was totally prepared, plans in order when he arrived that evening. He had chosen a home-style restaurant that specialized in Italian food, it was a local establishment and very popular. They each ordered a glass of wine with their meal, David chose Chianti, Jen selected a sparkling dry. Halfway through their meal Jen asked David if she could taste his wine, she'd never tried it before and said her curiosity was getting the best of her. He passed his goblet over, she passed him hers.

"This is very good David, how do you like mine? They switched glasses back again, Jennifer had a wide smile on her face, her plan was right on target.

David gave her a return grin, "Next time I'll order yours, Jen, it was delicious."

After paying the bill they walked to his car, an older Ford which he had inherited from his Aunt Rose. It was ten years old, had seldom been used and it had low mileage. It looked brand new and David loved it, a typical guy with their favorite toy having four wheels.

Before they reached the vehicle David became dizzy. "Jen, you had better drive, I don't know what's wrong but my head feels fuzzy. Maybe I shouldn't have had that wine."

Jen helped him into the car and then drove to his house in record time. She guided him to the door and then inside, locking the door behind her. Once she had maneuvered him upstairs she helped undress him. After positioning him next to the bed she gave him a shove and watched as he fell, sprawled nude and unconscious.

After she had David settled under the covers, Jennifer folded his clothing neatly and then undressed, placing her clothing beside his. Walking into the bathroom she smugly examined herself in the full length mirror, sure that what she was doing would accomplish her goal of trapping David. A glance at the clock assured her there was ample time before he awoke from the drug she had slipped into her wine. Turning out the light she folded back the bedcovers and slipped beneath them. She listened for a moment to his heavy breathing, he would sleep until morning. Pressing herself against him she too was soon deeply asleep.

Still half way in a dream, David was dimly aware of warmth pressing against the length of his body. He thought it the remnant of an erotic fancy, a figment of his imagination. Reaching out he trailed his fingers along the outline feeling definite curves and lastly firm breasts. He was sure now that he was dreaming, Sylvia would not have been so easy with her favors. He curled against the figure and slipped once again into a deep sleep. It would take the remainder of the morning before the effects of the drug wore off.

Jennifer was up, dressed, and out the door before David awoke. He gave a huge stretch and yawn, loath to leave the bed. He had slept like a baby. Finally realizing that he had to get to work, he crawled from beneath the covers and stood for a moment getting his bearings after a brief moment of dizziness. He must have drunk too much last night, the memories of dinner with Jennifer returned. Unfortunately, the only thing he clearly recalled was the dinner. He turned toward the bathroom, noticing for the first time a slip of paper sitting on his dresser. Puzzled, he picked it up and began to read.

Hi! Honey, I didn't want to wake you, you were sleeping so nicely. You about wore me out. I'll see you at work later. Love, Jen

The shock of what the note meant was so upsetting that David felt physically ill. He never would have cheated on Sylvia, he knew this. Yet the note proved otherwise. He didn't remember a thing about getting home last night. The only memory was having a harmless dinner with Jen, it didn't look so harmless now. Why had he asked her out to begin with? He crumbled the note in his fist and tossed it into the bathroom waste basket.

After shaving, brushing his teeth and showering, he felt more normal. He tossed yesterdays clothing down the laundry chute and then donned his favorite style jeans, cotton shirt and Nikes. He was out the door and on his way to the hardware.

Meanwhile, Jen had ridden home in a taxi. She showered and dressed in a demure outfit, something she knew David would like. She was waiting by the hardware store door when he arrived at opening time.

"What's going on Jennifer, what happened last night? I don't recall a thing except for the dinner itself. I read your note, are you telling me that you spent the night, we slept together?" David stared at her hoping for a sign that he was wrong.

"David, don't tell me you can't remember bringing me to your house, carrying me upstairs and hardly waiting until we were undressed before tossing me onto the bed? You were like a wildman, you even frightened me."

* * * * * * * * * *

CHAPTER 5

Rosemarie was heading back to Indiana, it was her instincts making that decision, and the only place she knew and felt comfortable traveling towards. As she pulled out of the driveway and waved goodbye to Sylvia, she had a moment of second thoughts, then shook them from her mind. She would NOT be sitting around waiting for Alex to regain his memory, she could not depend on his reaction to her. No more would she be a rich man's pastime, a toy he used at his pleasure. Those days were permanently over and she'd make sure they never happened again.

The miles slipped quickly away beneath her tires and as sunset loomed she stopped at a motor lodge and took a room for the night, she felt drained of every ounce of energy. Feeling slightly nauseous, she wandered into the attached restaurant. A bowl of chicken soup and a few crackers were consumed listlessly, but hopefully it should make her feel better. After paying the bill she returned to her room, disrobed, and dropped onto the bed drawing the covers over her shaking body, even her teeth were chattering. She fell into a restless doze, a feeling of intense heat made her pores open and shed copious amounts of perspiration which soaked the bedding. Her body felt on fire but she shivered with chills when the air touched the moisture that was filming her skin.

At noon the next day when the office manager unlocked the door, she could see that the occupant was very ill, this happened occasionally. She phoned the local police and let them handle the situation.

Officer Daniels arrived before the emergency vehicle. After checking that there was no evidence of foul play, he waited while the attendants loaded the woman into the ambulance. He retrieved her purse and luggage and followed the vehicle to the emergency entrance of the hospital. He watched as they took her vital signs and then hooked her up to an oxygen tank. It looked like she would be staying so he tucked her belongings on the storage ledge under the bed and left to finish his work day.

Rosemarie was delirious for two days. When she regained consciousness it was an unpleasant surprise to find she was in a hospital bed. Thoughts of leaving Sylvia was no longer a priority, she just wanted to get back home. They released her the very next morning.

All the way back home she remonstrated herself for being irresponsible, that was the trouble with her. She had run away when she was young and should know better by now. How old did she have to be to learn the lesson about facing difficulties?

By that evening she was pulling her car into the garage, anxious to explain to Sylvia what had happened during her absence and that she had decided to stay.

Sylvia met her at the door, she had been worried sick. Not a word had she heard from the time her mother had decided to leave.

"We have to talk mother. You may have the years over me but the way you're acting is irresponsible and downright childish, I deserve a little consideration. You could have at least phoned and let me know where you were and that you were okay. I'm really ticked off about this because you'd expect the same courtesy from me. In fact, you'd demand it."

Sy stood, feet apart, hands on hips, waiting for an explanation.

Rosemarie stood for a moment, shocked at her daughters' blatant display of anger, ready to lash out at her in retaliation, but seeing the indignant look on Sy's face and the aggressive stance she had taken, it suddenly stuck Rose as utterly comical. She couldn't help herself, she burst out laughing. When the startled, indignant look on Sy's face turned into bewilderment, Rose could not contain herself from outright hysterics, tears streaming down her face, her sides beginning to ache. The tears of laughter suddenly became tears of loss and regret. She reached out her arms and pulled Sylvia close to her heart holding her tightly.

"Honey, I'm so sorry for what I did. All these years, the very last thing I thought of was how it felt when I gave birth to you and the doctor laid you across my belly. You felt so warm, the heat of your body was a comfort to me because it was cold in the operating room and our connection was one of deep satisfaction. You were crying hard in anger, not liking the new environment you were thrust into. I loved the way you looked, I wanted you with all my heart. But then the rage I felt toward Alex surged anew and all I wanted to do was escape, run away, and that I did as soon as I was able. Each year, on the date of your birth I wondered what new experience you were learning, if you were walking yet, did you get your first tooth, were you starting kindergarten, and then first grade, the questions were endless. Yet, each time I found an excuse to stay away until suddenly I realized I was too late, I had missed it all. I promise I'll be here with you from now on, no more running away, no hiding from trouble. I can never repair the empty spaces we share though, they are lost forever."

Sylvia felt something deep down inside, loosen and dissolve away, a hurt she had hidden for years. "Mom, I love you, I always have from the very first time I realized you were somewhere in the same world sharing it with me. I used to dream of you walking in one day and telling me how much you loved and missed me. I can't believe you just now made that dream a reality." Finally they smiled at each other, their sadness soothed with the balm of love and forgiveness.

Rosemarie went to repair the damage to her face and erase the evidence of tears. When she returned to the kitchen she shared a coffee with her daughter and when, on the spur of the moment she decided to go see Alex, she told Sy her decision. She was back in her car and on her way before she could chance changing her mind. "Remember," she told herself, "no more running away."

Ryan was pleased to see Rosemarie and ushered her in immediately. Alex had been repeatedly asking for the "woman" who had visited them. He'd recalled kissing her and liking it immensely, it'd also brought a modicum of relief to him, as though he was back some place where he was supposed to be. Ryan couldn't figure it out.

Alex was in the family room watching television when Rose walked in. He didn't notice her immediately, not until he caught the faint fragrance of the perfume she had always favored. He turned his head in her direction noting the petite build, high heels and amber glints in her beautiful hair. His breath caught in his throat, his memory returning to the first time he had seen her. "You're here at last. I've been waiting and watching for you for so long. Every morning I anticipate seeing you walking to the bus stop, I hope I didn't frighten you away being so forward with my compliments." Alex felt the need to keep her close. "This time I won't run away, or…were you the one who disappeared and turned the world upside down?"

She loved him….no more evading the truth or making excuses for the past. The only thing she desired was to spend the rest of her life with him, the first person to see in the morning and the last at night. She had to wait until he regained his memory before committing herself to a relationship, if that was what he desired.

"What's your name beautiful? I realized we've met before but for some reason I cannot recall your name nor when it was that we met." Alex motioned to Rose to sit beside him. He wanted to talk to her although he had no idea what it was he wanted to say.

Rose made herself comfortable, she watched as Alex took her hand, inspecting her fingers and nails as though they were foreign objects, caressing them as though he couldn't stop himself from the pleasure it gave him. The same feelings a person would experience while petting their cat and listening to its resonant purr of contentment.

"We've sat like this before, haven't we? I remember…your name is Rose and I was in love with you, but it was a long time ago. True?" Alex watched the play of emotions that flickered across her face until at last she sat quietly gazing at him, her love evident for anyone to recognize.

"Would you like to take a drive with me Alex? I'll take you to some of the places we used to visit, maybe it will help restore your memory. At least it will get you out of the house for a while. I'd like seeing some of our old haunts, it would seem like old times."

Alex was already looking for his suit coat, a huge smile of anticipation lighting his face. It felt like he'd been inside forever. As they exited the door Alex looked at the blue sedan quizzically, "I expected something different, like a 1957 Corvette, a white one, in fact a convertible. Did you have one when we knew each other?"

"Actually Alex, that's what YOU own and it's sitting in your garage right now. Do you want to see it?"

"See it? I want to drive it. I'll take you for a little spin. You wait here while I get the keys." Alex's face was lit up like a neon sign. "I remember it now, that car was always my favorite, all white with beige leather seats and red interior. I liked that the canvas top stored nicely, tucked and hidden behind the seats."

They were on the road, Alex having no problems with the four gears, shifting smoothly, hands and feet working in perfect harmony. Rose's nervousness disappeared and she began to enjoy the scenery and her close proximity with Alex.

They stopped for gas and then for lunch. They bought ripe apples at a road stand and then sat at a nearby table enjoying the sweet crunchy delight. Talking endlessly, Alex was reliving more memories with each passing hour.

Rose, would you stay with me tonight? I don't mean sleep with me, I mean stay overnight. I want to see you first thing in the morning, have our coffee together and maybe work to tear down the differences that are keeping us apart."

Her heart felt like it was actually quivering at the thought of being under the same roof with him. All those years of sadness and here they were, together again. She could feel the wall she had built around her heart crumble into nothingness.

"There's nothing I'd like better Alex. I ran away once, afraid to face life, afraid to admit how much I loved you. I thought you had abandoned me when all I should have done was talk to you."

Standing, he pulled her close wrapping his arms about her.

Stay the night she did, sleeping in the guest bedroom. She slept better than she had for ages. In the morning, Ryan already had breakfast on the grill when she entered the kitchen, the aroma of Canadian bacon and griddle cakes made her realize how hungry she felt.

"Have a seat Rose, dad is on his way down. He overslept this morning which was good for him, he's been too restless this past week." Ryan was placing the serving dishes on the table as Alex walked in and made his way over to Rose. He sat down next to her. Turning her to face him he called to his son.

"Ryan, come over here, I want you to hear this." His son stood near, not unaware of what his father intended to do, knowing this was a long time coming.

"Rosemarie Fields, would you do me the honor of becoming my wife?" Alex watched the expression of surprise, and then the onset of tears as Rose nodded wordlessly, her unattainable dream becoming reality.

"Today we go shopping sweetheart, as soon as breakfast is over." And since neither one felt like eating, Ryan was left to have his breakfast alone.

By noon Rose had chosen her wedding ring set and Alex had selected his wedding band. They stopped in at a cozy tea house for a light lunch to make plans for their wedding. As usual, Alex had paper and pen handy in an inside pocket to keep track of everything. By the time they returned home, they were both anxious to tell Ryan of their plans.

The following weeks were a madhouse. While Ryan spent his time acquiring a banquet hall, orchestra, catering and miscellaneous accoutrements to accommodate the occasion, Rose was selecting her gown and those of her attendants. Sylvia would be Maid of honor and the two old friends of her mother Eleanor, Claire and Edna would be witnesses dressed in appropriate attire. The two old women were excited and very happy about being included in the ceremony.

Rosemarie insisted on paying for her gown and the attendants, although she had to fight Alex. He had insisted until she told him she would not be comfortable with him paying for everything, this was a two way relationship. When he realized how important this was to her, he relented.

The big day arrived. Sylvia was of two minds, she hated to lose her mother so soon after finding her, but gaining her true father and brother was such a huge prize that she truly looked forward to sharing Sunday dinners, Holiday celebrations, Birthdays and all the other times they would be together.

She and the attendants followed the bride down the aisle and then stood to the side as the two made their vows and were pronounced husband and wife. Suddenly it dawned on her, these two were her true parents, she was no longer alone in the world without roots and she even had a sibling, a brother now.

The wedding party arrived at the hall. Toasts with champagne, dinners of roasted capons, grilled Salmon, au gratin potatoes, carrots almandine was a success.

For the finale the German chocolate-French crème wedding cake for dessert. The remainder of the evening was spent dancing to the five piece orchestra who played all the favorite renditions.

Toward the end of the evening Alex and Rose disappeared while the party continued until almost dawn.

CHAPTER 6

Sylvia was still upset about seeing the lipstick on David's shirt. After serious consideration the realization dawned that if he had been guilty of cheating on her he would have made sure there was no evidence of it. She felt like a shrew recalling the way she had treated him. The least she could do was phone him and apologize.

When David heard Sy's voice and the apology she offered for the abrupt treatment he had received, a feeling of weight seemed to lift from his shoulders and settle comfortably within his psyche. He actually heaved a sigh of relief.

"I'm so glad you called Sy, I've been thinking about you so much and wishing I had taken more time asking questions instead of hurrying away like I did and becoming irritated. I'm so sorry for acting like that."

Sylvia paused, not wanting to sound like she was accusing him of cheating. "David, I realized afterward that you were not aware of the lipstick stains on your collar and shirt. Would you mind telling me how they got there?"

David didn't really want to tell her about the surprise he'd planned for presenting the engagement ring but it would be the only logical thing to do to clear the air of any misunderstandings.

"Okay, here goes….I bought an engagement ring and I was going to ask you to marry me that evening. I'd put the ring in my desk drawer at work but when I went to get it, it was missing. I started looking through all the drawers and then Jennifer came into the office and started helping me search. She slipped and I caught her before she fell, she must have gotten her lipstick smudges on me at that time. We never did find the ring. I've thought about you almost every day and I've missed you Sy."

Sylvia's intuition kicked into high gear, she knew without a doubt that Jennifer was plotting to try and hook David. The thing was, how could she prove it? There was only one resort.

"David, would you like to come over? It's early enough yet that I can fix a simple dinner and we can enjoy catching up on all that's happening."

"I'll be there in a jiffy Sy, and I'll pick up a bottle of wine on the way." David was out the door within minutes.

Sy opened a can of Red Salmon. She drained the liquid then put the contents into a large bowl, flaking it until it was well separated. She added a tsp. of dry minced onion, a sprinkle of parsley, and mixed in four large eggs. When all was well blended she hand-crumbled an entire tube of Ritz style crackers, mixing them in well. With her electric fry pan set at 250%, she used heaping tablespoons full of the mixture to fashion large round patties which she browned nicely on each side. It didn't take very long. She had sour cream as a topping if David so desired. A nice tossed salad and green beans as a veggie completed the meal. Leftovers patties were tasty sliced for a sandwich with mayo as a bread-spread instead of butter.

Sy greeted David with a kiss which broke the ice nicely, they were immediately at ease with each other. No serious discussions at the table, just light conversation. When the last bite was eaten and the table cleared Sy served coffee. That's when they began to delve into the problems that had surfaced, especially the one where David had awakened in Jennifer's bed, not remembering a thing that happened the night before.

David told Sy about asking Jen out to dinner. How he had tasted her wine and then within a short time had felt very dizzy. The only thing he recalled clearly was being helped to the car and asking her to drive. When he awoke in the morning he was shocked to see a note from Jen insinuating they'd made love. He couldn't call her a liar because he didn't remember a thing about the previous night but he did not believe her, he knew his body well enough to know the feeling of satiety. He told Sy everything. Before the evening was over they had reached an agreement that Jennifer was a trouble maker with ulterior motives. She also likely had something to do with the disappearing ring.

After David left, Sy finished rinsing the dishes and stacking them into the dishwasher. She wiped the counter, all the while thinking about Jennifer. Why, she wondered, would such a beautiful woman resort to such devious practices when she was a natural draw of men? It didn't make any sense. Sy had a lot of experience gleaned from the "Common Sense" column of what people were driven to because of events that had occurred during their youth, those fragile susceptible years. Whatever the cause, Sylvia would not tolerate the intrusion of Jen into her and David's plans.

She decided that she would confront Jennifer, find out what her problem was. If worse came to worse, David would fire her on the spot but for some reason, Sy didn't want things to go that far, didn't want to jeopardize anyone's livelihood.

Finally realizing the lateness of the hour, Sy made her way upstairs and readied herself for bed. Within moments she was fast asleep dreaming about Granny and the tape recorder.

Morning dawned gray and stormy. The rhythmic patter of raindrops against the window pane awoke Sy from her slumber. There was something comforting about lying in bed hearing the rain and wind outside while lying warm and cozy indoors. Giving a huge stretch, she swung her feet to the floor and then made her way to the bathroom. A shower would perk her up nicely.

After she was dressed, a light breakfast of toast and coffee sitting satisfyingly in her stomach, her umbrella opened, she made her way to the garage. It looked like it would be an all day rain.

The hardware store had just opened as Sy pulled into the parking lot. After locking her car door she hurried through the drizzle, closing the umbrella as soon as she entered the door. She could see Jennifer at the checkout register busy counting the cash, placing it into their separate numerical compartments. When she noticed Sylvia she went on alert.

"Hello, Jennifer, how are you this morning? You're looking beautiful as always. Did you know that David and I are planning on getting married? There have been some unusual occurrences happening lately and I think it will all be resolved after you and I have a serious discussion about what you possibly had to do with them. I don't want to involve the police but if that engagement ring doesn't show up, you'll have some serious explaining to do about doping David at the restaurant. He was going to call the police immediately after we talked last night but I convinced him to wait until I spoke with you this morning. By the way, he did find a few witnesses from that restaurant who saw you put something into your wine and then switch glasses with him. They also saw that you had to assist him when leaving the restaurant." Sylvia watched as Jennifer's face turned pale, but she wasn't one to beat about the bush when caught in the act. She'd learned long ago that as long as she had been truthful, she'd never had to suffer any consequences from her sly tricks.

"I'm so sorry Sylvia, I don't know what gets into me sometimes." Jen tried to look sorrowful and repentant, not doing a very good job of it because the gleam of triumph showing in her eyes was quite evident. "I was positive that David was interested in me and I wanted to get you out of the picture as soon as possible." She gave Sy a wicked grin. "Apparently I was mistaken, but don't hold it against me. I tried my best. As for your engagement ring, it was hidden in a safe place. If you watch the register for a moment, I'll get it for you."

Sylvia was irritated. She had expected Jennifer to make all sorts of excuses or even try to lie outright about what she had done, instead she'd owned up to it all. The person who ended up confused was herself and right now she had no idea about what to do or say, she was stymied. With a wry smile to herself she had to admit that a modicum of respect had surfaced for the way Jennifer had responded to the accusations, and there wasn't anything she had done that the police could be called about, not even the ring, which was somewhere on the premises. As for the witnesses at the restaurant noting Jen doctoring wine, there were none.

When Jennifer returned, David was with her, still admonishing her for taking the ring. She had also apologized for the ruse she'd played about the over-night stay over she had faked, admitting that nothing untoward had occurred.

"You do realize, Jennifer that I have to let you go? I cannot have someone working for me that I can't trust, and even though there was no permanent damage, the aftermath was upsetting, knowing it had all been a nasty ruse. I won't give you a recommendation, but I also will not mention what occurred should a future employer contact me. The most I will tell them is that you were good at your job and dependable. I think that's fair. Come to my office, I'll make out your paycheck, you can leave this morning."

Later they both watched as Jennifer walked out the door without a backward glance. They were happy to be rid of her.

THE THISTLE SEED

David promoted Billy Nash, the stock boy, to cashier and gave him a raise. He had tended the register when Jen was on a break or out to lunch. Dave would look for a replacement in the coming week.

That morning David took Sy out to breakfast then presented the ring to her, her eyes bright with unshed tears as she accepted his token of love. Now they could begin to make their wedding plans.

This was not the last of Jennifer however, she was making plans. Not one to let sleeping dogs lie there would be retaliation for the embarrassment they had caused her. She had a few clever ideas that would stop them in their tracks. She laughed to herself at the way she had suckered them into thinking she wasn't such a bad person, a maneuver she had worked on others many a time. If they knew what a can of worms they'd opened they'd be shaking in their shoes. This had worked out perfectly, she wouldn't be anywhere in the picture when it all hit the fan. All she had to do was keep her eye on the newspaper watching for the big announcement. She didn't think she'd have very long to wait.

After breakfast David dropped Sy off at her car in the parking lot. He kissed her goodbye and she watched as he walked toward the hardware store, realizing that he was the man she wanted to spend her life with. A sigh of pure contentment escaped her lips as she turned the key and drove off, heading home to do a little work on her news column which she had been a bit lax about replying to. She also needed to do a few loads of laundry. Sorting the colors she started the washer and as she turned to leave she remembered the recorder, realizing it had been a while since listening to one of the tapes. She took it into the kitchen and set it up.

Tape…We were staying at one of mother's brothers' house, Uncle Orville. They had a spare bedroom and I had cousins to play with, they even had a dog. I don't have a lot of memories from there, maybe we didn't stay very long. Mommy found a job, she started work very early in the morning, I remember because of her coming in to kiss me goodbye, I could smell the perfume she always. As an adult, I now know it was Coty's Emeraud which she favored all her life. I remember getting a permanent too, they said I looked like Shirley Temple. One vivid memory was of mom having me stand up in the bathroom sink while she gave me a sponge bath. It was a very old house with very old lightening. The light fixture was within my reach so I grasped it to help me keep my balance. Mommy didn't notice but it felt like my whole body was shaking and I could not let go of it and I couldn't even speak. When she saw what was happening she pulled me loose. My insides felt all funny and tingly, I wouldn't be surprised if my hair hadn't been standing on end either, but it wasn't painful at all. One day Aunty made a supper of liver and onions, mom was at work, didn't get home until later. I tried to eat but it made me feel ill and Aunty got really angry with me, told me I had to sit there until I ate it all. I did try but it made me feel like throwing up, so I just sat for a very long time, I didn't cry or fuss but although I wanted to please her I just couldn't get it down. I'm not sure but I think when mom got back from work she was angry because not long after that she took me to see a small basement apartment she had rented. It was pretty but I didn't get to stay there with her. She packed my things and took me to her sister Leona who was married and lived in New Collins, N.Y. Mom went back to Michigan and her job…end

Sy replaced the recorder. She put the first finished washed load into the dryer and started the second one washing. Returning to the kitchen she heated water for tea and then sat sipping it thoughtfully, feeling restless and upset about the tape, the sixth she had listened. She tried to figure out what was lacking, what the problem was. When the realization dawned she was surprised, it had been so evident. It was all so serious.

With the problem solved she'd have a new understanding of Granny and her down-to-earth homespun logic. She missed her so much but thank goodness for the years they'd had together. If only her mother had been here at the time what a great life it would have been, the three of them. In that instant she made up her mind, as soon as the laundry was finished she'd take a ride to visit her mother.

Within an hour Sy was on her way, Rose was expecting her. She stopped at a bakery and picked up a double-chocolate layer cake and a dozen lemon spice cookies.

When she pulled into their driveway Rose was waiting at the open door, Alex standing beside her. They ushered her into the kitchen where Rose gave her a huge hug, a warm welcome to her beautiful daughter. Alex was practically beaming with joy.

It seemed like an age since they had last seen each other. As they ushered her into the house and into the kitchen, Rosemarie gave Sy a huge motherly hug. "Honey, I was just about ready to drive over to visit with you. What in the world have you been up to with not even a phone call to let me know what's going on? I admit, we've been a bit busy doing some redecorating, giving the place a woman's touch which Alex is quite comfortable with. Even Ryan has helped select colors and fabrics, although he will be moving into his own home within the next week. He took the plunge and bought a place that had been standing vacant for years. When he gets back from the lumber yard ask him about it. He's really enthused about making the place livable so he can work on it while he's on site."

Sylvia hadn't realized how much she had missed her mother, just being with her eased tension she hadn't been aware of. She gave Rose an affectionate hug. "I missed you mom, that's why I dropped in, it seemed forever since we'd last talked, and dad, I'm not ignoring you either, you'll never know how much it means having my real parents right here where I can see you any time. No more wondering anymore, I've got the real thing right here." Sy had a wide smile, the pleasure she felt showing on her face couldn't be ignored and they couldn't help grinning back at her.

"Hey! Sy, you're lookin' great, what have you been up to?" Ryan picked her up and swung her around before setting her back on her feet. "Wow! That's some ring you're wearing, have you set the wedding date yet? Let me see it, David didn't rob the bank did he? Ryan grinned, seeing the blush begin to appear on Sy's cheeks. "Aw! Don't be shy sugar, you know I like to tease you. What have you been up to lately? If you're not in a hurry, how about taking a ride with me later on, I'd like your opinion on the house I just purchased?"

Sylvia gave a nod of assent as she turned to her mother. "So! Mom, you're looking fantastic, have you been using some new product that's giving you such a glow or is it the love-light shining from your eyes?" Sy gave her mother an affectionate hug, noting for the first time that she had gained a few pounds since the wedding.

Rose hesitated a moment before responding. "Actually honey, you're the first to hear the news, Alex and I are expecting a baby. I realize I'm a little old to be having a child but we're thrilled about it. The doctor said I'm in good shape and there shouldn't be any problem. In about seven months you'll have a little brother or sister." Rose watched Sy, waiting to see her reaction. At first there was just a stunned silence but then, when Sy realized what the future would hold for them, she couldn't help tears of happiness well up at the thought of a real honest-to-God family, her mother, father and even a brother or sister. She felt overwhelmed and pulled her mother closely into her arms, the love she felt for her overpowering.

When she stepped away she wiped her eyes with the back of her hand. "I'm so happy, Mom. When the time comes I'll be here to help you and I'll stay as long as you need me. You'll never believe how much I'll look forward to meeting my sibling. You're making my dreams come true, mom.

Ryan had been standing quietly, watching the interactions between the two women. Then he and Alex grinned at each other. They truly enjoyed not being the center of attention. From now on Rosemarie would be the main attraction. It was a while before Ryan could coax Sy into taking a ride to see his new home.

The house was only about a twenty minute ride away situated in a semi-rural area. Ryan said there were three acres of land surrounding the residence and even a small stream at the rear of the property. The description did not do it justice, Sy loved the look of the place. She could see that it had been neglected for years and was quite derelict but the possibilities were worth any effort of restoration.

It was a small mansion built of grey stone. It had an arched portico at the side entrance, and each set of windows were set with wide white stone edging which enhanced the look of the place, even the double front doors. It was two and a half stories high, the attic having a large half-moon shaped window set with multicolored glass. Windows were broken, one of the three wide steps leading to the entrance needed replacing and the slate roof was in bad shape. Sy was anxious to see the inside. They entered through the portico door. The choice was to either descend to the right down to the basement, or take the three stairs up. Sy chose the latter and found herself in an old-fashioned 1930s style kitchen which had been half-updated with a built-in oven set into the wall and next to it a four burner countertop cook surface. The cabinets, unfortunately had been painted, and the sink was an old iron enameled 4ft white elephant. The walls however, were real plaster and in good shape, ceilings 9ft high.

As Ryan escorted her through the home he gave her a running commentary on the changes he expected to make ranging from finding a professional to replace original type glass in broken windows, to matching any broken antique tile in the bathrooms. The library was a beauty with built-in book shelves of maple. The last place he took her to was the attic, accessed through a panel at the end of the upstairs main hallway.

The stairs were narrow and steep. When they reached the attic Sy was astonished at the multitude of castoff furnishings and miscellany scattered helter-skelter across the expanse of dusty flooring. There were several trunks, an old sewing machine, boxes of dishware, suitcases, lamps, everything highlighted by the multicolored panes of stained glass, half-moon windows set into each end of the attic. A veritable rainbow of colors casting a warm glow over all. The first thing that entered Sy's thoughts was that this had once been a Childs playroom. She could picture it clear as day.

"Did you check on who had previously owned this residence, Ryan? It must have been quite a popular gathering place for parties and family gatherings. I have to admit, you've found yourself a real treasure, I can hardly wait until you've restored it to its original splendor."

Ryan was anxious to get started on the place, more so now that Sy had voiced her opinion and support. "Would you like to have a hand in the restoration Sy? You have a good eye for decoration, maybe in your spare time you can give me some pointers. Make a list of things that you think should be changed or just renewed. It would be a huge help to me and it would allow me to get the work accomplished faster, rather than waste time trying to figure what should be done. What do you think?"

Sy knew she'd love the task, she didn't even need time to ponder. "It's a deal Ryan. I'll meet you here tomorrow morning with suitable work clothing, a pen and paper, and a slew of ideas. I think we're going to enjoy working together."

All the drive back to Alex's they were in serious discussions about the house and its restoration, eagerly enthused about accomplishing their goal.

When Sy told David about her new project he felt a slight twinge of irritation that her time would be devoted working on Ryan's house instead of their own. Actually, for the first time, he realized they had not made a decision on where they would reside after their marriage. "Honey, we've been postponing out wedding long enough. We waited until the hardware store business took hold, waited until Rose and Alex had their wedding and now, with Rose expecting, we'd better get our plans in order because you may be very busy helping you mom, not counting assisting Ryan with his fixer-upper. I think it's time we posted our wedding announcement in the newspaper and got on with our own life. What do you think?"

"I was wondering when you'd bring up the subject, didn't want to say anything because of you getting your store all set up and I agree, it's time. If you don't mind, I'd rather just have a small private, family oriented ceremony with a few good friends to invite, Sally Rose is one of them and my boss Ken from work."

They had been so busy with individual projects that suddenly the thought of marriage sounded like an excellent idea. They had successfully managed to keep a rein on their feelings when they became too overpowering. Their wedding day was what they were waiting for.

"Let's do it, then Sy. Get your calendar and we'll pick the day." David felt a surge of adrenalin, the prospect of planning his wedding a long awaited dream coming true. He had found the woman he wanted to spend his life with.

Sylvia couldn't believe what had happened, the ordinary day had turned into an adventure of planning a commitment, their entire future together as husband and wife. It seemed an immense step on such short notice but she truly did love David, couldn't think of going through life without him at her side. What did she think the engagement ring she was wearing meant? She had already given him her permission when she had accepted it.

The next few weeks passed quickly, the wedding announcement was posted in the news. A small reception, immediately following the ceremony, would be held at a small banquet hall with a sumptuously catered dinner. Sylvia found the perfect gown that looked like it had been made especially for her. The countdown of days dwindled until only two remained.

Jennifer was filled with envious rage, not only about the newspaper notices but about the obviously tasteful elegance of the wedding itself. This should be HER wedding day. David would have been a perfect mate, handsome, wealthy, already having a beautiful home and a thriving business. She wouldn't have had a care in the world, everything she desired at her beck and call. She felt physically ill thinking of her loss. There had to be something she could do to put a damper on the proceedings, something big, something shocking that would bring it all to a sudden stop.

She looked through her closet, finally selecting all black clothing including a black turtleneck. She covered her hair with a black rain hood and then slipped on black socks and shoes. She found her black eye-shadow powder, and dabbed it all over her face. She then pulled on black leather gloves. Looking at herself in a full length mirror she looked like a specter from a nightmare, this would be perfect. Picking up a few items from her dresser including her car keys, she left her apartment making sure no one saw her as she entered her car and drove away.

It was a moonless night as Jennifer made her way through the dark, empty streets, finally arriving at David's residence long before dawn. She had mixed feelings as she considered what she was about to do but since there wasn't one iota of affection involved, the feelings were only about the best way of escaping without detection.

She had to find some way of getting inside without leaving any signs of entry. This had to seem like an accident. Finally she noticed an open window in the dining room. Returning to the back porch, she retrieved the old fashioned wooden chair, a perfect height to reach the window. The screen lifted out easily and she was able to raise the window without a sound. She was inside and into the kitchen within moments.

"Ah! My lucky day," she mumbled aloud as she set about her work. Within minutes she was sliding back out the window which she quietly closed, replacing the screen and then the chair. There was not a sign that anyone had gained access. She hurried back to her car and drove away into the still dark night.

When she reached home she undressed and slipped into bed falling fast asleep in a very short time, completely contented with her night's activity. She didn't awaken until well into morning.

It was noon, she was watching television when a breaking news bulletin flashed about a house fire that firemen were having trouble controlling. They had managed to save the sole occupant whose name was being withheld until relatives could be contacted, but the home would be a total loss. The unnamed victim had been taken away by ambulance to the local hospital. There was no additional information on his name or condition. The source of the fire was unknown but an investigation would follow.

Jennifer sat wide-eyed listening to every word. The video pictures were mesmerizing, the fire burning hot and almost out of control. All that hardwood that older houses were built with sure created monumental infernos. She hadn't realized how beautiful the colors were. Orange, red, yellow with black curls of smoke making fancy designs in the air. Like an artist's creation, and it was all hers to enjoy while it lasted. Unfortunately the station went on to other news items that she wasn't interested in. She decided to drive over to the scene and watch the goings on with everyone else. She arrived there in record time.

She sat on someone's porch steps along with several other people attracted by the flames. It was like watching a movie with actors, directors and stand-ins. It was hours before the flames were extinguished. Only whirls of smoke were left rising into the air, and the smell of the burnt residue lingering in the atmosphere.

With a huge stretch of contentment, like the legendary cat that had eaten the canary, Jennifer rose and made her way to her car. For some strange reason she felt sleepy and drained of energy. All she desired at that moment was to go home and curl up for a nice nap. And that's exactly what she did.

* * * * * * * * * *

CHAPTER 7

When Sylvia received the phone call from David's parents about the fire and his injuries she was confused, thinking he had been injured while up north visiting them.

"Have you heard anything Sy? We just received the call from the hospital about David being injured in his house fire. We're on our way, leaving as soon as we get off the phone."

Sy was shocked and light-headed hearing that David had been injured. The idea that someone so far away had gotten news that she had been completely unaware of made her tremble, first with shock and then with angry disbelief, until the realization that his parents were listed as the ones to contact in an emergency finally dawned on her.

"Mrs. Kendall, this is the first I've heard about it. You and your husband can stay with me, I have plenty of room and it's so much more comfortable than being in a hotel or motel. We can go together to see David." Sy gave directions. They would arrive just after noontime.

By the time they were parking their car in the driveway, Sy had one of the bedrooms all ready for their stay with fresh bed linens, towels and miscellaneous bath items. She met them at the door and showed them upstairs to their room. She had a quiche baking in the oven that was almost done, something to tide them over until suppertime. After their light lunch they headed for the hospital, Mr. Kendall driving. They arrived just when visiting hours began.

It was a relief to know David was not in the emergency ward, a room had been available. One of the nurses said he was lucky to be alive. According to the police, the fire had progressed and the lower rear of the house was completely engulfed in flames. Thick smoke had filled the upper floor,

David was unconscious. Luckily a neighbor had seen the flames and called the fire department. They arrived in record time and were able to reach him quickly through the front window. If his bedroom had been in the rear of the house he would have perished. He would need to be on oxygen until his lungs cleared. They had him sedated, less stress on his system.

The three of them remained for only a short time, but they did manage to see his doctor who assured them David would recover completely. They would return each day until he was released from the hospital, agreeing that he would then be staying with Sylvia.

When David arrived at Sylvia's it was an old fashioned "Home Coming" celebration. His father had managed the store for him, Carol and Sy had become close friends and although their wedding plans had been postponed because of David's hospital stay, new plans had been completed. They were married within two days. It was everything they could have desired with his parents and all their friends present.

After all the celebrating, his parents back home up north, the wedding gifts opened and placed in cupboards, closets or drawers. David and Sy sat having their first breakfast alone together, their first "Love-knot" of married days beginning to string themselves together like precious pearls on a strong silken thread.

The final Granny Tape....
I liked living at Aunt Leona's which was out in the country. I had a real bedroom that even had a fireplace. Uncle Bob had a bakery route which he went to every day. They rented the upstairs of a big farmhouse. The owners, Mr. and Mrs. Warner lived downstairs. They were a very nice old couple. Mr. Warner had hunting dogs, I think they were pointers. I'm not sure but maybe he raised them to sell. They had all sorts of fruit trees and best of all they owned two goats. Every morning Mrs. Warner went to the barn and milked them. Sometimes I liked to watch. One morning she asked if I had ever tasted goats' milk, I hadn't. She poured me some so I could taste it. I was very happy that my curiosity had been satisfied. I told her it was very good and creamy and thanked her. Mr. Warner liked to sit on the big front porch and chew tobacco. Sometimes I'd sit on one of the steps and keep him company. He saw me watch as he bit off a piece of tobacco to chew, I guess he knew I was curious because he asked me if I'd like to taste it. Of course I said

THE THISTLE SEED

"Yes." He broke off a small piece and I put it in my mouth. At first it tasted sweet but after about two chews it got hot and nasty. I spit it out over the porch railing. I must have made a lot of noise because he was laughing very hard. Although I didn't laugh I felt satisfied that I finally knew what chewing tobacco tasted like.

One of the first things that caught my attention when I went there was a beautiful doll Aunt Leona kept on her bed. It was big, had a pretty face, her brown hair fixed into a fancy hairdo and a long silky green ball gown. Her dress belled out to almost cover the pillows. It must have been an antique because Aunty said I shouldn't touch it. I didn't but I sure liked looking at it, it was so pretty. I had so much fun that summer. This was in the country, hardly any houses just a few. I met a girl named Janet Goret who lived down the road a bit and we became friends. There was also another place, kind of old but there were about five kids that lived there. They had cows and we could swim in the stream that ran across their property. There was another house that Aunty sent me to for fresh churned butter.

That fall I went to school. It was a one room wooden building. There was a locker room where we hung our coats. The wooden desks had ink wells. There were about 3 different grades in that one room. I must have been in kindergarten because I didn't know how to read. The little town had the school house, a post office, a gas station, an ice cream parlor and a church. I liked going to church learning to sing their songs. One day my mother came to visit, we picked her up from the bus station. I didn't realize how much I had missed her. She could only stay one day because she had to go back to work. When we took her back to the bus Aunty asked if I'd like us to follow the bus for a little while. I saw Mommy through the window. Suddenly, for the first time in my life I started to cry very hard, I kept calling for her, I couldn't stop crying. Aunty must have been upset for mentioning following the bus but I couldn't help it.

When mother came for me the following year Aunty didn't have anything ready for me to leave, I think she wanted to keep me, but I went home with Mom.

Back home things were different. I had a step-father and we lived upstairs from his parents. We were there three years, by then I had a baby sister. We moved at a very bad time because of the war. We ended up in a one bedroom garage-sized house they paid too much for. When I was 14 step father told me I was nothing but a stranger in his house, I don't know why, I never caused any trouble. Maybe mom should have let me live with Aunty, maybe it would have been better for both of them. When I was old enough to babysit for a neighbor's kids, I loved it. I ended up doing the dishes and cleaning her downstairs while the kids were sleeping. I earned $5 my first wage. At 15 I got a summer job as cashier at a small grocery store. I learned to not spend money foolishly. Buy what you need, not just what you want.

Now, in my later years, I really don't know what to make of my life. What have I accomplished? I have warm memories of those who were kind to me, like the Warner's. Even my step-fathers mother, Marie, who was Belgian, had made buttermilk soup and let me taste it. Her husband Emil showed me the carrier pigeons he raised for sport. He kept them housed in a cote in his garage. But my outstanding memories of childhood were my green tricycle and a big Christmas tree, my childhood at Aunties where I loved being in the country, Mr. and Mrs. Warner, and oddly, the day I sang a song and got a nickel to buy a hamburger. I learned that things eventually pass and we move on. I'm glad you had me make these tapes Sy, I've felt very close to you talking about my life. I have loved my old age, the best years of all. I'm so happy we shared them, you and I....End

Sylvia sat for a while thinking how sorry she felt that there were no more tapes to listen to. She wished she had sat with Granny and talked, learned all about her while she was still alive. There were so many questions she would have asked. With a sigh of regret she bundled them together and placed them back in the cupboard. One day she would play them for Eleanor's great-grandchildren so they would get to know all about their ancestor, but for now she had better get her old work clothes on and head over to that house Ryan had purchased. The restoration would take a while and she had made promises to help. David had been a little irritated this morning when she mentioned it to him as he was leaving for the store but it was only because he'd wanted to come home for lunch. She couldn't help smiling about his slight show of disappointment.

Ryan was balanced at the top of a ladder in the living room, stripping water-stained wallpaper when she arrived, it was a mess. He had a liquid mixture of some sort that, after applying and letting it soak in, would loosen the paper. Sy got busy applying the liquid as high up as she could reach, then Ryan did the top section. Once they had completed the application of the entire room, they began peeling the old paper off….strips of it, until the entire room had been done. Only a few places needed the use of a putty knife. It took them an hour to clear the mess from the floor and wipe up the liquid spills. The walls were real plaster and in pretty good shape except for an area where water damage near the fireplace had occurred. Before any plastering, the slate roof had to be repaired and all work on the upstairs completed before doing anything downstairs. They sat having a fresh cup of coffee that Ryan had made with the coffeemaker he had brought. At least the electricity and water had been turned on, making their work day more comfortable.

"So Sy, what do you think? Are you putting together a few ideas about decorating? I don't plan on doing all this cleanup work on my own, I have a few people who are faster and more proficient at clearing up messes. I expect to have this ready for you in about a month. Here's an extra key, anytime you feel like inspecting the place, maybe getting a few new ideas, feel free to come over whenever you please. All the lighting is in working order and the plumbing too, although I'll replace some of the older water lines with copper."

Sylvia slipped the key into her pocket, the thought of exploring the place from top to bottom was exciting, and she loved to use her imagination. The main thing was not having intrusions while she planned colors and layouts of patterns.

"I'm almost as excited as you are Ryan, this will be a beautiful place when it's finished. I don't have much to do at home or my job to keep me busy, so you can bet I'll be here quite often." Sy loved to use her imagination and she was looking forward to going over the entire house from top to bottom. Now that Ryan knew the walls were plastered, there would be workmen to do the wallpaper removal on the rest of the house.

On the way home she made a hurried stop at the local butchers for steaks, she'd serve them with baked potatoes and a nice spinach salad for supper. David would be pleased, he loved beef.

At dinner that evening Sylvia couldn't stop talking about Ryan's house and all the work that needed doing. By the time dinner was over, David was too polite to voice his impatience with her but while helping clear the table afterwards he was more than irritated about her enthusiasm, he felt like a fifth wheel on a wagon, completely useless and ignored.

When Sylvia finally noticed David's silent withdrawal and the closed look on his face versus her enthused recital of the day's activities, she stopped talking immediately. Gathering up the plates and cutlery she headed for the kitchen, every step seeming to ignite the anger that was building inside. She was thinking of all the times she had sat quietly listening to him relate the day's activities at work, friction between a customer and himself over some minor error, or a delivery that was missing part of an order. By the time she reached the dishwasher she was fuming.

David, a few steps behind her, had no inkling of the fury building within his new wife. No inkling that is, until she turned on him like an angry cat. He felt the hairs on the back of his neck rise.

"Whoa! There! Sweetheart, calm down." He couldn't believe how that fleck of green in her eyes flashed like a beacon of warning. "Honey, I apologize. I was listening to every word you said, but you were so excited telling me about your day that it seemed every word was "Ryan" this, and "Ryan" that, until I suddenly realized how much time you two had spent together and I felt exceedingly jealous, which in turn made me angry because there was no earthly reason for it." He gathered her into his arms holding her close to his heart where he could feel the trembling in her body caused by her fury. At first she tried to pull away but then, with a huge sigh of relief she leaned into him and relaxed, the angry tension slowly fading away.

"We have to stop meeting like this," she said lightly, glad that anger hadn't escalated into a heated argument. "I'm sorry Davey, I got carried away with my enthusiasm, I know you trust me, I shouldn't have prattled on so much. As long as I know you have no problem about me working with Ryan then everything is okay. Right?

Sylvia slept like a log and when she awoke the next morning she could hardly contain her excitement about exploring Ryan's house from top to bottom. She loved the idea of finding unexplored areas that had been neglected for years.

After breakfast was over and David had left for the hardware store, she hurriedly cleaned up the kitchen and then set off for Ryan's old mansion. She planned on starting her search in the basement. She always liked to save the best until last and she adored the half-moon multi-colored windows in the attic.

THE THISTLE SEED

Arriving at the house she parked in the driveway. Entering the front door she stood for a moment looking at the expanse of the room they had worked on. It would be a magnificent great-room when finished. Wending her way to the kitchen she saw that the old cupboards and sink had already been removed making the room look much larger, the door to the side entrance and basement was closed.

Standing on the landing she noticed a wall switch which she clicked on. A bulb at the bottom of the stairway gave off a dim glow, just enough to highlight the stairs. She made her way down to the bottom.

Not surprisingly there was quite a cluttered mess. Cardboard cartons sat piled atop each other, shelves of empty canning jars lined one entire wall and this was just in the stairwell section. Outlines of piled castoffs could be seen in the shadowed recesses lit by dimly filtered light from a few narrow dirt-encrusted windows. Most of the basement lay in darkness. It would be a fruitless search without a flashlight so she returned to her car to get the one she kept in the trunk.

Now, purse slung over her shoulder because of workmen likely arriving, she was back at the stairwell not even bothering to turn on the uselessly dim basement light. Her flashlight cast a powerful beam.

Narrow aisles curved throughout the cavernous interior similar to a maze. Several times she found herself back at the beginning but she continued along the various narrow pathways until she reached a dead-end. A heavy oaken door, set solidly into the brick wall stood before her. Turning away, she cast her light over the various containers stacked so solidly, wondering what in the world could be so important about the contents that it all had to be stored so carefully. Maybe the secret was behind the door. She lifted the latch and began to tug it open. At first, nothing happened, but then with a slight rasp from disuse, it swung open silently on oiled hinges. As she stepped inside and passed the bright light over the interior, the door swung closed behind her before she could halt its progress. There was no latch, knob nor handle to reopen it.

It was a small room with no windows but a heavy desk and chair dominated, taking up most of the room. Another closed door was on the opposite wall, not as heavy looking as the first, but nonetheless built as sturdily. There was a wall switch she flipped on and a row of recessed wall lights lit the room brightly. She turned her flashlight off. She was surprised there was no dust on the furniture. Possibly because it was closed off from the rest of the house.

She went to the other door and tried the handle, it opened at her touch. Beyond lay a long tunnel completely lined with fieldstone. It was dry, built-in lights placed about every ten feet but she could not see its end. She pushed the chair over and propped the door open, she didn't want to be trapped twice.

She began to walk, haltingly at first but after about twenty paces she picked up speed and began to trot. Surprisingly, the air was fresh, not what she expected in such a closed up area. Around a curve in the tunnel she reached an area that had collapsed, the tunnel was blocked, but having no other options she began to dig at the rubble near the top of the pile. Soon the bright gleam of sunlight was visible and she reached up into the remaining debris clearing it away. Clambering out of the hole into daylight she found herself standing on the bank of the deep stream at the end of the property staring down at a half-submerged dock. She couldn't wait to find Ryan and tell him what she had discovered.

Workmen's vehicles were already parked in the driveway, thankfully they hadn't blocked her car. She headed for Alex's and Rose's residence, hoping Ryan would be there. Thankfully, he was.

"Hi! Mom….how are you feeling? You're looking good. When did the doctor say you'd deliver? I can hardly wait to have a baby sister." Sy gave her mom a big hug, smiling at the fact that she'd had to stand a short distance away because of Rose's growing girth.

"Honey, I have a long while to go before delivery. I expect that Ryan will already be moved into his new place by the time you have a sibling. We found out it's going to be a girl and I'm thrilled, so is Alex. We already have her room filled with all the baby things she'll require. I can hardly wait." Rose had a glow on her face that made Sylvia smile.

"Hi! Dad, is Ryan here? I was just exploring his new home. It's going to be a beauty when it's finished. I was exploring the basement, a very interesting set-up, not like anything a family would have. I was wondering if he had any information about the previous owner."

"You just missed him Sy, he left not even ten minutes before you arrived. You'll catch him back at his place."

"I'd better get going then." She gave him a quick kiss on his cheek and was out the door and back in her car so quickly that she didn't even notice them waving goodbye.

By the time she got to Ryan's, she felt like she had been running herself ragged, it had been a very long morning. Making her way up the wide stairway to the upper floor she could hear sounds of hammers and conversations of workmen. She found Ryan in the midst of the activity.

"You've got to come with me right this minute, Ryan. You won't believe what I discovered. Did you by any chance, do any research for the previous owner? I hope so because that person was a crook. Have you looked in the basement, did you see all those covered bundles? I'm at the point where I'd even believe that there are secret hiding places everywhere." All the while she was talking she was leading Ryan down the stairs and on the way to the basement.

This time after she opened the door, she secured it with a block of wood so it wouldn't lock behind them. Then she led Ryan through the tunnel and out to the stream.

"These were crooks, Ryan. They stole things, delivered their loot here, to the tunnel site. All those covered bundles in the basement are not items stored from the house, they're goods filched from all over. We have to notify the police right away."

Ryan couldn't believe what Sy was telling him but logic told him she was right. It was a perfect set-up for concealing stolen goods. No wonder he'd gotten the place at such a good price. They wanted it off their hands. The old man that had owned the property had passed away. His lawyer had handled the sale for his offspring who were known as shady characters with police records. They wanted to get out from under their illicit dealings that had been going on all the while the old man had been ill. Unfortunately, as soon as he had died the property had been locked up tight as a drum, no admittance until the will had been gone over by the attorneys. They'd had no chance to remove their last shipment of stolen booty. He wondered if they were still lurking around waiting for a chance to recover the goods and cash them in at a disreputable loan sharks. Anything was possible.

Ryan phoned the police. Within a short time two detectives arrived at the house. They had been working a dead-end robbery detail trying to find the perpetrators of a rash of major thefts. Maybe this was the break they'd been hoping for. Ryan took them down to the basement and then stood aside as they inspected a few of the bundled items. They matched product numbers against their list of stolen property, several matched. They finally had found the goods. The possibility of fingerprints would tag the thieves. They would arrange to have the stolen property picked up as soon as possible.

Later that afternoon a large van pulled into the driveway. Men had the basement cleared before evening arrived and now, walking around the emptied basement, Ryan felt a surge of relief. He had been uncomfortable seeing all those covered bundles and hadn't been in a hurry to open and investigate what was inside. He hoped whoever was responsible would be caught and quickly brought to justice. He didn't like the idea of his new home being the base of operations for a gang of thieves.

Sylvia was relieved. She loved her brother and was happy that the police, after being notified about the stolen property in the basement, had been satisfied that Ryan had nothing to do with it. "You've been working so hard, why don't you have supper with David and me? I'll make spaghetti, you love that stuff."

Ryan hesitated, the offer sounded good but he had a few errands to run and a new girlfriend to drop in to see on the way home. "Thanks sis, that sounds great but I have things to do. I'll take you up on your offer another time. Give David my regards and tell him I'll enjoy beating the pants off him at a game of pinochle once my place is finished and ready for company. Honest, Sy, you just can't imagine how much I'm looking forward to having my own home, it's way past the time for me to get out from under dads roof. The old days of kids living at home until marriage are passé. If you're still home at age twenty one you're an overgrown baby. The only reason I never got my own place was that I didn't want to leave dad alone. Now I'm free to do as I choose." Ryan had a wry grin on his face, a little embarrassed about revealing his deep love and concern for his father.

Sylvia put her arms around her brother giving him a big hug and a kiss on his cheek. "That's one of the reasons I love you, it's exactly what I would have done. We're two of a kind Ryan, love and respect for family before personal satisfaction. Come on, let's hit the road brother, I'll even walk you to your car." She tucked her arm through his and steered him through the door.

With a last wave goodbye, Ryan drove away. First stop, home to shower and change, then on to see his new girlfriend. She was a winner, he had a feeling she was the one he'd been hoping to find. He planned to take her to dinner then they'd go back to her place. He truly wanted to get to know her better. It had only been a few weeks that they'd known each other. They had met at the mall, both happening to make eye contact while looking at the "You are here" map in the rotunda. He knew the mall well since he and his dad had built it, but he wanted to check on where the new Paint 'n Stuff store was located. She, on the other hand, was looking for the Beauty Shoppe that had just moved in. Something between them had "Clicked." He had asked her to join him for coffee and that was the beginning. They had seen each other almost every day. He thought of her as his "Golden Girl," with her blonde hair and golden eyes. He couldn't stop thinking of her.

When he arrived at her tiny apartment the aroma of fresh coffee greeted him at the door. She had pulled the small table into the center of the room, the Scrabble Board was all set up and the two painted wooden chairs already waiting in place. They both enjoyed the competition, but this time he promised himself he wouldn't stay so late. She fixed their coffee, they seated themselves and the play began.

At midnight Ryan realized how late it was, time to get home. He was a bit stiff from sitting so long but it had been pure enjoyment, they had both laughed over some of the concoctions invented that wouldn't hold water. He pulled her into his arms and kissed her deeply, finally pulling away before emotions got out of hand. She resisted at first but then looked up at him, a sulky look on her face. She placed her hands on each side of his face and pulled him to her, warm lips opening beneath his, her breath coming quicker. For a moment he almost lost control, pressing himself into her warmth he felt her quick response. With a groan of misery he griped her waist with both hands and moved her aside. He bolted for the door knowing he wouldn't last another second. "I'll phone you tomorrow when I get home", he muttered hoarsely as she watched him disappear into the night.

Closing and locking the door, she couldn't help smiling at the tumultuous feelings that had been aroused, her's as well as his. She wanted him and that was the honest truth.

In the bathroom she stripped and stepped into the shower hoping the sting of water would relieve the stress she was feeling. Afterward she slipped under the covers, feeling the cool smoothness of the sheets against her nude body, almost like a caress. How much longer was he going to make her wait, this was driving her crazy. She ran her hand over her breasts feeling the nipples harden against her palm. Then, after a very short length of time she was fast asleep.

    Ryan tossed and turned, it seemed everything ached, and not only from all his hard work of the day. He'd never felt like this before, she was the first woman that seemed to encompass every waking thought of his day but he had no intentions of having sexual relations with her without a marriage certificate. He'd seen what had happened with his father. The next time he saw her he'd have an engagement ring in hand and a proposal of marriage. Hopefully he'd have the house restored in time to spend their wedding night there. He was in love with a wonderful woman. He could hardly wait for the nuptials when she would become Mrs. Jennifer Williams.

    It was almost dawn before he finally fell asleep and into a kaleidoscope of nightmarish dreams, beginning pleasantly enough with his marriage to Jennifer and then twisting into the horror of discovering, on their wedding night, that she was entwined in the arms of another. When he awoke, the feeling of disillusionment was lodged heavily in his mind. He lay for a while trying to analyze the meaning without success. Suddenly, he didn't want to rush into committing himself to Jennifer with an engagement ring. There wasn't any hurry, he'd get his house finished, furnished and then he'd move in. Maybe he'd even get a dog. He'd always wanted one, but with the hours he and his dad had worked, it hadn't been feasible. The thought brought a pensive smile of pleasure picturing being greeted at the door by a tail-wagging friend when returning home.

    By the time he had showered and dressed he was in a good mood. The kitchen would be finished this week. Plumbing pipes had been replaced with copper, the electrical wiring had been upgraded and a new circuit breaker box installed. Plaster walls had been patched, sanded and primed. Once the painting was finished, new lighting fixtures were ready to replace the old. He'd had the tunnel repaired and a sturdy locked metal door installed at each end. Eventually he'd have a new dock built. The basement would be the last project.

    Ryan decided to make a quick stop at his at his dad's house, he rang the bell and waited for someone to open the door. A couple more pushes without results and he turned away, wondering where they could be off to. With Rose pregnant they usually stayed close to home since it was getting near her time of delivery. He checked in the back, Alex's car was gone. A feeling of anxiety that something was happening had him back in his car and on the way to the hospital. He spotted his dads' new four door sedan he had purchased when Rose became pregnant, a gift for her. It already had a baby seat in the back.

"Alex is in the delivery room with his wife," the nurse said, "if you'll have a seat in the waiting room I'll keep you informed." So there he sat, wondering how the delivery was proceeding and then suddenly it hit him, a brother or sister to add to the family. He recalled when there were just the two, he and his dad. Then a sister, step-mom, brother-in-law, and now another sibling, life was becoming more interesting. One day he would have a wife and children, what a fantastically growing family it would become.

Just then his dad came into the waiting room, a big grin on his face as he put his arms around his son and told him he now had a new little brother, seven pounds, six ounces, they had named Scott Regan Williams. Rose had done an outstanding job in the delivery room, he was so proud of her. He didn't know how a woman could go through that much pain and then bring forth a new human being with a smile of joy. He'd feel like he'd be torn apart.

"She'll be in her room presently and then I'll take you in to see her, son. I never would have thought you'd have a brother to play with at your age. Life is full of surprises isn't it?"

The two men sat quietly, each deep in thought contemplating all the changes that had occurred in their lives. And to think it had all begun with a chance meeting at a restaurant.

Ryan was smiling to himself, the thought of having a little brother causing an amazing feeling of exaltation. He could only imagine what his father was feeling. Wanting to share the euphoria he decided to stop in to see Sylvia. He had seen her leaving the parking lot just as he had arrived at the hospital.

When she answered the door he could see she had been crying. "What's wrong sis, nothing's happened to Rose has it?" For a moment he could feel his heartbeat escalate until Sy gave a grin of embarrassment.

"No! Silly, I'm just happy about mom having an easy delivery and the thought that I have another brother. I'm also in a sentimental mood because I recently found out that I'm pregnant. Our babies will grow up playing together and being friends."

"Wow! Wait until dad hears about this, he'll be a grandfather and your mom a grandmother and I'll be an uncle. This is getting more than I can handle all in one morning Sy. In fact, I've decided this would be a very good time for me to move into my house. Enough work is finished that the little left undone won't hamper my comfort living there. My parents will appreciate having their privacy and so will I. Today is as good a day as any."

"Would you like some help, Ryan? I'm not doing anything and I'd sure like to see what you've done since I finished coordinating the color schemes for the painters."

"All I need do is get my clothes and sports equipment. If you bring your car, between the two of us it will only take one trip. I don't want you to carry anything, just let me do the work and you keep me company so I won't get bored, Okay?"

"Let me get my purse, I'll meet you at your dads. I'll leave a note for David in case he comes home for lunch."

Ryan couldn't believe he had moved so quickly. Sylvia had helped hang his suits, place sweaters and other garments in drawers. Everything was now put away. All he had to do was get used to where everything was so he wouldn't have to do repeat searches. His next items on the agenda were shopping for personal items and groceries. In fact, he needed dishware, glasses, utensils, and cookware. He was beginning to feel overwhelmed.

"Sy, would you like to go with me now to get kitchen stuff? At least I'll be able to make meals. I need to grocery shop too if it's not too much trouble."

"Sure Ryan, let's get it all finished at once. By the time you have everything you need, you'll be sorry you ever asked me for help. I'm a great believer in buying power."

When they finally returned to Ryan's home, the car was loaded with household items. Stainless steel kitchenware, utensils, a microwave-safe stoneware dinner set, glassware, wineglasses, and a multitude of other items to set up a home kitchen, bath and bedroom.

"Your grocery shopping can wait, Ryan. By the time you get all this put away in their permanent spots, you won't feel like cooking. Why don't you come over for supper tonight? Dave would be tickled to see you and we'd enjoy the company."

"Thanks Sy, I'll take you up on your offer, I'm starved. We should have stopped for lunch, I'm sorry, I was too enthused."

"Supper will be at six, don't be late, I'm looking forward to our visit."

CHAPTER 8

Jennifer Pryor sat contentedly, contemplating her well laid out plans to marry Ryan and have the life of leisure she had always craved but eluded her all her adult years. She had come close to it with David. But, just as well, she'd have more control over Ryan than David, who had been successful in running his own business and was used to having his own way. She planned on being a good wife to whomever she wed. But lately, she'd had the feeling that things were not what they appeared. There was something wrong and it definitely had to do with the way Ryan had been acting the past few days. On the spur of the moment she decided to phone, ask him to supper and hopefully get to the bottom of the puzzle. She listened to the repeated ringing. Just as she was ready to hang up, he answered the phone.

"Ryan, I was sure you must be out, I was just about ready to hang up and try you again later. I really need to talk to you, honey. If you're not busy can you drop over now? I promise not to keep you too long." It seemed to take forever before he answered but it was actually only a few moments.

"Jennifer! I was just thinking about you, I also want to talk to you. I can't make it right now, this evening would be better if you don't have anything else planned. How about eight o'clock?"

Disappointment was evident in Jennifer's response, the slight edge of anger making her cut off her words sharply. "Sure, Ryan, anything to please you. See you around eight then." Without waiting for his response she hung up the receiver.

When Ryan arrived later that evening she was prepared. She had made his favorite dessert, old-fashioned creamy rice pudding with raisins and fresh coffee with a hint of cinnamon that would put him in a relaxed mood. She had dressed carefully wanting to give the impression of an old-fashioned girl who hadn't been around very much. She had pulled her dyed honey-blonde hair into a ponytail and applied a very light hint of makeup. A light touch of eye shadow emphasized her golden eyes. Pale pink lipstick and the faint scent of musk perfume, a dainty white silk blouse that outlined her bust line and a gored A-line pale blue skirt that fell softly to below her knees completed her ensemble.

Stepping back from the door, she gave a twirl, the skirt belled out just enough to show an enticing glimpse of upper thigh. Ryan couldn't help noticing how beautiful she looked and felt an immediate attraction to her, stronger than ever before. As they sat at her tiny table eating the rice pudding and sipping coffee, Ryan couldn't stop his mind from assessing her attributes and imagining how it would feel being married to her. She was intelligent, a neat housekeeper, good cook, and sexy as any man would desire, he especially. What had he been thinking? No way would he want to lose her. She was all any man would want in a woman.

"Jen, I've been so busy working on my house that I've neglected you a bit. I apologize, it's just I wanted it finished as soon as possible. If you don't have anything planned this evening, how about taking a ride with me and I'll show you the place from top to bottom?"

She couldn't believe her luck. This was just what she had been hoping for, getting him alone at his own place where he would feel in control.

Jennifer rinsed the dishes and placed them, along with the coffee cups, in the sink. She picked up the pink sweater she had draped on her chair and Ryan escorted her to his car.

It was a cool evening, autumn just beginning with its fresh breezes and drifting leaves. The full moon looked like a huge globe of golden radiance that drew the eye like a magnet. It put Ryan in a very romantic mood.

Jennifer felt his hand reach for hers so she left it resting in his grasp. Occasionally he gave it a squeeze. She was beginning to feel quite confident about the outcome of the evening. This time she had a plan that she would stick with.

Ryan was glad he had put all the new purchases away. When he held the door open for Jen and clicked on the light switch, the wall sconces lit up the great room with a soft glow that made the room, although large, look very cozy. Two leather recliners with side tables sat before the natural fireplace that was built into the floor to ceiling multicolored sandstone wall. The slate hearth held a brass stand of fireplace tools and a wrought iron firewood holder. The remainder of the room held a long upholstered couch and two chairs with end tables and lamps, a bookcase at one end of the room with a cozy reading section plus, a stereo, television, grandfather clock, oil paintings and several live plants.

Jennifer's eyes were wide with amazement, she hadn't expected the house to be ready to move into. She imagined herself in this room, the lady of the house, curled up in one of the chairs in the reading corner perusing a good book. She would enjoy being the hostess of and greeting company that arrived. She looked at Ryan with new appreciation of his hard work and the understanding that he was someone who liked nice things and would work to achieve them. As for herself, she had worked all her life but even though she was careful with her earnings, she had never been able to get ahead. It had always been a hand to mouth existence and she was so tired of it. She was still young, wanted a family and a good husband but somehow had never gotten the chance, although she had tried to capture David but he had already been involved with someone else. Maybe this time she'd be lucky.

"This is beautiful Ryan, you've been working hard with not much rest and the results are outstanding. You've outdone yourself."

Ryan watched her face, noting the expressions of pleasure as her eyes found another area that drew her attention. She really liked the room.

"I knew what I wanted to feel when I walked into the house. Pleasure of course, but mainly a sense of calm relaxation. I achieved it with the help of my sister Sylvia. I'm so glad you like it."

He led her through the rest of the rooms finally ending in his newly furnished bedroom. "As you can see, the upstairs isn't entirely finished but it won't take much more labor to complete it. I decided I didn't want wallpaper, too much trouble removing it. With all the beautiful latex paint colors available, that's what I'll be using. The last of the wallpaper has been removed and any repair to the plaster walls has been done. Now it's just a matter of finishing the painting. I'm looking forward to buying the furnishings and getting the remaining rooms completed. I even have a sewing room tucked away in a corner of the upstairs attic, which is quite a remarkable place. I'll show you the next time you visit."

Jennifer gave a nod of assent, so overwhelmed at the imposing beauty of the home that she was left speechless. She hadn't realized what a good catch

Ryan would be, a hard working, talented guy who made his dreams a reality. She had to admit, she felt more than just attraction for him. It was like an invisible web being woven, the strands pulling them closer together. The disillusionment of thinking she would never meet the man of her dreams had disappeared, he was standing before her. A small icy core hidden within her being slowly began to dissolve until, without her being aware, it disappeared.

Ryan had been watching her intently, wondering what could possibly be so mesmerizing that she seemed to have drifted off in a daydream. He reached out and took her hand. At the contact she gave him a warm smile and followed him into the kitchen where he put the kettle on to boil and got out cups, sugar, cream and a canister of loose tea.

They sat before a large window overlooking the extensive rear property which was bathed in bright moonlight. The tea was an Earl Grey and between sips, they munched on crackers topped with a creamy bleu cheese while discussing the possibility of planting a few fruit trees, berry bushes and of course a vegetable garden. Just thinking about having garden fresh fruits and vegetables at their fingertips sounded impossible but very probable.

"Although it's far too late in the season for planting, there's still time to get the area ready for spring. We can sit down and make a diagram of what and where we want to plant. By the time spring comes I'll have the basement finished and install a commercial freezer that will hold all our fruits and vegetables. I think this is going to be fun, Jen. Are you up for it?"

She hadn't felt this enthused in a very long time, if it were possible she'd want to begin immediately. The thought of them working together made her feel lightheaded, and the simple fact of being needed and wanted gave such a lift to her ego that she felt giddy with euphoria.

"Ryan, you'll never know how ready I am to dig in with both hands. Just say the word and I'm at your beck and call."

He had never noticed how expressive her face was. He felt he could read every thought that crossed her mind. This was going to be a very interesting venture, one that would bring out each other's temperament, whether good or bad. Hopefully they would complement each other's

It was after midnight when he drove Jennifer home and walked her to her door. For a moment he was tempted to take her in his arms and kiss her until she begged for mercy but at the last moment he changed his mind. Better to keep things on a lighter scale, it looked like they would be spending a lot of time together. Why rush things this early in the game. He brushed a light kiss against her cheek then turned and walked away. He could see in his rear view mirror she was still standing in front of her door watching his departure. He couldn't help that a wide grin spread across his face at the thought of the confusion she was likely feeling. This time he would be the one who called the twists and turns developing in their relationship. He was very interested in her, maybe even to have her as his wife but she would be the last one to know. He planned on keeping her guessing.

Ryan awoke early, the patter of sleety rain against his windows promising the forecast of it changing to snow later in the day. The automatic thermostat clicked on sending a wave of warm air through the bedroom. Lazily he stretched, his body tensing momentarily as he extended his arms above his head flexing his shoulders and then sitting upright. Swinging his legs over the edge of the bed his bare feet hit the floor and he was up. After a quick shower and the usual tooth brushing, shaving activities, he pulled on a pair of jeans and a sweatshirt then headed downstairs to the kitchen. With his larder and refrigerator fully stocked, thanks to his sister Sylvia's help, he wasn't sure what he wanted, finally settling for a bowl of micro cooked oatmeal. He couldn't help grinning as he finished eating. Sylvia was the one who had placed the huge cardboard carton up in the cupboard saying it would be a perfect breakfast on a cold rainy day. How right she was. It warmed him from the inside. After rinsing out the bowl and utensils he placed them in the dishwasher. This reminded him of his intention of hiring a cleaning lady. Someone who'd come in a few times a week to take care of housework, laundry, and changing the bed linens. He'd check with his dad who might know of someone.

This morning he planned on exploring the attic, the sole remaining area to be refurbished. He flipped on the light switch at the bottom of the stairs and climbed.

It looked dismal because of the dreary weather outside. What a difference from when he was last here, the shadowy images looking strange without the multicolored reflections from sunlit windows. Slowly he wended his way around and through the miscellaneous castoffs, pulling away coverings, opening drawers, and investigating odd looking shadows. Opening one of the trunks he found marionette figures and several antique dolls, there was even a folding wooden stage for putting on puppet shows. He came across a small green tricycle that looked new, old fashioned roller skates with the keys attached with twine so as not to get lost. He found a beautifully built wooden doll house with all the miniature furniture inside. A large glass-door cabinet held a variety of books, a complete set of Tarzan of the Apes, Nancy Drew, Merlin, and other assorted youthful reading material. Apparently some youngster loved to read. Dolls and their outfits were wrapped and stored carefully away. A beautiful Lionel train set with all the accompanying buildings and scenery was packed in a huge leather case. Finally, Ryan removed the covering on an old rocking chair and sat down to contemplate the treasures he'd found. This looked to be just the tip of the iceberg. He hadn't looked into the trunks yet. It seemed there had been two children, a boy and a girl. He wondered what had happened to them and to their parents. Resting his head against the carved wooden chair frame he closed his eyes for a moment of contemplation and fell into a deep asleep. He began to dream.

Shadows seemed to shift about in the room. It could have been moving clouds filtering a small shaft of brighter skylight, but whatever the source, something in the atmosphere had changed. The morning drifted into noon and then into early evening.

Ryan awoke, wondering for a moment where he was, thinking he was in bed and it was morning. With a shake of his head he stood, the stiffness in his muscles making him wonder why he ached so much after just a short time dozing. It was then he realized he was in the attic, night had fallen, and he couldn't understand how time had passed so quickly.

Standing in his kitchen a short time later he still felt confused. Time had entirely disappeared and he hadn't accomplished a single thing in the entire day. He wasn't even hungry because it felt like the morning oatmeal was a solid lump sitting in his stomach. Feeling the need for something hot to drink he plugged in the coffee pot and started the brewing process. A strong feeling of restlessness possessed him, urging him to action, however there was nothing he could ascertain that needed his attention.

He sat, sipping at the coffee that he had fortified with a shot of brandy, contemplating the series of mental images he had retrieved from the dream sequences he had experienced during his long doze. It had been about toys and about a young boy and girl, brother and sister, who had played in the attic. He wondered why all the toys were still there. It would have been logical to take them along when the family moved. It was too late in the day to investigate further. Tomorrow he'd check more thoroughly.

The sound of the ringing phone drew his attention. His voice sounded distracted when he answered it.

"Ryan, I expected you to phone. We were going to make a diagram of where we want our plantings to go this coming spring, remember? I tried calling several times but apparently you were out someplace. When I still hadn't heard from you by evening I was getting frantic. If you hadn't answered this call I was going to phone the police."

Ryan could hear the stress in Jennifer's voice, she sounded close to tears. "I'm sorry Jen. You won't believe what happened but I swear it's the honest truth. I was looking through all that clutter in the attic and when I happened to uncover a great looking rocking chair, I sat down for a second. The next thing I knew it was evening and I had slept through the entire day. I'm just now having a cup of coffee trying to wake up completely. I'll likely be up all night."

"I'm sure you're kidding me Ryan. You sat down this morning, fell asleep and just now woke up? If I told you that same tale would you believe it? I don't think so. I'm sitting here, bored silly with nothing to do, so how about me coming over there to keep you company? At least we can be bored together."

When Jennifer arrived Ryan greeted her at the door. She had stopped for donuts at an all night diner and thrust the bag at him as she entered. He closed and locked the door behind her following her into the kitchen where she plopped down at the table and studied Ryan's face as he sat opposite her. He looked well rested but there was a hint of distraction in his appearance, a worried crease in his brow. She could detect no trace of subterfuge.

"Tell me what you were dreaming about, in detail please, even if it seems mundane."

So, between sips of coffee and bites of donut, Ryan went into detail about all he had discovered. The longer he spoke, the more Jennifer became intrigued, even nodding her head occasionally in agreement. She was entrapped in the minute description of all the various playthings that Ryan had uncovered. His voice, weaving a web of familiarity that caused her to actually picture each article as though she was standing before it, her hand reaching to experience the touch of ownership. It was a mesmerizing feeling that caused a glow of inner warmth she had never felt before. She wanted to see these treasures and could hardly wait for morning.

The night dragged by until they had ended up in the living room dozing in the easy chairs until dawn.

Ryan prepared breakfast. Cheese omelets with wheat toast, orange juice and micro-cooked bacon. He hated the mess frying made. After they finished eating and the kitchen was neatened, they headed for the attic.

The brilliance of the multicolored glass windows took Jennifer's breath away, suddenly bringing to mind the dim remembrance from long ago of playing under a rainbow with another child about her own age. She could almost remember her playmate.

Feeling breathless, her heartbeat accelerated as she meandered amongst items that were beginning to feel more and more familiar. That doll, the marionettes, and the wooden dollhouse Santa had brought the last Christmas she could remember. Her mind began a frenzied search for more and more memories until she became so dizzy she sat quickly in the old rocking chair to avoid falling. And even the chair felt familiar.

Helplessly she looked up at Ryan, a lost forlorn look on her face, unable to tell him what she was experiencing. She couldn't speak of the wealth of memories overwhelming her until she felt closed in, unable to express her anxiety and pain of recollection.

All she could think of was her loss, her sudden exodus from safety, warmth and love to the cold sterile environment of the orphanage. She had been three years old at the time her parents and brother had been killed in an automobile accident, at least that's what the supervisor eventually told her. The lawyer had sold off furnishings, two automobiles and jewelry to provide extras for her comfort until the only thing left had been the house. He had passed away and the house had slowly fallen into disrepair.

When she finally left the orphanage at the age of eighteen she had no memory of her previous existence. Her entire world consisted of the teachers and residents that made up her orphanage family. She had studied hard, learned bookkeeping by doing accounts for them. Her mind was quick and she was very good at her job.

She had felt resentful once she was out on her own. Everyone had someone to love, and be loved, except her. She was nothing. All she had were her looks and body which she had tried to use to advance herself. And now, here she was with a man she loved sitting in a rocking chair in an attic of long ago memories. The turmoil it created was almost more than she could bear.

"Talk to me Jen, what's wrong? You've been sitting there for at least the past five minutes not saying a word. You have the most forlorn look on your face as though you just lost your best friend."

"Funny you should say that Ryan, I just lost myself and regained my memory. I once lived here. These were the toys my brother and I played with. This was our playroom. Daddy had these special windows installed. He said we should always be at the foot of the rainbow having health, wealth and happiness. But my family died in a car accident and I lost the rainbow and all my dreams. I never realized what had happened, one day I was here, the next I was with strangers and I forgot my past."

Jennifer began to sob, it sounded as though her heart had broken. She was crying for her lost mother and father, the brother she had loved so much and all the years she could have had the treasure of their memories.

Ryan was stunned at the revelation. The sorrow Jen was feeling was almost like a solid wall that surrounded her, the depth of it expressed so vividly in her eyes that he couldn't help but pull her to her feet and fold her into his arms. He tucked her head against his shoulder and pulled her closely against his body hoping the warmth would give her a feeling of comfort.

"You poor kid, I wish I'd known about all this. Why didn't you ever tell me about the orphanage? You didn't think that would make a difference in the way I felt about you, did you? From the first moment I saw you I thought you were special, but you wore this hard shell that was almost like a warning to stay away. Then when I asked you out I enjoyed your company, yet there was something that seemed to tell me to be careful. I have to admit it was very confusing. Finally the breakthrough, when you really opened up to me, especially when we were talking about working together on the yard and planting everything we could think of. It was the house that intrigued you but you didn't know it. I'm just happy that you found me before you discovered the house, otherwise I'd never be sure of who you were marrying."

When Jen began to sob louder Ryan had no idea what to do about it. Not realizing that it was his proposal that had set her off.

"Come on honey, let's go downstairs. I'll fix you a nice cup of tea and we can sit in the living room in front of the nice warm fire that I'll light and talk about all the planting we will do this spring. How does that sound?"

A small hiccup, and then blowing her nose, Jennifer nodded her assent. They made their way down the stairs into the kitchen where in short order Ryan had a tray set with a tea pot, cups and saucers, strawberry jam and crackers. He balanced it on one hand while leading Jen into the living room. After setting the tray on an end table between the two leather chairs, he worked on getting a nice cozy fire going.

Finally Jen had her feet resting on a footstool, her legs covered with a colorful afghan, Ryan in the recliner chair nearby. Both sipping their teas and letting the peaceful aura calm and relax them.

"I've been meaning to ask you something, Jen, and this is as good a time as any. Do you think you could live here and be accepting about the loss of family you experienced? Even though I purchased the property because of all the taxes owed, you are basically part owner, at least as far as I'm concerned. If the lawyer hadn't died, the taxes would have been kept up and you would have inherited it. But I don't want you to be just a part owner, I want you to be my wife."

The silence seemed to extend into eternity as Ryan waited for a response, he was ready to rise and walk out of the room when he turned to look at Jen. She was fast asleep. The chaotic experience of reliving past memories had exhausted her mentally. The teacup, almost ready to tip its contents, was gently lifted from her fingertips. He tucked the afghan around her shoulders, picked up the tray and carried it into the kitchen.

Several hours later Jen awoke feeling warm, rested and much more able to cope. She refolded the afghan, draped it over the chair arm and then walked into the kitchen. Ryan was sitting at the table with a small ruler and pencil making squares and circles. She sat next to him, peering down at the drawing being revealed with each pencil stroke.

"We were going to plan our garden, Jen. I'm drawing the areas where we can plant our trees, berry bushes, vegetable and flower gardens. We'll have cobblestone paths that will look great but will also keep our feet dirt free when just going for walks to see how our farming attempts are doing. This will be trial and error but of course we can get advice from the pros. By the way, I had asked you a question but then discovered you were fast asleep so I'll ask again. Will you marry me?"

The question was asked while Jen was still absorbing all the information he had been describing, it took her a moment to realize what he had asked.

A sob caught in her throat and then she responded with a hearty, "Yes, with all my heart," and a huge kiss of confirmation.

Gardening was forgotten. They didn't want to wait long for their wedding. They simply wanted a small private ceremony with friends and family and Jen didn't want a fancy wedding gown either. She'd find something appropriate for the occasion.

As for family, Jennifer had none. She realized that she had some Making Up" to do with the people Ryan named as friends and family. Recalling the ridiculous things she had done to get attention and love she lowered her head in shame, not able to look Ryan in the face. She took his hand and began to walk to the great room, the thought of sitting in front of a cozy fire making her revelations seem less intense.

"I have a few things to talk to you about, Ryan, actions that I'm ashamed to even recall, let alone bring to light. It's something that needs to be said to clear the air so our marriage will have a healthy beginning without any hidden secrets, at least, on my part."

Ryan was mystified, wondering what in the world she could seem so uncomfortable about. Then slowly, the light dawned and he recalled the conversation he'd had with Sylvia about the incident with David and Jennifer. Sy had been mad as a wet hen when relating the tricky ploy Jennifer had cooked up. From beginning to end he'd listened, trying not to let his crooked sense of humor mess up the interesting tale. It was every guys dream. A fantasy not very likely to happen but David had made it into a real horror story for Sylvia.

Putting on a serious face, he pulled into his arms. "I know all about it, Jen. Sylvia told me quite a while ago. Sure, she was as angry as a hornets' nest hit by a stick, but she's not one to carry a grudge. She has the man she loves and if truth be told, has a huge sense of pride that she got the man someone went to such lengths to try and get. In fact, I think she'll be rather relieved that you'll belong to a fellow as handsome as me." Ryan had to choke back a laugh. Pretending to cough with emotion yet all the while grinning like an idiot, he didn't realize she had caught his facial reflection in one of the mirrors hanging on opposite walls. By the time he felt her body stiffen it was too late. The shove she gave him made him stumble backward, fall into the recliner which then tipped over tossing him into a summersault. He landed flat on his stomach wondering how it had all happened so quickly. He lifted his head staring at the upended chair and beyond that Jennifer, laughing her head off and subsiding into gurgles of delight.

Lending him a helping hand, once he was on his feet, both were chuckling at the antics that had occurred. They walked, arm and arm, back into the kitchen. Jennifer breathing a sigh of relief that everything had turned out surprisingly well.

"Jen, I'd like you to do something for me, I want you to move into one of the guest bedrooms. Why pay for another month's rent when we'll be planning our wedding? You'd be closer to work. There's really no sense in you traveling that extra five miles every morning and evening when you could be here." Ryan hoped she'd agree. He didn't like the idea of her driving home at night after visiting with him. They'd gotten into the habit of having supper together, he enjoyed cooking for her. "You'll have your own small suite with bath and dressing room. At least it's larger than your apartment. You'll have your private time to be alone and watch television, listen to music, or read. Whatever you desire, and when your door is closed I won't bother you. That's a promise."

Ryan made it sound very tempting. She detested her small apartment which almost made her feel she was bumping into herself. It would be pleasant having more space and she knew Ryan…he would not be knocking on her door in the middle of the night. Their togetherness would wait for marriage.

"You have a deal sugar, but if you don't stick to your promise I'll be out of here in a wink. You see, I've already made up my mind that our wedding night will be special. That will be the time when you have my permission to enter my bedroom." Jen gave a wicked grin at Ryan knowing she was making him uncomfortable by reading his thoughts. "That's okay honey cakes, think but don't touch." She watched a blush spread across his forehead. He was such a sweet guy that it almost broke her heart. She'd have to be very careful with him until he got used to her sometimes abrasive personality. Was it harmless? Yes. But to those who were not familiar with her moods, at times it was downright hurtful. She had to admit though, she loved him with every part of her being.

By the following weekend she was all moved in. A fellow employee had taken over the apartment, happy to be closer to work and not minding the limited space.

THE THISTLE SEED

They planned their wedding for the following month, a mid-October occasion. Ryan was having the reception at the house, caterers providing a sumptuous dinner. A small three piece band, the center of the great room cleared for dancing, would provide the music. It would be an intimate affair within the comfort of home. Only a dozen guests composed of family and friends would attend.

While Ryan planned the festivities, Jennifer planned her wardrobe. One of the first things she did was have her hair returned to its' original color. She had oil treatments to soften the dyed blackness to a more natural look and also a haircut, choosing a pixie style which gave her an impish look bringing attention to her golden-lioness eyes. It would be a breeze to take care of.

Exiting the salon she felt like a million dollars, now all she had to do was search for a dress. It was another week before she found one that looked made just for her. A soft, silky, beige confection looking like spun sugar, which fell just below the knees. It was perfect. She had a small headdress made of the same material, with a small spray of pearls on one side of it to set it off and finally, high heeled shoes covered in matching material.

She was able to get it home and in the closet before Ryan returned. Then, for the first time thinking about her wedding, she became nervous. This was a commitment she was making to one person. How could she know if she was doing the right thing?

It would be too late after the ceremony. A beading of perspiration began to form on her forehead, she felt like she was burning up. Maybe a nice warm shower would make her feel better. She dropped her apparel into the laundry chute, picked up her robe and then selected a towel from the linen closet.

She tempered the water and then stepped in sliding the shower door closed behind her. It felt heavenly against her heated skin. She began to soap herself thoroughly.

Ryan arrived home carrying supper. Carry out from their favorite Italian restaurant with all the trimmings plus a bottle of good Chianti. The aroma made his mouth water in anticipation. Taking the stairs three at a time he hurried to his room to change into something more comfortable. Jens' door was closed. That meant she was home. Good, the food wouldn't have to be reheated.

When he finished changing he tapped on her door. When she didn't respond he knocked a little harder. Finally he actually pounded on it. This time he didn't wait but opened it immediately. She was nowhere in sight but he could hear the sound of the shower. "Hey! Jen....what's taking you so long? HELLO!...JEN?...He felt a barb of fear shoot through his chest making his heart pound. He hurried to the bathroom and flung the door open, the shower doors were closed but he should have been able to see her outline through the glass but there was no image, with a shock he realized there was no steam either.

Jennifer was lying on her side, skin white and the now cold water splashing heavily over her. Quickly he turned off the spigots and grabbed a heavy towel wrapping it about her. When he lifted her limp form he couldn't see that she was breathing. Carrying her to the bed he laid her down then put his ear to her chest listening for a heartbeat. Thank God there was one. He dialed 911 then tried to revive her by rubbing her briskly with the towel but getting no response.

When he heard the siren getting closer, he carried her downstairs wrapped in her favorite robe. The attendants placed her on the floor, checked her vital signs, and then secured her on the stretcher and took her away, the siren wail trailing away in the distance.

He arrived in emergency five minutes later. It took a while to get any information until he explained that he was her fiancé and she had no other relations. He was then told she was in the intensive care unit, in serious trouble with pneumonia. He wasn't allowed in with her, it was a matter of priority in case of an emergency. "You may as well go home sir, there's nothing you can do. We will call you if anything develops."

He couldn't bring himself to leave. He hung around the waiting room until close to midnight finally becoming so exhausted he had to give up and head for home.

When he arrived he didn't want to go to bed. He stretched out on the sofa and eventually fell asleep dreaming that he was at a funeral and it was him in the casket as they shoveled dirt into it, slowly filling it to the brim.

He awoke with a start, the room filled with early sunlight. Running his fingers across his chin he could feel he needed a shave, a shower and change of clothing. The next half hour accomplished that. He dug out a roll of Italian bread from the carry out meal he had brought home the previous evening. He felt if he didn't eat something he'd drop like a lead weight, better safe than sorry. Sipping a fresh cup of coffee he felt much better. He grabbed his jacket and headed for the hospital.

Jennifer was finally in a room. He had made arrangements for payment of any expenses regardless of the cost. They had her on oxygen and an IV was slowly dripping its fluid into the tubing that connected to her arm. She looked pale but thankfully, according to the doctor, she was on the mend.

"Thank God you're okay, Jen. I was scared to death finding you unconscious in the shower. I have no idea how long you were lying there being drenched with cold water. It makes me nervous just imagining what could have happened if I hadn't come home when I did, you could have died."

"It DID almost happen, Ryan. They'll keep me here for a while to make sure the incident doesn't occur again before I'm recovered." Jennifer had a haunted look on her face which made Ryan nervous.

"So! What happened that put that odd look on your face, Jen? You're in the hospital for Pete's sake, the safest place to be. It couldn't have been anything that serious."

"Ryan, what happened scared the daylights out of me. After the examination, they said I would be staying a while. They had a room available and took me up on the elevator. Once there, the gurney was wheeled out. A nurse stayed with me while I put on the hospital gown. Suddenly my lungs stopped functioning, I only had enough breath in them to say, "Help me, I can't breathe." Another nurse was there immediately. She sat me on the edge of the bed, pulled the tray table over, laid a pillow on top and leaned me over it. She put a stethoscope on my back and I heard her say "There's no air going in." That's when the lack of oxygen caused me to pass out. I don't know how much time elapsed but suddenly I gulped in a huge breath of air as a nurse was pushing furiously on my back shouting. BREATHE…BREATHE…I opened my eyes to see four people standing around watching. They made sure I was okay before they left, that I was settled into bed. Later a nurse came in with a pencil and paper. She began to question me about my life, childhood, school, family and various subjects. It was only after she was gone that I realized they were checking for damage the lack of oxygen may have caused. I must have been in the danger zone but I'll never know. How can I remember what has been erased?"

They both sat in silence, the immensity of what could have happened forestalling any conversation.

"Jennifer, by the time you get out of here you'll feel like yourself again. I'm thankful that any loss of memory didn't include me, I don't know what

I would have done. Are you sure that you want to go through with the wedding? Has there been any change in the way you feel toward me?"

For a moment Jennifer sat silently, a forlorn look blanketing her features until she seemed to reach a conclusion. She drew in a deep breath of air and then, giving Ryan a loving smile, reaffirmed her love and commitment to him. She didn't want to mention that she had forgotten what her wedding dress looked like. She wondered what other memories she could have lost. This was something she would have to maneuver through. She didn't want Ryan, nor anyone else, to think there was something lacking in her. She'd rather die that feel inferior. She'd had enough of that after spending so many years in the orphanage, there wasn't much there to give a kid a sense of character. She'd just have to keep her fingers crossed and muddle through any future difficulties. When Ryan bent to kiss her goodbye, she reached an arm about his neck and pulled him to her. She didn't want to let him go.

Leaving the hospital, Ryan didn't feel like going home. He felt restless and uneasy, the idea that Jen would be in the hospital for a while was upsetting but he didn't want her home until she was out of danger. On the spur of the moment he headed for his dad's home, it had been a while since he had visited. In fact it had been just after Rose had come home from the hospital with the baby, his new brother Scott.

He could hear the chimes as he stood at the door impatiently pushing the button. It seemed to take forever before the door opened and his father stood before him looking a bit frazzled.

"Well! This is a surprise son, what brings you here on this cloudy, autumn day? I can't remember the last time you set foot in my door, too busy to visit or phone your dear old dad?" Alex stepped aside to admit his son and then closed the door and led him into the kitchen, the aroma of fresh coffee and bacon permeating the air and reminding Ryan of the hearty breakfasts they used to enjoy. Suddenly his mouth filled with digestive juices waiting for that first bite of flavorful bacon and eggs. With a quick swallow he hurriedly glanced at the stove. "Sorry, didn't mean to disturb your meal, dad, but that sure smells good."

"There's plenty here, son, sit down I'll fix you a plate. Rose will be right down, she had to bathe and change Scott while I fixed breakfast. You'll be amazed at how fast he's growing."

Ryan settled down at his old place at the table while Alex filled three plates with hash browns, Canadian bacon and eggs. A stack of wheat toast was carried and set in the center of the table. Ryan couldn't believe how hungry he felt but politely sat waiting for his father and Rose to join him.

When Rose walked into the room holding Scott, Ryan rose from his seat and went to meet her, taking his first look at the baby since he had been brought home from the hospital. Rose placed Scott in his arms and then went to sit at the table. She watched the expression on Ryan's face with amusement as his brow furrowed with a worried look, feeling uneasy holding something as delicate as a new baby. She couldn't help bursting out with laughter seeing the identical expressions that her husband had exhibited.

Alex took the squirming burden from Ryan, giving him a proud grin as he placed the baby over his shoulder and began to pat his back. Shortly, after a loud burp sounded, Alex placed his son in the bassinette that sat nearby. He then joined them at the table.

It was a leisurely meal spent catching up on all the latest family news. They were concerned to learn that Jen was in the hospital but that, however, was after Ryan had filled them in on all the other developments about Jennifer. Her loss of family, the orphanage and most shocking, that Ryan's house had once belonged to her parents.

It was late afternoon when Ryan finally headed for home, he couldn't recall the last time he'd enjoyed himself so much. His dad looked fit and enormously happy as did Rose. He hoped one day that his future would be as fulfilled. Hopefully, the first step would be taken at his wedding. When Jennifer was released from the hospital and recovered enough to stand with him as they took their marriage vows.

Evening visiting hours were at seven. Ryan showered and donned a fresh change of clothing. He planned to stop at a local florist and buy a bouquet of flowers for Jennifer, something colorful to cheer her up. She had been so depressed that morning.

Jennifer was dozing when he entered the room. She looked much better than she had earlier. He placed the flowers on the window ledge and then planted a kiss on her forehead before pulling the chair closer to her bed and sitting down to wait for her to awaken. Her coloring looked more normal and he noticed they had taken her off oxygen. He gave a sigh of relief, maybe she'd be home sooner than he'd expected.

Leaning his head against the chair back and letting his body relax, he could feel the tension draining from his system. He fell asleep, the anxiety over Jen and his restless night finally taking a toll on him.

He was in the attic. The morning sun, lighting the multicolored windows, caused a rainbow of hues to highlight all the assorted objects that had been accumulated over the years. It was beautiful. Every nook and cranny illuminated, the darkness swept away. He knew for certain he was asleep in a chair at the hospital, yet the feeling of reality seeing the half-moon lighted windows made him accept, without question, the fact that, indeed, he was also standing in the center of the attic.

His eyes scanned the contents, searching for he knew not what, but non-the-less seeking that which would hold his attention. Sight was drawn to a small wooden chest tucked in the depths of a shadowy corner. Like a sleepwalker, he made his way through the dusty obstacles until he was standing before it.

When he reached out his hand and his fingers brushed its surface, the lid slowly opened as though an invisible key had turned releasing its lock. He stepped closer to peer into the contents where a golden haze shimmered invitingly, asking him to enter it's realm of mystery. He accepted its invitation and took a step forward, a strong feeling of confidence making his decision unobjectionable. He was at the brink, ready to take his first step into the unknown when he felt something touch his shoulder, a pressure that he tried to ignore without success. Angrily he swatted at the intrusion but in moments, his eyes opened to the nurse gently shaking his shoulder to awaken him from his slumber. The feeling of discontent about the interruption to his seemingly lifelike dream lasted but only a moment, Jennifer was awake, looking surprisingly bright and healthy. The feeling of euphoria he had experienced standing at the brink of mystery reappeared. At that moment he knew, in the very center of his being, that Jennifer was going to be released. She would be going home with him that very day.

"Ryan, you were sleeping like a baby, I spoke to you several times trying to awaken you but when the nurse came in, she managed very easily. Honey! You'll never guess, the Doc gave me an okay to go home. It's a good thing you came when you did or I'd be here another day. He's signing my release papers even as we speak. You'll have to go home and get me some clothing. I can't wear that robe you brought me here in."

Ryan couldn't help smiling because he'd taken the robe home days ago. There were already garments hanging here in the closet for her to wear. He had been so anxious for her release that he'd done everything to prepare for it.

"Get dressed sweetheart. I'll go get the car and then I'll be right back to wheel you out. I can't wait to get you out of here and back home where you belong."

Within less than an hour they were on their way, neither could wait to walk in their front door. When they arrived Ryan carried Jen up the steps and set her on her feet. He opened the door and watched with a smile as she walked through it, a contented smile on her face seeing the familiar settings with a new look. This was where she belonged.

"Come into the kitchen, honey, I'll fix a light supper and then we can cuddle up on the couch in the living room and watch a movie or, if you prefer, just play a few games of dominos, whatever your heart desires.

Jennifer sat at the table sipping at a hot cup of tea while she watched Ryan stir fry some mixed vegetables. When they were cooked to his satisfaction he mixed in four scrambled eggs. When he felt the bottom was cooked, he flipped it over, added some shredded Swiss cheese, folded it in half and placed the cover over it. Five minutes later they were enjoying their omelets, a light flavorful meal that sat easily on the stomach.

Afterwards they remained seated playing their games of Dominos. Jennifer won the first game with a shutout, and then Ryan scored his win on the second. By then they were both feeling sleepy and decided to retire for the evening.

Morning came early, waking them with the sounds of thunder and lightning, a rather unusual occurrence at this late time of year. Rain drops turned into pellets of ice bouncing over the ground like miniature jumping beans. A blanket of white began to cover the surface when the sleet turned into snow, the first snowfall of the year.

"Do you realize, Ryan, that we've made no plans for Thanksgiving? I think it'd be a great idea if we had the entire family over for a grand holiday dinner. I'll fix a turkey with all the trimmings. Rose could bring the pies and Sylvia the salad and rolls. It'd be a hassle free day for everyone and we'd all love being able to catch up on all our family news. What d'you think, does that sound good?"

"I'm game, but we should let everyone know right away before they make plans. We've never gotten everyone together since before Rose got pregnant. I'll phone them right away." Ryan felt a rush of excitement, the thought of a family gathering at his new home, especially for a holiday, brought all sorts of ideas to mind. He wanted it to be an outstanding occasion, one that everyone would recall with smiles of remembered pleasure. He had to think of something original and different. It was then that a great idea bloomed. He'd have to contact a specialist but it would be a great surprise for all.

Before the day ended, acceptances from everyone had been received. Both Rose and Sy were happy to bring their additions to the holiday meal and Alex was bringing champagne to celebrate the occasion.

Ryan had brought his idea to fruition, he'd contacted a professional. Jen was unaware of his plans. On the day that Jennifer had an appointment with her hairdresser and a luncheon date with Rose, he put his plan into action. When she returned home she was unaware of anything unusual.

The days edged their way toward Thanksgiving. The day before was filled with pre-dinner preparations. Celery cleaned and sliced into 4" stalks filled with flavored cream cheese, the giblets simmered then diced into tiny fragments with plenty of onions and sage added, ready to be mixed into sage/onion croutons to make the stuffing. Deviled eggs, cranberry sauce and jelly, green and black olives, all in covered dishes stacked in the refrigerator ready to be placed on the table the next day. The formal table set with china, sterling silver, and etched stemware. All that could be pre-readied had been.

Thanksgiving Day dawned clear and cold with the forecast of snow for later that evening. Everyone planned on arriving around 2p.m. Dinner would be at three, late enough after breakfasts for good appetites to rekindle and appreciate a good holiday meal.

Rose brought two pumpkin and an apple, pies. Sylvia brought salad and two dozen home baked rolls, a recipe her Granny sometimes made. The aroma of baking turkey permeated the rooms making everyone anticipate savoring it. Ryan showed everyone around his home, through the upstairs and then even down into the basement which he was remodeling. They were full of compliments at the decorating he had done and of course, he gave Sylvia many compliments on the color schemes she had suggested to him.

They all enjoyed the tour with much conversation and even a few jokes about Jennifer having her own bedroom since the wedding had been put on hold.

By 3:15p.m. they were all at the table, a Thanksgiving prayer having been said and champagne toasts made for their health and happiness. This was the first family get-together ever, which they planned on continuing as a tradition every year. Dinner was devoured with gusto, everyone passed on dessert, suggesting that having it later with freshly made coffee would top the meal off nicely. It was then that Ryan gave a nod to Jennifer. She excused herself. Ryan led everyone into the living room where they settled into chairs or stood near the fireplace gazing into the warmth of the flames.

When the doorbell rang Ryan went to answer it at the same time that Jennifer came down the stairway wearing a beautiful soft, silky beige dress, with a tiny matching head piece. When she reached the living room the minister was already in place waiting for her. Everyone was astounded, never having had any inkling that they would also be guests attending Ryan and Jennifer's wedding. The ceremony was brief, vows spoken. They were now husband and wife. The minister was given an envelope and departed.

Alex gave his son a hug. The sudden thought that maybe in the future he could become a grandfather brought a huge smile. It was a joy that nothing could compare to. "Good luck, son. Just remember, marriage is very much like a roller coaster ride. There are ups and downs, but eventually, it all evens out. I'm here for you anytime you need me.

"Is everyone ready for coffee and dessert? Jen lead the way into the dining room. The women departed for the kitchen. Coffee was made and pies sliced with their ice cream or whipped topping. Two trays were carried in and set on the table, dessert dispensed to everyone according to choice. The evening was winding down.

After all the plates and utensils were tucked into the dishwasher, the crystal hand washed, dried and put away. It was time to bring celebrations to a close. Everyone agreed it had been an exceptional holiday, the marriage ceremony made it unique. They were very happy to have been included in the double celebration, a memorable day they would always treasure.

After the last goodbye, Ryan and Jen were alone. They both felt a little awkward, this was the wedding night both had awaited. With a last look around the kitchen to make sure all was neat, nothing left undone. They turned off the lights and made their way upstairs. Jen returned to her bedroom to remove her wedding apparel and don her special wedding night negligee, a light spray of perfume enveloped her as she made her way down the hall and into Ryan's bedroom. Dim candlelight and softly muted romantic music played from hidden stereo speakers. She could see a path of rose petals trailing from the door over to the bed. Covers were turned down, ready for the newlyweds. Ryan was already ensconced, head resting against one of the satin pillows, hair neatly combed, awaiting his new bride.

Jen blew out the candles and settled herself against his warmth. A muffled snore almost made her giggle out loud but controlling herself, she also was soon fast asleep.

When they awoke the next morning, almost at the same instant, Ryan couldn't believe Jennifer was tucked comfortably next to him. He didn't recall any romantic activities they had been involved in, therefore, he must have been sound asleep....and that was on his wedding night, the night they both had been waiting for.

"Aw! Jen, I'm so sorry, I ruined everything for you. I had all those romantic plans made and all for naught, I swear I didn't feel a bit sleepy. I wanted to save us some awkwardness, or at least I thought I was, by being in bed when you entered. Are you terribly disappointed? I know I can't change what happened since there's only one wedding night, but I'll do anything to please you and make up for it."

"Come here, dear husband of mine and give me a kiss, there's nothing to make up for. You can't imagine the comfort I felt when I cuddled up to the warmth of your body, the satisfaction of realizing I would never feel alone again because I have you. I've never slept that soundly in all my life, I think this must be the often spoken feeling of "Togetherness" when married people love each other and grow old together."

Ryan couldn't think of a word to say in reply, he gathered her in his arms held her closely and kissed her until she was breathless. The wait until their wedding was finally over, she was all that he had imagined and more.

Later, almost as though they had been doing it for years, they showered together, even washing each other's backs. Then, with towels wrapped about, they used the double sinks to do their morning grooming activities, glancing often at each other in the mirror with smiles of camaraderie and pleasure.

Jen went to her bedroom to dress, and then hurried downstairs to prepare breakfast while Ryan shaved. The most wonderful feeling of contentment had settled upon her making the day seem bright and sunny, although the weather outside was definitely winter like.

When Ryan entered the kitchen, fresh coffee had been brewed. The aroma of hash browns with onions, made his mouth water and Jen had also made him a fluffy cheese omelet. She was content having toast with orange marmalade after enjoying a soft boiled egg.

"I'll be away most of the day, Honey. Alex and I are in the process of developing another shopping mall out on the west side. What's nice is that we'll have 10% ownership in it, the same as the last one we did. Owning part of the two shopping malls will bring in enough income for both of us, ad infinitum, um, year after year, sorry, didn't mean to get wordy, sweetheart." Ryan gave her a whole-hearted kiss and a hug that took her breath away, and then he was out the door.

She realized not going away on a honeymoon suited her just fine. He'd had this appointment pre-arranged long before the wedding plans. They were both completely satisfied with their mutual decision.

After the kitchen had been neatened, the dishwasher cleared of all the Thanksgiving dinnerware which she put away, she placed that morning's dishes in their designated slots where they'd sit until the washer had been fully loaded again.

Back upstairs, she made the bed, picked up the soiled laundry and towels dropping them down the old fashioned laundry chute. This was so handy, no lugging dirty clothing down to the basement. After a quick cleanup of the bathroom, she was finished.

When the phone rang she expected to hear Ryan's voice and was surprised to hear it was Sylvia. "Hi! Is everything okay, Sy? I was just thinking of calling you. Ryan is working on a new development project. I'd caught up on all the minor housework and was feeling a bit restless not knowing what to do with all this spare time. Would you like some company this morning?"

"How did you guess, Jen? I'm bored silly. I've already taken care of my "Common Sense" column, the laundry is done, and I just cleaned house two days ago. How about if I come visit you? If I don't get out of this house for a while I'll lose my mind."

"Come on over, Sy, I'll even put on a pot of tea for you. I have a few new flavors that you'll enjoy sampling."

By the time Sylvia arrived she was in a very good mood and when Jen opened the door she gave her an impulsive hug. "Thank goodness, Jen, I need some one-on-one woman talk. Men just don't have any concept of the idea, they get bored awfully fast. So, what's on your agenda? Anything new you're considering venturing into?" Sylvia dropped into the kitchen chair, ready to have a good old fashioned girl talk.

"Nope, I'm in the same boat you are. One thing though Sy, I want to clear the air between us about how nasty I was trying to trick David. I've never apologized to you. I want us to be friends."

"Jennifer, David thought it was fantastic. He said it was something that guys dream about. When he told me about it, the more he talked, the madder I got until I thought I'd blow my top but David?....The more he related the incident, the more he smirked, until he was laughing out loud. I could have killed him on the spot but then I started laughing too and we couldn't stop. It was a side of him I never realized, just a typical guy."

They spent the morning becoming friends. Finally Jennifer took Sy up to the attic to show her all her family memorabilia stored there. It was still a mystery to her about the loss of her memory. It was seeing these old precious things that had restored her past and the loss of her mother, father and brother only now, after all these years, weighing heavily on her heart.

"I sometimes shudder to think that if I had not met Ryan, if he had not purchased this house, I would never have gotten in touch with my childhood. I would have continued to be a useless human being without any past memories of family to give me an anchor in life."

Sylvia put her arms around Jen with a hug to give her a measure of comfort. It must be a terrible blow to find that you once had a loving family but you can never talk to or renew family ties because they're all dead. Suddenly she was deeply thankful she had found her mother and father. She'd hate to be in Jennifer's shoes.

*   *   *   *   *   *   *   *   *   *

CHAPTER 9

Years had elapsed and now orders for the orphanage to close its doors had been followed until not a child remained. They had been disbursed to other institutions across the country that had room for a few new placements. Supervisor Gladys Cummings breathed a sigh of relief. The last door had been closed and she was safe at last. There was no way anyone could trace a path to her and the missing child. She had been forty five when she had made the stealthy move to take the boy, being first at the scene before the police or ambulance arrived. She had placed the baby, child seat and all into her own car, it had been so easy. And once the girl was placed in her care at the orphanage, she had told the child that her baby brother had been killed in the accident along with her parents. Gladys had named the boy Robert, after her own recently deceased child, she'd used her son's birth certificate. Robby belonged to her by law, at least that's how she felt.

Tomorrow, December 3rd Robby would turn 19. He was a handsome young man, black hair, beautiful brown eyes. He'd wanted to enter community college this past fall after graduating from high school in June but instead, had found a terrific job working on a new mall that was going to open in the spring. The builder had taken an interest in his mathematical skills and offered him good pay with possible future employment. Rob had jumped at the chance. Gladys thought it an excellent opportunity.

The first paycheck he'd brought home had almost made Gladys eyes pop out at the amount of money Rob had earned. She encouraged him to bank most of it, the first chance there had ever been extra money to save. She hoped he could eventually afford a car because her's was on its last legs, no longer dependable and too far gone to spend money on for repairs. She'd hoped to present him with a good, reliable, second hand auto for his graduation but was unable to find one she could afford. What was really nice about his new job was that they allowed him to use one of their pickup trucks. Occasionally the boss phoned and asked him to pick up something, sometimes it was breakfasts for the crew which he could charge on a special card the boss gave him to use. He even let him buy extra to bring home to her.

Sitting in the rocker Gladys dozed off, a half smile on her face recalling the day she had first brought Robby home from the accident. It had been the smartest move she had ever made. She could have cared for him in the orphanage but she wanted more for him than the dull routine that made up each endless day. She had been able to help Jennifer though, gave her extra lessons and finally allowed her to do the bookkeeping which had been a good experience for her. She'd been a hard worker and learned quickly. It was too bad no one had been interested in adopting her. At least, from what she had read in the papers, she was married to a good man and had the chance of a full happy life.

A soft snore issued from Gladys's lips. She was once again taking her afternoon snooze, comfortable that there would be no interruptions for the entire day. She'd awaken at her usual time and bustle about fixing something for Robby's supper. She had a nice lean beef steak to fry for him and would heat up the leftover fried potatoes and onions from yesterday, he loved them so much. It was a recipe handed down from the days of the 20's depression, a good old standby that everyone liked.

When Rob arrived home several hours later, Gladys was still in her chair sound asleep. He looked at her tired, lined, face recalling the many times she had soothed his aches and pains, tended his scrapes and read bedtime stories to him about knights in shining armor and brave young men off to seek their fortunes or rescue princesses in distress. He thought she was the best mother a son could ever have. Now that she was growing old, it was time that he took care of her. He showered, changed into jeans, a T-shirt and leather slides and went to the kitchen to prepare supper for the two of them. He saw the thick steak, perfect for two. Using a sharp knife he split the thickness into two evenly divided portions, seasoned them with a little pepper and placed them under the broiler. The potatoes he reheated on the stove. He set the table with plates, utensils and two glasses filled with milk. When the steaks were ready he went to awaken Gladys. With a startled snort she awoke but seeing her son kneeling in front of her, she took his face between her hands and planted a big kiss on his forehead. Robby tugged her from the chair and led her into the kitchen, a pleased smile on his face that he'd had a chance to surprise her.

"Oh! Sonny, what did you do? I was all ready to have that nice steak broiled for you and there I was, sleeping like a lazybones, and that, after you had worked so hard all day too. I'm ashamed of myself. I'll do better tomorrow, I promise. Where did you get the extra steak? Oh! You didn't....That was for you. After all that hard work you need good food and enough of it to keep your strength up."

Gladys tried to push her plate toward Robby, but he would have none of it. "Mom! Stop right now, you've been eating like a bird, you need this. You're forgetting that I get plenty to eat at lunch time, the boss's treat to the entire crew. From now on we don't have to scrimp on food anymore. I can start paying you some of my upkeep every week, and it's about time. There are so many things we need that I don't know where to begin. Some new dresses and shoes for you, that's for sure. Then, good grief, we sure need a good car. Another thing I'd really like to do is to get you out of this rental and into a real house. I know it seems a lot, but this job I have will last for a few years. I've heard that the boss is very good with bonuses too."

Rob had a mental list that seemed bottomless. Always something new to add, but for sure, he wanted to get into a new place, maybe a "fixer-upper." Something with good possibilities that he could work on while they lived there. At least it would be theirs. He hated seeing rent money fly out the window, a waste of cash when ownership put the money in your own pocket. Tomorrow he decided to talk to his boss and ask for his advice, maybe he knew of someplace for sale that was within his means. It was worth a try.

After their meal had been consumed Robby helped with the dishes. Afterward they sat in the living room watching the news on television. By ten they were both ready to retire. Robby kissed Gladys cheek, wished her a "Goodnight" and departed for the back bedroom. He was more tired than he had realized. He fell into a dreamless sleep. Dreamless that is, until a shadowy figure appeared on the outskirts of his memory and began to take shape. The more solid it became, the more fearful he felt, until he was inundated with dread. In his dream he stood outside the nightmare watching the events that unfurled. There was something so familiar about it, a memory that was trying to find its way back but he did not want to face it.

When morning dawned Robby did not recall his dreams, thankfully so, because they would have been upsetting to him. The aroma of bacon roused him from bed, his mom already preparing breakfast.

As soon as he finished eating he left immediately for his new job. He truly enjoyed working outdoors and the fresh air was invigorating, even though sometimes a bit too cold. Better though than that heated stuff all the offices were exposed to. He'd take fresh air any day of the week.

Today they were completing the last section of the exterior of the shopping complex. With the roofing on they'd have an easier time working inside. His boss was putting him to work alongside licensed contractors where he'd have a chance of learning the ropes and doing a good job. One of the regular contractors, Mr. Matt Lawford, had taken a liking to him. He was also a friend of Alex Williams, the man who had hired him. It was working out just fine. Anyone who needed extra help, Rob was available. He kept track of his hours and at the end of every day gave the information to Mr. Williams or to his son, Ryan.

That morning went well. Around noon Alex drew Robby aside and told him he would now be an apprentice to Mr. Lawford. After learning the craft as an apprentice, he'd be able to apply for a license. He sat with Mr. Williams and his son Ryan as they all ate lunch discussing the job and how well it was moving along.

"So! Rob, how is your family? Do you have any sisters or brothers who are looking for work? We can always use extra help keeping the work area clean. It's minimum wage but at least good for earning spending money. If you know of anyone wanting some part-time work let me know." Alex was smiling as he was looking at Robb. The kid was a hard worker and he likely had the same type of friends, at least that's what he'd learned about people a long time ago just like the old adage referred to, "Birds of a feather," sort of thing, it was so true.

"Nope! Mr. Alex, all I have is my mom and she's getting up in age. She said I was her "Change of Life" baby at age 49, I'll be twenty on my next birthday. You'll never know how much this job means to us. It was pretty tight while I was still in school although I did work some part-time jobs to help with expenses. One thing I'd really like to do is earn enough to buy a little house, one that's maybe a little run-down, inexpensive and needs work so we can own our own home instead of renting. It's such a big waste of money." Rob had a wistful look on his face, his dream of ownership showing for all to see.

Alex felt a tug at his heart. He was a good, hardworking kid. He tried to imagine what it had been like for him going to school and working to help pay bills, not being able to chum around with friends or even have time he could call his own. He made up his mind to keep his eyes out for just such a place, maybe help with the purchase price and also the fixing up. Just thinking about the pleasure it would give put a wide grin on his face.

Lunchtime over, everyone went back to work and at day's end, the structure was secured against intruders and everyone went home.

Alex, however, had his eyes peeled all the way home looking for a little house, in a decent neighborhood that could use a little tender, loving care. He was bound and determined to make the kids dream come true.

The last thing Gladys Cummings wanted was for Robby to get hooked up with the Williams family. She had followed Jennifer's activities since she had left the orphanage. The marriage between her and Ryan Williams, with Robby now working for Ryan's father, was tempting fate. She didn't know how to halt the friendship that seemed to be developing between Alex and her son. If Jennifer and Robby met, it's certain they would recognize similarities they shared and begin asking questions. It made Gladys feel ill just thinking about the possibility, there had to be something she could do. For the next week, almost every moment was spent pondering the danger of being discovered as a thief. The only solution, as far as she could determine, was getting out of town and moving as far away as possible. The problem was trying to convince Robert the move was necessary. Try as she may, she couldn't think of a way to do that, he liked his new job and the pay that went with it. She was stuck. Aside from doping him and dragging him away, there was nothing she could do to avert the fate that foretold the meeting of Jennifer and her brother. She tried to recall the brother's real name, it had been so long ago, it was…Ah! Jason. That was his name, the two double J's, Jenny and Jason.

Gladys dozed off, dreaming of police coming through the door, handcuffs ready to take her away. Robby angry, turning away from her and the pain it caused losing his love, losing him after all the years she had treasured him as her boy, the perfect replacement for the son she had lost. She felt her heart breaking and could not halt the tears.

Morning drifted into afternoon, until finally the song of crickets drifting through the opened window along with the misty scent of evening dew, signaled the lateness of the hour.

Robby was just getting home after working extra hours helping with a last minute emergency effort to secure the workplace after a major theft had been discovered from the previous night. Several expensive tools had been stolen that had hindered the day's schedule.

Reaching for the wall switch, he turned on the light and closed the door behind him. When he turned, the sight of his mother sitting asleep in the easy chair almost made him laugh aloud. She would be furious that she'd not had supper ready for him. When he bent to kiss her cheek however, and felt the coldness of her skin, he realized it was not a nap.

"Aw! Mom, I should have been here with you, I didn't have a chance to tell you goodbye, and that I loved you." He noticed a trail of tear stains on her cheeks and took his handkerchief out to gently wipe them away. "I wanted to find a little house for you Mom, something where you could plant flowers in your own yard, maybe have a little kitten or puppy to keep you company while I was at work. It was almost within reach if only things could have happened just a little earlier, if time had waited just a little longer."

Rob sat on the couch near her, tears streaming down his cheeks, his throat hurting from trying to hold in sobs. "You never complained, never asked for more. You were a good mom and I loved you very much."

He reached over and picked up the telephone to call the police. They were there in a very short time and the coroner soon after.

He couldn't sleep. There was too much to do and he didn't have the money. The coroner would have her for two or three days, then he'd have to have everything ready for her. He decided that cremation would be the best. At least he could get a loan and make payments for it. Then maybe take the ashes someplace pretty that she'd like, somewhere with trees and a brook which sounded peaceful.

He kept wondering if he'd missed something, maybe she'd been feeling ill and hadn't wanted to say anything. He felt a heavy burden of guilt weigh on his conscience. She'd never complained, but now he wondered if she'd been in misery and he'd been too self-absorbed to notice. Head in hands, he didn't notice a car pull up in front of the house, all he could see was his mother resting in the chair, cold and dead, gone forever, and his selfish self-centered ways of not paying enough attention to her.

THE THISTLE SEED

The sharp rap on the door shook him from his misery. When he went to answer it Alex was standing rigidly at attention, a look of deep concern on his face.

"The office phoned me, I'm here and whatever needs to be done we'll accomplish this morning. Come along Robert, we have things to do. Are you planning to have a funeral with casket and a burial or is there something else you have in mind? You've been a good worker, everyone likes you and I have plans to keep you around for as long as you like working for me, so don't be concerned about any funeral expense right now. We can have a payment schedule set up with my payroll clerk. No need to borrow money and pay atrocious interest charges when you can get the money from me without any fees. How does that sound to you? Right now we're going to my house. My wife Rose is even now fixing us a good breakfast that will tide us over for the time being. You're on paid leave from work, my son Ryan is taking care of business for me so you and I have all the time we need."

Rob was speechless. Everything was happening so quickly that he couldn't keep up with all that Alex had said. By the time they were sitting at Alex's breakfast table, eating pancakes and sausage, he was beginning to clear his mind and pay attention to what Alex was suggesting. When they had finished eating and the table was cleared, they continued to sit discussing what Rob wanted to do.

Cremation with a small ceremony at the funeral parlor and then Rob would take his mothers ashes to the closest stream to scatter them. She had always talked about loving to fish when she had been a kid and she loved being around water. He had a feeling this would please her very much.

Alex invited Rob to stay over with them, it would only be for a few days, then, after the funeral, they could figure out what to do next.

The following days were a blur to Robert. After having Gladys cremated, which took several days, he at last took her ashes to a stream located near an old cider mill which was closed for the season. The weather had not been cold enough to freeze and the stream was fast flowing, entering Lake St. Claire, the Detroit River, Lake Erie, over Niagara Falls and eventually into the Atlantic Ocean.

"Goodbye mom, I'm going to miss you so much. It will seem strange not seeing you when I walk in the door after work, or in the morning when I awaken and you're not there to share coffee time with me." With a swing of his arm her ashes were tossed into the wind and strewn over the water. He watched with heavy heart as an eddy swirled a moment and then floated the ashes swiftly away on the current.

When Robby returned to the house the entire atmosphere seemed changed. It felt empty. Not just that his mother was no longer there, but a definite feeling of vacancy. He felt like a stranger walking through the rooms, seeing everything as though for the very first time. He wondered how the absence of a person could create such a vacuum. It wasn't the same feeling as though the person had stepped outside for a moment, or was off shopping for a day, it was an absolute emptiness. He dropped down into the nearest seat realizing for the very first time that he was completely alone in the world, not a single living relative to share that feeling of continuity with.

Finally, a measure of peace settled upon him and he began to make plans. He didn't want to stay here, that was definite. All he needed to find was a small room with a bath. There was still three weeks to go on this months' lease but the landlord could have it in lieu of notice. There wasn't a thing worth keeping in the entire place, the only items he'd take would be the TV set and the strongbox his mom kept papers in.

Within an hour he'd notified the landlord, packed his clothing, and put the TV set along with the other items in the old car, sparkplugs replaced a few weeks ago and good for a few more miles. With a last glance at the deserted residence, he drove away.

The next few days, staying with Alex and Rose, were a great comfort to him. He shared his grief and feelings of abandonment with Rose who told him about her estrangement from her mother and how much she regretted not getting home in time to see her before her death. She talked about her daughter Sylvia who was expecting her first child, and about Alex's son Ryan who had recently married. The closeness of their family made Robby see that his life would be what he made of it. One day he too would marry and have children and he'd put his entire heart and soul into making it a happy home. He hoped he'd end up having a houseful of kids. The thought made him smile because he'd seen what having a new baby had done for Alex and his wife.

The next few days passed peacefully until Alex, while speaking to an acquaintance about having problems finding something suitable for Robby, learned of a senior couple who had an apartment available. Alex took Robby to see it.

It was small, furnished, and very reasonable rent with all utilities included. Alex thought it unsatisfactory but Robby liked it. Inside the front door there was a small entrance hallway. The door on the left was to the owners living quarters, the apartment door directly ahead.

On entering, the small, grey-carpeted, living room had a couch and chair. A white metal storage cabinet sat against the wall behind where the apartment entrance door opened. The small closet-sized kitchen was on the left-front wall of the room, a small 5 x 6 area without any door. On the kitchens left wall, right next to its entry, sat a small fridge. Next to it, a low metal cabinet where a toaster could sit on top with pots/pans stored on the two shelves beneath. There was a sliding-panel window in the wall over the cabinet. On the right side kitchen wall was a single stainless steel sink with a two door cupboard overhead. Next to the sink sat an apartment sized gas stove. The area in the center was about 5ft deep and 4ft wide, large enough to turn around in. Next to the kitchen door in the living room was a narrow 2 x 4 Formica-topped table with one chair. There were two tall windows in the living room. A narrow hallway ran down the left of the apartment, halfway down was the door to the bathroom and at the end, a room with bed, triple dresser and a nice long closet. A tall window gave plenty of light, the bedroom and hallway carpeted with a pretty blue. The entire place was bright and cheerful, the walls painted a soft white.

Rob could feel his spirits lift. The place was clean, in a nice neighborhood and most important of all, it was within his budget. "I'll take it. Do I need a security deposit? Mr. Alex can vouch for me, I work for him. For the first time, Rob looked at the apartment with the eyes of a tenant. It was perfect.

Ray Owens liked the looks of the kid. He was young, just about the age he'd been when Liz and he had married, he couldn't believe how long ago that had been.

"No! kid, no security deposit required as long as you keep the place clean, take out your trash and don't have any wild parties. You look like a sensible young fella, I can see that your boss likes you. It's $225 per month, first and last month's rent due now. You can move in immediately."

Rob sorted the bills from his pocket of cash and handed over the $450.00. Ray left to get a receipt. He handed it over, along with the keys to the front door and apartment, shook hands with Alex and then with Robert and returned to his own dwelling.

"Are you really sure you want this place, Rob? It sure looks small but I have to admit, it's been well taken care of and the rent's reasonable. If there's nothing else you need me around for I'm going to hit the road, I have to get back to the job. You can return to work on Monday, there's no sense showing up today, it's already half over and we're not working weekends. We're pretty much on target getting the job done on time." Alex gave Rob a friendly pat on the back as he headed for the door.

"Thanks Mr. Williams. I'll be there bright and early and thanks for all your help, I never would have found this place and I like it a lot."

Rob brought his belongings in and put them away in the dresser drawers. He placed the television set on the chair and plugged it in, adjusted the rabbit ears, and then sat back on the couch watching the news. When it dawned on him he had some shopping to do he checked the cupboards to see what kitchen items he'd need. A complete dish set was in the cupboard, pots, pans and utensils in the drawer and cupboard section of the metal cabinet. He looked into the tall metal cabinet near the front door, the shelves were empty but clean. Good for canned good, extra cleaning supplies. He had noticed a narrow door in the hallway. When he looked there were five shelves, a place to put towels and sheets.

When he headed out the door his head was filled with a list of all he needed. Of course, he didn't succeed in purchasing everything that first day. But he did stock the tall metal one with canned foods, bath soap, cleaning supplies, sponges. He bought new toothbrushes, paste, deodorant, shaving supplies. Towels and wash cloths, and an order of fried chicken with biscuits. When he finished eating he was exhausted. He wrapped the trash and set it in the fridge to put out in the garbage container in the morning. After making up his bed with clean sheets from home and taking a hot shower, he dropped into bed, almost asleep before his head hit the pillow.

The next day was a similar experience of making lists and purchases. The last thing he bought was a canister vacuum cleaner, easy to get under furniture. He was bound and determined to keep his place as neat as a pin. Shopping was over, it was time to take it easy and enjoy his new abode, but for the first time since his mother's death he had nothing to distract himself from the fact he was now completely alone. He had to get through the rest of today and then Sunday. Monday seemed a very long time to wait for.

He washed the dishes that were in the cupboard, two stainless steel pots and the Teflon-coated fry pan and stored them away. He decided to find the nearest Laundromat. He'd wash the two new bath towel sets along with the six pair of white work socks he'd purchased plus his soiled clothing. At least that should take up the remainder of today. He used two pillow cases to carry the items.

He sat listening to the two washers swishing and spinning. Then it was the dryers turn as they tossed and flung the articles hither and about until the bell signaled they were dry. After folding everything and trying to keep a semblance of neatness, he stuffed it all back into the same two, now clean, pillow cases. He knew there was yet another item he needed, a laundry basket. He wondered if the needing ever ended when one went out to live on their own. It had been one thing after another since he'd left the old house.

Back home, after the clean items had been stashed away in their respective places, he heated up the contents of a can of tomato soup for his supper. A few crackers scattered over the top of it in the old fashioned stoneware bowl made a satisfactory meal. He didn't feel very hungry. Later, he sat lethargically contemplating the empty hours remaining until bedtime. When he leaned his head back to rest it against the couch his eyes spotted the strongbox he had placed on the very top of the metal cabinet near the front door. He had forgotten all about it in his hurry to get settled in.

He pulled the chair up to the small table and then sat, staring at the locked box that he didn't have a key to. He had never seen its contents. The mystery made him wonder what had been so important that it had been put under lock and key. Maybe a pile of money, but knowing his mother, she hadn't had two pennies to rub together, only what he had given her. He knew for certain it had all been spent on rent, utility bills and food.

After staring at the thing for ten minutes he reached in his pocket for the old hunters pocket knife, the treasure he had found years ago when they had first moved into the house. He began to unfold and then reclose each miniature tool until he found one that looked suitable for the job.

Although the lock was rusty, it opened when enough pressure had been applied. He lifted the lid, not knowing what to expect.

A multitude of yellowed papers were jumbled together in a single heap, no order that he could ascertain. He lifted the pile out, pushed the emptied container aside, and began to sort. The old receipts were useless, as were guarantees on products. There were many copies of adoption papers, also two birth certificates, one for a Jennifer Pryor and the other for a Jason Pryor, both admitted to the orphanage on the same day. There was a birth certificate for Robert Cummings, born on December 3rd and a death certificate for the same Robert Cummings. He didn't find any adoption papers for Jason or for Jennifer but then a notice at the bottom of the pile stated that Jennifer had left the orphanage at the age of eighteen. Jason had disappeared. Robby now had a sinking feeling in his stomach. Gladys celebrated his birthday on December 3rd.

He wanted to ask so many questions but here he was, tangled in this web of deceit. It sounded like a soap opera mystery, leaving a person hanging until the next episode. One thing was certain, he was not Robert Cummings. He took out his wallet and extracted the items with his name listed. Drivers' license, health insurance, social security card, registered birth-certificate card, he was a stranger to himself. An odd way to put it, but he didn't know who he was and had no idea how to go about finding his true identity. It was beginning to give him a headache. He set the papers aside.

This was Sunday, the only person he knew available to possibly help him through this maze of deception was Alex. He stuffed all the papers into a small paper bag and headed for the nearest store with a phone. He called information, however the number was unlisted. He called the operator and when she answered he stretched the truth a little by saying there was a death he had to speak to Mr. Williams about. She asked for his name and told him to hold on. When Alex answered, the operator informed him about a death notification, would he accept the call. He agreed and the call from Robby was put through.

"I'm sorry to bother you today Mr. Alex, but I've found something that is puzzling and scaring the heck out of me. Would you check these papers over, maybe you can figure out what happened and if I'm really who these say I am."

"Whoa! Kid, what the heck are you talking about? You showed me all the necessary information I needed for tax purposes when I hired you. What's changed since then?"

"Sir, Gladys had a strongbox she kept locked. I decided to open it to see what was inside and there were all these adoption papers, birth and death certificates, and a few items that made me question who I am. It actually looks like I died. Please Mr. Alex, can you take a few minutes and look over these things, maybe you can make sense of them. The more I try to figure them out, the more confused I become." Rob waited, heart in his throat, hoping for a positive response.

If the boy hadn't sounded so stressed, Alex would have refused, instead he gave Rob his home address and told him to come on over. As expected, within a very short time he heard the rev of an engine as a car pulled in the driveway. He opened the door and waited as Robby hurried forward, a paper bag crushed in his fist and a harried look on his face. It must be something really drastic, Alex thought, to make him act so distressed.

Shortly they were both settled at the kitchen table. Robby opened the paper bag, dumped the contents out on the table and watched as Alex began to straighten and sort through them. There was complete silence, except for the rustle of papers, as Alex carefully read each item then placed them in separate piles.

"This pile has nothing of interest to concern you Robby, however these three documents tell a different story. You are not the son of Gladys Cummings. You're the son of Ronald and Regina Pryor who were killed in an auto accident, your sister Jennifer survived. Apparently Gladys had been at the scene and put you into her car before anyone else arrived. We'll have to get these documents corrected by the courts then you can live your life using your real name. I have to tell you son, I know your sister very well. She's my daughter-in-law, so in a roundabout way you and I are related." Alex sat back in his chair, a wide grin on his face. A new member of his growing family sat before him with a bewildered look on his face, confused and unsure about who he was and where he came from. It wouldn't take that long to reassure the young lad and give him back his confidence.

"Your name is Jason Pryor, your sisters' name is Jennifer Williams and she's married to my son Ryan. You just sit for a bit and make yourself comfortable, I'm going to phone her and tell her we'll be over to see her shortly. This is going to be a big shock to her, just as it is to you."

Alex dialed the number and as soon as Jennifer answered he began to talk. "Jen, sit down, I have someone here who would like very much to speak to you, and if you're not busy with any important appointments this morning, we'll head over there as soon as you hang up the phone."

"I'm not busy Alex, who's the person of interest? I can't think of anyone I'd want to talk to other than you or Rose, so, put them on. I'd bet I don't know them from Adam." Jennifer held the receiver close to her ear waiting. When the strangers' voice spoke, she didn't recognize it.

"Hello, Jennifer? You don't know me, at least you don't know me now, but you did a long time ago. You'll have to excuse me if I'm a little distracted. The lady, Gladys Cummings, who I thought was my mother just died a short time ago. I was heartbroken, I still am as a matter of fact because she was so good to me all those years. The problem is that she was no relation to me whatsoever. I just found out that she had taken me from an automobile that had been in a serious accident, many years ago. The same accident you were in when our mother and father were killed, I'm your younger brother, Jason. Alex has assured me that this is the truth. I brought all the papers to Alex so he could sort through them. I can't believe I have a big sister who knew me when I was just a baby. Is it okay for us to come over right now, you won't mind?"

Jennifer had to sit down quickly. A spell of dizziness, though short lived, had thrown her for a loop. She was speaking to her dead brother, the one she sometimes saw when she dreamed about playing in the attic, her mother sitting in the rocking chair holding Jason while she herself played pretend with the people and furniture in the big wooden dollhouse. She remembered the rainbow colors and the laughing baby boy that mother said would one day be her guardian angel, for that's what brothers did. All these years she had thought it just a fantasy. But now he was here, a real person of flesh and blood, she could barely control her excitement.

When the chimes sounded Jennifer was already swinging the door open, her eyes alighting on the young man standing beside Alex, a young man looking much the same as she. The same black hair and skin tone but the telling features were the eyes. It was like looking into a mirror, the same golden color as her own.

Flinging her arms about him she began to sob, "I remember Jason. You were strapped in the car seat sitting in the back beside me. I was making you laugh, tickling you. No matter where we were or who we were with, we always stayed close together. When you began to walk, you'd follow me about the house. You were my little shadow. I missed you so much. At the orphanage I sometimes imagined I could hear your laughter but Mrs. Cummings said it was my imagination, it was her son laughing. She'd never let me see you, she said it would make me feel sad because I didn't have a mother to care for me and I believed her." Jennifer could not let Jason go, her arms wrapped so tightly about him it was hard for him to breathe. She rested her head against his shoulder, her sobs slowly easing as she finally realized this was not a dream, this was her brother, now a grown man. She stepped back, swiped the tears from her cheeks with the back of her hand, and stood gazing at him in disbelief, he was truly here. Alive, healthy, and they were together again at last.

"I'm sorry, Jason, I've forgotten my manners. Here we are, standing at the front door making a spectacle of ourselves for the entire neighborhood to see. Come in, let me take your coats. Let's go into the kitchen where I can make a fresh pot of coffee and, since its lunchtime, I'll heat up the beef stew we had for dinner last night.

While the two men settled at the table, Jen set up the coffee maker. By the time coffee was ready she had already heated the casserole of stew in the microwave. She even had homemade cheesecake with cherry topping for dessert.

The conversation took up from when the accident had occurred. They both brought each other up to date on the missing years, and by the time lunch had been consumed along with the dessert, they felt comfortable with the fact they were indeed, brother and sister, at long last together again.

Tomorrow, Monday, Jason would be back to work. Alex said he would contact his lawyer and get all Jason's personal records registered back in his legitimate name. It shouldn't take too long since he had his birth certificate.

"Would you like to stay longer and visit with your sister, Jason? I'm sure she'd be happy to drive you home later. You two have a lot of catching up to do and I have a few errands to take care of. Rose wanted me to pick up more diapers so, if there's nothing else you two need me for, I'll be on my way."

Jennifer walked Alex to the door, thanking him profusely for finding her brother and bringing him to her. She gave him a bear hug and then watched as he descended the steps and got into his car. She waited until he drove away before closing the door and hurrying back to Jason.

Tugging at his arm she pulled him to his feet and led him to the stairs. All the while talking about how she had missed him every day and thought he was gone from her life forever. By the time they reached the attic steps she was telling him about how their mother loved to take him to the rainbow room and sit in the rocking chair holding him while he gazed with wide eyed wonder at all the colors scattered hither and yon throughout the entire room. As the sun moved through its cycle, so also did the colors, constantly changing the look, and even the shape, of all the various stored articles, an unending calliope of delight.

They spent the remainder of the day looking through old trunks, finding old toys that Jennifer told stories to her brother about, or how he had chewed the ear off or pulled the stuffing out of. They both found intense pleasure in reliving old memories. At least Jen did even though Jason had been a little too young at that time.

When the colors began to dim Jen realized it was getting late. She hadn't even started supper for Ryan. They both hurried downstairs, Jason saying he should be getting home and he'd call a cab, he didn't want Ryan to come home with Jen not there.

"Nonsense, you'll stay and have supper with us, and stay overnight too. You can ride to work with Ryan. He'll drop you off back home after the work day is over. What could be simpler than that? Plus we'll have more time to catch up on all those years we've been apart. Ryan will be surprised at what has happened, and happy to meet you as his new brother-in-law.

By the time Ryan arrived home, his head and coat covered with snow, Jennifer had supper ready. Italian-style breaded cube steak, spinach salad, hot-spicy rice and dilled green beans. She served the remainder of the cheesecake for dessert.

Later they sat in the great room before a blazing fire, sipping coffee and getting comfortable with the idea that they were all family. Slowly conversation tapered off until with a yawn, Ryan stated he felt ready to hit the hay. It had been a long afternoon getting last minute glitches corrected in time for Monday's work force. He'd left just before Jen had gotten the call from Alex. His dad left the majority of last minute problems for him to take care of because he didn't want to waste precious week-end time away from Rose and his new son. It worked out just fine as far as Ryan was concerned. He'd likely feel the same when Jen and he had their family.

The three climbed the stairs, Jen and Ryan stopped at their bedroom door to say goodnight to Jason, who then continued on to his room at the end of the hall.

THE THISTLE SEED

In the morning after the two men left for work, Jen stripped the guest bed and dropped the bundle down the laundry chute. She remade the bed with fresh linens. The next thing she did was phone Sylvia with all the latest news.

"Jen, if you don't have anything to do today why don't you come on over? I'm getting a little bored with this weather and with Christmas coming so soon, I thought we could get together and figure out what to do for the holiday dinner. Has Rose mentioned anything? She probably would like to have it at her place because of the baby. She was a little nervous on Thanksgiving but the baby was as quiet as could be and slept almost the entire time.

"I'll be there in about a half hour, Sy. I have some terrific news to tell you, and I'm still walking on a cloud. Is there anything I can pick up at the store for you?"

"No! But thanks for asking, Jen. Davey and I went shopping yesterday morning. I have everything I need and then some. You know how guys are, everything they see they want, and when you get to the checkout counter there are all these extra items that take you by surprise. I'm looking forward to seeing you, can't wait."

Jen turned on the dishwasher before bundling herself into her winter coat, boots, and also driving gloves. She was careful backing out of the driveway, visibility was limited. Once on the road she could only move slowly, the wind had strengthened blending the swirling the snow into a white out. She should have returned home.

Sylvia began to feel impatient. It had been well over an hour since she'd spoken to Jen. Maybe she was late leaving. Finally she tried phoning but after listening to at least twenty ringtones she hung up.

Jennifer was blinded by the whiteness. The wipers could not keep up with the onslaught. The windshield was a sodden thick blanket of white. She pulled the car over to what she thought was the side of the road and turned the wipers and lights off. The heater she kept on high, it felt like it was getting colder by the minute. She felt the beginnings of panic so she tilted her head back closing her eyes and trying to calm herself, it seemed for only a moment. When she opened them again her car was incased in white. The motor stalled, windows blanketed with snow, and that's when she began to panic when the door wouldn't budge after she'd pushed against it with all her might. She tried the horn and it worked. Every once in a while she sent it's signal to whomever could be in the vicinity.

While Jen had dozed a snowplow had thrown a much deeper covering of snow over her car. The last time she looked the light was fading, at least she thought it was the light because it was getting much dimmer inside. Her feet felt frozen and she could feel her body trembling. Once again she pushed on the horn, but this time it was much more muted, the drain on the battery having taken its toll.

So! She thought, was this the way it would end just when she'd found her brother and their two lives could again be joined? The thought should have made her angry but somehow a deep feeling of inconsolable sorrow surrounded her. Not fair, she argued. She thought of all the anger she used to carry within herself, the enmity toward those who seemed to have everything their hearts desired. Living in the orphanage she had tried hard to improve herself but she sometimes remembered the day she had been brought there, the dim memory of an auto wreck, a little baby crying, and a far different life than what she led in the orphanage. She had travelled so far since then. A wonderful husband Ryan, living in the beautiful home she had been born in, and now finding her brother Jason, after all these years. No! This was not fair, but if this was the ending she had always wondered about, it wasn't really too bad. She had all the good things to take with her, the last beautiful year of her life, all she ever wanted….and Love.

The feeble sound of a horn emanating from the massive snow drift caught the attention of the heavy set man making his way home from work. He'd been unable to get his car out of the parking lot. He used his strong arms to sweep the snow from the passenger side, eventually clearing the window where he saw a woman leaning over the steering wheel, apparently unconscious. The door was locked. He cleared the snow as best as he could, stepped back a pace and gave a fast, hard kick, breaking the window. He was able to open the door and drag the woman out, he hooked her purse at the same time and hefted her across his shoulder, slamming the door after.

In twenty steps he was on his porch and pounding at the door. His wife Hazel opened it immediately.

"Good Grief Ben, what have you got there? Hurry and get inside, the poor girl is frozen. And take those work shoes off before you mess up the carpet. Here, help me take her coat and boots off, and grab that afghan off the rocker while you're at it. I'll heat water for tea and honey and fill the hot water bottle to put on her stomach. That will warm her quickly." By the time

Hazel had finished with her ministrations Jennifer was coming around, the warmth of the hot water bottle seeming to heat her entire body.

"Where am I and how did I get here? The last thing I remember was thinking I was going to die." Jennifer peered at the couple, both in their sixties, grey haired and definitely Angels sent to save her. "I don't know how you managed to do it but thank God you did. Would you happen to have a phone that I can use? I'd like to call my husband and let him know I'm okay."

Hazel handed her the receiver from the old black phone on the end table. Jen had a little trouble dialing the numbers but as soon as Ryan answered, she began to talk.

She only got half a sentence out before he interrupted her. "Honey, there's no way I can come and get you. Radio and television alerts have warned everyone to stay in their homes and wait out the storm because it's going to get worse. The road crews aren't even trying to clear any streets until the snow eases up, it'd just be a waste of their time and fuel. You'll have to stay there. Let me talk to one of them." Jen motioned to Hazel to take the phone. She snuggled down under the afghan listening to the one-sided conversation.

"Hazel is my name. My husband's name is Ben. He heard her car horn and had to break a window to get her out. Yes! She's doing just fine. She's here on the couch warming up with a hot water bottle on her stomach and covered with my homemade afghan. Sure…we'd be glad to. We're not going anywhere and neither is she the way the weather looks. Yep! You have a pencil handy? …."

Jennifer didn't hear the last of the conversation. The cozy warmth had finally eased her tension and feelings of distress. She had dozed off.

"Come along Ben, she can sleep on the couch for as long as she stays with us. It's comfortable and a lot warmer downstairs than up. Besides, that old mattress in the spare bedroom leaves a lot to be desired for a good night's sleep. I wouldn't put my worst enemy in there."

In the kitchen Hazel pulled two chicken breasts from the refrigerator freezer. "Ben, Honey, go to the root cellar and get me a large onion, some carrots, five potatoes and that small head of cabbage. I'll fix a big pot of chicken stew for supper. She filled her stainless steel soup pot one-fourth full of water and set it on the range, heat turned on high. She dropped in the frozen breasts, three cloves of mashed garlic and as soon as she had peeled and sliced the onion, that went in also. While the liquid heated and came to a boil, she cleaned and sliced the carrots setting them aside. She also pared and diced the potatoes, leaving them in cold water to prevent their turning brown. When the breasts were fully cooked she removed them from the pot. A small can of tomato sauce was added to the liquid. Now she added the chopped cabbage, the vegetables and potatoes including the chicken breasts she had cut into bite-sized chunks. Once the mixture came to a boil she turned down the heat to let it simmer and thicken, a dash of salt, pepper and nutmeg added to enhance the flavor.

The aroma of something enticing awoke Jennifer. Warm, rested and downright hungry, she tossed the covering aside, swung her legs off the couch and wandered into the kitchen.

"Hello young lady. D'you think you could manage to climb outside a bowl of stew this evening?" Ben pulled a chair out from the table and motioned her to sit.

Hazel was ladling stew into old fashioned stoneware bowls. Homemade cotton napkins lay neatly folded beneath soup spoons. Three glasses of milk sat at each place setting and a basket of homemade biscuits in the middle of the table next to the butter tub.

Ben carried the pot to the table and set it on a wooden trivet. Hazel took her seat while Ben ladled out the stew into each bowl. After he took his seat, Hazel said grace and their meal began.

After the meal Jennifer asked for the recipe which she wrote out neatly and stuck into her purse. She had indulged herself, consuming two servings.

The blizzard lasted two days. By the time Ryan was able to pick Jennifer up she felt like she'd been away from home for a week. He had brought Jason along to clear the snow off Jen's car. They used cables to get it started, Jason would follow them home.

Jennifer promised Hazel and Ben she would come visit them when she was in the area. She liked them enough to keep her word. With a hug for each of them she followed Ryan to his car. He helped her in and closed the door.

All the way home she talked about the old couple and how thoughtful they had been. Once home she was out of the car in a flash and beat Ryan through the front door by a yard. He couldn't help laughing at her and when inside, grabbed her and swung her around like she was light as a feather.

"You act like you've been away for ages, Jen, I missed you too, Honey. From now on if there are storm warnings, I don't want you deciding to go visit somebody. You could have been frozen to death and nobody would have found you until after the weather had cleared. That was a stupid thing to do."

Jen had been listening to him harangue her with a half-smile on her face, but only until he'd used the word "stupid." Then her temper flared.

"I'm not stupid Ryan and I don't want to hear that word come out of that mouth of yours again. Who do you think you're talking to, some dumb kid? I got along fine before I ever met you and this isn't the first blizzard I've been stuck in either." She flounced across the room and into the kitchen, Ryan close at her heels.

"I didn't say you were stupid, I said it was a stupid thing to do, and don't walk away from me when I'm speaking to you. I don't like it."

"Well! That's just too bad, egghead, when did you get elected to be my boss? I don't have to take this aggravation from you or anyone." Jennifer felt like she'd lose her composure at any second, always having had a short fuse. She wanted to halt this exchange before her temper took control of her. She didn't want Ryan to see her dark side. The sudden ringing of the phone brought them from the edge, it was Alex.

"Hi! Son, what are you two up to? I thought I'd give you a call to make sure everything's okay. This storm was pretty bad. We lost power but thankfully for only a few hours. We were a little nervous because of the baby but just when I was ready to get a fire going in one of the fireplaces, the electric came back on. How about you, is everything okay?"

Ryan related the incident about Jen getting stranded and just getting her back home within the last few minutes. "We're fine now dad, home safe and sound. So! What's on your mind, need me for anything?"

"No! I don't need you for a thing, at least in this weather. It's just that I got a call yesterday from Oscar Hatch. Remember him? He was the sheriff I stayed with up north when I lost my memory. He wanted to know if we were working on anything and could we use some extra help. His youngest son Chris was supposed to begin college this past fall but the scholarship didn't go through, now he'll have to wait. We have plenty to do on that shopping mall. Maybe Jason wouldn't mind a roommate and getting a few extra dollars for rent. Think it over and give me a call tomorrow. I told him I'd let him know in a few days."

"Winter we can always use extra help, kids are in school now. Tell him okay dad, I'll get hold of Jason and if Jason doesn't want the company, I'll find Chris another place."

CHAPTER 10

Oscar Hatch hung up the telephone satisfied that his son would be kept busy the entire winter helping with Alex's building project. He'd had to get his son away from town for the winter after two young men had been found beaten to death, their bodies hidden in the woods. Two horseback riders had found the missing teenagers lying within 50ft of each other, their bodies preyed upon by scavengers. Ted Hunter and Sonny Jorgenson were their names, young men in their late teens and both hard workers. Ted had been employed at the Coney Island restaurant and Sonny at Riley's local drug store. Two hate filled crimes where the two had been beaten almost beyond recognition.

Oscar had checked for any strangers. There were none. The only other alternative was someone from another town but with only locals around during winter, there had been no new visitors. The perpetrator was someone living in the area.

It was driving him crazy trying to figure out a motive for the murders and who was responsible. At least with Chris working for Alex he'd be able to concentrate on solving the crimes without being worried about Chris becoming someone's target. He liked his job, but not if it endangered his family.

Patty brought in the latest Fax messages and laid them on the corner of his desk. "Want another coffee Oscar? You look like you could use a cup. You've been staying here too late at night and getting in too early in the morning. How does Angie feel about you being gone so much? It's going to be really lonely for her with Chris away for the winter too."

"No thanks, Pat. I've had enough coffee this morning to float me away. There's a limit to how much I can drink and I need my sleep at night more than those extra cupfuls during the day. Tell me Patty, do you have any intuitions about these murders? There's something these two young men had in common. If we can just find out what it was we might find the murderer. At first glance it looks like random killings but with the two so similar, I don't think that's a reasonable conclusion. Here, take a look at the scenes, see if there's anything that stirs your memory or maybe makes you think of a certain person."

Patty hated to look at the crime scenes. She'd had a look at them when the pictures were first developed, a lot of blood and too much missing skin on the faces, it almost made her want to puke. Reluctantly, she reached for the photos, glanced quickly at them to satisfy her boss, then handed them back.

"I can't say as anything comes to mind boss, they're such a mess that I really can't stand looking at them. I'm sorry, I would if I could."

With a sigh of resignation Oscar reached for the photos and replaced them in the envelope. "That's okay, Pat, run along and get your work done. If you think of anything let me know. Right now we're at a standstill, but sooner or later I'm going to catch the crazy s.o.b that did this and send him away for the rest of his life."

Oscar reached into his pocket for his pills. He'd forgotten to take his medication this morning and he could always tell when his blood pressure shot up. He could feel it in his head, a slight ache like all the blood was gathering there with not enough room to hold it all. The last thing he needed was a stroke, he'd better be more careful.

The person guilty of the crimes was a local. The thought that he was getting away with murder almost made him laugh out loud, not just one murder, but two. He'd had his eyes set on Chris Hatch as the next victim but unfortunately, that was no longer possible. He lounged back on the bench seat at the Coney Island, taking a swig of his Pepsi and ruminating about his latest escapades. Life was definitely not boring anymore. The exciting possibility of getting caught lent an element of danger to every waking hour. He loved life now, and the devil take him for it. He wondered how long this "High" would last. Whatever, when it wore off he'd have to create another and he knew just how to accomplish it.

He wandered over to the register and handed Ned a five dollar bill. Pocketing the change, he muttered "thanks" and slipped out the door, thinking that Ned would be a good candidate for his next project when boredom set in.

Swaggering down the street he couldn't help looking at passersby with contempt. What a dumb, stupid bunch they were. If they only knew who they had just walked by they'd have run for their lives. He broke out in a short burst of laughter, startling a young woman who had just exited the grocery store. She looked at him oddly wondering what was so funny since he certainly didn't seem like someone who had a sense of humor. In fact, he gave her the creeps. She turned quickly away before he could notice she was staring at him.

He turned around and followed her progress with his eyes, wondering where she lived and thinking that maybe it might be entertaining to catch her off guard and drag her into the woods like he had the two guys. He'd have to keep her from screaming, wouldn't want to draw attention. It was something he'd have to consider.

His spirits high he decided to get some gas in his car and take a ride to a neighboring town. He had a few extra bucks in his pockets, he'd taken the two guys right after they'd been paid, a very clever move on his part.

The ride was invigorating, windows down, cold air blowing with the forecast of snow by evening. He knew he'd have to be back by then but for now he enjoyed the feeling of getting away from that same old boring environment.

He spent the day doing a little shopping, scouting out the young men who worked at the various establishments knowing they might very well be on his endangered species list.

He got home just in time for supper. Meatloaf with mashed potatoes, canned peas and pudding for dessert. He sure couldn't complain about the cooking. Without a word of thanks he settled into the easy chair in the living room and clicked on the television.

Of course, there was nothing of interest on the local news except who had married, and who was buried. Without a word to say goodnight, he arose and went to bed, falling fast asleep immediately. He slept through the night. When he awoke in the morning the house was quiet, he was alone, exactly what he enjoyed. He knew he would have been hassled about looking for work again, he was getting sick and tired of it, in fact he was thinking of leaving her. What the hell, she was working, she could support herself, what did she need him for? He sure as hell didn't need her.

He picked up his keys and slammed the door when exiting, wishing he didn't ever have to set foot inside again. Snow had fallen during the night, it was a crisp, icy morning and he could see his breath fog the air. He smiled, he loved the cold.

Angelina Hatch stopped in to visit her daughter-in-law Darlene, her eldest son's wife. Will was also a policeman, a state trooper. He'd loved police work all his life because of listening to his dad's stories about cops, robbers, and all the excitement involved with catching criminals. Darlene and Will were expecting their first child, Angie and Oscar's first grandson. At first they'd wanted the gender to be a surprise but then, when the Doc asked if they'd like to see the baby's image on the monitor they couldn't resist. They were naming him William Oscar Hatch. She only had another month to go, the Doc estimated January fifteenth as the delivery date, but first babies could come earlier or later.

Darlene was happy for the company. She had quit her secretarial job when she became uncomfortable with her girth. Now, with all the extra time on her hands, she was bored witless.

The two women made themselves comfortable at the kitchen table. Angie handed Darlene a shopping bag and watched, a wide smile on her face, as her daughter-in-law ah'd and Oo'd over the knitted, newborn baby outfits. There were so many cute outfits at the store that Angie'd had a hard time resisting temptation. She knew these could only be used for a month or two at the most but this was their first grandchild, their first, to begin doting on.

The afternoon slipped away until Angie realized it was time to hurry home and begin fixing supper. Darlene planted a kiss on her mother-in-laws cheek, "I love you mom, thanks for the beautiful baby clothes. Tell dad hello and give him our love. We'll try and get over to see you this weekend. Will has been working a little overtime trying to put that extra money away towards the delivery expenses. We have insurance but there are always extra surprises that pop up out of nowhere."

"Honey, don't you worry about a thing, dad and I will help out with expenses. Tell that handsome son of mine not to work too hard, he'll need a lot of fortitude to help when the baby arrives. I love you too sweetheart, just be careful and don't over-tax yourself."

With a wave of her hand Angie was out the door and into her car. Darlene watched as she turned the corner and disappeared from view.

Angie was singing to herself all the way home. Not only did she know a lot of children's songs but she remembered all the fairy tales from her own childhood. It had been years since the boys had listened to her at bedtime, or even at times they didn't feel well. She'd always had a story or song to amuse them with. She could hardly wait for the new grandchild to arrive. It was a wonderful tradition to carry on for each new birth, something to tie all the generations together down through the years. The old stories were wonderful for children to learn from. They taught that good and bad things happened in life, that there were good people and bad people too. She knew there were some new-idea folks that wanted to change the rhymes and verses so all was sweet as honey, but life was not like that, however, to each his own as the old saying goes.

She parked the car in the garage and hurried into the house. Oscar would be home in an hour. She gathered the makings for a spaghetti dinner and started making the sauce. By the time her husband walked in the door the water was boiling and ready for her to drop in the pasta.

"You outdid yourself, Honey. That was the best spaghetti you ever made." Oscar pushed back from the table, picking up his plate and carrying it to the sink.

"You say that every time I make pasta Oscar, I always make it the same way." Angie planted a kiss on her husband's cheek as he handed her the last dish. She placed it in the dishwasher. It was full and ready to do a weeks' worth of dishes. Adding soap she started the cycle. They then both went into the living room to watch the local newscast. They'd stay up until about ten and then retire for the night.

As soon as breakfast was over it seemed the phone had been waiting to ring, Oscar picked it up. Angie listened to the one-sided conversation. Her consternation growing with each word Oscar uttered in reply.

When he hung up the phone the look on his face told her something terrible had occurred. "What is it? What's happened that's making you look so upset? Tell me Oscar, I can't be sitting here all day wondering what horrible thing has upset you so, I'm not a child." Angie waited impatiently, yet with a feeling of trepidation, to hear the reason for Oscar's obvious anguish.

"There's been another beating. The body was found behind Roscoe Jenkins gas station. They haven't identified who it is, but it doesn't look like it's anyone from around here."

"So far all the victims have been males but I want you and Darlene to keep a watchful eye out for suspicious characters when you're shopping or visiting friends. Whoever this person is, they have a tremendous amount of hate built up inside. There's no telling what he could do next, even include women in his murder list. This is the third homicide, at least that we know of. I'm going to issue an alert for the entire county. We have to stop this maniac as soon as possible."

"Oscar, you're looking a bit pale, did you take your blood pressure medication yet? I didn't buy that daily pill dispenser just for the fun of it Sweetie. Before you even reach for your coffee cup in the morning, you take your pill or I'm going to get awfully angry, and you know you'd hate to see that, right?"

He noticed the white, daily-pill-dispenser sitting on the counter near the coffee pot. He flipped open Monday's slot and popped the pill in his mouth swallowing it down with a big gulp of his now cold coffee. "There, does that make you happy? I have better things to do than worry about a little pill. But thanks Hon! This will help me remember to take the darn thing since I plan on being around for a long time yet. I have to get going Sweetheart. Keep the door locked, phone Darlene and your friends, warn them to be extra careful." With a quick kiss on her soft lips he was out the door and on his way.

Angie called everyone she knew. They in turn phone everyone they knew, and before noon arrived the entire town was aware of what had happened. The killer had the best laugh he'd had in a long time listening to his neighbor tell him all the gory details about the dead body behind the gas station. He planned on taking it easy for a while. The high he was on would last for a few weeks. When everyone calmed down and relaxed he'd have his chance again. There was always someone foolish enough to think they were free from danger. After all, everyone knew it never happened to them. It was always somebody else who was the victim. He felt like the cat that ate the canary, he licked his lips in anticipation.

Oscar sent alerts to the surrounding areas, there was no sense taking chances that innocent folks would meet up unsuspectingly with the monster. He felt relieved of his guilty conscience after sending the notifications.

The week passed without incident. On the following Monday Oscar interviewed two recruits newly graduated from the police academy. The time had come to have a full time law enforcement team so that he wouldn't have to have calls relayed to him on the weekends.

"You two fill out these applications, when you're finished drop them on my desk and have a seat. I'll interview each of you and let you know by this evening if you're hired. I'd like references and also the academy assessment of how you did. This is a growing community. We need people who will want to be a part of it."

While the two were busy with their paperwork, Oscar was making phone calls to the police departments of surrounding communities. There were no other incidents of beating deaths. The person responsible likely lived in the area, He hung up the phone, frustration making him feel irritable, the rustle of paper made him turn to look. The applications sat on his desk, the two new recruits standing by the door. "Come in Officer McRay and have a seat. I'll see you shortly Officer Murphy."

Patrick sat in front of the desk making an effort to appear calm even though he was more nervous than he could ever remember being, except maybe when he'd stood at the altar speaking his wedding vows to Tessa just last week. They had planned the wedding for after his graduation from the academy. He had searched for a position hoping for a small town opening and here he was. If he got the job Tess would begin looking for a suitable place to live. He studied the Sheriff's face as his application was being inspected, he looked tough but there was a sense of integrity and openness about him, a face that invited friendliness.

Oscar read that the young man was newly married, had done exceedingly well at the academy, he was ambitious, hardworking and loyal to the cause. Setting the application aside he turned toward the young man and openly studied the face framed by curly black hair. Dark blue eyes gazed back.

"When can you begin work, officer McRay? We'll order two sets of uniforms immediately, along with all the other necessary accessories. We'll have you ready to go in record time."

"I'm hired? I can start today, sir. I'll need to phone my wife to let her know."

"No! You have the remainder of the day to get settled, just be here tomorrow at eight a.m." Oscar stood and held out his hand, they shook firmly, sealing the deal. "You can send in that other fellow on your way out, I'll see you in the morning."

Oscar watched as Pat tapped his comrade on the shoulder. He waited at the door until the new recruit took a seat and saw that Patty had given a big smile of welcome to their new employee. She kept tabs on all the comings and goings of the office, he couldn't ask for a better helper.

Allen Murphy was single, thirty two years of age. He had lived with his widowed mother until she recently married a fine gentleman she had met at church. He'd always wanted to live in a small town and this was a perfect chance to do so. He enjoyed community involvement and planned to be an active participant. Just the type of officer that Oscar wanted. "You're hired. When would you like to start?"

"I need a few days to find a place to live and get settled in if that's okay with you."

Oscar couldn't dispute the need for time. "I'll order your uniforms, the firearms and all the accessories. How about Thursday morning? That'll give you two days. Check out our local paper, you may find a number of places you might like. We always have summer vacationers so in wintertime there are a lot of vacancies, nice ones too.

"Thanks Sheriff Hatch, that'll do nicely. I'll phone you as soon as I find a place suitable." Allen shook hands, and turned to leave. He paused at Patsy's desk on the way out.

"Hi! I expect to begin work here in a few days, my name is Al, Al Murphy and I just wanted to meet you now so I'll have a friend here who'll greet me on my first day. I'll see you then." He turned and hurried out the door.

Patty was surprised and thrilled at the sudden attention. Usually she was like an invisible person, no one noticed her very much but she had sure noticed him. He'd be hard to miss with that red hair and those green eyes. It was unusual he didn't have freckles. Her heart did a little flip inside her chest at the thought he'd seemed very interested in her. Likely just another of her daydreams of meeting prince charming on his white horse, but that never happened except in the movies. She couldn't be dawdling away time when she had work to do ordering new uniforms, weapons, identifications and shields for the new recruits. It would be nice having extra help, Oscar worked too hard. She hurried to complete the order and then turned to listing any tickets written during the weekend.

At the end of the day she felt unusually tired. When she got home Brad was watching television with a bag of chips in his lap, crumbs on his shirt and grease on his fingers. Sometimes she got so disgusted with him being sloppy but no matter how much she complained, it did no good. It was something rubbed off on him, a memory of his fathers' habits. She wondered why she had never noticed when they were going together, she must have been blinded by love, or so that old saying went. It was a joke, it hadn't been love, it was just that she'd wanted to be noticed.Finally. If she had it to do over she'd run away as fast and as far as possible.

With a weary sigh she hurried into the kitchen to prepare supper. Boston baked beans, hotdogs on buns with the beans poured over. It was eaten with a knife and fork, a hearty meal and quick. She hadn't been in the mood to stand at the stove cooking.

It was ten o'clock when she dropped into bed exhausted from the long day. Sometimes she thought it wasn't from overwork but from the boredom of her everyday existence that drained her energy. Likely, but nothing she could do about it.

She was fast asleep within a ten minute span of time, the television still on until all hours of the night, which she sometimes awoke to. He'd likely sleep most of the day tomorrow.

The furnace clicked on sending heated air into the rooms causing a film of frost to begin forming on the windows. When the sun hit it in the morning the ice would melt leaving a puddle of water on the window ledges. It was just another old house that needed insulation and storm windows but it was not likely to happen with just one paycheck coming in.

As soon as Brad heard the muffled snores from his mother, he pulled on his heavy boots, wool coat, made sure his gloves were in his pocket, and then slipped quietly out the door. He knew she'd sleep until dawn as long as she could hear the television. He'd learned long ago how to gain his freedom without all her pain-in-the-neck questioning.

The night was icy cold, his breath making puffy patterns in the air as he hurried toward town. He'd catch a late movie at the Cinema, an old film but one he liked. Then, after the movie, he'd stop in at the new Pool House where many of the single guys gathered shooting pool or playing chess, checkers or cards. It was the best thing that could have happened in a small town where everything usually closed up at nine p.m. He was earning a little money winning at pool. He was good at it but not too good to scare other players off. It was better than working a full time job wasting all sorts of hours.

It was midnight when he entered the pool hall. The air was filled with smoke from cigarettes and cigars and he detected the faint aroma of marijuana which made him ache for a joint. He liked the way it made him feel. Maybe he could take a hit off one, but looking at the group he didn't spot a friendly face.

He lounged about waiting for an opening or an invitation without success. Finally he gave up and went back home. His mother stirred and awoke for a moment after he turned off the television but then fell quickly back to sleep, never realizing that her son had left the house.

He decided that in the morning he'd look for a part time job. Not that he really wanted one but he needed money to spend. It had been a long time since his mother had given him any. She had learned it only kept him out of work.

In the morning Patty wore her prettiest blouse. She spent extra time fixing her hair which was naturally curly and tended to be a bit wild in humid weather. She used hair spray to tame it. A light touch of lipstick, a dab of her favorite Musk cologne, and she felt ready to meet the day. The thought that possibly Allen would be dropping in caused a breathless feeling and accelerated heartbeat. She saw herself actually blush as she turned quickly away from the hall mirror to pull on her coat and step into rubber boots, her shoes carried in a tote bag.

"I'm leaving, Brad. I want you to shovel the walk before you go anywhere. If you eat then please clean up after yourself, I don't want to come home to a mess. I'll see you later, honey. Please try to find a job today, Okay?"

Brad listened to the front door closing firmly and then the sound of the car motor starting, idling for a while, and then driving away. Once he was sure she was positively gone he crawled out of bed. He had to get away from here, if he went through another morning of her giving him instructions before she left for work he'd puke. He was sick of it and her too. She wasn't aware that he'd tracked down his father and found that he'd been killed on a construction job. They didn't have any family listed as next of kin so he'd been cremated and buried in Potters field. He didn't know why he never told his mother, maybe because he sensed she wouldn't care. Actually, he didn't either but for some reason he felt the loss anyway. He had hoped he could live with him. He drank milk from the carton, downed a hardboiled egg and a piece of toast. He went through his drawers stuffing clothing in an old duffle bag. When he had all that he intended to take, he put on his wool coat, boots and gloves. He slammed the door in hopes it would be for the last time. He went to the pantry and found the cardboard salt container she had removed the bottom from. When he turned it over wads of bills were pushed up inside. He took them all, stuffing the bills into his pockets, not feeling a smidgeon of guilt for stealing her hard earned money. He'd found it weeks ago when he'd looked for salt to put on the icy steps. Now he was ready. All he need do is stop for gas and then hit the road. Maybe he'd head down south, get away from this lousy ice and snow. He thought of leaving a note but could think of nothing to say. She'd know soon enough that he was gone for good. She'd tried to be a good mom, but for some reason he'd never felt a close connection to her. Finally he could call it quits.

When Patty returned home that evening she changed into her jeans and sweater before beginning to prepare supper. It was a treat tonight, spaghetti and meat balls with a tossed salad, Brad's favorite. The hours passed, she ate while the food was still warm but when it got on to eight o'clock and the food cold, she put it into the refrigerator. They could have leftovers tomorrow. This wasn't the first time Brad hadn't come home for supper. She was disappointed as usual but she had learned there was nothing she could do, he came and went as he pleased. She didn't have the fortitude to face him, there was always that hidden place where fear lurked, a reminder of her days living with his father whose temper erupted at unexpected moments taking her by complete surprise. He'd seemed to take great pleasure in the beatings he'd administered. Always apologizing afterwards, promising it would never happen again. She had been so happy after he left her. For weeks she had dreaded hearing the sound of his car or the door opening, but days had passed and gradually she had relaxed, the feeling of relief gradually turning into contentment.

She watched the late news, turned off the television set and went to bed getting a good night's sleep without bad dreams. In the morning she went to waken Brad. His bed unmade, she presumed he had left early.

The day went very well. One of the new recruits, Patrick McRay was busy becoming familiar with office procedure. He took phone calls, did some filing, and spent much of the day talking to Oscar and learning about a few of the characters in town that sometimes drank too much, abused their wives or even forgot where they lived when alcohol took control of them. Occasionally they spent the night in jail which gave a measure of peace to their family, at least until the next episode.

The day ended without undue public disruptions. The office closed, phone set up to transfer evening calls to Oscars residence.

When Patty walked in the front door, a strong feeling of "empty-house" syndrome overcame her. Instincts told her Brad was not home, hadn't been there and he had left for good. This was exactly what his father had done, but Brad had only just turned seventeen. At first she was almost frantic, ready to phone Oscar but then she recalled events in her own young life. At seventeen she already had two year old baby Brad. So if Brad felt he wanted to be out on his own now, at the same age as when she'd had so much responsibility, then she wished him luck.

Instincts were suddenly aroused. She hurried to the pantry knowing beforehand what she would find and sure enough, lying on the floor was the emptied cardboard salt container, almost five hundred dollars she had scrimped to save was gone. She wanted to cry but instead, she returned the carton to the shelf. She'd begin saving on payday. Repainting the house would just have to wait another year. She stripped Brad's bed and cleared out the dresser drawers. A few odds and ends she placed in the cufflink box on the dresser. Castoff clothing was hanging in the closet, not good enough to give to charity, so she scooped them up to toss into the trash. Something heavy dropped from a pocket and fell to the floor, a handsome gold watch, one she had never laid her eyes on before. She turned it over and peered at the back trying to read the inscription which was almost worn away from wear. She thought it was inscribed "Theodore" but it was so faint she couldn't be sure. Maybe someone lost it. Sheriff Hatch might be able to find the owner. She'd take it to work in the morning.

Replacing the bedspread and pillows on Brad's bed, she rolled up the window shade, took away the throw rug to wash along with the bedding, and ran the dust mop under the bed and over the floors bringing back the shine. The room looked neat now.

She headed down to the basement to do the laundry not caring how long it took, nor what time she went to bed. With her son gone it would take a while before she'd be able to get a good night's sleep. It couldn't be helped so she may as well make good use of the hours.

By one a.m. the laundry was folded neatly away, the floors were scrubbed, furniture polished and even the appliances had been cleaned. There wasn't another thing that needed doing. It was then she realized she hadn't eaten since lunchtime. She toasted bread, made a cheese sandwich and placed it in the microwave until the cheese melted. She sat at the table eating and sipping at a glass of cold milk.

By two a.m. she was sound asleep, exhaustion had knocked her out like a light. When the alarm went off at seven she felt surprisingly perky, the night's activities hadn't affected her. She made the bed, took a quick shower, dressed, and was out the door on her way to work with the gold watch tucked inside her purse.

Sheriff Hatch arrived at eight, his usual smile and greeting, "Good morning Patty, how are you this morning? It looks like we may get a little more snow. Did Brad shovel the walk for you yesterday? I recall you were a little peeved at him because you had to wade through a foot of it, you're way too lenient with that boy, he needs a firm hand to straighten him out before it's too late." Every time Oscar learned of Brad's laziness he got angry.

"Boss, I got a bad shock when I got home, Brad's clothes were gone and so is he. I hate to tell you this about my son, but he took the money I had hidden. I'd been saving for a year to repaint the house. I was planning on having it done this coming summer but now I'll have to start all over again." Patty forced herself to hold back the tears, almost succeeding except for the slight welling of moisture in her eyes.

Oscar felt helpless, he knew how careful Patty was with her money but that brat of her's took advantage of her instead of looking for a job. There was nothing he could do. He knew she wouldn't accept money or even a loan.

"This fell out of Brad's jacket. There's an inscription on the back but it's kind of faint, almost worn away. Maybe you can find the owner, it looks expensive and I bet somebody wants it back." I have no idea how Brad came to have it in his possession.

Oscar turned the piece over and checked the back of the watch, the shock of what he saw made his stomach do a flip. "Theodore Hunter, 35 years of faithful service. Best wishes on your retirement. Concord Lumber Company."

"Good Grief, Patty, I hate to tell you this but young Teddy Hunter inherited this watch after his dad passed away last year. He was one of the young men we found out in the woods, murdered, beaten to death beyond recognition. The other young fella was Sonny Jorgenson and later, the third victim was Clay Richards from Saginaw who'd been returning home from visiting relatives north of us and only stopped for something to eat. We don't know what happened to his car, we never found it. I'll send this in for fingerprints. I hate to tell you this, but if the only prints found are Teds, yours, Brads, and now mine of course, it's not going to look good for your son. The only reason I'm mentioning this now is so you'll have a chance to prepare yourself just in case."

Oscar felt terrible, he knew in his heart Brad was the culprit behind the attacks. He'd have to send out an APB to apprehend her son and every day that passed, Patricia would be caught between a rock and a hard place. Part of her hoping Brad wouldn't get caught, the other half hoping he would, without losing his life in the process. She was such a good person, undeserving of all the heartache that had invaded her life. Her skirt-chasing, hard-drinking husband and her lazy, shiftless, black-hearted son. Regardless what her days or nights had wrought, she had always been a cheerful, hardworking employee.

The APB bulletins were sent. Next would be his personal visit to Mrs. Hunter. A terrible thing after losing her husband to a heart attack last year, then her only son murdered. She was around fifty, a lot to lose at such a young age. Still, she was a strong woman, had found a job at the local department store right after her husband had passed away. She wasn't one to stay home and feel sorry for herself. Oscar headed over to the store hoping he could catch her during her morning break.

Lucille Hunter was sitting in the cafeteria having coffee when he walked up.

"Mind if I join you Lucy? I could use a cup of coffee myself but I've already reached my limit for the day. I wanted to catch you up on the investigation since new evidence has come to light. I thought I'd better tell you before you heard it from one of the gossips. News moves faster than lightening sometimes.

Lucy set her cup down carefully, the unexpected arrival of Sheriff Hatch had given her a momentary fright recalling his visit about her murdered son.

"What's happened Oscar? Did you find the person responsible? That's all I can think of these days, wanting the person punished for what they did. They took more than my son, they took my future. A daughter-in-law, grandchildren, great-grandchildren, family holidays, everything I looked forward to….all gone."

Her eyes bright with unshed tears, Lucy looked at him expectantly, hoping that at least one thing could be put to rest. The mystery of why her son had been killed.

"I have something to tell you, it's all I can do at this time, but I now have a very good lead to who committed the crime. I have fingerprints from your husband's watch. For now I have to keep it as evidence, but I have definite leads to the killer. I felt you deserved to know before anyone else. Would you please keep it to yourself, at least for the time being?" Oscar knew he could trust her.

A look of hope spread across Lucy's face, maybe, at last she could go to sleep at night and not spend hours wondering who was responsible. She had mentally examined every male living in town hoping to find a reason for her son's death without success and now, finally, a measure of peace of mind.

CHAPTER 11

Bradley Shields was on the road. He decided to head south, away from the small towns and close-knit networks that could track him down quickly. This time of year there were no vacationers to hide within. He traveled at night, parking in off road trails during the day, buying his food at night at drive-ins. Just before he neared the area he wanted to stay in, he located a fishing off-ramp, placed a rock on the accelerator and watched as his car drove into the water and disappeared from view. He didn't leave until he could no longer hear the bubbles. This was near the Blue Water Bridge where he knew the current was strong. With a sigh of relief he turned away, thankful that ice hadn't yet formed to block the ramp.

He remembered his mother talking about Alex, the fellow who had lost his memory. The Sheriff had located his family and sent him home. From what he'd heard her saying he was wealthy and was building a shopping mall. He wouldn't mind working outside, maybe he could get a job there, it wouldn't hurt to try. He doubted the fellow would recognize him, would never associate him with anyone from up north.

He was freezing, it was late, no traffic and not a residence in sight. Just when he felt he couldn't take another step, he saw a gas station in the distance. He picked up speed into a trot which helped get his blood circulating and generated a feeling of warmth throughout his body. He was going to make it just fine but when he finally arrived at the site the place was closed.

Not for long, he thought as he circled the building looking for an area of easy access. He spotted a window with screening inset in the glass. Searching for something appropriate he found a castoff wheel rim, just the right size and heavy enough to do the job. He arm was tiring from hurling the rim at the window but eventually the pane let loose and crashed inward shredding the wooden frame into splinters. He'd done it.

Once inside he made himself comfortable. There was a hot plate, several cans of soup, instant coffee, an aluminum pan for heating water or cooking. He ate well, even sampling a few goodies placed invitingly near the cash register, which was empty. He looked for a cash box finding one pushed back under the counter, it felt heavy but when he opened it there were only coins in the slots, the bills had been removed.

When he felt it was time to exit the premises, he filled a bag with miscellaneous items that would stem his hunger and keep his energy up, slung his duffle bag over his shoulder and left at four o'clock, wanting to be a safe distance away before the owner opened for business. Maybe he'd be lucky and hitch a ride with someone on their way to work and he did.

The young man accepted his excuse that his car wouldn't start, that he had to get to Highland to begin his new job and couldn't take a chance of losing it because of his old jalopy. He was dropped off near Highlands's city limit.

He had no idea which way to go but when he noticed the lights of an all-night diner he headed in that direction. He was confident that before the day was over he'd find what he was looking for.

When he arrived at the new mall building site, a young man was busy assembling supplies, stacking them on a dolly and wheeling them to the current work area. Brad watched for a while then dropped his duffle bag in a corner and began to help with the loading. They began to get acquainted while shuffling supplies back and forth between sites. When they finished Jason introduced himself and thanked Brad for the help.

"What are you doing here so early, Brad? None of the stores will open for at least another hour, although it was a piece of luck you showed up when you did. It would have taken me another hour to set up the work sites. Come on, I'll buy you breakfast, I was in too much of a hurry and didn't eat this morning."

When the two men entered Cozies Diner Jason ordered breakfast for the both of them. Scrambled eggs, two pancakes, sausage, hash browns, juice, toast and coffee, a super-size special at a reasonable price. Neither spoke while they demolished the food in short order. Finally pushing their plates away, they sat talking while finishing their coffee.

"I don't suppose you could use another helper on the job, could you? I just landed in town, don't even have a place to stay yet, but I need work before I run out of funds." Brad tried not to seem too anxious, he liked Jason and didn't want to seem like he was pressuring him. He waited for the negative response he expected, at this time of year he was sure they had all the help they needed.

Jason hadn't had such a great beginning to a morning since they had started building. It had been a tedious routine each weekday which he had come to despise intensely.

"I'll take you to meet Alex when he arrives, it will be up to him. He's the boss and has the last say. If he says no then I'll not argue with him, it'd be the final word."

"That's fair. At least I have a chance. If I don't find work with you I may find something at some of the retailers. What time do you expect him?"

"He's usually….Oh! There he is now. Wait here while I talk to him for a minute."

Jason hurried forward, intercepting Alex before he reached Brad, wanting privacy of their conversation.

"Hi! Boss, that young fella over there showed up early this morning and pitched in to help transfer supplies to the job sites. I didn't ask for his help, it was volunteered. He was a good worker and it sure saved time, he said he needs a job."

Alex inspected the young man who appeared strong although he was a little raggedy looking and needed a shave. All in all, with his muscular build, he'd come in handy shifting supplies about from place to place. Jason could be put to better use.

"Sure Jason, why not, we can use the help. You go ahead and start working with Ryan today. I'll get this new fella primed and ready to take over the miscellaneous duties you had been assigned to. I was considering hiring another gofer, I'm sure he'll do just fine. Go on, take off, I'll take care of this."

Alex strolled over to the young stranger, hand outstretched and a welcoming smile on his face. Brad knew immediately he had it made.

"You can start work tomorrow morning, or if you prefer right now, since I suspect you have some spare time to waste. Put your duffle bag in that office over in the corner. You'll also find a hard hat to wear, we practice safety, always. Make yourself useful keeping the workers supplied with whatever they need. I'll start you at ten dollars an hour beginning now. You can fill out the necessary forms on lunch hour. Get going, I expect a good day's work out of you."

Alex watched as the new hire walked away. He didn't recognize him, yet there was something that seemed vaguely familiar. He was sure that eventually the memory of where he knew him from would resurface. In the meantime, they could use the extra help.

The day passed and when evening loomed, the workers began to clear away their equipment and clean their work areas. Sawdust was vacuumed up, lumber piled neatly aside and tools stashed in the office. Brad extricated his duffle bag, taking note there was nothing available he could lift easily. At least he still had the money he'd taken from his mother and now, with the promise of a paycheck in his future, he was sitting on easy street. The only problem right now was finding a place to stay. He saw Jason on his way out the door and gave a yell in his direction.

"Hey! Jason, can you give me a lift to someplace where I can rent a room? I don't have a car, and I don't have any knowledge of the area for finding a place to stay." He watched Jason pause for a moment before turning toward him.

"Come on with me, Brad. I know just the place for you to at least spend one night, you can bunk with me and sleep on the couch. Tomorrow is Saturday, after work we can get the early Sunday News edition and find you a decent place in the area where you won't have far to travel. Maybe even a place handy for me to pick you up and drop you off every day."

Brad followed Jason to his pickup truck and climbed into the passenger seat. He had his duffle bag on his lap, ready to go.

"Do you want to stop off for something to eat Brad? Or, if you don't mind canned stew, we can just head to my place. It only takes a minute to heat it up and there's plenty for the two of us."

Brad was beyond tired, he didn't want to stop anywhere. "I pass on that offer Jason. If you don't mind, can we just get to your place? I'd like to take a shower and then after eating anything, get a good night's sleep."

"I was hoping you'd say that, Brad. We'll be home in short order." Within ten minutes Jason parked in front of a two story house. Brad hefted his duffle bag and tagged after him.

It was a small but neat rental. The couch looked long enough to accommodate his height. He was positive that as tired as he felt, he'd sleep like a log anyway regardless of its length. The first thing he wanted desperately was a shower, then food, and then sleep, in that order.

An hour later he was stretched out, clean, fed and already sleeping soundly. Jason was snoring lightly, their first day together ended.

When the clock alarm sounded they awoke at the same time, Jason went into his tiny kitchen to start the coffee while Brad used the bathroom. He hurriedly washed up, brushed his teeth and combed his hair. He decided to keep the sparse beard knowing that it would eventually fill out and disguise his identity nicely. He dressed in jeans, a blue wool shirt and had donned a tee underneath for comfort from the scratchy wool. He was ready to go.

"Coffee's good Jason, but I'll need more than this to make it until noon. Will Cozies Diner be open early on Saturday?"

"Yeah! It's open seven days a week. Some folks even use the mall on Sundays for jogging and they enjoy stopping there for coffee after their workout.

While the two were driving to the work site deciding what they wanted for breakfast, their boss Alex Williams was just finishing his at home.

"That was great, Rose honey. Why don't you come over here and sit for a while with me, have another coffee. I haven't had a chance to talk to you all week. Just as I'm sitting down for breakfast, you're off busy with little Scott. I think it's time we hired a Nanny. I know you said you didn't want a stranger taking care of our son but Rose honey, it would be so nice for times like this when we have a chance to be together. Please sweetheart, just think about it, a live-in nanny where we could enjoy getting out more often for a nice relaxing dinner or visiting Ryan and Jen or even a shopping day you'd enjoy with a friend. You've been stuck here without a break ever since our son was born. You're beginning to look tired, overworked and I don't like it. I want you to get some references from a few friends. Scott won't care who changes his diaper. No arguments sweetheart, I'm set on this. I want a fulltime nanny before the month is over. Agreed?"

Rose wouldn't look at him. She had her head turned away trying to still the quivering of her lip and the moisture gathering in her eyes. She adored taking care of her baby and found it difficult to imagine anyone else being as careful or tender with him as she. Finally she couldn't contain her feelings of deprivation thinking about a stranger caring for Scott.

"I'm his mother, Alex. Just the thought of him being in the care of a stranger makes me cringe. I'd be worried sick every minute of the day about him being cared for properly. I don't think I could stand that."

"I'll make a deal with you Rose. Let's find a good nanny and have a trial period. How about for two weeks? You can keep tabs on her and anytime you feel she's not doing an excellent job, you can fire her and I won't say a word. I promise."

Rose was stuck, there was nothing to disagree about and it sounded fair to her. At least she could always say that she had given it a try when she wanted the woman gone. "Okay! Alex, you have your way on this but only for a two week period. I'll start looking this very day. The nanny can have your old live-in maids' room. We haven't used it since Esther retired. It will be perfect."

Alex felt a weight life from his shoulders. He knew Rose would be very contented with a nanny. After all, he'd been raised with one and loved her, differently though than the love he'd had for his mother. He wanted time to spend with his wife without the interruptions of a crying baby who needed attention. After all, look how well Ryan had turned out. Scott will be just like him.

After Alex left for work Rose pondered who to call, finally deciding on asking the one woman she knew had used nannies. Mrs. Farthwald whose husband was the man financing the shopping malls development. They'd had lunch together several times and liked each other. They had the same type husbands who were always on the go.

On the third ringing of the phone the maid answered. Phyllis picked up the extension immediately. "What a nice surprise, Rose. What are you doing on this cold winters day? How about coming over for lunch if you're not busy?"

"That's something I need your advice on Phyllis. Alex has requested we get a nanny so I can be more independent. Do you have any references? Someone I can trust with complete confidence?" Rose waited, torn between wanting and yet not wanting to find a Nanny for Scott.

"I have several good ones Rose, but the best one of all was Audrey Johnson. I still have her phone number somewhere. I'll call you back okay?"

Phyllis returned the call within minutes. "She's interested Rose, said she could begin immediately once your interview is completed. She's 52, widowed with two grown children who are both in the medical profession. Her son, Dr. Ron Johnson, is a resident doctor at Baldwin Center, our local hospital. Her daughter Betty is a surgical nurse. I think you'll like her, she's honest and very patient with children. She must be good for both of hers to attend college and make a name for themselves." They chatted for another few minutes before hanging up.

Rose sat, deep in thought, analyzing the entire Nanny situation and what her true feelings were about having a stranger taking care of her child. It was a difficult decision to make yet she knew that Alex was unhappy. Of course he adored Scott but he wanted to keep the closeness the two of them shared just as it had been since they married. Rose picked up the phone and dialed the number.

"Hello! Audrey, this is Rose Williams. I'm calling to set up an interview appointment, Mrs. Farthwald recommended you highly. I believe you're just the type Nanny I'm hoping for."

"I'm available any time Mrs. Williams. In fact I can be there within a half hour if you'd like." Audrey held her breath, she really needed this position.

"That sounds perfect. I'll put on a pot of coffee." Rose sat back in the chair and took a deep breath, she couldn't halt the momentum, it was done. Hurrying into the kitchen she readied the coffee maker. Filling a serving plate with shortbread cookies, she set the table with cups, saucers, sugar, cream and napkins. She tuned the small radio to a pleasant musical station, the better to have background sound to fill in any unexpected silences. When the door chimes sounded she was ready.

"Good Morning, I hope I'm not too early." Audrey followed the attractive women into the kitchen. She felt nervous, although she shouldn't be. There wasn't another Nanny who could compete with her qualifications.

"Have a seat, the coffee's ready. We can get acquainted while enjoying a cup.

Just as they made themselves comfortable at the table, Scott made his presence known with a lusty wail of discomfort.

"This would be a good time for you to watch me Mrs. Williams." Audrey stood and walked into the dining room where the bassinet sat with the active little bundle inside.

"Well, aren't you the little talker, sweetie? Let's get you all taken care of so you feel happy again." She opened the diaper, immediately laying a cloth across Scott's thighs. Good thing she had, the touch of cold air had caused Scott to relieve his bladder, the cloth stopped it from arcing and wetting everyone. Rose had to smile remembering her first lesson in changing.

Audrey carried Scott into the kitchen and held him on her lap while she sipped at her coffee and nibbled at a cookie. Scott watched her, curiosity quite obvious at seeing a stranger who was not the familiar person he was used to. She liked Rose, of course, had made up her mind, she felt very comfortable with Audrey. She liked the confident way she had taken control of Scott's needs.

"When can you begin Audrey? I'll show you to your living quarters, anything you want changed we'll take care of immediately."

Suddenly Rose felt light hearted, an entirely new vista had opened for her. She'd be able to go shopping, meet friends for lunch, and even go out to dinner with her husband. Now she understood what Alex had been trying to get across to her.

"I like the room just the way it is, Mrs. Williams. In fact, if it's convenient for you I can move in today. Scott is already interested in who I am so that will give him a chance to get acquainted. I wouldn't be surprised if you and your husband feel like going out to dinner tomorrow, a short time for you two to be away and see how Scott adjusts. I have a feeling he'll be just fine."

By late afternoon Audrey was moved in and making herself comfortable.

When Alex arrived home a few hours later he was so pleased to see that Rose had taken his suggestion that he instantly asked her to go to a movie with him. "You can just wear jeans, Hon. We'll only be gone a few hours. I'll even take you out for a Coney Islands hotdog." He had such a gleam in his eyes that Rose couldn't help laughing.

"You have that same look on your face as when you first asked me out. If I'd known that hiring a Nanny would perk you up so much I'd have done it weeks ago." Rose was actually glowing with pleasure. Just going to a movie seemed exciting after so many weeks being anxious about Scott and not wanting to leave him in someone else's care.

"I'll phone you later Audrey, it's not that I don't trust you, it's just my first at being away for any length of time. I know I'll eventually adjust to the separations and be more comfortable."

Audrey couldn't help being amused since she had been through this with previous new parents, it was always the same. "Enjoy yourself you two, Scott will be just fine. In fact he'll be put to bed and fast asleep before you return."

"Help yourself to anything in the fridge that you fancy Audrey, if you don't see anything to tempt your appetite there are a variety of frozen dinners in the freezer. We'll see you later."

They enjoyed the movie, the popcorn and soda. Afterward they went to the same Coney Island where they had met after all the years of being separated. It was still a miracle they had run into each other. It almost felt like a first date.

They walked arm and arm back to the car with Alex planting a few kisses during pauses. When they finally drove off they weren't aware of eyes watching them and someone following.

The car parked down the street with lights off, the driver observing the two. It was a very nice neighborhood so chances were that pickings would be excellent. Next time they were out he'd make his move. People always had some type of schedule, Friday or Saturday nights set up for their entertainment. Today happened to be a short time away from their home. When they were out of sight he started the engine and drove away. The car ran quietly, it'd been a terrific deal buying from that old couple who'd had their license taken away, too old to drive safely anymore. There'd been no family to offer the auto to. He'd offered $500 dollars and the old woman had jumped at the deal. He'd looked in the Bluebook, the car was worth three times as much. Well cared for with low mileage but ten years old. He laughed about his windfall. "Lucky me."

Willy Crawford drove back to his motel, a smug smile on his face and larceny in his heart. This was the last place the coppers would look for him, he was originally from Minnesota and far, far, from home. He'd lucked out in the slammer when he was put in with old Ed Grogan who couldn't stop braggin' about his escapades here in this burg. He'd blabbed so much that Willy almost knew this town by heart. He even knew about the little hidey-hole up north where he'd taken the broad after he'd raped her. What a loser, a small time hood, a penny ante crap-head. He still laughed recalling hearing about the poison ivy episode Ed had experienced. Just for meanness he'd started calling him Rosy. When he'd been released from prison after having served out his time, he'd decided to head for Ed's old stomping grounds.

He'd found a lousy job but it paid enough to cover the cost of his ratty room and put food in his mouth. Good thing he'd talked his way into the poker game at Smitty's bar. Lady Luck had been sitting on his shoulders all night and he'd cleaned up good, walked away with most of their pay and been able to buy the car. He'd had an extra ace up his sleeve, so to speak. They'd suspected he'd been cheating but no proof. He'd make sure he kept a safe distance between him and Smitty's, he wouldn't want to end up with a busted head.

The Westend Motel was as far away from his marks as he could get. He parked, locked his car and checked the area for any suspicious characters before entering his room. There wasn't even a television but for the price he didn't care. He flopped on the bed, propped up his head on the pillow, lit up his camel and proceeded to contemplate his priorities. Who to do first? The broad Sylvia still lived at her grandmothers. He'd followed her to her mothers and then to her brothers. The houses were all prime for pickings, high end at that.

He almost caught himself on fire by dozing off, the cigarette fallen from his hand onto his stomach. The heat of it awakened him just in time, a stupid thing to do. Good thing he hadn't been drinking. He finally undressed and crawled into bed. Within moments he was fast asleep.

The sound of car motors starting up awoke him in the morning. It was late but he didn't have to hurry off, he'd paid for a week's rental and got a better deal. After a shower he felt revived, able to face the day and make plans, but first he needed food.

Scrambled eggs, hash browns, Canadian bacon, toast and coffee, he couldn't have asked for better. The place was a hole-in-the-wall diner but the food was good and plenty of it. With a toothpick in his mouth he paid at the register and sauntered out into the cold. It looked like more snow was on the way. He snugged his collar closer about his neck and hurried to his car. There was no place to go except back to the motel. He stopped at a drug store to purchase a pint of whiskey, a deck of cards, a bag of pretzels and threw in a six pack of Pepsi on the spur of the moment. He had all day to kill.

At six o'clock that evening he got into his car and drove away. He parked down the street from his objective and didn't have long to wait before he saw the couple leave.

Audrey thought Alex or Rose had forgotten something. When she swung the door open the stranger stepped inside quickly closing the door as he held her by the throat and pinned her against the wall. "Don't make a sound babe unless you want your face messed up. I won't hurt you unless you give me trouble. Where did they go and when will they be back?

"Please don't hurt me, I have a baby to care for, I'm only the nanny. I've just moved in and I have no information whatsoever about the house or where there would be money or a safe and I'm not sure when they'll return." Audrey was frightened but for some reason she didn't think the guy would seriously harm her, he didn't look mean. If she'd known his criminal background she wouldn't have felt so confident.

"I didn't ask you about money or a safe, where's your room? Let's go, make it snappy, I haven't got all day." He kept his hand about her neck as she hurried upstairs, he right behind her even stepping on her heels as he kept her under his control.

When they reached her room he pulled out his gun and stepped away. "Pack a bag sugar, everything you'll need for a long trip." He kept his eyes on her every move making sure she didn't have a weapon hidden amongst her belongings. When she'd gathered everything into her suitcase and she had latched the lid, he told her to pack everything needed for the baby. That's when she became fearful of his plans.

"Please don't do this, the baby is a newborn, only a few months old. Take me if you want but not the baby. I'll do anything you ask except this."

"You'll do exactly as I say unless you want to be found flat on your back with the baby gone. I'm taking him. The only reason I'm taking you is to care for him. If he was older I wouldn't need you would I? What do you think I'd do then, take the baby and kiss you goodbye? You'd be dead meat, I wouldn't leave any witness. You got that sugar? Now get your dead ass busy and pack juniors stuff."

She felt the first stirrings of real fear. The cold, hard look on his face brooked no resistance from her, she knew in her bones he wouldn't hesitate to kill her to gain his ends. He was in a hurry and she couldn't stall anymore.

"Okay, I'm hurrying." She loaded two large bundles filled with diapers, formula, extra bottles and nipples, baby blankets, baking soda for diaper rash and anything else she could think of. Last was the portable bassinet with the sleeping baby inside. Within ten minutes his car was loaded up and they were driving away. The last thing Willy did was leave a short message.

"No cops. Good thing you have a Nanny, she'll take care of your baby. I'll contact you in two days. If you call the cops, you'll never see either of them again, I guarantee."

They were far away on an interstate highway by the time Alex and Rose returned home. Rose became hysterical when she found Scott and Audrey missing. She thought Audrey had taken him until Alex showed her the note. Alex had a hard time trying to calm her and keep her from contacting the police. At last she heeded her husband's warning.

That night they couldn't sleep. They sat in the kitchen in mutual misery drinking too much coffee with nothing to say to each other except to wonder aloud why everything had happened, why to them, and would their baby be well and safe until they got him back. Morning came with grey skies and snow. Exhausted but not able to sleep they finally went to their bedroom and slipped under the covers trying to warm their shocked, cold bodies by huddling close together. They finally dozed off but only for a few hours. When they arose it was only to again sit waiting in the kitchen for the hours to pass and the phone call to come with the instructions. The call did not come until the second day while other calls had been quickly shuffled aside with plausible excuses

All were accepted without question, yet the sense that something was out of the ordinary left its inquisitiveness suspended in the atmosphere.

Before its second signal the phone was picked up, Alex listened to the instructions but before he could ask about baby Scott and Audrey's welfare, the call was disconnected.

"He told me to withdraw two hundred thousand dollars from the bank, the denominations to be in old twenty and fifty dollar bills. He warned us against contacting the police and said he'll phone again with further instructions. This is the wisest thing to do Rose. We have no idea if he has someone watching our every move and I don't give a damn about the money, he can take all I have. I want our son safely back home and once he is I'll get that bastard if it takes the rest of my life."

Rose felt numb. The lack of sleep and anguish over her missing baby was unbearable. She was near the point of a breakdown and it was taking all her inner strength to maintain her stability. The last thing she needed was to be drugged into oblivion and not know what was going on. She absolutely had to hold herself together for Alex's sake. He had enough on his mind dealing with the devil that had invaded their lives. She was also worried about Audrey, poor woman. What must she be going through trying to protect Scott and at the same time deal with the madman who had taken them? She tried to picture herself in the same situation without success. She sent a silent prayer for the safe return of them both. She knew Scott was in good hands as long as nothing happened to Audrey. Thank goodness they had hired a professional instead of having a regular babysitter. Just the idea of what the outcome could have been sent shivers down her spine. She rested her arms on the tabletop and dropped her head down on them, only to rest for a moment. She fell sound asleep.

Alex let her get the small measure of rest she needed so desperately, a few moments of blessed reprieve from the agony of their loss.

Rose slept for an hour. She awoke with a startled movement that almost felled her from her chair. With a gasp of shock at realizing where she was, she broke into deep sobs of despair. "I had Scott safe in my arms. I was running with him as fast as I could when a hand reached out to drag him from me, I would not let him go. I'd almost made it to safety." The dream and reality merged, she felt as though her heart was breaking, the pain and loss unbearable.

"I have to do SOMETHING, Alex. I'm going to the police. I know you don't agree with my decision but we're wasting time that could be spent finding our son. I won't change my mind, instincts tell me this is the right thing to do. If you won't come with me, I'll go alone."

"Rose, honey, don't be foolish, I can't let you do this. If I have to tie you up to keep you here I will. The deal has been made. I phoned the bank, they were curious about the large amount but I told them I was planning a charity event. They'll have the money later today. Settle down my love, if we get the police involved things could get messy. I want our son back home by tonight, and it's possible if we follow instructions."

Rose was not satisfied. She knew deep in her being this was the wrong way to go. She had to make him see the logic. Once the money changed hands, where was the reason to put oneself in jeopardy by returning the baby? They'd never see their son alive again. She had to figure a way to get Alex to agree, but he was stubborn once his mind was made up, there was only one possibility. She watched as he prepared to leave for the bank. Dressing hurriedly but making sure that he looked as self possessed as usual and as neat as a pin. He gave her a quick kiss on the cheek and then was out the door. It was then that she picked up the phone and dialed.

"I'd like to speak to the officer in charge please. Thank you, I'll hold…. Yes! This is Mrs. Rose Williams, my son and babysitter has been kidnapped. My husband Alex is, even now, on his way to the bank to withdraw the ransom. He doesn't want the police involved. He'll be very angry with me but I feel strongly that I'll never see my son alive again if they're given the money. Please help us. I want my son and Audrey home safely."

"What bank is your husband going to, Mrs. Williams? I'll send detectives immediately. What make of automobile is he driving? We'll intercept him as soon as he leaves the bank and meet back at your home. If the phone rings in the meantime, please do not answer it. If it's the kidnapper we want everything set up before any further conversations between the two of you. I'm sending detective Sharon Atkins to stay with you. She'll be there before we arrive with your husband."

Rose was shaking badly as she hung up the phone. The feeling of dread and shock seemed to creep into every pore of her being. It was not only fear for her son's safety, but that she had no idea what Alex would do, or even forgive her, for going against his decision. She wouldn't have long to wait.

Detective Atkins arrived not long before Alex and his accompanying undercover officers. Rose felt a small measure of relief knowing someone would be at her side when Alex faced her, not that he would ever raise a hand to her. It was having someone there to hopefully stem the tide of vindictiveness Alex was sure to vent at her betrayal. She prayed she had done the right thing.

Within a half hour she heard several cars pull into the driveway. With her heart lodged in her throat she went to open the door.

Alex walked quickly past without a glance or word of greeting, his features frozen into a mask of denunciation and anger. He tossed the money packet onto the kitchen table and then turned to face Rose, his eyes hard, lips set into a curl of contempt.

"What have you done? Do you care so much about money that you'd sacrifice our son? I'll never forgive you for this Rose. We would have had Scott returned to us on this very day, safe and alive. When they find that the police are involved, there's a possibility we'll never see him again." Alex turned quickly away but not before she saw tears well in his eyes, the anxiety and love for his son tearing him apart.

"You don't mean that, Alex. You're not the type of man who can turn your feelings off and on so easily. You're upset, but it would have jeopardized Scott's life if you had paid the ransom. They'd of had no reason to return him. For God's sake, I'm his mother and I don't care a damn about the money, just my son's safe return to me. This is one thing you will do my way, Alex, I'll not back down. If you thwart me on this and Scott is harmed, then I'll never want to set eyes on you again."

Rose hit the floor at an awkward angle, her arm twisted under her in an unexpected faint. The alarm Alex felt at her collapse made him realize that regardless of their dispute over what to do about Scott, he loved her with all his being. That was one thing that would never change. He gathered her into his arms and carried her into the living room where he placed her on the sofa.

Meanwhile, the police were setting up their equipment, detective Sharon Atkins in charge. When all was ready, she tapped Alex on the shoulder. "When the phone rings we both pick up at the same time. Keep the person on the line as long as possible while we try to trace the call. Above all, keep calm. We'll get your son back, just do as you're told and don't do anything foolish. The kidnappers are only interested in money, we have to insure there is a trade off."

The hours dragged by with no call. When evening arrived a mounting feeling of dread settled on Rose. Even Alex, trying to console her and give her hope, felt fear building that he would never set eyes on his living son again. Slowly fear began to change into rage at the person who would dare put his son in danger. He wanted to feel his hands around that person's throat and squeeze the life from him. He realized in that moment that he was entirely capable of murder, at least where the safety of his family was concerned. It was a side of his nature he had never been aware of.

"Rose honey, how about fixing something to eat for everyone? I'll even give you a hand, I need something to keep busy and get my mind off what's happening. The day seemed so long with nothing happening about getting Scott and Audrey back safely."

They spent the next hour making a spaghetti dinner. The kitchen counter was set up buffet style with seating at the kitchen table. The five officers took turns eating and monitoring the phone. When everyone had finished and the kitchen had been returned to its original neatness, no call had come in. It was now late, not likely that any contact would be made by the kidnapper. Two officers remained at the home. They would take turns monitoring the phone. Rose and Alex were encouraged to retire and try to get some rest. Their bedroom extension could be answered by them should a call come in, the police could listen in on the main line and try to trace it.

Although they didn't think they'd sleep, both Alex and Rose fell into deep exhausted slumber. They had not undressed but had stretched out on top of the bed thinking they would just try to relax for a while. It was predawn, not even a hint of sunrise color touched the eastern horizon. Alex lay awake listening to Rose's gentle breathing, hoping she would stay safely lost in sleep for a little longer. He couldn't bear to see her in such misery worrying about Scott. At least this respite would give her strength to bear up under another day of stress. At last he let the tears have their way, he'd managed to appear composed during the fearful worry of Scott and Audrey's abduction but now, their release seemed to ease just a little part of his misery. Silently he kept swiping them away, an unrelenting stream of pain and sorrow that seemed endless. He couldn't let Rose see this weakness, he had to stop this somehow but try as he may, the burden was too much to control. Deep sobs began to shake his body, the realization that he was as helpless as Rose to recover their son seemed to strip his manhood away making him feel completely worthless. It was then that Rose reached out and wrapped her arms around him. "Hold me Alex, we need each other to keep faith that we'll get our son back. Tears are a good thing, they wash away the doubt and worry, and show that we have a tender heart. I've always known about your kind heart, my love. That's been something you've never been able to hide from me. We are two of a kind, Scott is a part of us. I know we'll have him back with us very soon.

Their tears blended as did their bodies in the age-old expression of love. It seemed every fiber of their being was drained of energy. They both fell asleep, awakening when the morning sun shining through the bedroom window, warmed their faces.

The bedside phone shattered the silence. With a shocked gasp Rose picked up the receiver. "Hello?"

Willy Crawford was surprised into momentary silence hearing a woman's voice. It was so soft and young sounding that he almost thought he'd dialed a wrong number, and then he realized it was the baby's mother.

"Are you ready to deal lady? You want your baby back as much as I want the money, right? Let me talk to the man of the family, I don't deal with dames."

Rose handed the phone to Alex, a look of fear and anger making her mouth twist into a scowl of contempt for her feeling of helplessness.

"This is Alex. When can I have my son?"

"Do you have the money Mr. wise guy? No money, no son."

"The money is ready, waiting for me to pick it up. I'm not dropping it off anywhere, get that? This will be a straight out switch. You hand me my son, I'll hand you the money. That's the only way I'll pay and the nanny better be included in the switch too, you're not keeping her."

Willy was stumped. He had to figure how to get the money in trade for the kid and nanny. "I'll call you again tomorrow with plans." Willy hung up before any trace could be completed. He had an idea the police were in on the deal now, there'd been a funny echo on the line, likely a monitor.

Meanwhile Audrey was locked in a room caring for baby Scott. Willy had supplied formula and diapers. She was able to keep the baby comfortable and fed. She, though, was feeling pangs of hunger. It had been several days since her last meal. Taking a chance that her captor might feel sympathy or concern that she wouldn't care properly for his little captive, she rapped sharply at the locked door. When there was no response she began to kick vigorously at it. The noise couldn't fail to draw attention.

"Stop that racket or I'll come in there and shut it up with a few good whacks to your noggin. If I hear another sound out of you, you're askin' for trouble." Willy was ticked. Dames were nothin' but trouble.

"Mr. If you want this baby taken care of you better get me something to eat before I pass out unless you want to change his diapers and feed him yourself. I'm getting really dizzy even as I speak and I can't hold out much longer." Audrey did feel faint. She had been attempting to hold herself together for Scott's sake but she could feel waves of giddiness trying to take hold. It was only a matter of time before she lost consciousness.

Willy looked at the cheeseburger sitting in front of him. He was still a little hungry but rather than take a chance she'd faint, he decided to give it to her. "Get your butt over to the other side of the room and start tappin' on the wall so I can tell where you are. When I hear that, I'll open the door and put somethin' on the floor for you to eat. Don't even think of tryin' anything 'cause I'll knock you silly." As soon as he heard the tapping, he opened the door a notch and dropped the burger on the floor, quickly slamming the door closed and relocking it. He heard the footsteps hurrying close and then the rustle of paper being unwrapped. A moan of pleasure sounded as she took a first bite. He relocked the door and walked away.

A spurt of digestive juices flooded her mouth as she almost choked in her hurry to consume the delicacy. She forced herself to take smaller bites and chew each well, making the feast last longer and feel more filling. When finished she truly felt as though she had consumed a satisfying amount of food. Scott was sleeping soundly as she curled up in a moldy smelling armchair and dozed off.

Willy was ready to place the phone call the next morning. He checked his watch making sure it was wound up and running. He'd make sure he severed the connection too quickly to be traced. His plans were sure fire.

Alex picked up the phone on the first ring and listened to the instructions. "Bring the $200,000 in a canvas bag. Take a Taxi out to the old mill road and then send the cab away. If I see any sign of cops I'll shoot the kid and the nanny too. When we meet, I'll send the nanny over to get the money. When she gives the money to me I'll hand her the kid then they're both all yours, any questions?"

"No questions, I'll see you in the morning." Alex hung up and turned toward the officer who had been listening on the extension. "I hope you guys know what you're doing. If anything happens to my son or his nanny you're responsible." He had a grim look on his face as he turned to his wife and pulled her into his arms. "We have to hope all goes as planned sweetheart. There's nothing we can do but wait."

The night seemed to drag by. Finally when dawn streaked the eastern sky blood red, Alex and Rose dressed and headed downstairs. The police were ready and waiting for them. The money was packed in the canvas bag, a tracking device hidden inside as a precaution. The Taxi was waiting outside, a police officer dressed as the driver. Rose kissed Alex goodbye and watched as he entered the cab and it drove away. She hurried to the phone, the police would keep her updated on developments.

Alex watched the taxi drive away. He couldn't see any sign of the kidnapper so he stayed where he was waiting. It seemed a very long time before he saw movement at the end of the road near the mill. Then he saw Audrey step into view, she was holding Scott. When she spotted him she immediately handed Scott to the man standing near her and began to walk toward Alex. He handed her the canvas bag and watched as she returned to the man, placing the bag on the ground near his feet. She took Scott from the man and hurried back toward Alex. It was then that hidden police officers closed in and arrested the kidnapper. Willy Crawford just had his last fling at freedom. He would be going to prison for a very long time.

When Alex returned home Rose was frantic. She had called the doctor who was there to check out Scott and Audrey. Neither was the worse for the ordeal but Audrey was starved. Both had baths, a change of clothing and were fed. Scott fell asleep immediately. Audrey talked a blue streak while she ate but finally exhaustion took over. She stumbled upstairs to her room and dropped onto the bed, fast asleep before her head hit the pillow.

With a sigh of relief Rose and Alex indulged in a glass of wine. Arm about each other they wended their way upstairs to their bedroom. Within moments they had undressed and were cuddled together under the covers, the relief from their shared moments of torment drained them of energy. For a while they held each other closely until sleep settled upon them. They drifted into dreamland, not to awaken until dawn.

CHAPTER 12

Bradley Shields had found a place to rent. He liked Jason well enough but just the thought of his wealthy upbringing made jealousy burn like a poison. He couldn't stand being around him for very long. Why hadn't he been lucky enough to be born into a rich household? It was his parents fault and he didn't plan on ending up like them, poor as church mice.

It was a basement apartment with a separate entrance through the side door. Spacious enough so he wouldn't feel like a mouse in a trap. The floors were all vinyl tile with throw rugs in the living room and bedroom. The bathroom wasn't large. No bathtub, but the corner shower was roomy with a sliding glass door. Two doors on opposite walls of the bath gave access to the kitchen, the other to the bedroom.

The apartment walls were completely wood paneled which gave the place a cozy atmosphere. There were even a few pictures hung. The furnace and hot water tank were enclosed in the center of the area separating the living quarters into two separate spaces. The living room and kitchen were on the left side wall of the basement stairs and the bedroom on the right side wall of the stairs. At the center of the far wall of the basement was the bathroom, with access from both the kitchen and bedroom, very convenient when having company, as if he ever would. The rent was reasonable, $200 a month but on the condition he would do a few odd jobs like setting the garbage out each week for pickup and when there was heavy snowfall, shovel the front walk. He signed the agreement, satisfied he could hold up his end of the bargain.

He put his clothing away in the bedroom dresser drawers, hung shirts and jeans in the closet and then headed for the nearest supermarket.

This was the first time in his life he had shopped. He wandered the aisles not sure what to buy until feeling foolish, he bought a pen and small notebook, parked himself at a table in the cafeteria, ordered a burger and fries, and between bites wrote down the necessities and food he'd need. When he'd finished eating, his list was complete. He was home within an hour stashing everything away. Living alone was more involved than he'd anticipated. He realized he'd missed buying toilet paper. Thankfully he'd bought Kleenex because he had the sniffles. He'd purchased a pot and a frying pan a 4pc dish set, 4pc setting of utensils, two drinking glasses, 2 bath soaps, a set of sheets, 2 pillows and cases, a blanket and two towels/wash cloths. He'd started out with a $400.50 paycheck and after rent and partial shopping spending $180 he only had $20 left. He'd have to fill up Alex's truck with gas in the morning too, good thing he'd taken that kitty money from his ma or he'd be flat busted. He had bought everything except food.

Too tired to do anything except make the bed and drop into it, he was soon deep into dreamland not to awaken until morning. When he arose there was nothing to eat. He'd stop at Cozies on the way to work. He also had to remember to thank Alex for letting him borrow the truck. Jason was already at the work site when he arrived. "What's up Jason, you look angry. I'm sorry I'm a little late, I had to put gas in the truck."

"I'm not ticked at you Brad. Alex's son has been kidnapped along with the nanny. I'll be taking charge while he's away. If you see any problems that I happen to miss let me know immediately. It's easier to fix mistakes at the beginning of a project."

At first Brad was shocked, he'd never imagined stuff like that happened to people he knew, but then he thought of the opportunity this presented. Jason was not the wise know-it-all that most bosses were. Maybe he'd have a chance to line his pockets, albeit carefully, while Alex was away. Not actually stealing money but maybe supplies. He'd have to wait and bide his time, this was a gravy job and he didn't want to mess it up.

Jason watched Brad, feeling a tinge of suspicion at the secretive expression that had dropped like a shade over the new employee's face. Something told him that maybe, with Alex away, he should be more aware of what was happening at the job site. After all, what did he really know about Brad? He wanted his boss to have complete confidence in his ability to handle this responsibility. He'd be damned if he'd let him down.

Brad noticed Jason straightening his shoulders, a look of determination settling upon his countenance. "So! Boss, what do you want me to start on today? I can begin unloading that new pallet of supplies before the rest of the gang gets here. You name it and my time is all yours for the next 8 hours."

Jason couldn't help smiling at the title. Suddenly he felt he'd been fretting over nothing, likely it was just the worry over Alex's missing baby boy. He clapped Brad on the back as he walked with him to the supply site. "I'll give you a hand until the rest of the workers arrives. You're doing a great job Brad. At first my boss wasn't sure about you, but I told him about watching you sweat through your first day. He felt that you'd be no slouch at hard work. I'll let you in on a secret, you keep this up and he'll put you in charge of something. He wants to spend more time with his wife and son. I'll be taking his place and you, if you continue like you are, will take mine, second in command. You'll make a very good living and if you enjoy the work, you'll likely end up retiring from the company with a good pension. Just think, you thought you were just getting a part time temporary job but you may end up as someone in authority."

While Jason was speaking Brad had been listening, becoming more amazed with each sentence that was spoken. The last thing he'd ever imagined in life was being a boss of someone. Suddenly his future seemed illuminated with a golden sheen of luxury and wealth, something he least expected.

The conversation had continued during their unloading of the pallets. The work force had arrived.

When lunch time arrived Jason invited Brad, his treat. This time they went into the mall and visited the Mexican restaurant. Brad had never tasted anything with a south-of-the-border zing so Jason ordered. Burritos, refried beans, and tacos, there was also a generous sized dispenser of hot sauce to use as they preferred. Jason ordered a glass of milk, Brad preferred water. He secretly hoped it would cool down the spiciness.

It was hotly seasoned and delicious, Brad planned on eating there again. "This was great Jason, thanks pal. To think I've missed this terrific food all these years, what a waste of time."

"It grows on you Brad. You'll be subject to a sudden craving for a burrito or those refried beans and you won't be satisfied until you indulge yourself." He gave a wicked laugh and a wink at his friend as they made their way back to the job site.

At day's end, the job site cleaned up, everyone went on their way. Jason let Brad use the company pickup truck. It was only sitting at the site so may as well let Brad use it until he could afford his own transportation.

Although Brad was not in the mood to shop, it was either that or wait until morning and not have breakfast when he left to shop with an empty stomach. He grinned to himself knowing that would be a huge mistake, he'd end up buying everything except the kitchen sink. When he reached the supermarket there were plenty of parking spaces, maybe no long waiting lines at the checkout. That was fine with him, he felt a bit tired.

Bathroom tissue, bread, eggs, butter, milk, peanut butter, strawberry jam, he headed for the meat counter. Next came Canadian bacon, pork sausage, he felt his eyes were bigger than his stomach, he'd better slow down. He wandered down the frozen dinner aisle. This was fantastic, anything and everything a person could desire.

An assortment of dinners and meat entrees finished his shopping spree. By the time he arrived home it was dark. It took two trips to tote everything downstairs and by the time it was all stashed in the fridge and freezer he was starved. The only quick solution would be a glass of milk and two peanut butter sandwiches. He closed his eyes in ecstasy, the milk tasted like cream. The meal was consumed within a very short time.

After a shower he retired for the night thinking, as he snuggled down into bed, that the next time he bought sheets, he'd launder them before using them. He was even too tired to itch.

In the morning, hurriedly dressing and then fixing eggs, bacon and oven toast, he realized he needed a few more things to make life more pleasant. Like a toaster, a coffee pot and an alarm clock. Didn't this ever end….this neediness? There was a list of items beginning to run through his mind and it was driving him crazy. All he really wanted was to be comfortable. He decided he would not go shopping again until his next paycheck. That was final. But he should buy another set of sheets and pillow cases so he could wash them before having to sleep on them…what in God's name was happening to him, this was nuts. He almost felt like gnashing his teeth in frustration. For a moment the sudden image of his mother flashed through his mind. He saw her stripping his bed, doing laundry. He remembered her asking him to take out the trash and shovel the walk. For the first time ever, he felt himself in her shoes and how she must have felt when he'd just walk out ignoring her. All the way to work his conscience was tormenting him. Sure, he'd do chores for his landlord but not for his mother? She had always been good to him, even getting him a car. But it was too late for him now, he couldn't go back. What was that old saying, "You can never go home again?" That was it, he couldn't. He'd killed somebody, more than one, and all because of his crappy attitude about life, like they all owed him something. There was great satisfaction in working for your paycheck. Now he knew what his mother had been trying to teach him, pride in accomplishment, earning those dollars honestly. The magnitude of his mistakes overwhelmed him. He could spend the rest of his life in jail and there was no way he could rectify what he had done. He didn't realize he had already arrived at the job site. He tried to get himself under control.

When Jason spotted Brad walking onto the work site he could see something was wrong. He looked pale as a ghost and seemed to be in physical pain. "Hey! Pal, what's the matter? You look sick as a dog. There's no sense sticking around and passing your illness on to the rest of us. Get the heck out of here. Go home, go to bed and don't come back until you feel better. I can't afford to have the entire crew out sick."

"I'm not sick, Jason, it was likely those scratchy sheets I slept on. I never thought of washing them before use, that's the first thing I'll take care of after work today."

Jason doubted Brads excuse but decided to let it pass. Within a half hour he had finished assigning work sites to the crew. Everyone drifted away to their jobs, Brad included.

At noon Brad did a quick disappearing act and was late checking back in, Jason didn't say a word. This was the first lapse in ethics since he had begun work. Everyone deserved a little leeway occasionally. Fortunately, the remainder of the week went smoothly.

At the end of the week Friday paychecks were being handed out. Everyone was anxious to be on their way. Brad had just tucked his into his pocket and was half way out the door when he spotted a familiar face heading in his direction. He ducked quickly behind a stack of drywall and watched as Sheriff Hatch's son Chris made his way to where Jason was passing out the last envelopes. He was close enough to hear their conversation. He didn't wait to listen to it all but hurried to the truck that Jason had let him use and sped off. Plans were formulated and solidified before he reached his apartment. He had the entire weekend. He'd be a thousand miles away before anyone became aware of his absence. He'd dump the company truck as soon as he found a car. He packed all his possessions, no way was he leaving this for somebody else to enjoy. It was quite a bundle but it was his.

When Monday morning arrived Chris was early, he waited outside the entrance and watched as Jason pulled into the parking area, locked his car, and then unlocked the mall doors. Chris followed him to the office.

"Nice to meet you Chris, Alex has talked to your father letting him know you got here safely. You can bunk with me. My bedroom's large enough for a fold-down cot, they're fairly comfortable and since you'll only be working here through the winter, it won't cost you a dime except for your share of the food. How does that sound?"

"I'm happy to pay my way Jason. Dad gave me enough money to last until I got my first paycheck with some to spare. I'll try to stay out of your way, I'm quiet, I like to read a lot and maybe, once in a while, watch sports on television. One thing, though, I don't know how to cook. Mom wouldn't let me anywhere in the kitchen. I think it was because I tried to fix her a surprise Mother's Day breakfast when I was younger. Didn't pay attention to how high I had the heat under the eggs. I got distracted and they burnt to a crisp, smoked up the whole downstairs. The fire alarm went off and both mom and dad thought the house was burning. When she didn't see me in my bedroom she became frantic, was in such a hurry to get down the stairs that, thankfully the stairs were carpeted, she slid down all the way on her fanny and because she had a nighty on, she got carpet burns on you know where."

Chris had such a serious look on his face that Jason smothered his laugh as best he could by pretending to cough. He almost choked in the process.

After he showed Chris the site he was to work at and introduced him to his co-workers, he hurried back to his office muttering aloud to himself. "I wonder where the heck Brad is, he's usually here waiting when I arrive. Maybe he had trouble with the company truck, sometimes it's hard to start, probably needs a tune up or new spark plugs." Jason wasn't overly upset, yet, but as the clock edged toward nine o'clock he knew something was wrong. He decided to take a ride over to Brad's apartment.

Arriving at the property, the company truck was nowhere in sight. He must have missed him while on the way over, but instincts told him to check with the landlord. He had a sinking feeling that things were about to take a turn for the worse. He went to the front door and rang the bell. After a few moments an older, heavy set man answered the door.

"Good Morning sir, I'm sorry to bother you but my employee, Brad Shields hasn't shown up for work, I was worried something had happened to him. Have you seen or talked to him this morning?"

"So, you're the boss Brad has mentioned. You're darn nice to let him use the company truck. He told me last Friday evening that you were sending him down to Tennessee to check on a shipment of drywall you'd been waiting for that was holding up the job. It musta been around eight in the evening when he left, already dark. I heard the truck start up and take off. He seemed a nice enough young man but, to be honest with you, it always felt like he was hiding something. He said he wouldn't be back until next week." The man waited expectantly, watching Jason with anticipation.

"Would you mind showing me his apartment? I never sent him down to Tennessee, either. I don't want to draw any conclusions but I have an idea that seeing his living quarters will help solve one of the problems." Jason was positive about what he'd find.

Mr. Rhodes walked him around to the side door and then down the basement steps into the apartment. It was empty of everything but the basic furniture. Not a scrap of evidence remained that anyone had lived there.

Jason tried to control his anger. He had been more than generous to Brad, had even let him use the company truck for his personal use after work hours and this was his reward. The truck was gone, only God knew where. "Thanks Mr. Rhodes, I hope he didn't owe you any money, he sure wasn't worried about taking the company truck. I'll have to notify the police as soon as I leave here.

Jason strode away quickly while a list of "things to do" began sorting themselves in his mind. First the police then find access to another pickup truck. They had been thinking about buying a new one, having two trucks would have been convenient but they had stalled about buying during the winter, they'd planned the purchase for spring. The more he thought about the inconvenience, the angrier he became. Wait til Alex hears about this, he thought, he'll hit the ceiling, poor guy. Things were just settling down after baby Scotts' kidnapping. Jason felt almost ill with apprehension.

After he phoned the police and gave all the details, he drove to his bosses' home. For a moment he sat in his car. Then realizing that stalling wasn't solving anything, he exited the vehicle and rang the doorbell. He listened to the chimes echo and a moment later Alex opened the door. One look at his employees face told him something had happened.

"Come in Jason, things can't be that serious. You look like you lost your best friend. I doubt it's anything that bad for you to become upset about." Alex draped his arm about Jason's shoulders and drew him into the kitchen where Rose was feeding the baby. He poured a cup of coffee for Jason and topped his own cup off. "Would you like more coffee Rose?" She shook her head in a negative response, too busy wiping the cereal off Scott's face and watching him laugh, to give a verbal reply.

"Okay Jason, what's so important that you show up here on a Monday morning looking like you ate sour grapes?"

"Brad stole the truck and skipped town. This happened last Friday so he's had over two days to hide his tracks. Since he didn't have a car I let him use the truck. I'll never trust anyone again. He made a fool of me."

Alex could see that Jason was experiencing not only hurt feelings, but also loss of trust in his fellow man.

"Well! First thing we should do is notify the police, give a description of him and the truck. Is anything else missing from the work site?"

"I don't know boss, as soon as I found out he'd left I came right here. By the way, Sheriff Hatch's son Chris started work today. He seems like a nice kid. I'm letting him bunk with me. My bedroom is big enough for one of those fold-up heavy duty cots that have a mattress. I remember Ryan has one up in his attic, I'm sure he'll let me borrow it. I'll stop over to see him this evening. How is he doing at the new construction site? I sure miss having you two around, but this has been good experience for me, I'm learning the ropes and enjoying every minute of it."

"You head back to the job Jason and I'll take care of phoning the police. I'll give my son Ryan a call and have him drop that cot over to your place, he has a pickup truck. He can do that as soon as he gets home from our Westside project which seems to be coming along nicely. You're doing an excellent job Jason. You have a permanent position with us for as long as you desire."

Alex walked Jason to the door and watched as he drove off. He was a diamond in the rough. He'd be a very important part of the company once he learned all the ropes. Eventually he, himself, wanted to retire and spend more time with Rose and baby Scott. Ryan could take the helm of the company, maybe even by next year. Alex had a spring in his step when he returned to the kitchen. Scott had finished eating, Alex picked him up and carried him into the living room, balancing him on his knee as he sat in the rocker and began to hum a song to him. Scott gave a big smile then up-chucked part of his meal. With a sigh of regret Alex went to find Rose, playtime was over for today. Rose gave a knowing smile as she retrieved her son, Alex would never listen. You do not bounce a baby around after he has just eaten.

By the end of the day an APB had been sent out for Brad Shields and the stolen truck. By the next morning information had come in that he was also wanted for a triple homicide. The search would now intensify.

Jason had calmed down a little. Once he learned about Brad's background, he considered himself lucky. Maybe he'd escaped being one of Brads victims. Work went on as usual and the drywall shipment finally arrived, several weeks late. They were now in the process of finishing up the last of the retail stores. Soon windows and doors would be installed, once that was done the final cleanup. The men would then be sent to the Westside location which was almost ready for construction to begin.

Alex picked up the phone and dialed. "Good morning son, how's that Westside site coming along? We're about finished over here, ready to send you labor."

"Not completed yet, dad. The weather held us up from finishing the footings so maybe another few days to make sure the last of the poured concrete has set completely. The area has all been graded though. Workers can begin roughing-out on the far side of the complex. I hope this project goes as well as yours did. It will be a relief when it's roofed and enclosed, keeps weather out and thieves from walking off with supplies."

"How's Jenny doing? Did she finally decide what she wanted to do about the old couple that found her in that snow drift? Lucky for Jen, she could have frozen to death and they wouldn't have found her until that pile of snow melted. She shouldn't have been out in the weather to begin with."

"I know dad, but she's stubborn. She won't give up on the idea of doing something extra-special for them in return for saving her life. I'm at the point where I'd rather let her have her own way than argue. But I don't think she'll be venturing out in any snowstorms again, it scared her more than she let on."

For a minute there was silence as both men contemplated the disaster that had been avoided. If Ryan had known what Jennifer was thinking of doing he would have had a panic attack.

"How's my new baby brother doing, dad? I'm sorry I haven't been over to visit. If you and Rose aren't busy this weekend maybe Rose might like to get out of the house. How about coming over for dinner on Sunday? Jen will be glad for the company, she's been feeling a bit dejected. The two women will be able to catch up on all the latest gossip."

"I'll let you know, son, sounds good to me."

Right after Alex hung up the phone it rang. "Did you forget something son?"

Instead of Ryan, it was a stranger's voice. "This is Officer Edwards. We've been contacted by the Oregon State police. They almost had Brad Shields in custody however your pickup truck was totaled in the pursuit. The felon managed to escape on foot. They feel it is only a matter of time before his capture."

Alex hung up the phone after thanking officer Edwards for his courtesy call. He'd feel much better when Brad was taken into custody, what a mistake he'd made by hiring him. Intuition told him to phone Oscar Hatch with this latest news.

"Hello, Patty, this is Alex Williams. Remember me? I was the fellow who had amnesia last year. Is Oscar around? I'd like to talk to him if he's not busy."

"Hi! Alex, it's good to hear your voice, you sound happy. He's on the phone, it will only be for a short time. So how are you doing since you got back home? I've thought of you many times."

"Everything is back to normal Patty. In fact I even have a new son Scott. My wife and I are thrilled. It was an unexpected, welcome surprise."

"You should bring them up here for a vacation, Alex. Everyone liked you and would be tickled to meet your wife and family. Remember that old abandoned resort you stayed at after you had that accident driving off the cliff? Someone bought it and it's been rebuilt into better than new. It's brought visitors here in the summer which invigorated our economy. We even have new people taking up permanent residences."

"That's an excellent idea Patty. I'd forgotten about vacations since I got married, it's been a big change in my life having a wife and child. I'd bet she'd love to get away from home for a while, enjoy a little respite from the everyday humdrum of life. In fact, who would I talk to about making reservations for this summer?"

"That would be Roscoe Jenkins, the fellow that owns the gas station. He still owns it and it's a great place to advertize his resort. If you want to make reservations I'd suggest you talk to him, much better than phoning the resort. You'd have a hard time with them they're so busy."

"Thanks Patty. I'll do that after talking with Oscar." It was only another minute and then Sheriff Hatch was on the line.

"Alex, son-of-a-gun, I was just thinking about you. I got a call from the Oregon State police about Brad Shields. They're hot on his trail. I wouldn't be surprised if he was in custody before the week is over. He can't get far without transportation. I feel sorry for Patty though. Even with his stealing her money and treating her so badly, he's still her son and she loves him." Oscar couldn't help feeling upset, Patty was such a good person and she didn't deserve this sort of worry about that no-good son of hers.

"I called you to bring you up to date on the latest information, Oscar. I should have realized you'd have your fingers on the pulse of all the action. Say! Your son Chris arrived, he'll be bunking with a fellow employee, Jason who's my daughter-in-law Jennifer's brother. We'll take good care of him Oscar. I'll call you often to keep you up to date."

"Alex, I sometimes think of how different fate would have been if you hadn't had that accident and spent some time with us. So many lives have been intertwined. I sure wish you could come up here and visit sometime. I'd love to meet your wife and sons. What did you name your new baby? Chris had phoned and told me all the latest news of you and your family. I was shocked to learn of the kidnapping too. Of course Angie told all her friends and then word got around."

The longer Alex talked to Oscar, the more it felt like he was back with him and his family and all the good people in town. He had really enjoyed living there, even working at the Coney Island and meeting everyone. A pang of longing gave him a twinge of regret at leaving.

"I sometimes miss being there Oscar. Weird, but that was my first time just being an ordinary fellow trying to make a living working for minimum wages. I wouldn't trade that experience for anything."

"I'm glad we met Alex, the chance you're giving my son Chris to earn a living while finding out what it feels like living and working in a big city is a tremendous break for him. I won't worry about him as much as I would have if he was off and away with complete strangers." Oscar felt the vacancy left by his son's absence, but it was nowhere as bad as it could have been if he'd gone off to work with a stranger. With a sigh of relief, he concentrated again on the conversation. "Thank you Alex. You're a good man."

When final goodbyes had been said, both were contemplative after hanging up their receivers. Fate had a hand in their meeting, Oscar thought, he wondered what she might have up her sleeve for the future.

Alex was also reflectively reviewing their conversation. Ryan was doing an excellent job of supervising the building. He'd grown up hanging around the developing sites after school, learning by watching and also giving a hand to workers during school vacations. He'd turned into a knowledgeable, competent supervisor. Alex felt he wouldn't have to worry if he turned the project over to his son while he took his family on vacation. The more he thought about it, the better the idea became. In fact, maybe, if they left soon, they'd have a jump on the other vacationers and get a cabin near the lake. They could stay there during the summer with Alex returning to the worksite occasionally to check in with Ryan. On the spur of the moment he dialed Oscar's number and when Patty answered was transferred to her boss.

"Hey! Oscar, I just had a brain storm. What is that resorts phone number? I'm going to make reservations for the entire summer. Rose will enjoy spending the days relaxing in the sun. Right now the baby is no trouble since he's so young. Once he begins crawling about, she'll have her hands full."

Oscar couldn't believe what he was hearing. Many times he'd been tempted to take a few days off work to drive down and visit Alex. He'd finally realized the reason he'd missed the guy so much. This was the first close friend he'd had since becoming sheriff. For some reason folks were a little uncomfortable being around him even when it was after working hours. Over the years he'd become used to being somewhat of a loner until Alex had shown up, amnesia and all....it had been an eye opener for him to realize the male companionship he was missing. Oh! It wasn't that he didn't enjoy his sons company it was just, different with them. He was their father and was treated as such.

When Patty glanced at her boss she noticed his face was practically alight with pleasure. She wondered what the news was all about to create such delight. She didn't have long to ruminate.

"Patty, you won't believe what's going to happen. Alex has decided to bring his family here for vacation. He's planning on spending the entire summer at the resort. God! Help me, I can't believe how excited I am about seeing him again. It wasn't until he'd returned home that I began to realize what an empty space he'd left in my days. I missed his company the very first day he was gone." For a moment Oscar recalled his best friend Joe Murphy who had been killed in an auto accident when an escaping felon crashed into his car. Joe had just dropped him off after their cadet training classes. They had decided to become police officers. When he had learned of the accident he'd wanted to quit but remembering the dedication Joe'd had about becoming a cop, he decided to finish the course as a memorial to his friend. It was the wisest decision he could have made, he'd never regretted it either. Suddenly Oscar realized why he felt so close to Alex, he reminded him of Joe.

Oscar picked up the phone and called his wife Angie to tell her the news. After that call was completed he contacted his son Will who was a State Trooper. Then, deciding to visit the Coney Island for lunch, he looked forward to seeing the expressions on folks faces when he told them that Alex would be around for the summer, bringing his wife and new baby on vacation. Before the ending of the day the entire town was abuzz with the news and of course, Angie had phoned all her friends also. There would be a count-down until the Williams family arrived on the scene.

The days passed quickly. June arrived and they were packed and ready for the trip north. It was unbelievable how many extra things were needed for the baby. Rose added a multitude of packs of disposable diapers, worried she wouldn't find the same brand up north. To Alex it seemed enough to last a year, however Rose assured him they would all be used before their return home.

They left at dawn. The trip would easily be completed before the day was over even with numerous stops to change the baby and dispose of the soiled diapers. It was a leisurely trip. At midmorning they stopped for breakfast, dawdled over their meal while Scott slept on the seat next to them. At noon, although neither felt hunger, they tarried at a Coffee Shoppe to enjoy a fresh baked pastry. The coffee was superb. They passed farmland with high growths of corn, wheat. Rows of sprouting vegetables such as cabbage, cauliflower, green beans. Orchard trees were rife with flowers soon to become apples, cherries, pears or peaches. The occasional scent of fertilizer was carried on the breeze wafting through the car windows. Several pastures of dairy cattle dotted the landscapes they drove past. There were hills and valleys, picturesque farms with huge old fashioned barns visible in the distance, and everything looked so green and fresh. The air itself was invigorating.

It was almost dinnertime when they turned onto the road leading to the resort. The road had not been surfaced and the forest was lush with the chatter of birdlife and squirrels. The scent of earth, leaf mold and vegetation permeated the air like it had for a multitude of years. A feeling of intense pleasure enfolded the two adults. Alex reached for Rose's hand and pressed a kiss on its palm. She felt a spark of pleasure heighten her awareness of him and how handsome he looked, how much she loved him. If he had turned to look at her he would have been surprised at the look of longing on her face. A look put there at the memory of all the years they had missed being together and the yearnings she had tried to overcome after she had run away from home and him so many years ago.

Scott began to make a fuss, it was changing time again but since they were almost at their rental, it could wait a few more minutes.

When Alex exited the tree line he couldn't believe his eyes. This couldn't be the same place where he had spent so much time after escaping from his sandy prison between the rocky walls at the water's edge. It was absolutely beautiful. The old log building had been saved. An upper floor was added plus an extended addition turning it into a main lodge with a dining area. He parked at the rear of the building. Taking baby Scott they entered the lodge. Alex settled Rose and Scott on a bench while he rang a bell that sat on the counter to signal the manager.

Roscoe Jenkins tapped Alex on the shoulder. He had a wide grin on his face knowing he had surprised him.

"Alex, you son-of-a-gun, Oscar told me you were on the way. I saved the better of two new cottages for you, right near the water too. You won't recognize this place, a lot different than when you were stuck here. We have living quarters upstairs for the hired help and a new camp ground area with a dozen small log cabins for vacationers. I already signed you in. I'll have one of the men help with your baggage, we'll have you all settled in quickly. Is that the little lady and your son I've heard so much about?" Roscoe hurried over to greet Rose. "Come along darling, we'll have you comfy quicker than a cats wink." Alex carried Scott while Rose followed Roscoe. The cottage he led them to was far enough away from the water's edge that winter lake ice wouldn't damage it during harsh winter months. No other structure hindered the view of the lake.

Teddy, the young gofer, already had the contents from their auto in hand, ready to place them inside. He then made a hurried departure back to the lodge.

Roscoe only tarried a moment or two. Just enough time to welcome them to his resort and answer any questions they had. "Meals are at eight in the morning, twelve noon and at six for supper. In fact, you're just in time. Supper is being served as we speak. I'll see you there." With a wide grin he turned and was out the door on his way to the lodge.

The tempting aroma of roast beef wafted to them through the screened windows of the log building. The combination of fresh, pine scented air, lake breezes and a good dinner hurried their steps along as they followed Roscoe.

There were at least a dozen or so diners sitting at the red-checkered tablecloth- covered tables. Small candle-lit hurricane lamps gave a warm glow to animated faces while the buzz of conversation and laughter permeated the atmosphere. For a moment Alex recalled the barren look of the place when he had been stranded here, then a wide grin lit his face seeing a few familiar faces smiling at him with recognition. He felt immediately at home with the surroundings.

They settled down at a corner table, an extra chair held the baby carrier where Scott slept peacefully, the hum of conversation a lullaby.

It was the first leisurely dinner they had enjoyed since leaving home. Rose was relaxed, looking forward to a restful vacation and even an invigorating swim in the clear fresh waters of Lake Huron in the morning. For tonight though, a good dinner and a solid night's sleep would suite her just fine.

By the time they were finishing their meal Rose was yawning, trying to hide it behind her hand. Alex picked up Scott, handed the waiter the check and some bills, told him to keep the change, and Rose followed him out the door. Within a half hour they were tucked into bed sound asleep.

Alex nudged Rose from sleep by passing the cup of fresh coffee under her nose which began to twitch with anticipation. Her eyes popped open and a wide smile spread across her face. "You must have ulterior motives this morning sweetheart, you know exactly what I need and I don't even have to wait for the coffee maker." She pulled herself erect, leaning against the pillow propped against the headboard. With the first sip a sigh of contentment escaped her lips. "This feels like heaven, honey. Coffee in bed, I didn't expect this on our vacation, you're spoiling me." She glanced over at Scott who was playing with his toes trying to stick them into his mouth. The flexibility he possessed amazed her. "Even Scott is in a good mood this morning. You must have already changed him, right?"

Alex gave a nod of agreement. It had taken him quite a while after Scott's birth to control his gagging convulsions when trying to help by changing his son's diapers. He still remembered Roses side-splitting laughter when watching him. Sometimes, even now, he had moments of queasiness but time and repetition had strengthened his resolve, he was almost a pro at changing time now. He gave his wife a smile of relief, he was overcoming his weaknesses.

Rose took her time dressing. She donned jeans and a sky-blue tee, comfortable leather sandals, her hair pulled back in a ponytail, Alex was stunned. She looked as she had when they'd first met years ago. The infatuation he'd felt at the time seemed to possess him once again. She was beautiful, and she was his. Suddenly the deep love he felt for her jolted his entire being into a painful realization that he truly needed her, she was part and parcel of his life and he wouldn't want to be without her. For the first time he felt a twinge of fear. What if something should happen to her? He doubted he'd want to go on alone. The unsettling feelings were uncomfortable. He tried to stop the asinine guessing game his mind had conceived, a ridiculously lonely scenario that wasn't worth wasting mental energy on. With a smile he picked up his son and placed a kiss on his forehead, then urged Rose toward the door.

They enjoyed a light breakfast of cereal, toast and juice. Then off to the boat ramp where visitors were loaded into a cruiser to see the colorful rock facings towering over the lake. Alex pointed out the sandy strip where he had been stranded and the peak he'd driven off on that dark night he'd gone over the cliff in Ryan's Jeep. It seemed a million years ago but memories were as fresh as if it had happened only recently. Somewhere down there that jeep was resting deep under the water, he might have been with it. With a mental shake he pulled his mind away from the troublesome thought. Why was he in such a morbid mood this morning? It was a beautiful day, not a cloud in the sky and Rose looked contented and happy.

He turned his face toward the prow of the boat, putting his morose thoughts aside. This was a vacation, straighten up for God's sake, enjoy this leisure time with Rose. The boat ride was enjoyable, the rock cliffs unbelievably beautiful and worth the trip.

That afternoon they packed a few supplies for Scott. Alex was taking Rose to see the town, visit the local establishments and maybe even Oscar Hatch if he wasn't too busy. He felt a spur of excitement at seeing his friends again. They had been so good to him.

His first stop was the sheriff's office. Patty was still there, busy as usual. She looked good, not as frazzled as he remembered. Then he recalled her son Brad and what he had done. Patty didn't have to contend with him anymore, he was gone from her life forever. He noticed an engagement ring on her left hand. "Hello! Patty, remember me? This is my wife Rose and son Scott. You're looking very pretty this morning. I was sorry to hear about your son Brad though. It must have been very hard on you."

"Oh! My! Gosh! JD…er! I mean Alex, you'll always be JD to me, it's hard to change your name after knowing you as JD for so long."

"Patty, this is my wife Rose and son Scott. I'm taking her around to meet everyone. I'm excited about seeing all the folks again. Where's Oscar this morning? Off solving a new case? Say! That's a beautiful engagement ring you're wearing, from anyone I know?"

"Al Murphy, a new recruit Oscar hired a while ago, not sure you met him. I sold my house, Al insisted I keep the money. For the time being I'm living in our new home getting it all ready for after our wedding. Choosing the paint, carpeting, furniture, making sure the work is done to my satisfaction. I'm still in a daze not believing my good luck at finding such a wonderful guy. I love him to pieces and can hardly wait for our wedding, but we're doing it all properly, it's the way we both want to begin our life together." Patty was actually glowing. Alex couldn't help smiling recalling his own anticipation when he'd finally captured Rose's heart.

Just then Oscar walked into the office. Spotting Alex he did a double take then reached for him, encircling him in a bear hug. "I heard you had arrived. This must be Rose and baby Scott, come along into my office and have a seat, would you like some coffee?" Oscar tried to control his emotions at seeing Alex again. The connection they'd made, becoming such good friends, made him realize anew how much he'd missed him. True friends were hard to come by. Being Sheriff, folks were extra polite when speaking to him but somehow everyone kept their personal distance. He'd grown used to the solitude over the years but when Alex appeared, memory gone, depending on him for help, they'd formed a bond which they'd both benefited from.

Alex made introductions. Rose sat quietly holding the baby while the two men caught up on the latest developments they had experienced. She could see the friendship that had developed during Alex's amnesia, his trust and affection for the older man. It was then she realized he had never spoken to her about his father. She had never thought to question him.

Oscar contacted one of his officers to take charge of the office for the remainder of the day. He was taking Alex and Rose home, Angie was already preparing one of her memorable Italian dinners. Alex followed Oscar in his own car.

Time seemed to disappear too quickly. Dusk was making an appearance, the call of crickets and pond frogs carried on the evening breeze. Alex recalled falling asleep to their music, the serenade had never failed to lull him into dreamland. He realized the muffled quiet back home of hearing only occasional street traffic or the hum of the air conditioner, was not as welcome as the night song. These were living creatures creating harmony, a comfort to listen to until sleep began to curl around mind and body, softly muting the sounds until only silence remained.

The drive back to their cabin was pleasant. Car windows open to the night air, a huge moon floating in the sky and stars so bright they almost seemed within reach. They were both relaxed, still full from the spaghetti, roast chicken and spinach salad dinner Angie had prepared. Rose made sure she got the recipes before they left. She had enjoyed the visit very much, the friendliness and homespun atmosphere a refreshing change from city life. If she had her choice this would be where she'd like to spend summer vacations. She could hardly wait to tell the family about it. It was nice not having to worry about any upkeep either. Roscoe had local women earning extra money working as maids keeping the cabins neat.

That night they all slept well, even Scott. The sun was barely peeking over the distant eastern edge of the lake when they began to stir. The purple, rosy glow of dawn spread across the sky brightening quickly, a few fluffy clouds suspended in the atmosphere. It looked like a beautiful day.

CHAPTER 13

Ryan sat pensively drinking his last cup of morning coffee while watching Jennifer wipe the counters and load the dishwasher. She was in an expansive mood this morning happily discussing her upcoming shopping trip with Rose and Sylvia. They planned on visiting the new woman's clothing store, "Stacks," that had just opened at the local mall. It was a high-end shop with all the latest styles. Not that the women catered only to the most expensive stores, but the "Grand Opening" sales were too tempting to resist. Ryan tried to act serious and hide the smile that kept trying to spread across his face. He could not imagine why the women were so interested in store sales when they could afford to purchase anything their hearts desired. He'd never understand their logic. Jennifer didn't notice, thankfully.

Draining the last drop of coffee, he handed the cup to Jen and picked up his jacket hastily shrugging into it. Planting a quick kiss on her lips he headed for the door. "Have fun Hon, if you're not back by dinner don't worry, I plan on picking up a pizza on the way home." He hoped she'd be late, this was the first chance he'd have to retrieve the film from the hidden cameras he'd had installed before their wedding on Thanksgiving Day. He hadn't mentioned them to anyone. The thought of everyone's surprise when he handed out the fancy albums with copies of all the photos, filled him with the anticipated pleasure of seeing their astonished faces.

Within moments of Ryan's departure Jennifer headed out the door. She adored the cute little 1949 Plymouth coupe Ryan had surprised her with on her birthday. He'd handed her a small, prettily wrapped, box but when she opened it expecting jewelry, there was a set of keys instead. She'd leave the car at Rose's. They'd take her sedan to the mall.

The day seemed to slip away too quickly. Rose had her nanny caring for baby Scott, Sylvia, several months pregnant, was in a very good mood to shop for baby items, and Jennifer, still remembering the secretive expression on Ryan's face that morning, was in the mood to spend money, retaliating for the mystery he was withholding from her. She knew his moods and hadn't liked the feeling she'd gotten from him that something was being hidden from her.

When they eventually arrived back at Roses it was late and traffic heavy so neither Sylvia nor Jen wanted to stay for coffee. With a wave goodbye to Rose after retrieving their packages from Roses car, they each went their separate way homeward.

Ryan arrived home. Thankfully no lights were on, Jen was still off shopping. He quickly retrieved the film tapes from the hidden cameras and secreted them in his jacket. Tomorrow he'd take them to get developed. This was turning out better than he could have planned. When the phone rang, expecting that it was Jennifer phoning to let him know she'd be late, he was surprised to hear Roses voice.

"Hi! Hon, let me talk to Jen, she forgot a package, I wouldn't want her to worry that she'd lost it somewhere in the mall."

"Rose?....Jen isn't here, how long ago did she leave?"

"I'm jumping the gun, Ryan. She'll likely be pulling into the driveway any moment. Just tell her I have one of her packages. I have some errands to do tomorrow and I'll drop it off to her, Okay?"

After Ryan hung up the phone he felt a weird premonition begin to tweak his psyche and at the same time a warm touch on his shoulder, but when he turned to look, no one was there. He grabbed his jacket and hurried out the door. He should have remained at home. The telephone began to ring the moment he drove off. After a while it stopped, then began again a few seconds later.

Ryan headed toward his father's house. When he crossed the main street at the light, a huge semi truck was pulled to the side of the road. The crumpled remains of a small blue coupe were sitting on one of the crosswalks and several police cars were stationed to guide traffic around the accident. He pulled in behind the semi, exited his pickup and made his way through the scattered debris toward the closest officer.

"Keep moving, don't block traffic." He shouted at one gawker, while waving other autos forward, traffic slowing for a few minutes then proceeding again at regular speeds once past the mangled metal.

Ryan tapped the officer on the shoulder, panic making him raise his voice, as he asked what had happened to the driver of the small blue car.

"Who are you? I don't give out information regarding the accident. Unless you have a legitimate reason for being here I suggest you get on your way."

"Please officer, that's my wife's car, where did they take her? Was she okay? She went shopping with friends and should have been home long ago."

The sudden expression of sympathy on the policeman's face caused Ryan's face to turn pale with dread. Another quick glance at the crumpled wreck intensified the feeling of impending doom at the officer's reply. Ryan felt a strong hand holding his arm.

"The ambulance just left a few moments ago. I expect they took the woman to Community General, I'll check on this for you. The officer pushed the call button on the small black pager hooked to the shoulder of his uniform. "Luke here, double checking on where you took the accident victim from 4th and Slocum. Right….Thanks."

"It was a pretty bad accident Mr. Williams, they took her to Community, I'll drive you there. Your truck will be fine just where it is, it will take a while to clear the area of the debris."

By the time they arrived at the hospital Ryan was prepared for the worse news, that Jennifer had been declared DOA and that there had been nothing the emergency team could do to save her. It felt like every fiber of his body had frozen into screaming disbelief. He wanted to wake up again in the morning, decide to take the day off and go browsing at the mall with his wife. Or maybe, coax her into staying home with him while he showed her the films from the cameras he'd hidden about and they could relive that special day again in memory. Before he was aware, the police car was stopped, motor turned off and the officer was sitting quietly waiting for him to return from his reveries.

Officer Luke walked Ryan into the hospital emergency ward where he was told his wife had been transferred to a regular room. When he arrived at her bedside Jennifer lay pale and wan, leg in a caste hoisted up in a sling. Ryan took her hand trying to rub some warmth into it, the relief that she was alive making him want to gather her into his arms and keep her safe from pain and worry. It was then that the love he felt for her overwhelmed him, he had never realized the true depth of his feelings for her.

The next morning Ryan arrived at the hospital happy to see that his wife was awake. Jen had been under an anesthetic the previous evening, had slept the entire time he was there.

"I never saw the truck coming, the light had just turned green for me, I was half-way across when the truck come out of nowhere and slammed into me. I spun around several times but then something caused me to black out. When I came to I was in the ambulance on the way to the hospital." Jennifer felt tears well up as she thought of the little blue coupe she loved so much. "Did you see my car, is it too messed up to fix? I should have been more careful but when the light changed I didn't have any warning not to drive on, I didn't see the truck trying to stop."

Ryan already had the car at a repair shop. Thankfully the frame was okay but the replacement parts would be expensive, it would also need a new motor. He didn't care about the cost. He just wanted it fixed and by hook or crook, Jen would have her little prize back as good as new. He smiled at his wife with secret pleasure knowing that when the caste was finally removed his greatest delight would be presenting Jen with her restored coupe.

Eventually Jen was released from the hospital. The caste, of course, would remain on for the next several months. The awkwardness of getting about was eased by having an electric wheelchair which Jen enjoyed scooting around on downstairs. She was able to prepare meals standing on one leg, chair handy behind her for quick rests. Ryan hired a maid for cleaning, laundry and for doing shopping from lists Jen made. In fact, Jen was getting a little spoiled with the extra help but that was fine with Ryan who occasionally thought of the close call Jen'd had, he could have lost her.

Ryan enjoyed helping Jen with her shower. He'd encase the caste in plastic wrap then they'd undress and he'd help her into the shower. He'd scrub her back, and then she'd scrub his while he kept a firm grip so she wouldn't fall. When they were dried off and he'd rubbed lotion on her, he'd carry her into their bed. The caste didn't hinder their lovemaking and afterward they slept like babies.

Days drifted away and the time to remove the cast finally arrived, not a moment too soon to suit Jennifer. She was sick of the weighty cumbersome thing. Of course she now had physical therapy but at least she could move about easily again and happy to see the electric wheelchair gone from sight. Somehow though, she wasn't in a hurry to rid herself of the maid who had turned from a convenience into a necessity.

When at last therapy was completed, she was pronounced able to return to regular activities. That was when Ryan took her by the hand, placed her in his truck, and took her for a pleasant drive. While they were gone the local repair shop returned the newly painted and restored coupe to the family driveway.

Jennifer thought she was daydreaming when they returned home. She sat so quietly that Ryan felt a moment of consternation. He turned to her only to discover her eyes were welling with tears of disbelief and happiness.

"Oh! Honey! What have you done? I thought it was gone forever, especially since you never mentioned it or the accident again. You know how much I love that little car. I feel like a princess when I'm driving it. It's small, cute and I adore it. How did you ever manage to make it look new again?"

Ryan didn't mind the kisses or hugs one bit, "I did it for you sweetheart. It was easy.

I didn't have to lift a finger either, just had it taken it to my friends repair shop." Ryan couldn't help the grin of pleasure at seeing Jennifer's excitement about having her car back. "One thing though, I don't want any more scares about any accidents. From now on you look before taking a green light for granted. There's always some jerk who'll try to beat the red light."

Jennifer turned away to hide the guilty expression that she could feel showing on her face. If her husband knew her secret he'd forbid her from driving at all. She had been tempted to tell him she thought she was pregnant just before the accident, but had decided to wait a few more days to be sure. Now, however, she'd wait a long enough time for him to get over the upset before telling him the good news. She was thankful the accident hadn't caused a miscarriage, but then, she was only a little over two weeks late for her period. For some reason an old proverb popped into her mind... "Oh what a tangled web we weave when we practice to deceive." A sudden eruption of goose bumps, the fine hairs standing erect on her arms caused a chill, a premonition of impending disaster. She felt deep in her bones that if she told Ryan about being pregnant he'd stop her from driving. There'd go her freedom, the feeling of independence, the right to pick-up-and-go any time she felt hemmed in. She'd never told him about her feelings of entrapment right after they married. She'd felt she had to account for every moment of her day. However, being able to jump into her car and take off for places unknown had been a release from the feelings of bondage, a very silly way to think of marriage but fact as far as her personal feelings were concerned. There was no way she could explain this all to Ryan without deeply hurting him. The only recourse was to continue to keep her feelings secret. Still, this caused resentment on her part. She loved him, her oft times soul-search confirmed that, so what was she to do?

"I have to get to work, Honey. I'm glad you're so pleased with my surprise. I originally had an idea to buy you a new sporty little car but after seeing how upset you were about your coupe, I had no other choice but to get it fixed as good as new for you. Don't bother cooking, I'll stop off and pick up a pizza for our supper. Go enjoy yourself today, maybe visit Sylvia or Rose. I'll see you around six."

She watched Ryan drive away in his truck with mixed feelings. She had to admit he was exceptionally good to her, even when she happened to be in one of her bitchy moods, which wasn't that often, at least she didn't think so.

After making the bed and neatening up the house she dressed in jeans, tee and a denim jacket, picked up her purse adding a handful of twenties from her stash of cash hidden and tucked up in the open bottom of a tomato soup can sitting on the back shelf of the pantry. With a last glance around she headed out the door. Settling onto the front seat of her coupe it felt like she was home again. The motor purred to life and with a screech of tires she was away, heading for she knew not where, at least until she'd reached the expressway. With a spur-of-the-moment decision, she headed north. When she almost passed the side route to Port Huron she made a quick right turn soon arriving at the Blue Water Bridge to Canada. All she needed was her driving license to pass into foreign territory, she'd worry about everything tomorrow but right now all she wanted was a straight road into nowhere. She turned north knowing that at some point she would again have access getting back into the states, she just didn't

know when or where. The miles seemed to flow past mesmerizing her into a relaxed mood. When the realization that she'd not eaten breakfast nor lunch finally created hunger pangs, the thought of the embryo growing inside caused her to take notice of her surroundings and look for a fast-food eatery or restaurant. For the next few miles not one place available until finally a small grocery store in a small town had to suffice.

She bought bagels, cheese, tangerines, apples, crackers, small cans of apple juice, an old fashioned can opener, tomato juice, bottles of water, orange juice and a small roasted chicken which she had watched turning on a spit near the meat counter. She also bought two huge rolls of paper towels. A large wedge of cheddar cheese was the last purchase.

Wiping the chicken grease from her face and hands Jennifer felt a thousand times better, her enthusiasm about the trip intensified into pure excitement. She decided to continue northward until she reached the northern entry to upper Michigan, via Canada. It would be a long haul but she'd phone Ryan about the time he'd reach home. The problem was, she didn't have a map, only her instincts to guide her to her destination. As the sun began to set she found a small inn and rented a room, totally exhausted from her long drive. She fell into a deep sleep as soon as her head hit the pillow and didn't awaken until morning. When she tried phoning Ryan there was no answer. Discouraged, she hung up, intending to try calling again later at mid-morning. There was a Tim Horton's restaurant across the road. She headed there for breakfast and a hot cup of coffee.

By the end of the day she felt bone tired of driving. She hadn't stopped anywhere for food, instead she nibbled at the cheese, bites of apple and drank an entire bottle of water. She was fortunate to find restrooms at petrol stations when needed. When she finally spotted a sign for Sault Ste Marie she felt her spirits rise knowing that she'd soon be back in Michigan, although there was no way she could get back home before evening. It was a very long drive from the northern shores of the Upper Peninsula down to her suburban home. She had been unable to reach Ryan and finally realized what a stupid thing she had done by just driving away without leaving any note of explanation. If he had done this to her she'd have been more than furious, she'd be ready to kill him. Thankfully, this was the last night she'd be renting a motel. She showered, washed her hair and dropped into bed, falling asleep immediately.

After breakfast the next morning she was on her way home, picking up interstate 75 which would take her all the way without any side trips.

The fewer miles there were to drive, the more nervous she became realizing Ryan would be more than just angry, yet she could think of no plausible excuse. Could this be like some of those stories told about the raging hormones that pregnant women experienced making them do outlandish things? God! She hoped with all her heart it would be so. Maybe it truly was....when had she ever done anything so ridiculous? But then she recalled the ruse she had played on David. But that was when she had been a different person. She was changed now, not the same as when she had felt so alone and lost. Only wanting to find someone to love who would love her back with their entire being. She had found that person in Ryan. Why did she leave without saying a word? She felt that old fear rising within her. Had she ruined the good life she now had, driven away the only man she truly loved. She felt a cramp begin in her side and travel to her stomach. Please! She thought, this can't be happening now, I have to get home or Ryan will never forgive me. She felt tears well up but tried to stem their flow.

When she arrived home there was a police car parked on the street in front of the house. She pulled in behind Ryan's truck, slammed the car door and hurried up the front walk. Just as she arrived at the door it opened, Ryan caught her as she began to fall in a dead faint. Lifting her in his arms he carried her into the living room and placed her on the couch.

The police officer standing at his side recognized the symptoms that the young woman was experiencing and told Ryan to elevate her feet. A short time later the cramping stopped. When Jennifer opened her eyes Ryan was sitting next to her holding her hand. The officer had left, the missing person no longer missing.

"Ryan, I'm so sorry for causing you worry. I don't know what got into me. It was a spur of the moment decision that got out of hand. I must have put on a thousand miles in these two days. I tried phoning you several times without success. Where were you all this time?"

"When I got home from work and you weren't here I called Rose immediately. I was so worried and upset, I couldn't figure where you had disappeared to. Finally, Rose told me your secret, she had seen the baby items in that package you had forgotten to bring home. She told me all about what she had gone through when pregnant, and about the hormones that had driven her crazy. She suggested that I just relax and wait for you to come back home when you felt ready. I hardly slept a wink last night from worrying. Sweetheart, from now on anytime you get upset or feel trapped, call me and I'll be here in a flash to help you through it. You should have told me you were pregnant. I think this is the greatest news I ever could have wished for. We'll be busy now fixing up one of the bedrooms and buying all sorts of things to make caring for him easier on you. Actually, I should say "Us" because I want to help too. Are you as excited as I am?

Jennifer was resting her head on her arm watching Ryan as he was speaking to her. There was a definite glow in his eyes and energetic gestures with his hands when describing the things he wanted to do with the baby's room. If she'd had any idea at all how excited he'd be about the pregnancy, she'd have told him the moment she discovered she was expecting. Suddenly, the reality that within a year she would be mother to a real live baby brought a stab of fear and a feeling of inadequacy. Would she be able to cope with the responsibility? Would Ryan? The only person she could get information from was Rose. For a moment she thought about her mother and wished she was able to confide in her, talk to her about the worries that were nagging at her. She must have gone through the very same feelings when pregnant with Jason and her.

For the very first time Jen realized how much she missed her mom and how much she could have learned from her. That empty void seemed to expand with every passing moment. Ryan's voice drew her back from her reveries.

"So! Let's start on the baby's room tomorrow, okay, Honey? You pick the colors, wallpaper, furniture and I'll take care of the rest but for now, you relax. I'll fix you a nice hot cup of tea...." Ryan's voice drifted away as he hurried to the kitchen.

The sweetened cup of fragrant lemon tea soothed Jens nerves and settled her stomach. Exhaustion from sitting in one position for so many miles suddenly seemed to drain every ounce of energy from her. All she wanted to do now was insert her tired body onto a nice firm mattress and stretch out her cramped leg muscles. A good night's sleep would solve some of her misery.

Ryan picked up the drained cup and returned to the kitchen. He wiped off the counter, placed the cup and spoon in the dishwasher then returned to the living room. Jennifer had fallen deeply asleep. He turned off the lights except for the lighted stairway, cradled Jen in his arms and carried her upstairs. After placing her in bed he covered her, planted a gentle kiss on her cheek, whispered "Goodnight sweetheart," and soon the only sounds heard were his muffled snores.

In the morning Jennifer was in a better mood after the long night's sleep that had restored her into a positive attitude about her pregnancy. She knew she'd be a good mother and she had no doubts about Ryan, he'd likely exhibit the same attitude and actions as his father Alex. The way he'd reared Ryan was the way Ryan would also raise his own children. With a smile Jen began to prepare breakfast knowing Ryan would be surprised that the morning sickness she had been experiencing was finally over with. In fact, she felt darn good this morning. Maybe it was the change of scenery she had enjoyed the past few days or maybe the deep concern Ryan had shown about her absence. He loved her more than she'd imagined and that put her in an exceptionally giddy mood. She felt like a schoolgirl experiencing her first crush.

Ryan settled down at the table, eyes wide with surprise at the sumptuous display Jen placed before him. A stack of pancakes, a platter of sausage links and Canadian bacon, sunny-side up eggs and buttered whole wheat toast, he was famished, not having had much of an appetite after Jens disappearance.

Jen sat quietly watching him while nibbling on a piece of toast and sipping at a glass of orange juice. She felt more relaxed about her pregnancy now that she wasn't spending the mornings bent over the commode like she had in previous weeks.

She had another doctor's appointment on Monday. He was going to do a scan of her abdomen and show them what the baby looked like. Ryan was going with her, she could hardly wait.

Ryan arrived with her at Doc Murray's, too curious about the scan to wait to see the pictures they would bring home. They both peered at the screen trying unsuccessfully to decipher the image revealed until the doctor pointed the outlines of two babies entwined, hands moving, feet pushing against the encompassing walls. The shock of carrying twins almost undid Jennifer until Dr. Murray reassured her that birthing two would be over almost as quickly as giving birth to one.

Ryan was excited yet worried about Jennifer carrying twins. She was a delicate woman, light as a feather for him to carry. How in the world could her body manage to house two new lives, feed them from the food she ate, yet manage to sustain itself in a healthy manner? Of course he wanted a family but not at the risk of losing his wife. He took the Doctor aside and proceeded to question him intensely. When all the answers had been assimilated, Doctor's assurances and sensible replies so reasonable Ryan was finally put at ease about his concern for Jennifer.

The days drifted into weeks and then into months. The closer Jennifer came to her delivery date, the more her expanding girth gave her trouble sleeping. Her ankles became swollen and her back was killing her along with other miscellaneous miseries.

Ryan could hardly wait for their birth. He had already made arrangements for a nanny, had gotten a great reference from Esther, the maid who had cared for him when he had been a young lad. The new nanny was Esther Rodgers niece, Penelope, her brother's child, a well trained woman of thirty who had been taught as a young teenager by Esther. It was a worthwhile lifelong profession that they both took pride in. Penny was already in residence, fully prepared for the twins' arrival, everything in doubles except for the bathing apparatus and rocking chair. The babies would be bottle fed, no worries about having enough breast milk for proper growth.

Jennifer answered the phone, happy to hear Doc Murrays voice. She had been packed and ready for the past several days waiting for the phone call that would give her a timetable for release from her misery. Tomorrow morning was delivery day. They wanted her at the hospital this afternoon. She had felt restless all night, had gotten up several times to go to the bathroom but it was just pressure on her bladder. Toward dawn her stomach had done a sort of roll-over, and she could feel the baby had turned, she was unaware she was already in the first phase of labor. By the time they arrived at the hospital she felt waves of cramping although no actual pain.

Three hours later after a spinal had been administered, two healthy babies were delivered, a girl, Angela Louise Williams, 5 lb. 2oz., and a boy, Matthew Ryan Williams, 5 lb. 7oz. Ryan had the boy circumcised. The three would remain in the hospital for two days.

Ryan was stressed, he wanted his family home. The two days seemed like 4, the hours dragging along as slow as molasses. He really wasn't much of a cook and neither was Penny so he had brought pizza home the evening of the afternoon Jen had left. The next two days saw cheeseburgers, fries and milkshakes for one day, Chinese food for the last night. Neither he nor Penny had much appetite so there was plenty leftover for lunches. On the day Jen was expecting to be allowed to come home, Ryan decided to fix an oven pot roast. He seen Jen fix it enough times to give it a try. Roaster pan, 5# beef roast, in went baby carrots, peeled chunks of potatoes, an envelope of dried onion soup mix sprinkled over everything, and finally an 8oz tin of tomato sauce diluted with water to make 16oz. was poured over all. The roasting pan lid went on and the oven set at 350%. In three-four hours or so dinner would be ready.

The three adults and two babies were on the way home. Two carriers held the twins in the back seat with Penny sitting between. Once they arrived at home Ryan carried the twins upstairs where Penny would change them and give them bottles of formula. He escorted Jen into the house, the aroma of the roast beef permeating the kitchen. Jennifer felt she could eat a horse, as the old saying went. She felt she hadn't had a decent meal in ages. Hospital food was nothing to brag about.

The three of them sat down to dinner at 5pm. The roast was perfectly done and Ryan was enjoying the accolades for his cooking prowess. Jennifer already knew what she'd fix for tomorrow. The remainder of the roast would be made into a perfect stew that would be enjoyed immensely. A completely different meal created from the same ingredients, only the addition of a tin of tomato sauce and a can of peas necessary.

Within a week friends and relatives began to arrive to view the babies bringing gifts. Ah'd! And Oh'd! Over, the babies slept peacefully the entire time, well fed and scented with baby powder. Jennifer could not stay away from them more than an hour. She was almost ready to speak with Ryan about not keeping Penny for a nanny when Ryan decided it was time for his wife to enjoy a night out on the town. He took her shopping for a new outfit. He had made arrangements at their favorite restaurant to have a private dinner for the entire family to celebrate their new parenthood. Absolutely no gifts would be accepted, only the attendance of the invited. The entire evening was pure pleasure. David, Sylvia, Alex, Rose, Ryan and Jennifer, even David's parents Carol and David, Sr., had been able to attend. They were staying a few days with their son and daughter-in-law Sylvia. After dinner the entire family congregated at Alex's home. The men retired to the game room to play pool while the women relaxed.

Sylvia tried to keep a smile on her face even though the entire evening had been pure misery for her. The entire conversation had been about "Babies, Babies, Babies," until she thought she'd scream from frustration. She and David had tried everything they could think of to get her pregnant. Every month it was another disappointment. The Doctor told them they should just forget about getting pregnant. As soon as they relaxed it would happen, he'd seen it many times when couples were sure there was a problem. He couldn't count how many pleasant surprises he had witnessed but somehow Sy could never relax and forget, it was a constant worry that they'd never have children. Even David's parents kept asking when they'd start their family.

Sy had finally, without mentioning it to David, gone to a fertility clinic and been tested. The results were that she'd had previous infections in her fallopian tubes, likely she thought from the rapes by that creep that had kidnapped her. They were so scarred that the chances of her becoming pregnant were very slim, almost nonexistent. Sylvia was heartbroken, only that is, until she thought of artificial insemination. If they could get a healthy egg or two from her, David was fine regarding his sperm. It was time for her to make up her mind and talk to David. The sooner this could be accomplished the sooner she and David would have their own child. Maybe even two if the Doctor would agree. She decided at that moment to not waste another day. Just making that decision seemed to give her some peace of mind. Who knew, maybe with the coming year she and David would have their long-awaited family. She felt a smile twitch at the edges of her lips.

Two months later they did the process. In the mean time she had taken multiple vitamins, followed a good diet regimen to promote health, made sure she regularly had a good night's sleep. She felt physically and mentally strong and ready. Two weeks later after three of her fertilized eggs were implanted she missed her period. Now it was a matter of waiting. The Doctor had said there was a chance one or two of the eggs wouldn't take and he was right. Sylvia was pregnant and didn't care what gender it would be as long as the baby was born healthy. She'd follow every instruction to make sure.

It would be a spring birth. The round of baby showers from her newspaper "Common Sense" co-workers, to friends and family filled the nursery with every single necessity. Multiple items of layettes, diapers, bottles, everything and anything needed. Now it was only a matter of waiting for the delivery.

CHAPTER 14

    Bradley Shields watched the scene below realizing how close he'd come to being arrested again. His stomach muscles felt tight as a drum and he tried to relax his jaw, the ache of clenching his teeth unnoticed while watching the ongoing search. His stolen car was being towed away at that moment. The cops thought he'd hitched a ride with someone, not finding his footprints anyplace other than near the car and beside the road. This was the second time within the past year that he'd been able to elude them but now it was time for him to move on to new territory. He'd spent the past winter at an old hunting cabin where he'd found a nice cache of food, guns and ammunition, even a great pair of hunting boots. The place was used mainly in autumn, the October page of the calendar hanging on the wall, a perfect month for deer hunting, told him so. Now he had to worry about hitching a ride or stealing another auto. He recalled seeing smoke from a distant chimney a few weeks ago but the woods were so dense he hadn't seen any reason to go searching, being perfectly contented where he was.
    After the tow truck left with the car and the cops disbursed, he waited another hour before struggling his way through the dense upper pine tree branches to a clearing where he could safely work his way downward and then drop to the thick layer of pine needle debris below. He had a general idea of where that chimney smoke had come from. He kept to the edge of the road until he came to a narrow trail wending its way into the forest. Within moments he was out of sight and sound of the highway making his way slowly upward, swatting through swarms of mosquitoes that were having a feast drawing blood from his exposed skin. He recalled his escape shortly after he'd been arrested, they'd almost had him for good except that the vehicle taking him and several other felons to the maximum security

prison had skidded and crashed on the icy road. The other three had been recaptured. He'd been lucky to find an all-night Laundromat where some stupid jerk was killing time at a nearby bar while his clothes dried. They fit perfectly, even the denim jacket. He'd taken his prison garb and disposed of them in a trash bin a few blocks away taking the precaution of first stuffing them into a paper sack. He'd die before he ever went to prison he promised himself. He meant it with every fiber of his being.

He stood, secreted behind the massive evergreen boles, surveying the log structure in the nearby clearing. It was a two story building with a large picture window in the downstairs center room, a massive chimney that hinted at more than one fireplace, and multiple windows throughout the upper level. It reminded him of the hunting lodge that many of the men back home belonged to, even Sheriff Hatch and his sons. It was a place other than the local taverns, where family men could congregate to play a few games of pool, cards, checkers or chess without being pressed to buy drinks. When he'd been a kid he'd imagined being a member there and having a fun place to go when life got dull and boring. A member fee, paid each year for upkeep, was a lot less expensive than hanging around the pool halls or bars.

There was an old jeep parked under a T-roofed enclosure but no other vehicle in sight. He couldn't pick up any scent of wood smoke either, the place seemed deserted.

Cautiously, he edged up to the large center window and peered around it into the shadowy interior. It looked vacant. At least he couldn't see anything that would signify that somebody was in there. All looked neat and vacated for the winter. He suddenly became aware of a sharp chill in the air as the wind began to buffet the treetops and clouds began to scud across the now darkening sky. Another snow storm was on the way. Checking around the outside of the building for an easy access site he finally gave up and used his elbow to break out a small pane of glass in the rear door. Within moments he was inside searching for something to eat finally finding metal canisters stacked in the pantry that were filled with cornmeal, rice, dried beans, sugar, flour, jerky, coffee and a short row of tinned spices. He stuffed a few pieces of the beef jerky into his mouth, chewing until it softened enough that the flavor suddenly burst forth making his stomach growl with hunger. At least his hunger pangs would be silenced for the time being. There were no canned goods. He didn't know much about cooking but he remembered his mom making bean soup, it couldn't be that hard. The water pump at the metal sink was self-priming. He filled a pot with clear water, dumped several scoops of the dried beans into it and added some dried onion. He tried the stove, realized he had to open the propane connection for it to work. When the burner was lit he turned the heat to low, covered the container and walked away. It would likely take the rest of the day to cook.

He went on a search of the lodge, not being a person to pass up any opportunity to enrich himself. There was nothing of monetary interest downstairs so climbing the steps he began to inspect the upper level. It was much larger then he had anticipated. There were three individual bedrooms and one large bunkroom holding at least half a dozen double-decker bunk beds. He was beginning to get a feel of the place, this wasn't a regular lodge, it was more like a summer camp place for kids. The fathers used the lodge in autumn for hunting. He felt a rush of jealousy remembering his own father. It must be great having somebody bring you here for vacations. He tried to still the anger that welled up. He finally succeeded in tamping it down and hiding it away.

He was just ready to check out the last room, swinging the door open when a muffled sneeze almost made him wet his pants. Somebody was in the corner bed covered head to toe with a thick comforter and they weren't aware he was there. A thin film of nervous perspiration dampened his brow as he tried to think what to do.

Quietly he edged over to the bed. It wasn't a large outline bundled under the covers. In fact, he'd have sworn the person was nowhere as tall as he. Taking a chance, he grabbed the edge of the blanket and tossed it aside revealing the huddled form of a young lad not more than fourteen or fifteen years old, very thin, malnourished and looking sick as a dog. The kid was frightened so badly that his eyes suddenly rolled back in his head and he passed out cold turkey.

Brad stood for a moment shocked at finding he wasn't alone then he burst out laughing so hard his sides hurt. By the time he had himself under control the youngster had regained consciousness and was glaring at him.

"What the hell's so funny mister and what're ya doing here? This is a private 'stablishment." Brad was getting inspected from head to toe, a suspicious glare making the young boys face look hard and tough as nails.

"Hey kid, I'm here for the same reason you are, just getting out of the cold. I don't give a rat's ass what you got to say so shut your trap. I'm cookin' up some bean soup, if you want some when it's ready you're welcome to it but don't give me a hard time. What's your name kid?"

"Everybody calls me Red cause of my red hair but actually my name is Rory Malone. I like Red better though."

"Fine, I'll call you Red then. Why were you in bed, you sick or something?"

"Nope! Just got so hungry that I felt sick, I haven't eaten anything for maybe three days. I crawled in bed and covered up 'cause I felt cold, I might as well sleep if I can't eat, right?"

"Get your butt out of bed and help me get a fire started. It's dark enough that we can enjoy some heat without worrying about someone spotting the smoke. The soup will be done soon and then we can both enjoy a good hot meal. Do you know anything about this place? Does anyone come up here in the winter? I sure don't plan on staying here very long. In fact, it's time for me to move on to someplace as far away as I can get. Maybe even Alaska, that's a pretty good distance. Where are your parents, kid? Do you have any relatives you can live with? You're too young to be out on your own. There are a lot of creeps out there just looking for prime meat like you."

The conversation between them continued while they stacked cordwood they toted in from the lean-to. Soon a crackling fire was warming the room nicely.

The large stoneware soup bowls were filled to the brim. The two sat close to the wood fire enjoying the warmth from both the food and the flames. When they finished eating each stretched out on one of the double sofas arranged near the fireplace and fell asleep. They slept until morning. Brad made cornmeal mush for their breakfast. He'd made up his mind he was leaving that very day. He hoped that old Jeep would start. At least there wouldn't be a problem stealing it, they may not realize it's gone until spring.

Brad packed up the beef jerky along with a tin of crackers. The remainder of the soup he poured into an empty milk carton that had been used for dried peas. At least he wouldn't starve. As Brad assembled his food items Red stood quietly nearby watching. There wouldn't be a thing left for him to eat. He made up his mind to go with Brad and he wouldn't take no for an answer either. Brad might act tough but he hadn't given a second thought about sharing his meal with a stranger. Besides, he didn't have any family left. It was either hit the road or end up in an Orphans Home until he turned eighteen.

He'd rather rot in hell, he'd heard about those places a million times from his father. Every time he'd gotten in trouble his Pa had described to him in detail where he'd end up if he didn't straighten his ass up. Pa should know, that's where he had grown up.

Brad had everything stashed in the Jeep, only a last, quick look around to make sure he didn't leave any evidence and he was ready to hit the road. He'd started the jeep earlier in the morning. A little priming and the motor had purred like a kitten. He felt almost happy. He had food for a few days and a good ride, what more could a fellow ask for?

After he closed the lodge door and made his way to the parking structure he spotted Red sitting in the passenger seat. "Hey! Kid, get out of there, you are not coming with me, I've got enough trouble taking care of myself without having to worry about you.

He grasped Reds collar by the neck, pulled him out of the seat and shoved him to the ground. Hurriedly he started the engine and backed swiftly out of the enclosure. Red tried to grab on to the side of the jeep but Brad gunned the motor stepping on the accelerator and Red was left holding nothing but air. Brad looked in the rear view mirror as he drove away, the thin figure growing smaller with distance. At the very last he watched as Red dropped to his knees, hands pressed against his face, shoulders hunched forward. Brad could have sworn he saw those shoulders quivering.

Ah! Shit!....Brad brought the jeep slowly to a stop. Where would he be if those guys at the Alex' job hadn't been so good to him? He remembered how Ryan and Jason had helped him out. He'd ended up stealing their truck but they had been good to him. He had to admit, he wasn't a very good hearted guy himself but there was something about Red that sort of got to him. With a sigh he put the jeep into reverse and began to back up. He hadn't gone very far when Red came into view jogging as fast as he could. As soon as he spotted Brad he picked up speed and in short order dropped breathlessly into the passenger seat.

"I was going to follow you, Brad. I didn't care how far or for how long, you're the only person that has ever helped me. I don't have a soul who cares about me but you, a complete stranger, gave me food, treated me like a real person, and never raised a hand to me all the time we were together. If you can stand my company I'd like to stick around for a while, at least until I find a place I feel comfortable at. Is that okay with you?"

"Red, understand this, I'm not the friendliest person. I don't like to talk a lot, and I don't like to be yakked at a lot either. As long as you can mostly keep your trap closed except for something important to say to me, then I'll be able to tolerate having you around. Think you can do that?"

Red had a warm gleam in his eyes as he nodded in agreement. Suddenly, he had a friend, somebody who really cared what happened to him, even though he'd deny it. He felt a strange sensation in his chest as though a warm flame began to thaw out a chunk of ice that had been lodged inside for most of his life. What a nice feeling, he thought, having never experienced anything like it before.

Brad glanced at his new travel companion noting the lack of tension in Reds jaw, the relaxed posture, and a half-smile twitching at the corners of Red's mouth. Geez! It sure didn't take much to make the kid happy, he thought, just a ride, maybe into the next town. But who knew? Actually, it was kinda nice having a traveling companion who wasn't a blabbermouth. A person to watch the road for turnoffs and keep an eye out for hidden cruisers that were waiting to drop a ticket on some unsuspecting driver.

Around noon time Brad pulled into a rest stop. They sat at one of the picnic tables and shared the cold bean soup pouring it into two cups Brad had taken from the lodge. They both chewed on their pieces of beef jerky, the best either had ever tasted. After slaking their thirst at the water fountain they returned to the jeep and were back on the road.

That evening and for several afterwards, they slept in the jeep, a tight squeeze, but at least the weather was mild enough that they could tolerate the outdoors. Brad was making his way up the coast through Oregon and eventually Washington state. He planned on sneaking into Canada and then up to Alaska. If luck held out, they would both have a new life waiting for them when they crossed back into the USA.

In northern California Brad was able to roll a drunk who'd stumbled out of a bar across the street from where they had parked for the night. He'd gotten $67 dollars and a credit card. The first thing he did was fill the jeep with gas, and then they ate their fill at a local diner. He headed for the shady side of town and was able to sell the credit card for $100. At least he was out of the deal and safe. By the time the card changed hands several times he'd be in the clear. They got another $20 for giving a guy a ride to the gas station. He had stalled out with no cell phone and was glad to give them the money.

It was about this time that Brad began to feel uncomfortable about reaching his destination without the use of a roadmap and at least a minimum of traveling equipment. When next he spotted a shopping mall he headed for the sporting goods store he located at the "You are here" map in the atrium. That was the luckiest move he could have made. He bought a map atlas, and while on his way out of the store, he noticed two older guys deeply involved in a conversation having coffee at a small kiosk. They were so intent on their discussion that they were not paying attention to their shopping parcels sitting on the floor behind their stools. Brad gave a nod to Red and they each picked up a package and were out the door without incident. They dropped the items into the back of the jeep and then sped away. That night and for several afterward they could afford a motel room and have cash for gas from the money found in the wallet at the bottom of one of the bags. They also had warm wool sweaters, socks, and sweatshirts that were in the packages. Although Brads fit fairly well, Red needed much smaller sizes.

The Atlas had much more than the roadway information Brad needed. He was bitterly disappointed to realize there was no way he could sensibly travel to Alaska. The distance through Canada had been a shock, and the wilderness areas were too vast. The entire notion had been a ridiculous pipe dream. The idea of Canada still felt right though and by tomorrow he should be able to maneuver his way in.

That night they slept well-fed and anxious for the morning's activities. Red was all for the Canada trip. He hadn't mentioned to Brad how he thought Alaska sounded like it would be cold most of the year. He wanted a place with warm summers and fresh- water lakes to swim in. He didn't want to worry about shark bites or jelly fish stings, and he didn't want his skin coated with a layer of salt when he exited the water either. His father had told him what it felt like and how salty the water really was when he was stationed in San Diego. Pa hadn't wanted to re enlist even though they could have used the money. He'd traveled home, found work as a handyman doing odd jobs. He started drinking too much and that's when his temper changed. First turning ornery and finally getting downright mean taking his frustrations out on Ma and him. After ma ran away to her brother, it was time for Red to hit the road. He had no intentions of living with his ma's brother and wife. The lodge had been a safe haven for him. Brad showing up when he did was a prayer answered. He'd been so hungry he thought he was going to die.

He watched the sky turn brighter through the crack in the window drapes, lying quietly so as not to awaken Brad. He heard Brads breathing change and shortly a cough sounded as Brad swung his feet to the floor and gave a stretch. He sat up, yawned, and then rose from the bed pulling on his jeans, tee and sweater. Today was the turning point of the journey. Before they left town they stopped at a fast food restaurant for breakfast and when they left, Brad carried an order of burgers to go. The bad mood he had awakened with was still with him, even breakfast had not alleviated his nasty disposition and Red was beginning to get on his nerves. It wasn't that the kid was too talkative, it was just that he had to include the kid in all the plans he was making. He'd never been a sociable guy, he liked his solitude, liked not having to cater to someone else's whims or foibles. Now that he wasn't going to Alaska he didn't need any company, in fact, before the day was over he intended to be a solitary traveler once again. He glanced at Red and for the first time a calculating expression flashed over his countenance, gone quickly but as luck would have it, Red had caught the look before Brad turned away.

It was a look Red was very familiar with, a look he seen enough times on his Pa's face when he was planning retaliation for some minor infraction. He felt a cold chill edge up his backbone. There was trouble in the works except he knew it wasn't a beating that was being planned for him. He recalled the icy look he had witnessed on Brads face when he had found Red concealed under the covers at the lodge, a cold penetrating gaze with not a hint of humanity or ordinary curiosity. It had frightened the wits out of Red. His intuition now took precedence, he decided he would not be traveling with Brad any further, he felt it a matter of his survival.

After Brad filled the jeep with gas and went inside to pay, Red grabbed his new duffle bag he had packed with everything they had accumulated and lit out. He hid behind the station and watched as Brad looked for him. When Brad noticed Reds possessions were gone, he gave a careless shrug, climbed into the jeep and took off. Just to be on the safe side, Red stayed hidden for the next half hour.

He was cautious the remainder of the day, always worried that Brad would come back looking for him. By evening he began to relax. When he saw the lighted windows of the church and the banner of the banquet celebration he slipped in the side door and hid in a closet. It was warm, dark and quiet. He stretched out, laid his head against the duffle bag and was soon sound asleep. He slept until morning when he heard noises of someone moving around which awakened him. He had planned on being gone before anyone showed up, too late now. He cracked open the door and peeked out.

Parson Wells was pouring himself a coffee from a large blue thermos. He leaned back in his swivel chair with a tired sigh. Yesterday's banquet had been very successful with enough money finally raised for the church's new roof. It had taken two years to save for it. With the second sip of his coffee he almost choked hearing a cough from the closet. He stood and quickly stepped to the closed closet door. "Who's in there? Get your hide out here this minute or I'll phone the police."

Red was terrified. Why had he fallen asleep? He'd had every intention of being gone long before daylight. He pushed himself upright and opened the door. His face pale as a ghost, lips trembling, he pulled a handful of singles from his pocket and held them out to the elderly man standing before him. "I'm sorry sir, I was so tired and didn't have anywhere else to go. I saw the church with all the people gathered and I thought it would be a safe place to stay the night. I didn't take anything, sir. You can take this money, there's about $20 there, that'll pay for me using your closet to sleep in.

"Why! You're nothing but a kid. How old are you and what are you doing out all night by yourself?" Parson Wells had a soft spot in his heart for anyone who needed help. If there was trouble in the family he'd make sure everything was sorted out and order restored.

Red was tempted to fib but being as the man was a preacher he didn't want to burn in hell for telling a lie. "I don't have a family, sir. I ran away from my father who drinks too much and beats me. My mother ran away too but I didn't want to go with her so I lit out on my own. I'll be sixteen on my next birthday."

"Where does your father live, son? I'll have to contact him about you. If he's an unfit parent you don't have to stay with him, we can find a good home for you."

"I can't take the chance of telling you that, sir. I'd rather die than go back with him. Anyway, he'd find out where I was and beat me within an inch of my life. Here, take the money, I'll be on my way. I'm sorry for any upset I caused." Red dropped the bills on the desk and turned away picking up the duffle bag and heading for the door. Before he could exit, he felt his arm grasped by a strong hand and he was pulled back to the desk.

"Hold on a piece sonny, I can't just let you disappear like this. You're too young to be out on your own, you can't provide for yourself, you're too young to get a job without identification and you don't have a place to stay or even enough money to feed yourself for a day. How about making a deal with me?

"That depends what the deal is. I definitely won't go back to my father."

"First, what's your name sonny? We can get this all straightened out legally. I have a couple of good lawyer members who've offered their services to me any time needed. If your home life is as bad as you say, we can get you a different guardian instead of your father. Did you notice that house next to the church? That's where my wife and I live. There's room for you too if you've a mind to try it. You can help with chores, that way you won't feel indebted to us, and you'd have your own room. Our two daughters are married and both live in other states so you won't be subjected to any sibling rivalry or jealousy. Just say the word and we can get a head start on your problems. Besides, I can't have you wandering around like a lost sheep. You might have to do something illegal that would get you into trouble and maybe even jail."

Red couldn't believe his good luck, all because he'd decided to sleep indoors in a closet. "What do I call you, sir? My name is Rory Malone but everyone calls me Red."

"I'm Pastor Jeff Wells but you can call me Preacher. That's what my dear wife has called me for years when she likes the sermons I preach every Sunday. Many of my parishioners call me that too and it suits me just fine. Grab your bag there Red and lets go, we'll get you all settled in before you start work. A nice breakfast would likely set well with you too." Jeff couldn't help grinning at the youngster, he looked a little over-whelmed.

Laura Wells was not surprised at having a new visitor. This happened occasionally, except usually not to so young a person. Red settled in immediately, first enjoying a nice hot bath. He donned some of his stolen garments, overlarge but clean at least. The breakfast was better than any he'd ever eaten, pancakes, sausage and scrambled eggs. He helped clear the table and then followed Preacher back to the church where he was kept busy the remainder of the day. The work was easy and he had to admit, the Preacher was as good as gold with never an angry word or action.

As the days passed Parson Jeff and his wife became accustomed to having the youngster about. Their days became adjusted to young Reds needs and their concern for him and his welfare grew by leaps and bounds until a few months later they finally accepted the fact he would be a permanent resident of their home, a foster son they could guide along the righteous path in life. He was more than contented to follow their advice. The peace and quietude of life with them had brought a measure of comfort and fulfillment he had never experienced before. He intended to spend the rest of his life with them, or at least as long as they would tolerate his company.

Occasionally, his thoughts dwelt on his traveling companion, Brad. The bad feelings he had experienced still remained to remind him how lucky he had been. There was no doubt in his mind he would have been stretched out in an alley somewhere dead as a doornail. He'd have to keep an eye out for Brad from now on. He'd do anything to protect his new family, at least that's how he thought of them. If he'd known folks like them were out in the world he'd have hightailed it away from home years ago. His jaw clamped shut almost grinding his teeth in anger thinking of what Brad would have done to the Parson for the money collected from the banquet for the new church roof. It was fate that led him to the church. He promised himself he'd do everything the preacher requested of him and more. They were already teaching him school subjects he'd failed at because of scanty attendance and poor grades. For some odd reason everything seemed easier, even interesting now. A completely different attitude than he'd had when living at home. His pa had never cared about school subjects, didn't even care if Red never learned a lick of school teachings. Parson Jeff was different and so was Mrs. Wells. Every morning after he finished his chores the books came out and the learning began. Oddly enough, he enjoyed it. Maybe it had something to do with the praise he got when he did well. Life wasn't just about today. It was about tomorrow and the tomorrow after that. What he would accomplish by the time he was as old as Preacher Jeff.

With a sigh he continued reading the story he had been assigned. Mrs. Well expected him to give a report to her in the morning about what he'd learned from the tale and how it could apply to life. For a moment his conscience began to bother him about the shopping bags Brad and he had lifted from the two old guys at the mall. He remembered the name inside the wallet he'd found inside the shopping bag, Paul Winston, and the address. The sales receipt was for $125. When he earned that amount of money he planned on sending it to the guy.

Turning the page, he once again became absorbed in the story about a Prince who lived in a castle. In his favorite room a pretty canary sang in a cage, beautiful flowering plants grew in the bright sunlight streaming from all the windows and there was even a musical waterfall, but the prince didn't notice anything but his reflection in all the mirrors throughout the room. Every day that passed the windows became narrower but the prince didn't see…Red's head drooped and finally came to rest on his arm that was stretched across the desk.

"Red, honey….wake up. Aww! You poor kid, Jeff must be working you too hard. It's lunchtime Sweetie." Laura gave a shake to Reds shoulder.

Rubbing his hands across his eyes gave her a smile as he stood to follow her.

CHAPTER 15

Jason was still smiling the next morning recalling his visit to see his twin niece and nephew Jennifer had given birth to. They were fraternal twins, didn't look at all alike. This was their second day at home. She was going to have her hands full that's for sure but at least Ryan had hired a nanny. Against Jens wishes until Ryan complained that he wouldn't be able to abide seeing her continually exhausted and dragging about the house like a pale ghost of herself. Jen had finally relented.

He still couldn't believe the turn his life had taken after finding he had an honest to goodness sister, lost to each other all those years when he was being raised as the son of the orphanage mistress. He shuddered to think what he would have missed if he hadn't gotten a job working for Alex. Now his life was full, he was anchored with a family having a great brother-in-law Ryan, his father Alex and of course his wife Rose. Those lonely years he'd had with Gladys Cummings, the woman he'd thought was his mother, seemed like a long ago dream. Thankfully Jennifer and he had more in common than they had anticipated, even though they had spent most of their young years apart.

He fixed himself a bowl of oatmeal and two pieces of toast. After breakfast was eaten, he washed the items and placed them back in their respective places. He was out the door, into his pickup truck and on his way to work. Alex had said this was the last shopping mall project he was bidding on. They had begun it last fall. It would be completed at the end of summer. He already had a job lined up for when it was over. Alex's daughter Sylvia's in-laws lived up north and desperately needed a trustworthy person to manage their hardware store. Sy's husband David had already contacted his parents giving Jason a good recommendation. They were expecting him there as soon as the mall was completed. He'd never lived anywhere other than a city and was excited about experiencing what it would be like living in the country. He was looking forward to autumn.

The day went quickly keeping him busy stacking supplies and learning a few basics of the building trade. It always amazed him how quickly walls were erected and dry wall installed creating enclosed spaces in a very short time. He'd noticed the main tools before constructing anything were a level and ruler. As long as everything was squared away, any applications could be included easily, even applying wallpaper. Everything would fit perfectly if measured. He had all this information stored away in his memory bank in case he needed it one day.

"Hey! Jason, do you have any plans for tonight?" Alex was making his way down the newly installed escalator, too impatient to stand quietly waiting for the landing, watching as Jason hurried toward him.

"Nope! Nothing planned. I was going to stay in this evening, maybe read a little or watch television. Did I tell you I went to see my new niece and nephew last night? When I think what I might have missed in life it scares me. It's going to take me a mighty long time to become confident about having my sister back and all my new family."

I'd like you to follow me home after work, Jason. You can have supper with us while I discuss a new project with you. Is that okay with you, Jason?"

That evening after a fantastic dinner of grilled steak, baked potatoes, salad and apple pie, Jason sipped his coffee while listening to Alex discuss the tree house he wanted Jason to build for his young son Scott. In not too many years Scott would enjoy playing up there with his friends. That was the one thing Alex had desired passionately when he was young. At least now he could provide that pleasure for his son, even though Rose thought the tree house should wait until Scott was older. The way years seemed to slip away so quickly Alex had decided to build it now. The more he added to the design, the more excited he became to have the building begun. It had started out as a very simple sketch of an enclosure attached to weight bearing limbs. Then, an upper lookout tower had been added to the design along with an extension to the pole ladder. There was even to be a flag to fly from the highest level. It was everything Alex would have wanted when he'd been an adventuresome lad and daydreaming of impossible schemes. He could hardly wait to see the finished project. It would even be large and sturdy enough for him to occasionally surprise his son with a visit. He couldn't help smiling at the thought. By the time Jason left with the plans he had caught Alex's enthusiasm.

The following week lumber was delivered. Alex supplied the tools and accessories needed for the building. For the next month, weather permitting, Jason found extreme pleasure working with the hardwood Alex had ordered.

Rose enjoyed Jason's attendance each day at suppertime. The two men mostly discussed the tree house but the obvious pleasure in the meals Jason exhibited was a balm to Rose's attempt at cooking a variety of menus to please his appetite. Apparently his pseudo mom Gladys had not been very imaginative.

When at last the tree house was completed Jason spent several days applying a double coat of wood preservative.

Two weeks later Alex stood outside in the late afternoon sun admiring the tree house construction. On a whim he grasped the pole ladder and began to climb. When he reached the first level he pulled himself onto its deck and sat in the opening, feet dangling over the edge, enjoying the extended view of the surrounding area. The smile that lit up his face at the wonder and joy of being elevated above the ordinary human activities of life seemed to instill a feeling of euphoria and physical freedom from the boundaries of earth. He felt like an eagle perched at the edge of his aerie. If he had wings he'd spread them wide and soar up into the blue stratosphere. It was an invigorating feeling, one he wanted his son to experience. It made one open one's mind to unfamiliar vistas willing to try that hesitant step into territory strange and unknown. He loved the sensation, he felt able to accomplish anything his heart desired. With a sigh of regret he swung about, set his foot on the first circular extension of the pole, and then descended quickly to ground level.

When he sat down to supper Rose couldn't help seeing the distracted look on her husband's face."Is there something wrong Honey? I saw you looking at the tree house. Don't tell me you found something else to change on it. You've already decided to add screens and a screen door to keep bees and wasps from building nests in it. Next you'll want an A/C and a furnace…I'm sorry Alex, I didn't mean to sound nasty. It's just that watching you sitting up there and seeing the way you looked made me feel left out of your life for a moment. It took me back to when you left me when I was expecting our daughter. Even though that was years ago the feeling is still fresh in my memory."

Alex looked at his wife, surprise and a shamed expression showing on his face for a moment. "I was only enjoying the feeling of being at the top of the world, Rose. I'd always wanted a tree house when I was a kid. This weekend I want you to pack us a lunch, bring along a blanket and we'll spend this Saturday up there having a picnic so you can get a feeling of how wonderful it is being up above the ground where the birds dwell. I bet you'll change your mind and opinion about that tree dwelling."

"Don't count on it sweetheart, I'm not an easy sell, and have never been one but I'm game and will take you up on that offer. Before I do though, please put those screens on, I'm willing to wait as long as necessary."

Alex couldn't help that a grin lit up his face knowing Rose would do anything to stall her climb up into the tree house. He'd already ordered the screened window and door frames weeks ago. They were to be delivered the very next day and all would be installed before the weekend. Yeah! He thought, it was likely silly of an adult male like him getting excited about something so mundane but he liked that feeling of height. Maybe he should take flying lessons at the local city airport. In fact, this coming week he'd check in with the flight instructors there to see what they had to say about it. He resolved to do just that but in the meantime he'd not mention a word to Rose, she'd likely have a fit if she found out.

On Saturday Rose and he spent the entire morning in the tree house. They enjoyed the lunch Rose had packed too. That was when Alex realized a basket attached to a rope and winch would be handy for transporting items up. The more time that passed, the more things he added. An insulated built-in cooler, inside shutters that could be closed during strong winds or rain storms, and shingles installed on the roof. He put a stop to Rose adding curtains though. The very last items he added were an air mattress and a thick, red acrylic blanket folded neatly on one of the shelves. It was finished.

That week he did stop at the local airport and inquire about flying lessons. The man he spoke to was a retired USN flight captain who had taught lessons for the past seven years. He signed the contract. The lessons would be twice a week on Tuesdays and Thursdays. He could hardly wait to begin.

He found he had an aptitude for flying. The instructor was pleased with his progress and the lessons passed so quickly that he was soloing before he had expected to. This was one hundred times better than the tree house. The expectations were beyond his wildest dreams.

When their plans for a vacation were once again being discussed it was again to be at Roscoe's Resort up north. Alex took the bull by its horns and told Rose about his flying lessons and his license. He was shocked to discover she already knew about his escapades at flying. She had spotted his car at the City airport and waited, curious as to why he was stopped there. She had seen him take off and fly a plane. She had left before he landed, at first very angry he'd not said a word to her, then accepting of the fact he had tried to spare her worry. However, she had no intentions of putting neither Scott nor herself at risk being in a plane with him. If he liked, he could fly to the resort, she of course would drive the auto with her son safely at her side.

Alex reluctantly gave in, they would take the car to Roscoe's.

When Sylvia hung up the phone after hearing her mother Rose complaining of how worried she was about Alex having his flying license, she had stopped herself from telling Rose the doctor was planning to induce labor in a few days. She was so hugely pregnant that she could barely manage to walk, and two weeks overdue at that.

The pain in her back was getting worse. She decided to phone David at his hardware store and ask if he could manage to come home a little earlier. She was just reaching for the phone again when water began to trickle down her legs then something let loose. God help her, labor was starting and she was home alone. She hurriedly pushed 911, gave her address, and then dialed David. He did not reach home however until after the ambulance had taken her to the hospital.

He hurriedly leaped back into his car and sped off praying he would arrive before the baby was born. He'd had a feeling that morning Sy was due because of the discomfort she was experiencing but she had been adamant about him going to work and not making her a nervous wreck by being at her elbow with every step she took. When he arrived at the hospital he parked in the emergency lot and hurried inside. They had already taken her into the operating room. An aide guided him to the waiting room where he alternated between pacing, looking out the window, and trying to find something to read that would hold his interest. Finally he just sat quietly staring at the television, not really noticing what the program was about, his entire being concentrated on what Sylvia would be going through. Maybe he was already a father to a little boy or girl. The enormous responsibility of guiding another being to adulthood suddenly overwhelmed him and he wished with all his heart that his own dad were there at that moment to give him moral support and ease his worries.

For a moment he had been so distracted with his mental anguish he hadn't heard someone call his name.

"Mr. Kendall, Mr. David Kendall? You may see your wife now. She resting comfortably in her room, I'll take you there."

David glanced at his watch, disbelieving the amount of time that had elapsed. He hurried after the nurse thinking he should have brought some flowers for Sy, he recalled she loved those yellow flowers he had once given her, were they Daffodils, or were they called Jonquils? They were a very pretty yellow whatever their name. He'd find out and bring her some this afternoon. The nurse left him at the door of Sys room.

Sylvia held her baby girl carefully, she seemed fragile but the Doctor had assured her that she was a full 6 lb. 7oz. full term baby. She had a head full of black hair just like David's. The delivery seemed to go quickly although the actual time had been about 5 hours.

"Sy, are you okay, how do you feel, is the baby okay? The nurse said we have a little girl." David felt awkward, not knowing what to say or do. The bundle Sy was holding seemed awfully small which made him wonder if everything had been normal for the delivery. He was embarrassed to ask.

"Sit down over here by me Davey and hold out your arms. It's time for you to meet our daughter, Penelope Ann. I think the names we choose suit her perfectly." Sylvia placed her daughter snuggly in her husband's arms and then leaned back to rest against the plumped pillows watching the amazing display of emotions exhibited on David's face.

As for David, he felt he was holding a precious, delicately fragile piece of himself and Sylvia. At that moment he felt someone move out from behind him and then reach for the baby taking her from his arms. A huge smile beamed forth as Rose cradled her little grandchild against her breast.

"Sorry Davey, I couldn't control myself when I saw you begin to tremble. I know what you're feeling my dear son-in-law, it's a mighty powerful sensation holding your own flesh and blood in your arms and wondering what the future will hold." Rose pressed a kiss on the baby's forehead then passed her back to Sylvia.

"Alex will stop in this evening, honey, he sends his love. His business appointment was too important to cancel. He knew you wouldn't be upset with him. He said he was having a gift for the baby delivered to the house, you'll see it when you get home. He didn't tell me what it is I just hope it's something useful. You know your father though, he has outrageous ideas that we would never dream of." Rose settled into a chair next to the bed ready for a long, pleasant morning visit.

David kissed his wife goodbye, promised he'd be back in the evening. He gave Rose a peck on the cheek and was on his way out the door.

As soon as he arrived home he called Roses house to speak with the nanny. Now supplied with the phone number of a reliable house cleaning agency, he also got the name and number of a trustworthy babysitter. He couldn't help the grin that lit up his face thinking of the surprises he had in store for Sylvia. The last two months she'd had such a rough time with her pregnancy that they'd both become worried. Thank heaven the delivery had gone well and she looked wonderful. Not back to her old self yet, that would take a while, but at least almost normal.

Early morning on the third day David picked up his wife and daughter. They were on their way home, the baby sleeping peacefully in the rear carseat. David had gone grocery shopping using the list Sy had made out the previous afternoon. How she kept track of everything was beyond his conception and even though she kept a running list of needed items there were those "Extras" that were always handy for unexpected circumstances, like drop-in visitors.

"So! What did Alex get for the baby, Davey? I can't imagine, we already have everything we need." Sy loved mysteries, trying to guess sometimes led to fantasies so extreme they would burst out laughing. Like a stationary baby's motor cycle, a baby's hot air balloon to ride in when tied to a tree. The more ridiculous items sounded, the harder they laughed.

When they reached home David honked the car horn before he retrieved the baby from the car-seat, he cradled her in his left arm while steadying Sy with his right. As they reached the front door it opened.

Sy felt shocked for a moment but only until she found herself gazing at Esther Rodgers, the maid who had practically raised Alex's son Ryan. She had been a full time housekeeper and cook for them. Esther greeted Sy with a warm hug, while David put Penny in the basinet he'd earlier set on a chair in the hallway waiting for the baby's return from the hospital.

"I made fresh coffee Mrs. Kendall. With your approval, I'll be taking care of the housework, helping you with the baby and even cooking when you're not in the mood." Speechless, Sy was let into the kitchen. David hung up her jacket while Esther poured Sylvia a cup of coffee and placed a plate of fresh baked biscuits, a butter dish, utensils and a jar of strawberry preserves in front of her.

At that moment Sy broke out in such deep sobs that it sounded as though she was crying her heart out.

"What's wrong, Ms. Kendall, are you upset because I'm here? I'm so sorry my dear. I guess we should have waited before assuming so much, I'll be gone and away before you even blink twice." Esther was on her way out the kitchen door before Sy could catch her breath and respond.

"Oh! No! Please wait, Mrs. Rodgers. I'm not at all angry having you here. When I left the hospital this morning thinking about all my new responsibilities, I felt over whelmed with fear that I wouldn't be capable of handling it all. Then, when the front door opened, you were standing there calm and organized. Suddenly, I was sitting comfortably at my kitchen table, fresh coffee and all the fixings set before me, and all my load of heavy worries quietly disappeared. Thanks to you and your kindness. I'd like it very much if you'd stay. My mother and dad have only praise and high esteem for you and all the wonderful work you did for them."

By the time Sy had dried her tears and coaxed Esther to sit with her and enjoy the fare, the three were laughing and totally at ease. David especially, since he'd thought for a time he was in hot water.

While Sy went to nurse Penny, David chatted with Esther making arrangements for her to provide him with shopping lists for anything the baby needed. He'd already stashed a supply of diapers, rash cream, baby powder, baby soap and shampoo, a rubber-bulb siphon for clearing mucus from the baby's nose, bottles and rubber nipples for juice and water. He didn't forget a few pacifiers either.

"Whew! I never expected babies needed so many things Esther, how long does this last?"

Esther couldn't help laughing at the expression on David's face, like a poor lost soul wandering in the woods. "At least two years, David. She'll likely be weaned when she's a year old. By the second year it's potty training, learning to eat better using utensils. By age three she should be going to preschool. But, we're getting way ahead of ourselves, Penny just came home today from being delivered into our way of life. It's going to take her a while to adapt."

When Sylvia returned she noticed the serious expression on her husband's face. "What's happening, Honey?" She looked at him quizzically, and then noticed the grin on Esther's face.

"I was just telling him about a baby's growth, the phases they go through. I think it surprised him how long it takes for them to become self-sufficient. One thing I'll need to pick up for you very soon Sylvia, is a breast pump. You'll soon be going shopping with friends, out to dinner or movies with David. You'll be able to have a supply of your milk on hand for when you won't be here at feeding time."

Privately, Sy didn't think she'd ever want to leave her baby for any length of time but she nodded in agreement.

David left to go back to work at the hardware store, Sy went upstairs to shower and freshen up, and Esther changed Penny's diaper. Washed and powdered, wearing a clean the little nighty, the baby slept. At last, Esther thought, I can be happy again.

Rose and Alex were thrilled, this was their third grandchild. They were already indulging Jen and Ryan's twins, two month old Angela and Matthew. They still couldn't believe the babies didn't look alike. They were fraternal twins, not identical.

Alex was waiting to hear from Sylvia hoping she'd like the gift he'd bought for their daughter, Penelope. He couldn't help smiling at the thought of what Penny would do when she was a few years older and able to ride the spring mounted pony-sized Palomino. It was so sturdily built that 80lb kids could enjoy the feeling of being on a galloping horse. He had bought it on the spur of the moment thinking if how much fun he would have had with it when he was a kid.

A feeling of restless energy seemed to overwhelm him. He couldn't bear the feeling of having nothing to do. Rose was visiting Jennifer, she'd wanted to see how the twins were faring, plus she had felt housebound and needed some woman talk with another female who was experiencing the same emotions she was feeling. He hadn't been in the mood to go with her. He decided to head out to the airport and enjoy a few hours of flying. It was perfect weather, clear with only light winds. He scribbled a note for Rose and anchored it with his coffee cup, then went upstairs to change into Levis, a light sweater and Nikes. As a precaution he also grabbed a denim jacket, tossing it over his shoulder.

Within an hour he was taxiing down the runway and then soaring up into the blue. He circled overhead and then headed north, away from town and over the countryside. He vowed that somehow he'd get Rose to fly with him if it was the last thing worth accomplishing in life. She'd love it as much as he. Once Scott was old enough he'd even have him enrolled for flying lessons. Teach him there was more to life than being anchored to earth and its boundaries. The exhilaration of being airborne was indescribable.

Alex had not filed a flight plan, only wanting to have a little airtime to calm his edginess and unwind. He was enjoying the scenery, the feeling of power he had maneuvering his craft to either follow a stream or check out a fishing craft where someone was reeling in a catch. The peaceful serenity that infused his entire being had dulled his awareness of the instrument panel. It was too late when the motor began to sputter and he checked the gas gauge. The needle sat at empty.

There was not a field in sight, only an endless forest of evergreens beneath him and the lake in the distance too far to even attempt to reach. He quickly donned his denim jacket and then cut the power to the motor. No sense chancing sparks that would set off a forest fire. He guided the plane as best he could, hoping to reach any sort of clearing where he could land.

The last sound he heard was the shattering of window glass and the crunch of metal as his plane entered the towering treetops.

Cold rain wetting his face and clothing, Alex awoke. It was pitch black, he couldn't distinguish a thing or even if he was in a precarious position. He recalled aiming the plane into the treetops but that was the extent.

"Rose is going to kill me," he thought. The, "I told you so" she would be assailing him with made him cringe. Somehow he had to get out of this mess and get home, the problem was he couldn't see how far up he was. He'd have to wait for morning. Edging into the back part of the plane out of the rain, he curled up and fell asleep.

During the night rain finally eased and eventually stopped but Alex was not aware, he slept the deep sleep of the weary.

Meanwhile, Rose was frantic with worry. Alex's note hadn't said where he was going or how long he'd be away, only that he had some errands to run and he'd be gone a while. She phoned Ryan and then Sylvia. Neither had any inkling where Alex could be however, without telling Rose his intentions, Ryan decided to take a ride past the airport to see if his dad's car was there.

When Ryan pulled up into his parent's driveway he sat for several moments hating the fact that his father was missing and he was the one who had to tell Rose the bad news. He felt sick with worry and dread that possibly this time his dad wouldn't make it home alive. He recalled the amnesia Alex had experienced and the months he'd been missing after his last escapade up north. He'd thought for sure that his dad was gone forever. The devastation and depression that hit him thinking he'd never see Alex again had almost been more than he could bear. Now, here he was worrying again. When would his father grow up, act his age and accept the fact that he had a wife and young son to care for? The more Ryan dwelt on the irresponsibility of his dad, the angrier he became.

Finally, knowing he couldn't postpone the inevitable any longer, he exited the car and made his way to the front door. It opened before he could ring the doorbell and Rose stood before him, pale as a ghost, waiting for the bad news she had expected hearing since Alex's disappearance.

He felt his eyes well with tears he'd been trying to withhold as he pulled her to him and felt her tremble uncontrollably as he told her about seeing Alex's car at the airport.

"It's too early to begin worrying Rose, give him until late evening before thinking something bad has happened. You know the way he is, he may have landed at some private airstrip to visit with friends and didn't notice the passing of time. He has several pals he keeps in contact with who also fly. Maybe they knew of a nice place to hunt or fish that they wanted to show him. Come on now, Rose, sit down, I'm calling Jen and Sy to come keep you company. They'll bring your grandbabies to keep you occupied while I do some investigating."

Rose sat at the kitchen table listening to his conversations with both women. When he hung up he filled the tea kettle with water and set it to heat. Searching for the canister that held an impressive assortment of tea flavors in neat disposable tea bags, he selected Chamomile, remedied to be a very good calming agent. For an additional health bonus he added a teaspoon of honey then set the cup down before Rose and watched as she sipped at the hot beverage.

Sylvia and Jennifer arrived at the same time. Ryan held his son in his arms while Jen made Angela comfortable in the playpen that sat in the dining room. She then also placed Matthew next to his twin sister. By the time Sy put Penelope down and settled her next to her cousins, Jennifer had tea ready for the both of them.

When darkness fell with still no sign of Alex, Ryan placed a call to the airport telling them of the missing person. They checked for a flight plan and found none had been filed. They then began to contact outlying airfields. The hours passed without any information about plane crashes or notifications of finding the missing pilot.

The family spent a sleepless night. In the morning, with dwindling hope and no word of the missing plane, Ryan phoned the family doctor to ask him to make a house call and give Rose a sedative so she could sleep. While there, he did a quick inspection of baby Scott then hurried off to complete his office appointments, promising to stop back that evening.

Jen and Sy shared one of the spare bedrooms. Jennifer invited her twin's nanny to come and stay with them to help with the little ones while they all waited with Rose for word of Alex.

When the third day passed without news, it was time to take their babies home. They phoned Rose often, every day, hoping for a positive sign that Alex was alive but as the days passed, hope waned. Eventually, at the end of an entire two weeks, the only information expected was that a body had been discovered or a wreck located.

Rose felt numb. Where was the man she married, the life they had created together after all those years they'd spent apart? What would Scott know of his father? Only those stories told and memories revisited years from now when curious questions were asked and answered? Not fair!…What sort of nasty trick had fate again played on them? Drawing them together after years of separation then, twice, putting their future in jeopardy. That accident and amnesia Alex had experienced, Rose had endured but had almost made her lose her mind. Was this another episode with Fate flaunting her power?

Suddenly, Rose felt rage well within like a tidal wave. She would not act like a cringing mouse at the whim of whatever the future would hold. She was tired of tears, silence, depression, withdrawal and most of all, hiding in the house waiting for dreaded news about her beloved. Alex would be ashamed of her behaving like this. Whatever happened she had to hold her head high and move forward.

Leafing through her little black book she phoned the local spa and made an appointment for the "Works," sauna, masseuse, manicure, pedicure, brow wax, hair style, color and cut. Then off to shop for several new outfits which Alex had been urging her to do saying just because she gave birth to a child didn't mean she couldn't look chic, well dressed and hot, was his expression.

That evening, returning home, Rose felt much better. Not happier…that wouldn't happen unless Alex returned, but feeling better about herself. It was amazing what a little pampering could do for a woman. Truthfully, she expected Alex would be home eventually, just like last time. She wanted to look her best for him. He was the love of her life.

It was a month later that a pilot spotted a plane wreck in the tree tops in one of the National forests. They sent in a crew and recovered the body of the pilot, later identified as that of Alex Williams. An autopsy confirmed he had died of pneumonia.

Rose had his remains cremated. That summer she and the family met up north at the resort where Alex had taken refuge when he had managed to escape from the isolated sandbar where he had been stranded after driving off the cliff.

Rose sailed through those several months like a zombie walking on air. She walked, talked, ate and slept but those who knew her realized she was on automatic pilot. Doing and saying the correct things however her mind and heart was lodged elsewhere, resting beside the man she loved with her entire being.

CHAPTER 16

It was a year since Alex had died. Rose still had problems sleeping, her mind endlessly reviewing the circumstances of Alex's death when he had been trapped in his plane wreckage 100 feet high in a treetop, exposed to the elements and unable to find a way down to solid ground. The thought of the misery he must have gone through caused her such heartache that she was often unable to cope with the requirements of everyday living, even sometimes neglecting to care for herself properly.

Scott's care was given over to Esther who had quickly found a replacement nanny for Sylvia's baby girl Penelope. It had been a matter of survival for Rose and little Scott since Rose's ongoing mental distress. Eventually, Esther had the entire home back to its normal operations after hiring a housekeeper to come in twice a week.

With Alex gone, Ryan and Jason'd had their hands full and at last they were within weeks of completing the last shopping center Alex had contracted for.

Ryan and Jennifer were planning a memorial service for Alex when the shopping center was completed. It was to be at their home where the entire family would congregate. Ryan also had a surprise for them.

The final weeks of completion went quickly. The men were paid their final wages plus a bonus for finishing ahead of schedule. The final clean-up, tools and equipment packed up and carted away to be stored at the company warehouse where a guard and watchdog would see to its security.

That evening, after a shower and early dinner, Ryan sat with Jennifer having a last cup of coffee discussing their plans for the family get-together on the last weekend of the month of May. Even the babies and nannies would be attending although in a separate part of the house so there would be no interruptions during the special presentation. Ryan felt nervous, he wondered if there was a possibility he was making a mistake, yet it felt right to him.

Almost too soon it was the day of the family dinner. Ryan had it catered. A simple five course meal served with champagne. Shrimp cocktails, a delicate crème of asparagus soup, surf and turf with twice baked potatoes, fresh spinach and ricotta salad, and Crème Brule for dessert. They retired to the family room where Ryan had seating set up before a large screen with a movie projector. Everyone was curious about what they were going to view.

"It's a surprise, everyone. Something I've been planning for a while so make yourselves comfortable, the film runs for a few hours." Ryan felt nervous, maybe he was making a mistake, yet, for himself, he felt very good about what he had viewed. He only hoped everyone else would feel the same.

The lights were dimmed and the film began. Ryan's front door opened and there was Rose toting a pumpkin pie, Alex right behind holding what looked like an apple pie. Next came Sylvia holding a plastic bag of baked rolls and David carrying a plastic container filled with salad. Everyone sat rapt watching the interaction of a family enjoying a Thanksgiving get-together. When the doorbell rang they saw the minister who performed the wedding ceremony for Jennifer and Ryan. Alex gave his son a hug, "Good Luck, son. Just remember, marriage is very much like a roller coaster ride. There are up and downs…" It was at that point Rose felt the tears begin to slide

down her cheeks, tears of release from the terrible prison she had locked herself into after losing her beloved husband. He would never want her to mourn for him at the expense of her health and son Scott's well-being. Hearing his voice, seeing him put his arms around her while placing a light kiss on her neck and pulling her close to his side filled her with such a deep sense of peace and confidence in his commitment to her that for the first time she realized how very lucky she had been. They had loved each other with every fiber of their being.

When the film ended everyone sat in silence unable, or unwilling to break the spell that had been woven while watching the loving relationships generated by all the family members. It was, in part, a revelation of what an outsider would see and feel, a picture of love and interaction between close-knit relatives perfectly at ease exhibiting their devotion.

"Ryan, whatever induced you to have hidden cameras throughout your home for that get-together? It must have been fate taking a hand in it. We've never filmed any family festivities, what a wonderful idea." David was enthralled by the idea of having a record of family holidays or outstanding events to pass on to a younger generation.

"I wanted a recording of our wedding, something that we can show our children one day when they become curious about us, how we fell in love and when we got married." Ryan glanced at Jennifer, the love he felt for her evident for everyone to see. I wanted to leave something for our kids, a living, walking, talking picture of their mother and I that shows how a true marriage looks to others. Not something acted out like a stage play, but real feelings that show how we felt about each other."

Rose, by this time, had pulled herself together realizing she would always have memories but her main concern would be caring for Scott and raising him so he'd be instilled with all the good characteristics of his father. She felt renewed, able to look forward to the future, whatever it would hold.

When the evening ended it was on a much lighter mood felt by the entire family. Ryan stood at the front door waving goodbye to everyone. He had presented each with a copy of the tape, something for their memory books. Pure luck he'd decided to place those cameras for his wedding day, he'd never be sorry.

Rose arrived home in a better mood than when she'd left. After tucking Scott into bed she went into the kitchen to put on the kettle for a cup of tea. It was still relatively early, not quite ten p.m. and there was no way she could go to bed at this time and expect to fall asleep. Not that she'd be up all hours like she had lately, but somehow she expected to sleep better tonight. Without doubt it was seeing the tapes Ryan had shown. She still had that warm feeling of Alex's presence standing next to her while viewing it. Not that she believed in ghosts, but there definitely had been a feeling of closeness with her husband.

Sipping the hot tea she fell into reverie not noticing when her tea began to cool or that muffled light noise was coming from the front door area. She was unaware when the shadow of a person stood near the kitchen door watching her. Too late, when she felt a cloth pressed over her mouth and nose, the sharp stench of ether gagging her. Senses reeling she began to lose consciousness and was eased back in her seat. Strips of toweling bound her legs and arms to the chair. She didn't awaken for several hours.

The smell of ether seemed to infuse every fiber of her being. She felt she was having a nightmare of some sort. It wasn't until she opened her eyes and saw a stranger sitting at the table across from her eating a sandwich and drinking a glass of milk that she realized she couldn't move. When she tried to speak she found that a gag was secured across her mouth. Frantic, she struggled against her bonds which only made them tighten more. Finally, realizing she was securely bound and at the stranger's mercy, she quieted her struggles and began to analyze her precarious predicament and what the man's intentions could be.

There was something familiar about him but she couldn't place where she recognized him from. Whatever or where ever, right now she had more worries to think about, nanny Audrey upstairs with Scott, they were both in jeopardy.

"Listen lady, I'm going to fix myself some food to go and also take any cash you have handy, as much as there is. If you cooperate and tell me where to look, I'll be gone before you know it. Fair?"

Rose gave a vigorous nod and watched as he came closer to loosen the gag over her mouth.

"If you make any noise I'll hurt you, real bad…just tell me where the money is."

"I promise I'll be quiet, just go into the dining room and look in the bottom cupboard of the china cabinet. You'll see a fancy metal box sitting in the back right-hand corner. There's about four or five hundred dollars there, that's all the cash I have, honest. Please, don't hurt me.…I'll do anything you want. You can take my credit cards, I'll even make out some checks for you to cash but please, take what you want and go away, I won't even call the police." Rose was desperate to have the man gone as soon as possible.

"Take it easy, lady, I'm not stupid. Keep your credit cards, there's nothing I need to buy with them. Cash is what I'm interested in and the more the better." Brad felt like laughing, he got such a high just listening to the bitch whine and moan. The cash was great, that'd take him a ways plus there was plenty of stuff in the fridge so that he'd be very well fed for a while. He began to assemble sandwiches he made with the corned beef that had been covered neatly with saran. He loved the stuff but never bought it at a deli, too expensive. He used the entire leftover brisket to make half a dozen sandwiches. He dropped crisp dill pickles into two sandwich bags and secured the tops with plastic ties. There were six bottles of water he grabbed along with a few apples. The peanut butter kisses stashed in the freezer were the last prize he found. Before leaving he replaced the gag. At least that'd give him til morning before the alarm was sounded.

When Audrey, the nanny, awoke the next morning she carried Scott downstairs almost dropping him when she saw Rose bound and gagged sitting at the kitchen table. After untying her and then fixing her a fresh cup of coffee, she listened in disbelief to the story about the robbery and the unmitigated gall of the thief making himself a lunch for the road, by then the police were there also listening to the tale.

Along with a description of the culprit, an all points bulletin was released to the media. Success of capture was however not expected, too many hours had passed.

Sheriff Hatch, reading the APB recognized the description of the murderer of three young men. So....Brad Shields was on his way home. This was good news. He'd be on his way back to home ground expecting to hide out at his mom's. What a surprise he was in for. His mom was remarried to Allen Murphy, one of his top officers no less. She was also expecting a child. There was no place here for Brad to hide out and go to ground.

Picking up the phone he dialed Allen and when his call was answered he began to relate the latest news about Brad. Too late, he found he'd been speaking to Patty who, although distressed to learn Brad was on his way home, decided to leave everything in her husband's and sheriff Hatches' hands. She had distanced herself from Brad immediately when he had left with her hard earned money, and then finding the watch and learning he was also a murderer, she'd washed her hands of him entirely. She was looking forward to this new child that was within two months of being born. She didn't want to know the gender but hoped it would be a girl.

When Al came home from work he led her into the kitchen, sat her down at the table and began to talk....

"Honey, Sheriff Hatch told me all about Brad and the sort of son he'd been to you. The mean things he'd done like taking your hard earned money when he left, the three murders that were solved by the watch you'd found and given to sheriff. He was a bad apple, sweetheart. There's no way he could have learned to do all this bad stuff from you. It's a fact that some folks are born with a bad seed inside that takes root and grows into something evil that takes control of their lives. It touches everyone near to them. You don't have a mean bone in your body, I can swear on the Holy Bible to that. This is the very last word I want spoken about Brad. He is no longer a part of our family or even your son. I will not have you hurt by his actions, you did all you could raising him, loving him, buying him a car, giving everything you could to try and get him to love you but that's something he has no concept of, he wouldn't know it if it slapped him in the face. So, darling wife, listen to your loving husband who'd move heaven and earth to please you. Don't worry one hair of your pretty head about that trouble maker. Let Sheriff Hatch take care of everything. Once he's safely in prison you won't have to worry about him anymore. Agreed?"

Although Patty knew Al was right about Brad, she still couldn't close him off completely from her heart. She recalled what a sweet child he'd been, but then little by little as he'd reached his teens he'd become moody. She thought giving him a car would help, he could take friends out for rides, even go to nearby towns for a change of scenery. For a while it had seemed to work, he'd been in a good mood but then, it wasn't long before he was back to his old self. Mean, selfish, and self-centered, too lazy to even shovel the walk for her. His taking her last $500 was the final straw. Finding that watch from one of the murdered boys, she'd been sick to heart learning it was Brad who was responsible for all the killings. How could her son have done such a terrible thing?

Well, she hoped to never see him again. All he'd ever brought her was heart-ache. She had a new life now with a good husband who loved her as she loved him, a new home and a baby on the way. This felt like paradise, something she had never expected out of life. Surprising what unexpected things arose when a person changed a few seemingly inconsequential things in life. This all happened because Brad decided to leave with her savings.

Meanwhile, Brad was thoughtfully tucking a stolen gun into his belt. He'd never owned a revolver before, it felt heavy and dangerous, a nice fit in his hand. Just holding it gave him a feeling of power and infallibility. He was "The Man." He felt there wasn't a person walking this earth that could defeat him. He intended to head back home but he needed a car, he'd ditched the jeep long ago and had been hitchhiking across the country. He didn't look the same as when he'd left home. He was sun-browned with a beard and moustache, his hair shoulder length and curly. He had squint wrinkles around his eyes making him look older than his 18 years. He was also thinner than when he'd lived at home and even his mother would have had to take a second look to recognize him as her son. He was aware of the APB Hatch had sent out on him but wasn't worried. He'd since learned a lot about living and evading the law. He now had identification taken from a drunk he'd found passed out on a park bench in Nevada and with his longer hair the License picture was a close match. He'd also memorized the vital statistics just in case, since cops were always suspicious about hesitations during questionings. Even that broad Rose, Alex's wife, wouldn't recognize him as the same man who had robbed her. He couldn't help laughing to himself, she hadn't remembered him from when he'd worked with Alex, or even that he'd stolen the company pickup truck. Enough of this reminiscing…he had to find transportation.

The sun had set as he made his way to the local hot-spots. Sooner or later he'd find what he needed. It was almost midnight when a tipsy senior staggered out of a tavern heading toward an old Ford pickup truck. He crawled in behind the steering wheel then tried to put his key in the ignition without success. His head eventually dropped back against the seat and soon loud snores began to emanate from the opened window.

Brad opened the door, slid the old man over to the passenger side, and then made himself comfortable behind the steering wheel. He plucked the keys from the old man's hand, started the motor and listened to the rumble of the well tuned, powerful engine. Bingo…Lady Luck at last. He couldn't have picked a better ride. Popping it into gear he eased it out of the parking lot and onto the road. When he found a secluded place to stop he searched the old guys' pockets for a wallet and money. It must've been pay day, a whopping $326.00 dollars which he pocketed along with the registration. He then checked the address on the driver's license. Taking a chance, he checked the glove box knowing many kept a road map handy. Yep! A typical old fart, there it was.

There were no lights on at the rural farmhouse when he finally found the location thanks to the map. Brad pulled into the back yard near the barn, turned off the motor and cut the lights. He sat for a while but when no one came to the door to see what was taking the old guy so long, he figured it was safe. There were at least half a dozen keys besides the trucks on the metal ring. He flipped through them until he found two that looked like house keys. One of them fit the back door.

A thorough search found the house empty of any other occupant except for a black mongrel that wagged its tail with an enthusiastic greeting.

Brad brought the old man inside and placed him on the sofa, and then he checked through the entire house making sure no one else was there. He placed the truck keys on the kitchen table then stretched out on the leather recliner next to the sofa and fell fast asleep. Someone was shaking his shoulder. He thought it was his mother waking him, the aroma of fresh coffee and frying sausage permeated the air.

"Hey, fella, take it easy. It's just me. You brought me home last night and I have to thank you for that. I'd a ended up in a ditch for sure otherwise. You must' a been in the bar when I left and seen how tipsy I was. I should a eaten something before stopping in there. I don't make a habit of drinkin' so much but time just seemed to slip away an next thing I knew, the 'tender cut me off without so much as a bye-your-leave."

Brad was still half asleep, but leery until he recalled the truck and its owner. Sunlight was streaming through the kitchen windows and extending into the living room. He could see the kitchen table was set up with plates, cups and utensils for two. The rumbling of his stomach was so loud the old man began to laugh, slapping his thigh vigorously and then pulling Brad by the arm and settling him at the table.

"You set there fella, I'll dish out the food." A stack of buttered wheat toast, platter of bacon, sausage and ham were placed in the center of the table. A fry pan of sunny-side up eggs was carried over and a spatula ladled them out onto the country plates. The only sounds were the clink of silverware as the two men managed to climb outside of the bounteous meal. When sated, they quietly sipped their hot coffee. The mutt lay by the old man's feet waiting for any leftovers, while the sun climbed higher and the stove clock edged toward eight a.m.

"That was the best meal I've had in ages, I almost ate the dish, guess I was hungrier than I imagined. Thanks, you're quite a cook, old man."

"You're welcome, I used to like cooking for my wife on weekends, bless her heart. It was my treat to her for all the work she did during the week. By the way, my name's Sam, Sam Watson. I still do a little farming but I like to work on motors mostly. Folks usually call me when they run into problems with their farming equipment or vehicles. I'm cheaper than the town repair shop. What's your name and what sort of work do you do young fella?"

Brad couldn't think of a single thing he was talented at, and for the first time in his life, a powerful feeling of embarrassment made him cringe at the thought of being completely useless. He recalled his new ID. "Uh! My name is Frank Daniels."

The old man was quick to spot folks reactions. "Eh!…what'm I doin' sitting here like I have all day to loaf about, how about giving me a hand with these dishes then I'll take you along with me. That is, if you don't have anything pressing or someplace you have to be?"

"Nope, nothing planned, in fact I was just passing through town and was about to stop in at the tavern when I saw you coming out."

"Where's your vehicle? Did you leave it at the bar?"

"Actually Sam, I wrecked my car two weeks ago so I was hitch-hiking. Lucky for me that I just happened to be dropped off where I saw you needed some help."

The two washed and dried the dishes and then Sam fed Moby some table scraps mixed with regular dried dog food. He also put fresh water in the drinking bowl. "You be good Moby, don't go chasing any rabbits." Moby gave a wag of his tail. He had his own swinging doggy door Sam had put in special for him.

Sam packed a generous lunch for the two of them. Within moments they were on the highway heading toward the near-distant hills. The windows were rolled down letting the breeze, fresh with morning dew, fill the truck's cab. This was the first time Brad had ever gone anywhere with a man who was old enough to be his grandfather, he was the right age. "Hey, Sam, I almost forgot. I have your $326 dollars. When I was carrying you in the house it was falling out of your pocket, I have your registration for the truck too. I don't know why I thought I should put that with your money, but I did. I'm glad I was able to help you."

Sam glanced at the young man. He wasn't born yesterday, He'd known his money had been taken and was waiting for any forthcoming words on the subject.

"Thanks kid, I appreciate that. I withdrew the money from my bank yesterday knowing I'd be driving up into the hills today, I thought I'd misplaced it. I'm taking you to my secret Hideaway. Whenever I get edgy or out of sorts with everyday hassles I pack a few things and disappear for a week or two. We'll only be gone until tomorrow, otherwise I'd have brought

Moby, he loves it there. It's named Secret Blue. You'll see why when we get there. Years ago my grandfather staked a claim to it when he found a trace of silver in the stream that flows into the lake but nothing ever came of it, only got enough to buy the site just before the vein petered out. At first he thought of selling but after spending the entire year living there he got so attached to the place he decided to keep it. Good for me he did."

Sam took a narrow turnoff into the dense pine forest they had been driving along the edge of for the last half hour. The trees were so dense it was impossible to see more than twenty feet into their midst. Now he understood why Sam's old truck wasn't all painted and polished. Branches brushed and bounced against the fenders making screeching sounds and leaving traces of pine needles that were quickly erased by the next noisy swipe. The bends and turns of the path quickly hid them from the main road.

Just when Brad thought they'd never get out of the thick greenery he noticed a brightening ahead and almost in the blink of an eye Sam pulled his truck to a stop at the edge of a sheer drop-off, the tops of another dense pine forest rising a few feet above the cliffs rim.

The truck stays here. If I had provisions with me I'd lower them by rope to the clearing below rather than tote it. We hoof it, not too far either. Sam took their lunch pack, swung it over his shoulder and started walking along the rim's edge, Brad close at his heels. About twenty feet further a winding path wended it way downward, Sam took off at a fast pace, Brad keeping up with him.

The lower forest was not as dense nor as large and when the two men broke through edge of the trees Brad almost lost his breathe at the beauty of the scene before him. The clearing was abloom with wildflowers, Queen Ann's Lace, Buttercups, and the bright blue of Chicory weed. The lake must have covered about five acres, it's color matching the blue of the sky and the water as clear as glass. Near its center a swirl of water disturbed the surface.

"The lake is spring fed, Frank, drinkable too. Sam led the way to where two dwellings stood spaced about twenty feet apart. One was made of logs, the other of stone. "The log cabin was my gramps. He built that while he was looking for silver. I built the stone dwelling. I worked on it every time I came here for a stay, whether short or long. I wanted something permanent. I completed it about a decade ago." Sam had a grin a mile wide. "Wait til you see the inside, it's my heaven on earth. If I didn't need to work I'd have retired here years ago."

"Do you bring many friends up here, Sam? Seems it would be a great hunting lodge, or I bet you could even rent it to vacationers it's such an ideal get-away spot with that beautiful lake for swimming."

"Years ago my best friends Ray, Bud and I would spend our weekends here. This was from the time we were teenagers. Even after they married it was our place to relax when everyday pressures got too much to bear. Then time changed us. You know how it is, there's things the wife wants done around the house and it has to be done on the weekends, not after a day's hard work. Little by little the guys got tied up going to little league games, taking the family on picnics or just relaxing at home. Family ties win out every time. We drifted apart, still friends but different now. Especially since I'm the single fella who, according to their wives, needed a mate. I got tired of all the "fixing," invited to their family dinners with the maiden aunts or older sisters looking me over like I was prime meat on the hoof. Embarrassing, that's what it was. Little by little I accepted their invitations less and less until they finally ended."

"Didn't you ever think of getting married, Sam? You're still not too bad looking, even for an old guy. What stopped you?"

"Nothing stopped me. The woman I fell in love with and wanted to marry didn't feel the same way about me. We were an item in high school, Sam and Edie....went together like bread and butter, meat and taters. Where one of us was, so too was the other. After graduation Edie went to university nursing school. We were going to marry after she graduated. In the meantime I took over my family farm. Pop was in poor health but ma took good care of him. Things were working out well."

Sam looked pensively off to the forest gathering his memories.

"Edie's schooling took four years. When she graduated she began to work at the local hospital. We dated but somehow things weren't the same between us. Maybe her being away to the big city all that time, seeing all the newfangled things, going to movies and out to dinner, changed her outlook on farm living. After she stopped accepting dates from me, it wasn't long before her engagement was announced in the paper. She married a young resident doctor at the hospital, she's still with him to this day. Her three sons and daughter, all attended college and now her grandchildren are in college too."

Brad could have sworn Sam's eyes looked brightly moist, like tears were ready to gather but he turned quickly away, taking a fast swipe at his face with the cuff of his shirt sleeve. When he turned back again he had his emotions under control.

"She was right, you know. I never could have given her the sort of life she deserved, let alone send our kids to college. She had a better conception of what life with me would have been like. Livelihood depended on the success of the crops. Well! Enough of this reverie, how about some lunch, Frank?"

It took a moment for Brad to respond to his new name. "I'm starved Sam, I thought you'd never ask." He followed Sam into the stone cottage, his eyes traveling the interior, surprised at all the work Sam had accomplished.

They seated themselves at a sturdy pine table. Sam opened the bag of sandwiches also placing two old fashioned plates on the table. He filled two glasses with fresh water from the self-priming pump and opened the plastic container of dill pickles.

The heady aroma of vinegar and dill made Brads mouth water with anticipation. They made quick work of the lunch, several sandwiches left wrapped for supper later on. Sam had decided they would stay overnight and head back home in the morning.

The remainder of the day was spent sweeping out both dwellings. Brad helped Sam cut and split some firewood to warm the stone cottage when temps dropped during the night. Sam also cut two thin green boughs, each about three feet long, and trimmed the ends with his pocket knife. This was for a little surprise he had planned for later that evening. When they were finished neatening up the entire area, leaves, broken branches piled and burned, it was beginning to turn dark. The sun slipped behind the tall forest and night began creeping closer across the eastern sky. Birds had settled into their resting places while a few croakers began their nightly serenade. Crickets joined in with the occasional hoot of an owl.

Brad yawned, suddenly tired, realizing it had been a very long day, but he felt good. Not that there had been any really hard labor, just continually being busy until the hours had slipped quickly away, the day over.

Sam opened the spigot to the propane that supplied the cooking stove. After air in the tubes had vented he lit the burner and set the big aluminum coffee pot on to boil. The logs were beginning to burn nicely in the stone fireplace sending welcome warmth into the chilly room. He watched Frank, sitting on one of the wooden stools before the fire, give a huge yawn. The kid had done well today. He wondered what he looked like under all that facial hair. He still wasn't comfortable about trusting him either. There were other things that bothered him too, like sometimes catching a certain calculating look just before the kid turned quickly away hiding his emotions. He'd be alert, his sixth sense a constant warning bell telling him to be on guard against a danger that was as threatening as a storm cloud where you couldn't see the lightening until it struck. He might be old but he wasn't stupid. At least he was in good physical shape, better than the kid who didn't look like he'd had much experience with heavy labor. He'd take a farm any day for keeping in healthy condition. Better than all those machines where you only toned one muscle at a time. He couldn't help grinning at the memory of watching a few folks doing workouts at a fitness facility. The windows were clean as a whistle, the people sweaty and frazzled looking. Where was the pleasure? At least with farming there was sunlight, fresh air and scenery.

"Want some coffee, Frank? I'll put some sweetener in it to perk you up. It'll taste good with the last of our sandwiches. Plus, if you look in the flap of my pack you'll find a bag of marshmallows. That's what those two peeled green switches are for."

Brad hadn't had those since he was a kid. It brought back the times his mom had been busy cleaning, catching up with laundry. She would light a big candle, sit him in front of it at the kitchen table with a long handled fork and a saucer of marshmallows, to let him enjoy toasting the treats while she finished her housework. He loved watching the flame melt the mallow turning it brown. Just before it caught fire he'd pull it away from the heat, blow on it a little and then let the sweet puffiness melt away in his mouth.

Later, after the two men were sated with sandwiches and toasted mallows, Sam pulled two plastic bags containing blankets out of the storage cupboard along with two pillows. "You get the top bunk Frank. Sleep tight kid, I'll see you in the morning. We'll
 head back home at first light. I know a great place to stop for breakfast, been going there for years."

When Sam heard the heavy breathing telling him that Frank was soundly asleep, he quietly arose, slipped on his boots, put his belt back on, and then slipped silently out through the door, thanking God he had thought to oil the hinges as he pulled it gently closed. He then hurried to the path through the forest to his truck. He always relied on his instincts since he'd realized, years ago when he had been in the service, instincts were there for a purpose. He'd

THE THISTLE SEED

saved his life more than once by heeding them. His instincts had warned him about Frank, although this time it had taken a while for him to take the warnings seriously. He actually had thought it was the age difference between him and the kid, that he was getting too old to comprehend the makings of someone so young. Geez!...there must be at least fifty years difference.

Within a half hour he was back in his truck. Another half hour he was out of the forest and on the main road home without even a stop for breakfast. There was someone he wanted to see the very first thing this morning. By the time he finally reached town, Sheriff Randy Delaney was just parking his cruiser and entering the police station.

"Hey!, Randy, hold up a minute." Sam slipped out the truck door, slammed it, and hurried toward the sheriff who was waiting at the station door, still holding it half opened.

"What's your hurry this early in the morning, Sam? You look like you just crawled out of bed. Having some trouble around the farm?"

"Not sure Randy, but I want you to do a little checking for me. A few nights ago I got loaded over at the tavern. When I came to, I was on my sofa and a stranger was fast asleep in the chair next to me. My $326 I'd withdrawn from the bank and my truck registration were missing from my wallet. It ended up I fixed breakfast for both of us. The kid eventually apologized saying he forgot to give the stuff back but there's something amiss with this young man. I think he has a bad streak and meant me harm. I took him up to Secret Blue and left him there when my instincts began to pester me too much."

"Come on into the office, Sam. Give me a description of this character and I'll check the APB's I have in the folder. Maybe we can get to the root of your worries."

Sam felt some of the tension ease up. Randy was good at his job, if there were any troubles involving Frank, there would be alerts sent out to police throughout the country.

Randy sorted through the folder putting at least a dozen wanted photos aside. He then passed them over to Sam. "Take your time, I'm in no hurry. How about a cup of coffee while you're checking them?"

Sam nodded intent on inspecting the photos. However, when Randy sat a cup of the offices best coffee next to him, he stopped his perusing and gratefully leaned back to enjoy the wake-up beverage. He really needed it after lack of enough sleep and the long drive.

Eventually he set the cup aside, continuing his inspection of the wanted pictures. He could feel the hair stand up at the nape of his neck when he saw Franks picture, except his name wasn't Frank, it was Bradley Shields, a murderer of three young men.

"Good God! Randy, this is the young man I trusted enough to take to Secret Blue. I had to be nuts to put my faith in a perfect stranger. He's still there, he has no transportation out."

"Go home Sam. Thanks to you and all those good times my teenage friends and I had on summer vacations when you'd take us there for weeks at a time, I remember the way there perfectly. I'll call in my off duty deputies right now."

There were six officers who readied themselves to capture a dangerous escapee. Two officers were left behind to take care of any town business that happened to arise.

At about twelve-noon three squad cars were finally wending their way through the narrow forest toward the drop-off where they would leave their autos. At least the lower forest hid them from being seen on this high ridge. As they made their way along the downward winding path, they were not aware that their subject was already hiding not far away, waiting until they were out of sight and sound so he could take one of their vehicles. He managed to hot-wire it quickly and was gone before they arrived back and discovered their loss.

When Sheriff Delaney saw one of their squad cars missing, he immediately put out an APB to be on the lookout for the stolen police vehicle.

Outside the next town an officer, parked behind a signboard waiting to nab scofflaws, noticed a police car speeding by driven by a scruffy bearded man dressed in a tee shirt. He took chase immediately, at the same time getting an APB alert over his radio about the stolen police vehicle. However, when they reached speeds of close to 100mph and were nearing the outskirts of town and the local school, he backed off and radioed ahead to alert other officers. He hadn't realized he had been gritting his teeth, even his stomach muscles felt sore they had been tensed so long. Whoever the jerk was he needed to be stopped but unfortunately, it wouldn't be by him. The silent cusswords did not ease his anger at losing the perp.

Brad was aware he was going to get caught unless he thought of something immediately. He had to ditch the car, but where? It was getting toward dusk, seemed like the day was here and gone too fast. Just then he happened to pass a boat launching site for the local fishermen. A quick glance around showed not a soul in sight, likely everyone had gone home for supper. He pulled up to the ramp, rolled down the windows, put the car in drive, and closed the door. He watched with immense satisfaction as the car inched slowly forward, water creeping upward, auto settling deeper and deeper until it disappeared from view. At least he now had more time. It would be a while before they found it but now he needed to rid himself of the beard and get a haircut. An all night drug store satisfied his needs. He bought a pair of scissors, shaving cream, throw-away razors and instant suntan lotion.

The rest room of a gas station was perfect. It took him an hour to get rid of all the hair which he flushed down the commode. He rubbed the tanning lotion over his face and neck also making sure he got around his ears good. It blended well with the tan on his arms. Great! He couldn't even recognize himself and neither would Sam or anyone else from around here. It was time for him to hitch a ride with someone. He headed for the highway selecting the side where he would be heading east. Within an hour he had his sucker, a young teenager, on his way to see a friend in the next town.

Once the town lights were left behind and an empty highway stretched ahead, Brad asked the teen to pull over to the side of the road, he thought he was going to be sick and didn't want to mess up the kid's car. As soon as the car came to a stop Brad gave a quick elbow to the kid's neck which caused a gag reaction. That was all it took, he was quickly on his way alone, the teen laying in a ditch unconscious with possible brain damage, his pockets emptied of his weekly wages working after school and on weekends.

Brad was heading home. There wasn't anywhere else he could go to ground except at his mothers. She'd take care of him and at least he'd have a place to sleep with decent meals. Besides, she had never refused him anything. The confidence he felt gave a sudden lift to his spirits as he pressed the gas pedal a little harder, speed picking up a notch but not enough to get pulled over by a cop.

The next morning he bought cheese, lunchmeat, bread, mustard and two six packs of spring water at a highway gas station. This would be enough to get him where he was heading for. No need to risk stopping at diners or places where people congregated…too risky. He'd also sleep in the car again.

The miles slipped away and he was, at last, passing through Highland where he'd worked for Alex and stolen the company pickup truck. By tomorrow morning he'd be back up north and close to home where he'd pull into the woods during the day to hide the car. As soon as it got dark he'd head for his mom's.

That night was clear with bright moonlight, so bright in fact that he cast a shadow as he made his way back home, slipping behind anything handy whenever he spotted a car with someone just getting home from work. He was as nervous as a kid trying to ride a bike for the very first time.

Eventually he slipped into his own backyard. He could see lights coming from the kitchen window and his mother standing at the sink that sat underneath it. Maybe she was doing dishes. Just as he was ready to mount the stairs and knock at the back door, he saw a man appear and place a kiss her on the neck. Brad felt a shock that seemed to paralyze his entire body. "Who the crap is that," he muttered aloud feeling rage begin to mount and sending his blood pressure sky high. He'd never seen the guy before. He didn't look like a wimp either, not someone he could bulldoze to the ground and beat the hell out of. He stood quietly contemplating what his next actions should be. He had no choice but to act so he went around the house to the front door and rang the doorbell. It was the man who opened the door.

"Is Patty here?"

It took only a moment for Allen Murphy, Patricia's new husband, to recognize the young man standing at the door. He didn't have his gun handy so he acted accordingly.

"She's doing dishes right now. You must be here about the rummage sale that's planned for this Sunday to raise money for the new school gymnasium. Come on in and have a seat while I get her." Allen closed the front door then turned toward the kitchen. He should have been more suspicious of Brad. As soon as his back was turned Brad hit him on the head with the handle of the revolver he'd had tucked into the back of his belt. Al dropped to the floor, the reverberations through the structure alerting Patty that something was wrong. She was drying her hands with a dishtowel as she hurried into the living room to see what the commotion was all about. When the body of her husband came into view with her son Brad standing over him, a feeling of intense rage seemed to take total control of her emotions. With a quick flip of her wrist the end of the dishtowel snapped into the air and whipped its edge into Brad's eyes, the sting of the cloth across his opened eyes causing such pain he had to turn away rubbing the closed eyelids, trying to ease the intense irritation. It didn't help.

"You sick minded brat, who do you think you're dealing with? I'm not the same woman you ran away from taking my hard earned money. I gave you everything I could afford but it was never enough, was it? You had me browbeaten and catering to your every whim and now you march in here attacking my husband and you think I'll just accept it?" Patty wrested the gun from Brads hand and with a wide swing of her arm brought it smashing down against his head. He dropped to the floor like a stone.

Sheriff Hatch arrived with one of his deputies within minutes of receiving her call. Patty already had Brad trussed up like a pig in a poke, never again would she trust him. Allan was sitting in the easy chair, a cold compress on his head to relieve the pain and swelling.

"He caught me pretty fast boss, he was hardly in through the door when I turned to call Patty and he cold-cocked me. I was out like a light. Patty's awfully good with that towel, she sometimes surprises me, keeps me on my toes, so to speak." Allen gave a bashful grin, embarrassed about mentioning the little games they enjoyed sometimes.

Brad was handcuffed and wrestled out into the squad car where they also hog-tied him as a precaution. There he was on his stomach in the back seat, feet and wrists forced together above his back with plastic restrainers. He wouldn't have a chance to plan any sly moves. This time he was going to the maximum security prison to spend the remainder of his life.

The next morning Sheriff Hatch contacted Sheriff Randy Delaney in Utah to let him know that Bradley Shields was in police custody and would be tried for three murders.

That evening, after supper when he and Angie were enjoying a cup of coffee which seemed to top off a meal nicely, he considered phoning Rose and letting her know what happened with Brad Shields. His own son Chris Hatch had called him when Brad had stolen Alex's company truck. Chris still worked with Ryan, they'd become good friends.

"Hi! Rose, it's been a while since we last spoke, how's that kid of mine doing working with Ryan? Hmm! That's good to know, he always did like to earn extra for spending and also putting a little aside into savings. He's handy, learned a lot by helping me with any projects that Angie wanted done. He likes working with wood also. I have two beautiful wooden Mallards, a pair he hand-carved and painted that look like the real thing. Well! Rose, the real reason I'm calling is I wanted you to know that Brad Shields is in custody. You don't have to worry about him showing up on your doorstep anymore, he's going to jail for the remainder of his life. Everyone around here is relieved, even his own mother. I feel sorry for her, she tried so hard to raise him right but some are just born to be bad."

"Thanks for calling Oscar, and please give Angie my regards. I may come up there again this summer bringing my daughter and our little ones. I still can't get over Alex being gone. It will take me a lot more than a year to be able to bear his loss. Thank God for family, otherwise it would be impossible." With a catch in her voice, she said a

hasty goodbye and hung up.

Rose sat quietly, her mind traveling back weeks, months and then years, suddenly recalling the beloved face of her mother Eleanor, remembering the words of wisdom she had tried to instill in her and the taped messages that Sylvia had coaxed her grandmother into making. If only she hadn't run away and left Sylvia, if she had stayed maybe Alex and she might have married back then. Life would have been so different.

Her mother, Eleanor, had always told her that life was like a thistle seed which regardless of the type soil, grew into a strong plant laden with sharp pickers and beautiful flowers. A person had to be mindful and deal with those sharp stings in life, never knowing when they would unexpectedly cause hurt. But wounds healed and life went on…The End

There's a huge pine tree off the end of my patio and when I began writing this story each day I noticed something sprouting under its drooping branches. Whatever the plant was it grew quickly, heading up into the pine tree branches above. Finally I asked my husband to see what it could be. It was a Thistle plant with a pretty flower just blooming. Where or how it happened to germinate there was a mystery, but it gave me the incentive to write my novel. D. J. Lane